Jaded Loyalties

Kristine Endsley

ALSO BY

THE EXILE'S PARADOX

Jaded Loyalties
A Twisted Fate
Book 3 coming in 2025
Series Novella
Shattered Fate

Copyright © 2024 by Kristine Endsley

All rights reserved.

No part of this publication may be reproduced, distributed, or transmitted in any form or by any means, including photocopying, recording, or other electronic or mechanical methods, without the prior written permission of the publisher, except as permitted by U.S. copyright law. For permission requests, contact kristineendsley@gmail.com.

This is a work of fiction. Names, characters, places, and incidents are either the product of the author's imagination or are used fictitiously. Any resemblance to actual persons, living or dead, business establishments, events, or locales is entirely coincidental.

Jaded Loyalties

The Exile's Paradox Series/Book Two

http://www.kristineendsley.com

Cover art and design by Cristiana Leone

Editing by

http://www.arrowheadediting.com

Published by KE Fantasy

ISBN: E-book: 979-8-9897685-5-4, Paperback: 979-8-9897685-7-8, Hardcover: 979-8-9897685-6-1

First edition: November 2024

To the men who helped me become the person I am today.
Terry, Don, and Gene.

contents

Index of Common Words	XI
1	1
2	13
3	19
4	32
5	43
6	51
7	59
8	71
9	80
10	86
11	95
12	108
13	117
14	121

15	128
16	144
17	152
18	161
19	171
20	179
21	188
22	199
23	205
24	218
25	225
26	235
27	248
28	259
29	270
30	279
31	293
32	300
33	315
34	324
Epilogue	328
Author's Note	334

Acknowledgements	335
About the author	336
Fullpage image	337

Index of Common Words

Aeminan— Citizens of *Aemina*
Aemirin— Language of the *Aeminan* people
Ai— Expression or exasperation, like "oh"
Amura Ore— Governing council in *Aemina*
Aore— Senior *Amura Ore* assembly member
Enda— Elf
Endae— The elven realm
Endaen— Elven
Hallë— This is Nolan's name for Hally, only he uses it
Imolegin— An *enda*'s magical signature
Laro— Father
Loret— Junior *Amura Ore* assembly member
Meril— An *endaen* magical amulet
Muranilde — Rare soulmate-like bond Hally and Nolan share
Murë— Mother
Nol— This is Hally's name for Nolan, only she uses it
Rosava— Earth
Sajé— A comforting word like "shh"
Savile— Title of an exile (again, not capitalized when using gender version)
Yalurë (Yalu)— Paternal grandmother (Grannie/Grandma)
Zayuri— Org. of samurai-like warriors

Word Endings:
-ë— female
-o— male
-e— neutral or title
-i— plural

Remember! These are English translations for the convenience of English speakers. Please don't assume the characters are speaking English just because you're reading English.

For a full ever expanding and evolving translation list visit my website: https://kristineendsley.com/extras/

1

I NEEDED TO GET out before I lost my mind. Yelling would only result in hurt feelings and regretful words. But damn it, they wouldn't let me do anything. Nol kept fussing over me. Charlie jumped up to help whenever I tried to get something. This cast needed to come off sooner. My doctor cleared me of my concussion a couple of days ago, but Nol still wouldn't let me get up on a ladder, and neither of them wanted me to be on my phone for long.

The little bell jingled as I opened the front door to my tattoo shop, Yula's Quill. My shoulders relaxed as I inhaled the scents of tattoo ink, antiseptic cleaners, and Lewis's cologne. Perfect.

"Hello!" Lewis called from his station, unable to see me through the repaired saloon doors separating our workstations from the lobby. "Be with you soon. I'm in a session."

"*Bonjour*, Lewis," I said in an exasperated rush. I walked past our gray couch, coffee table, and glass display case in the bright lobby. All new-to-us, thanks to my former tattoo mentor's drug-induced rampage three weeks ago. Not fun.

"Hally?"

"Yep." I pushed the saloon doors open and slipped through without disturbing them as much as possible. I dropped my purse in the bottom of my toolbox, then rolled my swivel chair into Lewis's cubicle. A thirty-something bearded, bald customer was lying on his side, getting a side-view image of a realistic heart crushed in a fist amongst broken rib bones on his rib cage.

"Girl, I thought I told you not to come in here until your wrist is healed." Lewis looked up, his reading glasses at the tip of his nose and his machine held right above his client's skin.

"I'm hiding." I dropped into the chair and crossed my arms as well as I could with the cast.

"Aren't you not supposed to turn off your location anymore?" He continued shading the bones.

I grumbled, "I didn't. It's—they're driving me crazy."

Lewis snorted, dipped his cartridge in black ink, and kept going. The client was staring at me—a stranger had come in, invading his tattoo session. He didn't seem offended, with his half-lidded eyes looking at my boobs.

"Hey, up here." I gestured to my face.

His eyes rose. "Hi," he purred.

You have to be kidding me. "Hally—co-owner, tattoo artist, and not interested."

"Where's your tats, then? Aren't all artists supposed to be covered in them?" He looked back down at my boobs.

I didn't answer. His disrespectful attitude did not deserve one.

"Don't be goin' disrespectin' my partner."

The guy's mouth closed, and he set his jaw. If he kept going, Lewis would stop. Don't ever piss off your tattoo artist. Ever.

"So why you goin' crazy?" Lewis lifted his machine and wiped at the tat, all in one practiced move

"I can't stand how much they're fussing over me. They're treating me like—"

"Like you almost died." The whites of his eyes stood out as his eyes widened.

"Not fair. We thought Nol was dead first, and no one is treating him like an infirm."

"Infirm?" We continued ignoring the client.

"They ain't. They're tryin' to take care of you, and you're not used to that."

"Hmm." I tapped my knee. "I needed a break."

"I get that." His lip stuck out as he focused on the tattoo. "You two have been apart a long time. Gettin' a new groove won't happen in a day."

"I know, he knows. It's just we've never been at odds like this."

"Maybe this is a good thing, then. Fightin' and figurin' things out bring people closer."

"Sure." I swiveled back around and went to my little tattooing area with its standing silver toolbox covered in stickers from tattoo conventions and a "whining costs extra" magnet. My rolling drawers for ink and other whatnots were stuffed in the corner between the client chair and the partisan wall.

"You're not gonna go workin', are you?" Lewis called over the buzzing of his machine.

"No, just fiddling. Promise."

I picked up the purple ink bottle from my drawer. Gil had been playing with it before he kissed me. A day after that, a bitch of an *endaë*, who thought she could play goddess and infect my people with her curse, killed him. She'd come over from the Endae realm to find me and destroyed...everything.

My chin quivered, and I tapped the bottle against it. That was what Nol and I were really dealing with. We missed Gileal, and it hurt to talk about. I set down the bottle, scrubbed my face, and probably ruined my make-up. Where'd my mirror go?

"No complaining 'bout how I set up your shit. I did the best I could."

"It's not that. Ah-ha!" I found the mirror in the toolbox's bottom drawer. It should've been in the plastic drawers.

Aswryn, that *endaë* bitch with the goddess complex, killed Gil and my ex-mentor three weeks ago while destroying my shop. To be fair, Ian, the mentor, had started destroying it first, but she was worse. She broke my right wrist and gave me a concussion. Since then, Lewis had been holding down the fort.

Lewis finished up with his client soon after, while I slouched in my chair and doodled on a sketch pad.

"Hally?" Lewis leaned his beefy arms over my partisan wall. His frown deepened the lines in his umber skin. Why did humans age so fast? "Tell me what's really goin' on with your elf drama."

"You already know," I mumbled.

"Nah, you talked to your grandma yesterday, didn't you?"

She and I had a schedule. We met in her dreams—dream-walking—twice a week to stay updated. Because I was banished, no one was supposed to know about them, but it seemed that Nol's parents, my parents, and several *Zayuri* knew about our meetings. Honestly, I was beginning to wonder if they cared whether the *Amura Ore* found out.

I huffed and tossed the sketchbook on the toolbox. "Besides missing Gil? The curse still hasn't dissipated."

Lewis grunted. He and his girlfriend, Yumi, came to my house every Sunday for dinner, so he was familiar with the situation. "No."

"What?" I lifted my gaze from my cast to glare at Lewis.

"That ain't it."

The bell above the door jingled, and the glass door flew against the storefront window—thankfully without any glass shattering.

"Hey!" Lewis bellowed. We were tired of our shit getting ruined.

Three tall men invaded our shop. Two headed toward us while another one shut the door and locked it. Some trick of the light made the storefront windows look matte black. For a moment, I thought the doorman's hair was the same color. I blinked as it went back to a natural dark brown—not matte, because that would be weird.

The loud smack of the saloon doors hitting my partisan wall brought me out of my mental lapse on reality. The shortest man, and first through the doors, came right up to Lewis. His brown-haired head only came up to Lewis's chin.

"Are you Hally Dubois?"

I blinked. My reaction time was so off. Their third man, about Lewis's height with dark blond shoulder-length hair and leaf-green eyes, glared at me. He'd asked a question. Shit.

I swallowed and assessed the people in front of me before I answered. What would resolve this in the calmest way? A shuffling from the front distracted me. At first, I pictured someone jumping over the pass-through behind the display case and into my station. But no, the one in the front shifted so he could see me and his green-eyed asshole friend.

He looked different from the other two. Paler, dark brown hair, and almost black eyes. He didn't ooze that thuggish vibe like the other two. He clasped his hands in front of him and watched with an almost bored, "can't believe I had to come along" look.

"Hey!" Leafy-green barked, jerking my attention back to him. "Are you Hally Dubois?"

"Yes." I set my hands on my hips, cast notwithstanding. "You can't just barge in here—"

"We need to talk." He nodded to his companion beside him.

The shorter man thrust his right arm out and grabbed Lewis by the throat. The next thing I knew, he'd lifted Lewis off the ground. All three-plus hundred pounds of a six-foot-four black man. Holy shit.

"Lewis!" I screamed. "Let him go!" I tried to run out to help my friend, but Leafy-green shoved me into my toolbox. Lewis went limp, and the brunette dropped him. A crash came from inside his cubicle and Wyatt Earp, Lewis's skeleton-on-a-pole, hit the partisan panel as his body hit the base.

"Lewis! You killed him!" My voice was rough from screaming.

"The human is fine. Once we're gone, you can untwist the spell. He'll remember nothing."

Spell? "Who are you?"

Leafy-green towered over me as the metal handle poked into my shoulder blade. He jutted his chin out to intimidate me, but I was used to everyone being bigger than me. And I was more pissed than scared. Call me stupid.

"Hally Dubois?"

My teeth clenched as I leaned in. "We've established this."

"You and your *Zayuri* partner are in direct violation of the Earth-*Endae* treaty."

"What—"

"Silence!"

Yeah, I'd be quiet, and seething—and a bit scared.

"You kinda need her to calm down to comprehend your words, Brodrick."

Brodrick turned his head around, and his hair followed, hitting me in the face. "Quinn—"

Quinn, the one blocking the door, raised his shoulders to his ears, shoved his hands into the pockets of his black peacoat, and turned away, unimpressed.

"As I was saying." Brodrick squared his shoulders. "You are hereby summoned to appear before Her Majesty, Queen Orlaith, Ruler of the Sidhe."

"I don't know what fucking game you're playing, but you need to wake up my friend. Now."

Brodrick's shoulders dropped, and he blinked a slow, deliberate blink. "Like we'd do that and have this conversation with you."

"Conversation? You attacked us." I gestured toward Lewis's cubical.

Brodrick's eye ticked at a choked-off laugh from the front.

"You will appear at the start of the first hour this fourth day prior to the birth of the new year."

I stepped back, hiccupping. That was not a human way to count days. That was *endaen*—elven—as in not of Earth.

"If you fail to appear, it will be considered an act of war."

"Wait—wait." I waved my hand in front of him. The gig was up. "One, that's bullshit. If you're going to summon someone, you must give a formal written statement."

"Oh, right, my bad." Quinn straightened from his slouch and jogged in, reaching over the pass-through and into my cubicle. He handed me an envelope and went right back to his post.

I took a breath, calming my racing heart to think. "You must give me time to review it before I agree to any of this shit."

"There is no agreeing—"

"Forty-eight hours is standard."

That got me another eye twitch. "You are the ones breaking the treaty. That gives us the right to choose the time and date. The address is on the paper. Four days prior to the birth of the new year."

Fuck. What day was the spring equinox this year? "I'm not meeting anyone anywhere I don't feel safe. We will meet on common ground for this."

"No—"

"Do you want your meeting or not? Pioneer Perk."

"That small place?" Quinn balked.

I narrowed my eyes at him.

"Pick your people wisely," I told Brodrick. "That's where I'll be. Now, leave. If you ever touch my friend again, you'll be so far up in paperwork you won't celebrate until next spring."

"You—" He shoved his chest into me.

I stumbled, but rolled my eyes up to meet his, refusing to show how scared I was.

Quinn appeared behind Brodrick and grabbed his arm. "Don't touch her, Brodrick. We're done."

Brodrick curled his lip at his buddy, but the finality in Quinn's expression stopped him. He yanked his arm out of Quinn's hand and shoved the saloon doors open.

Quinn grabbed the swinging door and met my eyes. "We'll be in touch."

"Get out," I growled.

Quinn opened the front door and let the brunette out. He paused, met my eyes, and dipped his chin with an air of respect before leaving.

"Lewis?" I yelled as I sent out a tendril of my magic to lock the front door and ran to his side.

He lay with his neck against his skeleton's post. Poor Wyatt Earp was knocked over against the back panel. I couldn't move him—Lewis, not Wyatt—and I couldn't move the pole without hurting Lewis. They'd said I could release him after they left. How?

I patted his face. "Lewis. Lewis, wake up. Oh, what do I do?" Water? I ran to our small break room, grabbed a cup, and hurried back. Did I just throw it? I poured it on his face and waited.

"Come on, Lewis."

I pulled my phone out and found the number I wanted. It rang once and went to voicemail. That jerk. I called again with the same result. So I texted: *911. Lewis is hurt.*

Ten seconds later: *Call the doctor.*

"Are you kidding me?" I yelled at the phone like Nol could hear. With a quick check on Lewis, still breathing and still out, I called my niece, Charlie.

"Hey, Tatie. What's up?"

"Is Nol there?" My words sounded a bit panicky.

"Um...no." She hesitated, but recovered. "What's wrong?"

"Do you know where he is?"

"No...you sound stressed." She whispered something off the phone. He was too there, and he had told Charlie to tell me no.

"Let me talk to him. This is an emergency."

There was a rustling. "I thought we weren't talking tonight, Hallë," my pain-in-the-ass *muranildo* said, as if this phone call proved his point in our earlier argument. A stupid argument that, if I were honest with myself, I'd blown way out of proportion. He didn't need to know that, though.

"Yeah, well, three people coming into my shop claiming to be Sidhe and knocking Lewis out with a spell I don't know how to untwist kind of supersedes it."

"What?"

"I need you. There was...there were people here, and they did something to Lewis. They weren't *endai*, but they weren't human. The one just lifted Lewis off the floor, and he...they said it was a spell. He picked Lewis up, Nol!" I took a breath, expecting Nol to say something. "Nol? Are you there?"

"I'm already leaving," he said in a quiet, emotionless voice. "Do not leave."

"I won't." I dropped the phone and went back to Lewis's side.

Three weeks ago, everything came to a head. Ian, my old mentor, ruined my shop and Aswryn destroyed my fake identity. Part of that destruction involved my magic. Aswryn shoved so much of her magic into me that it broke the one-hundred-year-old magical block I'd cast on myself. The results almost killed Lewis when he caught me off guard. It scared me enough that I ran away.

"Hallë—" Nol walked in from the break room in the back. He'd used his *Zayuri* magic, traveling through shadows between my house on North Beacon Hill and Pioneer Square in downtown Seattle.

"Here!" I shot up, waving my hand like a madwoman.

"Let me get to him." His training had conditioned him to void his face and voice of emotion. Nol gave me one glance, his ice-blue eyes meeting mine, as I backed up to let him crouch down beside Lewis. From behind him, I watched Nol check on Lewis, both physically and magically. Nol checked his breathing and then placed his hands over his torso. Nol's magical signature rolled out as he cast a spell.

"It's a simple spell to lose consciousness. An'di did them when her patients were hurt and she needed to provide intense medical treatment."

"Can—can you wake him up?"

"Of course." Nol sat back on his heels and shoved his cinnamon-red hair out of his face.

Lewis's eyes fluttered open, and I gasped. Before Nol was even out of the way, I'd dropped to Lewis's side.

"Lewis? Are you okay? Are you hurt?"

"What happened?" Lewis asked, his voice scratchy from the guy's hand crushing his windpipe.

"Those people, remember?" I nodded, trying to get him to respond.

Lewis squinted at the lights, at me, and then up at Nol behind me. "What people? Why am I on the floor? And why is my face wet?"

"Erm, that last one was my fault. I tried to wake you up with water."

"Humph," he pouted.

I looked up at Nol, who stared at us, his eyes distant.

"I don't know who they were. They came in here and—knocked you out cold with a spell."

"Spell?" Lewis asked.

"Yes," Nol said. "You could have done what I did, Hallë."

"Like hell." No way would I touch Lewis with my magic again.

"You would not have hurt him."

"Not the time," I said through clenched teeth. "You know my stand on this."

"Excuse me?" Lewis waved to get my attention. "Dude on the floor over here? What the fuck? Move, Hally."

I scooted back and popped up, but stayed close, ready to help him if he needed it. Nol scanned the floor, his magical signature spreading out again.

"Damn, woman! I ain't no baby. Stop hoverin'."

"Are you sure you're okay?"

Lewis rubbed his bald head over his cowboy skeleton tattoo. "Guess I'm getting a bump here."

"I can go get some ice and Tylenol," I offered.

"You got other shit to figure out. Get over there and help him do his—" He waved his hand around. "—magic. I'll get my own damn meds."

After Lewis stood and I was sure he was stable, I went to the front where Nol held his arms out, palms to the floor and fingers spread. Although he wore mostly human attire, jeans and tennis shoes, he'd grabbed his henna-brown leather jacket—the part of his *Zayuri* uniform that he wore the most, because the sheath to his sword was attached to it. "Tell me."

"These guys were nothing like I've ever seen before. They know who and what we are. They said they knocked Lewis out to talk with me."

"About?"

"About...um." My brain, worried about Lewis, had shoved the entire conversation to the back of my mind. "We are summoned by some lady who thinks she's a queen. There's an envelope." I ran to my area and found the paper on the floor under my swivel chair. "This."

Nol, right behind me, grabbed it and ripped the envelope open. "What is a treaty?"

"An agreement between two countries." I bumped into my toolbox, reminding me of Brodrick standing where Nol was now.

"Who are the fae?" he asked, his eyes still on the letter.

"Fae?"

"Yes, Hallë. The fae—these, High Court and Queen Orlaith of the Fae."

"What? The guy said *Sidhe*. There's no such thing as fae."

Nol lowered his arms and his emotions bloomed on his face. He gave me an exasperated, flat look. His uncharacteristically impatient attitude lately was one of the reasons I'd needed a break tonight.

I set my hands on my hips and glared at him. "Like the fairies in the books we read Ray. They're yay big." I held my hands close together. "And they have wings."

"That is fae?" Nol frowned. He enjoyed reading to Charlie's daughter most nights, and one of her favorites was some fairy book with a do-gooder moral of some sort. I never read that one.

"Yeah. This is ridiculous." I shoved my hair back.

"Look through the letter." He folded the paper and handed it to me. "Political papers are your expertise, not mine."

"I do not do paperwork." But I grabbed the letter anyway.

"They want us to go to Fauntleroy Boulevard. Where is that?"

"Oh no." I waggled my finger. "I changed that. If they were going to demand a meeting, I wanted it to be on neutral ground."

"Where, then? Do not say the cafe. Please don't." Nol pressed his temples with a thumb and forefinger.

I stayed silent.

He raised an eyebrow, expecting an answer.

"You said not to say the cafe." I shrugged.

"*Ai*, Hallë. Why that place?"

"I feel safe there, okay?" I reached for my bracelet as irritated, pale blue eyes glared at me. "The coffee shop is neutral, and they can't do shit with everyone there."

"In the first hour?" Nol asked.

"Huh? There's plenty of people there at one a.m."

"The first hour of the day," Nol chastised me.

"Yeah, and?"

"Of. The. Day. It is *endaen* timing."

"Oh...when is that?"

"You don't know? *C'yo*. When is sunrise?"

"No fucking way." That was ridiculous. No one should wake up before sunrise.

"On the fourth day prior to the birth of the new year? Spring is in five days."

"So tomorrow morning? You have to be fucking kidding me. They gave us no time. Why would they do this? We've done nothing."

"We will find out everything in a few hours." Nol groaned as his eyes darted behind me.

"Whachya goin' to find out about?" Lewis mumbled, shuffling in with an ice pack on his head.

"We have to talk," I said.

"And what we're doing now isn't?"

"No, everyone. I'm not leaving anyone out of this."

"I'll call Yumi," Lewis murmured. "She's not gonna be happy."

"Join the club." I pulled my phone out of my pocket. "I have Mateo and Sam."

Nol lifted his head from his phone. "I told Charlie."

2

Lewis was right. Yumi was pissed that we hadn't called her sooner, but when she got here and I explained why I'd called Nol first, she calmed down.

"I don't understand who cast a spell on Lewis. You or Nolan? Aswryn isn't back, is she? She's dead. Right?" Her dark brown eyes widened, but were vibrant with conviction. She'd fight if she had to. Good.

Some might not take Yumi seriously. A woman shorter than me, with short, blue and green spiked hair (this week), facial piercings, and tattoos, but never mess with Yumi. As a nurse, she could be the sweetest person imaginable, but she scared me when she got pissed. I think it was a nurse thing, kind until she had to be tough.

"No more secrets, right?" she asked, but it felt more like an accusation.

"Right. We're just waiting for Mateo and Sam."

We'd all agreed that there would be no more secrets between us when I told them what I was—after three years of friendship and me pretending to be human.

"I don't want to keep this from you, Yumi. I promise."

As I said that, the back door opened. Mateo and Sam were arguing about something to do with raspberry and lemon flavors. Sam, my height, came in first, pushing back the hood of his tan jacket. The rain still managed to get on his glasses. A few wet golden curls stuck to his forehead. Mateo followed him, his moussed faux hawk still spiky and dry thanks to the umbrella he was shaking out. I hurried over and grabbed their arms. Mateo stopped arguing and stared down at me.

"*Ojitos*?" His brown eyes searched mine before I kissed both of his cheeks, then Sam's. He called me *ojitos*, after his mother had proclaimed it when I first met her. She loved my dark green eyes, and the name stuck.

"Come sit and I'll tell you." I guided the two to their seats.

Every wall in the room was covered, and adding six adults filled it to the brink. We didn't dare go out front, with all the windows and these odd magic people who knew way too much. Our couch ran the length of the left side of the room. Above the couch, we'd taped sketches, artwork, and posters from door to door. On the right side, the oak computer table took up the back corner, and a kitchenette was stuffed in the opposite one. Locked cubbies for our belongings were between them, and in the middle of the room was a tiny round table with four metal chairs.

Mateo sat down, balanced on the edge of the couch cushion, while I stood in front of him. Everyone else settled down, Sam beside Mateo, and Charlie perched on the arm beside them. Yumi sat beside Sam, and Lewis sat in his computer chair closest to the door. Nol took one of the metal chairs with the thin cushions, spun it around, and sat next to the desk.

Oh boy, now the fun part.

I backed up to the rolling TV stand, pulled out the VHS connected to our security cameras and popped it into our small VHR/TV combo to watch the footage from a mere two hours ago. "Okay, this is going to look crazy."

The black and white show started, and as they watched, their expressions remained the same until Lewis fell to the floor.

"Oh, no! I thought you said someone knocked him out with a spell." Charlie shoved her hands between her legs and leaned forward.

"Yeah—right there. See?"

"He fell to the floor, talking to those men." Sam pressed his lips into a thin line.

"Sexy men," Charlie purred.

"What do you mean, he fell to the floor?" I grabbed the remote and rewound it. Yes, we still had VHS, because Lewis refused to let us have a digital security system. The better to keep private. On the screen, Lewis rose, the saloon doors shut, and I pressed play.

"Watch."

The same thing happened on and off the screen.

"Nol? You see what he did, right? You see the three guys?"

"Hallë, two men come back, and Lewis falls. No one touches him, although the one in front of him crouches to check on him."

Blair Witch Project vibes made me shiver. Holy shit. I let it play a little longer. "There's the third."

"I don't see a third one." Nol's eyes darted to me, then back to the screen, seeing something completely different from me.

"He's right there." I pointed to Quinn leaning on the front door. "And this guy here picked Lewis up and knocked him out."

They all shook their heads, and I was about ready to cry. I rewound the footage again.

"*Arrêt!*" *Stop*, Charlie yelled in French—my niece's first language.

"Tatie, let it play." She waved her hand as if that would make the tape move.

I stopped. The brunette dropped Lewis, and they still didn't say anything. Charlie got up and tugged the remote out of my hand, fast-forwarded a ways, then rewound it.

"Watch," she said, her eyes glued to the screen as she brushed her long chestnut hair back behind her.

Yumi gasped. "How did they do that?"

"No fucking way. Do it again, Charlie." Mateo waved his arms in excitement.

"Mateo, this isn't movie night!"

He ignored me. They watched the event several more times, forward and backward. I kept seeing the same thing, but everyone else saw the real footage in reverse.

After the thousandth time—or more like tenth—I grabbed the remote back. "You seriously can't see this forward?"

They all shook their heads.

"You will need to explain, Hallë." Nol grabbed my arm, and his thumb rubbed the inside of my wrist, trying to calm me.

I dropped into the metal chair next to Nol and started from the beginning. While I explained what had happened, I let all of them read the summons.

"Wait, so if fairies are real, could vampires be real, too?" Mateo asked.

Sam rustled Mateo's hair, knowing that his fiancé was only half serious. He'd asked something like that when I told him I was an *enda*—an elf in human terms. But at this point, it was a fair question.

"I hope not. That's just too much for my old brain to comprehend." Lewis leaned forward, the ice bag in one hand.

"Vampires? Are those the things that change into animals?" Nol asked, tipping his chair onto its two back legs.

"No, those are werewolves," Mateo answered. "Vampires suck your blood."

We were not getting into this. "Guys, please," I begged.

"How do they know about you, though?" Charlie asked.

No one said anything for a while.

"Did they call Nolan by name?" Yumi asked, now behind Lewis, rubbing his shoulders.

I thought back. "Um...no. They said, '*Zayuri* partner.'"

"Why do they say it like this? 'First hour of the fourth day prior to the birth of the new year'? What day is that, exactly?"

"In *Endae*, we celebrate the spring equinox as our new year," Nol answered Yumi. "And our calendar reflects that. I honestly think it was a stupid way for them to say it."

Yumi rested her arms on Lewis's shoulders. "Maybe they're not sure if you're familiar with the American calendar."

"Or they're stuck-up assholes," I muttered.

"So, when is it?" Mateo shook the note at me.

"Tomorrow at seven a.m."

"Sunrise is at seven twenty, Hallë. They said, 'First hour.'"

"Whatever."

Nol grunted. I wasn't in the mood to be literal or corrected.

"That's in like six hours. You need to get home and pick something to wear."

Please, help me, Mother. "What difference does it make what we wear, Mateo?"

Mateo sat up straighter. "You have to look like badasses. Leather up and boots with heels and shit."

I stood blinking at Mateo's wild imagination, fueled by lots of books and movies.

"No."

"Ah, come on. Nolan's gonna do it!"

"I'm going to do what?" Nol straightened in his seat and looked at Mateo with interest.

"You're gonna dress up, right? We can't put you in leather pants, but those black jeans we bought last week will go with your jacket and boots." He really wanted to see Nol in leather pants, bringing it up every chance he could.

"What is he talking about?" Nol mumbled to me. His look held a smidgen of worry.

"Nol will be wearing his *Zayuri* uniform—you do have your full uniform, right?"

Nol gave me the "ask a stupid question, get a stupid answer" look. "You should find something similar to *Aeminan* clothing to represent our country properly."

"It's no longer my country. Besides, acting as a diplomat—which I shouldn't do—I need to dress for the occasion and respect local customs. I'm just not sure if that's human locale or if they expect something else."

Mateo turned to Nol. "You need to prove you can't be walked all over. Wearing a suit and blah heels won't do that. Is *Aeminan* clothing badass?"

I rubbed the bridge of my nose as a headache began to form. Why did they always gang up on me?

"We have to find you something that screams you mean business." Mateo popped up off the couch. "We're gonna show those damn fairies not to mess with you."

I looked up at the ceiling and grumbled. Was he serious?

"Yumi?" I pleaded with her, knowing Charlie would agree with Mateo if I asked her.

"I can't come over and help. Mateo, don't go too outrageous. Professional badass. Is that a thing?" Yumi stood, and Lewis followed suit. Mateo rallied up his forces, pulling on Charlie and Sam until the two of them stood.

My shoulders fell. "Professional badass? Really?"

Yumi gave me a smirk and rested her cheek on Lewis's arm. Payback for not calling her sooner. Damn it.

"Hallë said I'm a badass already." Nol's eyebrow went up as he gazed around the room. I was never going to live that down, and I wasn't even the one who'd said it!

"Yes, you are." Mateo came over and pinched his cheek, knowing the entire situation. DEA Agent Zack-ass had proclaimed Nol a "badass" after picking us up following the fight with Aswryn. Was it badass to be kidnapped? No, no, it wasn't. If anything, I was the badass for taking Aswryn's magic away and finding them.

"Kill me now," I mumbled and went out to the front to grab my purse out of my toolbox. I wasn't wearing anything other than professional clothes that blended in with the human customers at Pioneer Perk. Abso-fucking-lutely not.

3

Nol and I agreed on the way home that telling my grandmother, and maybe getting help from *Endae,* was more important than the right clothes. Sorry, Mateo, but politics came before fashion. As I dreamwalked, Nol had roped them all into searching for fairy information on the internet.

"Tell them nothing until I can grant you permission. How much of your training do you remember, little crow?"

My grandmother and I walked together in a field she thought she recognized, but when she woke up, she probably wouldn't. Dreams were odd. It didn't look familiar to me.

"Some. What will I do if they ask me my name?"

Yalu paused and thought. "You'll have to give it to them. I don't want you telling them about your exile. Get to know them better first. Essentially, in *Aeminan* terms, your exile makes you a convicted felon."

"Agreed, but I don't feel comfortable using Inara. It's not my name anymore. If *Aemina* finds out, I could get in trouble."

"You're exiled. Our laws don't pertain to you as rigidly."

"I am still—I didn't—"

"I know this is overwhelming, but you can do this. At this time, you are our interim diplomat. Let them do the talking. Your job will be to listen and gather information for us. Make sure they are aware that you are holding back information. However, it is only because you haven't been able to contact the *Amura Ore.*"

"But they might consider you—"

"Yes, and that is my official order. Be cordial, and when they ask you anything about home, tell them you can't answer until you get permission. Hedge on the details of how long you've been there. You want to collect as much information about them without giving them anything. This will be a full council discussion. Nothing in our records has said there are any magical species over there."

"But Rassel—he told me there are other magic users over here who won't see my magic as a threat. He told me that as he, *Aore* Junae and *Loret* Maeson, sent me to Earth." Rassel, the teacher who hated me, should never have been my grandmother's proxy for the local council. To this day, that was what I hated most about my "trial," more so than it not even being a trial in the first place.

"Rassel told you that?" She looked out into the distance. "I will call upon him, then. He will need to tell the council what he knows."

"It sounded like Rassel knew more about Earth than the two members. He said *Aemina* hadn't heard from them in a long time, so he wasn't sure I could find them, or if they were still here. Perhaps he thought they had left Earth as well? Are there other realms I'm not aware of, Yalu?"

"I don't—I will speak with everyone about this information."

"He might deny it. This was after we left the courtroom."

"Yes, because what they did, and how they did it, was illegal."

"Does that mean more delays?"

"There is no telling. I hope to guide you on how to move forward within the day. However, there are other issues. The entire assembly has determined that Aswryn's death did not break the curse. It just isn't leaving. After all this time, they all have had to admit that Aswryn had a partner in forming and casting the curse. There is no other reason." Nol had broached this subject soon after he'd reached adulthood and after Aswryn had kidnapped him. Many of the members were too stubborn and proud to admit they were wrong, no matter if Nol was right nine times out of ten.

"Hally—" Yalu hesitated, then looked away. "Never mind."

"You can tell me."

She patted my cheek and smiled a smile that did not reach her eyes. "No, little crow. I will wait until it is more definitive. I feel myself stirring. Lean on each other. You're *muranildi* for a reason."

"Yes, Yalu." But I wasn't sure if she heard me before her dream flickered, and I was in a void between her mind and mine. The loneliest and freakiest place.

I felt the night terror coming before I saw anything, like a twitch on your back telling you there's something out there. Waiting. The faceless thing, I'd seen it before. It couldn't hurt me—my consciousness knew that—but this place was something between awareness and not. The solid space below me disappeared, but I couldn't scream. I just flailed in silence. Then someone grabbed my hand. I looked up, but the relief from being rescued was torn away when I found the faceless thing that lurked in the back of my mind and in all my night terrors.

No sound came out as I screamed and jerked to get out of its grip. I dared not use my other hand to force it to let go, in case it grabbed that one, too. Nothing was working, and I felt myself rise as it pulled me closer. I bucked and my hand slipped, so I bucked again. Falling for eternity was better than being with this thing. A third buck and I was free, falling fast, faster until I landed.

I gasped awake and bolted upright, trying to get enough air. The feeling of the thing holding on to me trickled away. With one last shake of my arm, I focused on my heart rate to calm down.

My phone said three twenty in the morning. Not that I could call a dream-walk restful, but it wasn't as draining as *Olauvë*, where council members who weren't in the capital went into a meditative state to be present at required meetings. Time to go give my report.

Nol was pacing across the living room when I came down. In full uniform. Except his jacket, which wasn't in sight. I'd actually never seen him wear the whole thing. The sleeveless black-and-brown shirt wrapped around his body, crisscrossing to tie at the small of his back, right above his clasped hands, as he continued to pace. I'd always wondered if the damn things were comfortable. Weren't they worried about them untying?

Seeing him now, while he looked...handsome, it reminded me of his uncle. And Tolwe scared me. Thankfully, he kept his cinnamon hair loose instead of in a tight braid like Tolwe, but it also hid his face from me. Still, the pacing was a sign.

"Nol—" He stopped and snapped his focus to me instead of his thoughts. It looked like he'd needed out of them anyway.

Nol opened his mouth to respond, but Mateo interrupted him. "Oh good, she's finally up." Mateo got up from the couch, tossing a packet of papers on the coffee table. "I thought you'd sleep through your meeting."

I raised my eyebrows, wishing that were possible. "I'm going to start a fucking war."

Mateo paused in his stretch, his dark brown eyes wide with surprise. The others stopped their research and waited for me to continue.

"There is no way I can remember everything Yalu told me in her official orders to act as interim diplomat." The gravity of what she expected of me closed in. I doubled over to suck in enough breath.

Nol was there in a moment, placing his hands on my shoulders. "I have no doubt in you. This is what you wanted to do—"

"As a kid. It's been a hundred years. She wants me to use my name, Nol. My name."

"*Astur*." *Okay*.

"She doesn't want me to tell them I'm exiled, but she wants me to be honest. How do I do that?"

"You do your best with what you have been given. Call upon what you remember and what she told you. I will be beside you the entire time."

"I can't do this. I can't be responsible for starting a war."

"Let's get your mind off this." The ice clinked as Mateo downed the last of his water and headed for the kitchen. "We'll go pick out your clothes."

"Mateo!" I whined and dropped my head back to stare at the ceiling. "That isn't going to work. Give me work or something."

"There's nothing that hasn't already been found." Sam dropped his papers on the coffee table, next to Mateo's. "We can't tell the difference between real and myth. Through the centuries, people have copied other people's work. It's information overload."

"But that doesn't mean we stop researching—"

"Hallë, you would not be able to determine if what you find is something we have already read." He tried to look apologetic, the dimple between his eyebrows dinted. "Truly, let Mateo distract you. Get dressed."

"But—"

"Come on, *ojitos*. Let's go find you an outfit." Mateo grabbed my arm and started toward the downstairs hallway.

"Help me?" I tried to look as pathetic as possible as I begged the others.

Nol picked a tablet up from their pile of papers and ignored my plea. Sam waved, but Charlie, my wonderful niece, stood up and followed. Thank the Mother.

Resigned to my fate by the bottom of the stairs, I marched up between Charlie and Mateo, missing the creaky step, even though Mateo stepped on it. He didn't care, but it always bugged me, and I didn't want to replace the real wood throughout the house.

Mateo headed straight to my closet while I watched them from the middle of my room. While Mateo didn't know my walk-in closet inside and out, he'd been through it a few times.

"This isn't going to work."

"You wound me, Hally. I will find you the perfect outfit."

"What if Nol is right? What if they do make a scene?" I wrung my hands as I watched Charlie and Mateo push around my clothes.

"Stop second-guessing yourself, Tatie," Charlie spoke up, half muffled from the clothes-covered walls. "They're hiding from the humans."

I walked over and leaned on the doorframe.

"Exactly." Mateo poked his head out of the clothes and looked at Charlie. "They can't risk getting noticed."

"What am I supposed to say if I can't tell them anything? There is no way I can do this all."

"Try this on." Mateo shoved a halter top at me.

"I'm not wearing that. No halter tops. No skirts with high boots either."

Mateo scoffed. "You're no fun. You have excluded almost every piece of clothing in here, then."

"Not true." I walked in and pushed him out of the way. As a tattoo artist, I didn't have much office attire—okay, none. I owned one pair of black jeans without holes and nothing that wasn't sheer, lacy, sleeveless, or ripped. You get the picture, right? I was a tattoo artist, and gothic was my persona. I did not go all corsets, straps, and almost naked. But my clothes were a bit...revealing to show off tattoos I didn't get to have. Plus, fabric got in the way of tattooing.

"Here. This is professional." I shook the sweater and saw the deliberately tattered stitches and holes. "Never mind."

"You have to go in, intimidating and confident, otherwise they'll force you to do what they want." Mateo shoved some shirts around.

"How do you know this, Mateo?" Charlie crossed her arms and cocked a hip, frowning at him.

"Books, duh. Plus, Sam has to look authoritative whenever he goes into courtrooms and trial conferences."

"Nol's lucky," I grumbled. All he had to do was pull out his uniform.

"Tatie, what about your green shirt, the one with the red flowers? I love that one." Charlie pushed off the door frame and went to look for said shirt.

I thought back. It was a satin tank top, with a sheer green arm cape—the ones that covered the arms and shoulders. "No. The only skirt that goes with it was ruined. But! I have something similar." I pulled out an all-black sheer tank top with a chain of velvet black dahlias snaking up the torso to hide the middle of one breast. The other side only had one flower to hide my nipple. "I wear a camisole with it."

"It could work." Mateo shrugged. "Oh, what if..." He dug around in my top drawer. "Where's your—ah-ha." Mateo pulled out a halter-top bra with a similar pattern. "Put it on. Let's see."

The shirt combination held merit. I grabbed the two items and tossed them on the bed. Mateo had already pulled out three pairs of pants since I'd left. All with holes, zippers, or laced-up sides. None of that would do.

"Here!" I pulled out the one pair of jeans without holes in them.

Mateo glanced my way for a moment. "No." He went back to looking.

I rolled my eyes and left the closet to try everything on. He meant well, but I couldn't think of anything else. "Come out here and look, both of you."

They poked their heads out like two naughty children making sure the room was clear.

I checked the mirror hanging on the inside of the closet door. "I'm wearing these."

Mateo's lips puckered, but he knew I was right. He was irritated because that meant I couldn't wear the boots he thought were the "badass" vibe we needed to have.

"Now can we please get back to the war issue?"

"War?" Mateo's eyes widened. "You are not going to war."

"When they think I'm lying about everything, we will. What am I supposed to say if I can't tell them anything? There is no way I can do this."

We left my room and stomped down the stairs, Charlie in front this time, holding on to the banister. "Your grandmother and Nolan have faith in you. You are the most qualified of all the *endai*."

"All I can tell them about is myself. I know nothing of recent politics."

"Is she still going on about that?" Sam yelled from the living room as we got to the bottom of the stairs.

"Yes," both Charlie and Mateo said together.

I groaned.

Sam came into view from the hall. "Clothes usually do the trick."

It wasn't like we'd gone shopping. "We weren't going to spend three and a half hours in my closet, Sam."

"Let's watch a movie, then." Sam started walking toward us.

I placed my hands on my hips. "That's not going to work. Did you not hear what I said before?"

"Impending war and end of the world as we know it. Come on. We'll watch *Lord of the Rings*. Nolan hasn't watched it yet, and he can mock the fake language. You love that movie, Hally."

"LOTR?" I squinted at him. "Are you nuts?"

"It's perfect!" Mateo rubbed his hands together and grabbed my elbow. "A full three hours of distraction, and you'll leave right after it's over."

"I don't want to rush out of here. That's ridiculous."

"Then what's your suggestion?"

I grumbled as I tried to think of another activity. Board games wouldn't work. Then I realized their attempt to distract me had worked, which brought me back around to why they wanted to distract me. "Ugh, I can't do this."

"You can and you will." Charlie moved to the side and let Mateo guide me back up the stairs

"Nolan, stop pacing and get your ass up the stairs. We've got something else to research!" Sam's voice echoed through the back of the house.

I was so screwed.

Nol was looking up Tolkien's languages as soon as he heard Arwen speak—oh, and after he had stopped laughing at how "mystical" elves were supposed to look. Mateo almost kicked him, until I smacked Nol for the third time for his outburst of, "*Ai, sae felineda!" That's not possible.* I didn't feel guilty one bit, either. The guy tried, okay? Tolkien was a genius and Nol needed to shut up.

"How was this research?" Nol asked as the credits rolled. Well, he'd asked it before under his breath during the movie in *Aemirin*.

"Middle Earth could be their Underhill," Mateo offered.

I checked my phone. Six thirty-seven. "Fuck. It's almost time to go."

"We established that's when the movie would be over." Mateo pinched the back of his neck and yawned.

"Shush, you're not helping." I rubbed my palms on my jeans.

I walked over to the TV to turn it off manually. The fish tank next to it bubbled away.

"You've got this, Tatie," Charlie said as I stared at the lid.

"What if I don't? Yalu said to listen, be cordial, and tell them I can't say anything without permission. How won't that piss this lady off? It'd piss me off to no end."

Charlie walked up to me, her jaw set. "Look at me."

Charlie shook my shoulders once and made me look her in the eyes.

"I know you're scared, but this is not the time to fall apart. You have to be strong. There isn't another option. People are depending on you, and you will not let them down. Do you hear me? You've never let me down and you aren't about to start now." Her words started to sink in. She was right. There wasn't another option and no one else to rely on. "So get your fucking head in the game and fall apart on your own time."

I nodded and stared back into the beautiful brown eyes of this woman. My niece had been strong enough to bring her daughter to a new country when she'd been falling apart. When all she'd wanted to do was lie down and give up.

"All right," I whispered. I gathered my thoughts and focused. Nothing else mattered except getting through this meeting. "*Merci, Charlie.*" *Thank you, Charlie.* She let me go so I could compose myself. "I'm better. You're right, love."

"I just learned from the best." Charlie hugged me. "Are you ready?"

Fuck. Charlie held me until I got my breathing under control. "Okay." I pushed down my shirt, not that it needed any smoothing or anything. "We have fifteen minutes?" No one said anything. "We need to be clear on what we're doing, otherwise I might freak the fuck out. Everything we do must be deliberate. Nol, have you gotten any better at politics?"

Nol scowled at me. "Why do you think I carry a sword?"

The sound of a throat clearing came from the dark hallway outside of the upstairs family room, followed by the appearance of Sam, his hands shoved in his trouser pockets—rumpled trousers—and he gave the room a lazy smile. "I made coffee."

"So that's where he ran off to." Mateo jumped up and headed to his partner to kiss his temple.

"*Mon ange.*" My angel. "Thank you, Sam. Well, Nol?"

"I suck at it," Nol grumbled.

"Then you won't say a word."

We clambered down the stairs, Mateo in front, going way too slow, in my opinion.

"How did you do that?" I caught Nol whispering to Charlie.

"It's mostly what she told me when I was upset about Remi's death." She didn't bother to keep her voice down.

"She told you that?"

"Mostly, *oui*." Charlie, a stair above me, squeezed my shoulder. "Right, Tatie?"

"Pretty much, yes. Sometimes we need that, sometimes not."

While there was time to drink coffee, there was no time to enjoy it. Unless we wanted to be late. Less than ten minutes later, five mugs were drying on the rack as we headed to the back. We shoved our feet into boots and shoes, the rain pattering down on the roof of the mudroom in the back of my house. I grabbed the trench coat that Mateo had said not to wear and slipped it on.

"You'll take Sam's car—" Mateo started.

"We will?" I asked at the same time Sam asked, "She will?" Sam liked his car.

"Their options are the old Volvo or your Audi, dear."

"There's nothing wrong with the Volvo," I said.

"Do we have to make Hallë drive?"

For the record, I was a great driver—Nol just thought vehicles were too big for me. To be fair, the Volvo was a boat. Irritated as fuck with the whole situation, I blurted without thinking, "We could take my bike."

Everyone shut up and turned their heads in slow motion, except Charlie, who knew about it. The hush of rain was the only sound as Sam and Mateo processed this new development.

"You have a motorcycle?" Mateo's voice broke.

I lifted a shoulder as I rolled up onto my toes, and the leather of the boots creaked. "Charlie and I brought it out of storage a week ago." I paused. "Um, just don't tell Agent Zack-ass." The agent who had given me shit for years, because he'd tried to connect me to my old tattoo mentor's drug dealing. Besides, transit was not that bad, but Friday on King County Metro at seven in the morning—um, no thank you.

"Is that a yes?" There was no need for confirmation, and I withheld my chuckling as I switched my trench coat for my red leather riding jacket. I flipped the hood up and buttoned the front. The thing was pretty warm, but it did nothing for the bottom portion of my body. I used to have riding pants, but Charlie and I couldn't find them in the storage unit. "Ready?"

"An improvement," Mateo noted and hooked Sam's arm to walk out together.

"Where was I when this happened?" Nol asked as he thumped down the stairs that led to the backyard.

"You were shopping with Mateo," Charlie said as I opened the lock to the flimsy metal shed. I planned to get a better shed this summer. "Tatie and I decided she needed a way to travel in case of an emergency."

"But I didn't want to get another car—" I added.

"So I asked about the bike."

"I'd almost forgotten about it, to be honest." I shrugged and pulled the key back out.

The boys came closer, but we couldn't all fit inside. Nol cast a small sphere to keep the rain out.

"Why didn't you do that when we left the house?" Mateo chided.

"Our coats do an exceptional job. Just because we have magic at our disposal does not mean we use it for everything. Try running everywhere you go, Mateo. Or carrying around twenty-pound weights all day. Magic can be draining. Even the small spells, if held for too long, grow tiresome."

"You sound like my mom," I told Nol without really thinking about my words.

Nol turned to me, a smile on his face. "Where do you think I learned it from? My mom?"

"Fair." Wennië wasn't a nagger. My mom, on the other hand—every child needed nagging according to her. Nol, Gil, and I had never gone a day without her input, be it about homework, chores, or voice level.

"Why are we just finding out about this?" Sam's eyes were about as round as his fogging glasses, and he had trouble picking up his jaw.

After a moment of confused silence, I realized Sam was talking about the bike, not my mother. "None of you have one, and I figured you'd never imagine me with one. Remember, I try to blend in. Don't be so shocked. There's a ton of shit you don't know about me."

"Like what?" Mateo asked.

Charlie giggled.

"We're getting off topic. Nol, Charlie's helmet might fit you."

"*Ai*, I am not getting on that."

"Tell me one thing," Mateo demanded.

"You'll have to wait." Hiding my smirk, I shuffled into where my black 2007 Ninja was covered, along with two helmets. I handed Nol Charlie's helmet, but he didn't take it. "Charlie will be pissed if you drop that." I let go, making him scramble to catch it. So un-*Zayuri*-like of him.

"Hell yeah," Mateo said as soon as I lifted the cover. It wasn't that badass, but it was better than a 1982 brown Volvo station wagon.

They moved aside as I pushed my Ninja out, and Charlie opened the gate. She kissed my cheeks.

"What about your cast?" Sam asked.

"I drove it here fine." I wiggled my fingers. Sure, it had been a little difficult, but I'd managed.

"Yes, and with a concussion," Sam pointed out. Now he sounded like Yumi.

"It was just a few days before the doctor cleared me. It's fine. No!?" I offered one last time.

"Nope." He could take the shadows and be there before me.

"Ah, you probably wouldn't fit, anyway."

Mateo and Sam continued to stare at me and didn't respond as I waved. Charlie hadn't stopped smiling since I'd blurted out my secret.

4

I REMEMBERED WHY I didn't ride my bike in Washington. First of all, lane splitting was a no-no. In my experience, Washingtonians were much less considerate. Less than ten minutes after leaving my house, I parked my bike against the building close to the coffee shop—one good thing about bikes. Yes, I did speed and lane-split through a few places. I was careful; I promise.

I tucked my helmet under my arm and went inside. My favorite coffee shop was on the second floor of the Pioneer Building. Sometimes people missed it, walking by, more interested in the underground tours or Cherry Street coffee shop. They were cool too, but Pioneer Perk was open twenty-four hours. And they let dogs in here! How perfect was that? If I ever got one, I'd bring it in here.

The velvety, nutty smell of coffee beans permeated the stairwell. Usually, I took my time, checked out the posters of new music artists and band flyers, but not this damn early in the morning. Instead, I shrugged out of my riding jacket, laid it over my helmet, and surveyed the cafe. I didn't see any of my unwelcome visitors from last night or anyone that screamed, "Magical fairy over here!" Nor did I see Nol.

"*Oyi,*" *Hey*, Nol whispered as he grabbed my elbow.

I jumped. "Fucking-A, Nol. Don't sneak up on me like that," I whispered back.

"I can't believe you drove off on that thing. You're going to kill yourself."

"English," I hissed. "I've ridden a motorcycle for over fifty years and I'm not dead yet. What is it with you not trusting me?" Off and on at least, but he didn't need to know that.

Nol stood straight and rolled his shoulders back. "I trust you," he continued in *Aemirin*. "It is the machines you navigate that terrify me. You are so small."

"Stop right there. My size doesn't matter in the slightest. You of all people should know this."

He puffed his cheeks out. "As Charlie says, I'm working on it. They can do so much damage if they fail. To you and whatever is around it."

"You're *Zayuri*."

He bobbed his head, waiting for me to continue.

"How are they more dangerous than Sanae?" How much more dangerous could it get than riding a dragon?

Nol went to speak, but paused and dropped his eyes. *Yeah, that's what I thought.*

I hitched my helmet and jacket up my hip and got in line. "Do you want a mocha?"

"Please," he muttered, hands behind his back while scanning the area.

The barista was unfamiliar since I never came in at this forsaken hour in the morning. We moved up, giving me a better view out the window. The sun had risen high enough to set the new green leaves of the trees aglow in The Square and deepen the gray and red of the Life Mutual Building across the street. I smiled, remembering what Pioneer Square used to be like.

"What are you looking at?" Nol asked, in English, resting his chin atop my head.

"Just remembering old times. Léon didn't believe me when I told him they'd put the totem pole back up once they were done fixing the road. He'd lost faith in so much by then, and this one simple thing—after his tatie had told him he was finally safe—they took it away from him."

"They put it back, obviously."

"Hm-mm."

"Ma'am?" the barista called, bringing me back to the here and now.

We moved up and ordered. A drip for me, too early for anything fancy.

I leaned against the end of the counter, looking around while I waited for our coffees. The café was sparse, with just a few half-asleep people. Two women at different tables stared at their phones. The faint displacement of air brought my head around as two men in business suits came in. Then I found Nol leaning against the condiment table, stir stick in hand, eyes up and roaming the room. The sunlight, reflecting off the windows of another building, made Nol's cinnamon-red hair glow.

"Hally!" the other barista yelled.

Nol pushed off the table and was at the counter in a few long strides, picking up our coffees before I made it several feet closer from my spot. He handed me my cup and muttered, "I think they are here. Do not look."

"Where? Those two women don't strike me as fairy material."

"The right back. The other side with the step-up thing with books and games. At the large table."

The platform in the back? "When was the last time you slept? You keep messing up your words and your contractions are fading."

"I'll be fine."

Sure, that proved it. "I just want to make sure you're okay."

"It does not matter right now."

"Fuck them. Answer my question. How long has it been since you slept?"

He pursed his lips. "A few days."

"Crap. Why didn't you say something?"

"What can you do about it?"

"Is it the city noises?"

"I think that is most of it. Come."

Before he could get ahead of me, I got in front of him and stopped.

"Hallë—" he hissed.

Like invisible smoke on the floor, I let my magic roll out around us, feeling the energies, the lives of the four people with their coffees, and the two humans behind the counter. We moved only after my magic swept the area. I pushed it over the step onto the platform and felt their ward. My feet tapped against the step, and I raised my voice without allowing the humans to hear. I forced a smile. "Unless you want to risk me sitting in your lap, I suggest you drop your ward." I paused for a few breaths. "Please. I'd prefer to find a seat without someone in it."

Nol rested his hand on my shoulder as they dropped their glamor—no, enclosed us in their glamor. I felt it at my back, like a soft force field. Did that mean we couldn't get out? One tall but slight woman sat at the table, and four people stood behind her. Two close to the wall held their hands behind their backs, while two had positioned themselves behind her shoulders, hands clasped in front of them. All four assessed Nol, with no-funny-business-bodyguard faces. Fun.

One moment, they all appeared human, and the next their ears were pointier than mine and Nol's. Their bone structure was sharper than ours, too, which was to say, inhuman.

The woman, who I assumed was the queen, wore her silver-blonde hair in a pixie cut. Her hair wasn't blonde enough to call human but not silver enough to shine in the light. Wait—did it? As she shifted, I checked for any flashing. Nope. That would have been distracting.

She wore a cream pantsuit, darkening the beige hue of her skin and lightening her pale sienna eyes. She uncrossed her ankles and sat up. I wished I owned more business-casual clothes, damn it. I wasn't sure if I was supposed to speak first. The last political class I'd taken was one hundred and nineteen years ago. Then again, I knew nothing about fae customs either.

I bowed a polite business bow that I hoped was acceptable.

"Good morning. Hally Dubois, is it?" She got the French accent right, even with her Washington accent.

"Good morning. I assume, per the summons, you are Her Majesty, Queen Orlaith, Ruler of the Fae. Or is it sidhe? Brodrick announced you as sidhe; however, the letter said *fae*."

She dipped her head. "Both are correct. You may call me Orlaith in public. I would say welcome; however, I cannot. Do you know why?"

Did this count as public inside her ward? "According to the summons, we are in violation of the Earth-*Endae* treaty?"

"Exactly, and breaking agreements isn't good, is it?"

"No, it's not. Orlaith, if I may say something?"

She waved her hand, a little flick.

"Since we only obtained your summons eight hours ago, I have not been able to discuss the situation with *Aemina*. I am not in the position to give you many answers."

"Of course, you haven't been able to tell them about the summons. Do your people know that you never contacted me?"

I shook my head. "We were unaware of whom to contact or how to do so. *Endai* haven't been in contact with this realm in so long that they didn't know what awaited me."

She turned to the guard on her left, who nodded. "My truth seer says you are not lying. It has been a while now, hasn't it?" She paused, testing my reaction. I wouldn't answer. "It was brave of you to come here without any information. You're quite young, both of you. To send such a young team means they don't consider Aswryn a high priority or *Aemina* lacks politicians." Again, she waited.

My stomach flipped at the mention of Aswryn. What had that evil *endai* done to these people? "I would love to give you answers; however, without *Aemina's* permission, I can't say. I'm sure you wouldn't want one of your people speaking on behalf of the fae without consulting you first."

"You're lecturing me on how I consult with my diplomats?"

"That wasn't my intention." I fumbled to recover from my faux pas. Damn it. "Please, forgive me. I just don't want to get into trouble with *Aemina*."

"They send an inexperienced diplomat to explain with a *Zayuri*. Is—was Aswryn a nuisance to you? Is that why it took them so long to send someone over?"

I stared at my shoes, then remembered my classes: *act like you know what you're doing; even if you don't, be confident; and only give away what you know they already know.* "Aswryn was never just a nuisance. She was a real threat, which we've handled."

"About that. If you were here to kill Aswryn, why are you still here? What else are you planning?"

"Well—"

"Pardon me? Hallë? Orlaith?" Nol dipped his head.

I stared at him, wide-eyed, wishing I could hush him.

"I would not speak, except I feel it is important to defend Hallë's position."

She raised her chin. "Which is?"

"Hallë is still healing from the injuries Aswryn inflicted on her before I could reach her. The human doctors cleared her three days ago of her concussion."

"You have healers there—far more skilled than human ones."

Nol gave a shuddering breath. "There are not many healers left. Aswryn killed most of them, including my sister."

Damn it, he was giving too much information away.

Orlaith waited, nodding as she looked between us. "My condolences. What is your name?"

"Nolan."

"Your full name?"

"Twynolan Madoraen *Rudairn, Hasin Zayuri*."

"Madoraen *Zayuri* family line? Interesting. I knew some of your ancestors, Nolan. How did you reach *Hasin* so fast? You've had, what, forty years, fifty at most. You can't be older than two hundred and fifty."

"Approximately thirty. Anger is a strong motivator. I wanted to stop Aswryn after she killed my sister."

"Ah, so that is why you came with Hally—or met her here? Revenge."

I straightened but tried to keep my nerves from showing. They'd done their research. How far had they traced my presence here? Oh, how I wished I could shut Nol up.

"I chose to come here, yes. You remember much about *endai* and the *Zayuri*."

"I would hope so. Before the war, we were friends for centuries upon centuries. You don't forget that." Orlaith's eyes widened a fraction as she realized what she'd given away. She smiled, keeping it slow and lazy, like she'd meant to give us that information. But I knew.

"You speak English better than he does, Hally. I can see the advantage of coming before Nolan—risky, if Aswryn found you. You're impressive to have remained hidden from us and Aswryn for so long. Right under our noses, in California and then here. And you make friends fast. I assume you came in through the Redwoods?" She paused. "A sting operation—do you know the phrase?"

"I know the phrase."

"But when Aswryn came to you, you sure announced yourself. You're powerful. But that is to be expected, given your family."

My lungs seized, and it broke my focus. "I—I'm sorry. My family?"

"I knew your ancestors. A grandmother several times back. Before the war." How long did these people live? "She was my friend—I missed her for quite some time."

My mind went blank. "Oh." Such an intelligent, diplomatic answer. I was screwing this up. It took me a moment to recover. But then I could have slapped my forehead. My family line wasn't hard to determine, as one female from every generation carried the same traits. The black hair and dark green eyes, so unlike the rest of our people, accompanied our magical traits.

"I assume the *Amura Ore* continues to keep a close eye on your family. This is another reason I'm curious to know why they sent you. If you tell me what Aswryn did there, I will tell you what she did here."

"Are there lasting effects from what she did here?" I asked.

"You could say that."

I bit my lip. She'd tricked me into giving information—although it was more of a tit for tat. Aswryn had been wreaking havoc on both our people. My jaw tightened as Nol cleared his throat. What was he doing now?

"She killed many *Aeminan* citizens."

I couldn't take my eyes off Nol as he blurted out shit he knew he shouldn't. Hadn't I told him not to talk?

"She was part *Mellori*," Orlaith said. "I'm not sure what else."

Nol glanced at me, lips pressed hard, and the worry line between his brow deepened. "There is evidence to support that her father is or was *Aeminan*. But I also do not think she was working alone."

Orlaith laughed. It appeared sincere, but if she was older than dirt, she'd had time to perfect her reactions. Which was why her slip earlier was peculiar. "No, she was not. Do you know who she worked with in *Endae*?"

"The *Zayuri* have been searching, yet no. She was detained for over two years before someone helped her escape."

Her thin eyebrows shot up. "So, she had people in the *Zayuri*?"

"Not us. The *Aeminan* guard."

"What damage did she do over there?"

I shook my head a fraction when he met my eyes, but he turned back to Orlaith and continued. "Hallë, I will not get in trouble for telling her things like you will. It is a...looped hole?"

Orlaith lifted a shoulder. Not her problem.

"Her curse was specific to *Aemina*. The more powerful you are, the faster it is to latch on."

Orlaith's eyes darted to me, and she sat up straight. "It was more dangerous for you and your family. Was it not, Hally?"

I gave her that grin again. "Aswryn was a threat to many." Yes, my family's magic was powerful, but it was also different from other *endai*.

Orlaith touched her chin and peered from Nol to me. "Hmm. Hally, I will grant you twenty-four hours to get in touch with *Aem-*

ina. I will have an escort meet you at your home at eight on Saturday morning if you feel safer now?"

"Yes, Your Majesty. Thank you."

Orlaith held her finger up. "Ah-uh, never thank the fae. You are in our debt if you do. I'll give you this one." She winked.

I gave her a slight bow.

"Wait, you said you would tell us what Aswryn has done here," Nol almost whined.

"I will." She sat up, her back off the chair and her face full of raw honesty. "Just not now."

At Nol's naïve expression, I couldn't hold in my laugh. I patted him on the arm as he watched me with an innocent, confused expression I hadn't seen since he was a child.

"Hallë?" He leaned closer.

"I'm sorry." I tried to stop laughing but couldn't. "You look so confused, and it's so rare for you. She really got you, didn't she?"

Orlaith started laughing with me, but a gentle laugh, not to make fun of Nol, but at the situation.

"You knew she would do that?"

"Why do you think I told you to stop? Oh, man, this is perfect. I love you, but please leave the politics to me."

Nol glanced up at Orlaith, who was still laughing. The guards continued looking forward as if they couldn't hear, giving the British Royal guards a run for their money. "You truly are not telling us now?"

"She'll lose her only bargaining chip."

Nol looked at Orlaith for confirmation, and she lifted her shoulders in an apologetic shrug. "Oh dear, I am sorry, but Hally is right. I think I will enjoy working with you two."

"Your Majesty, if you would lower your ward so we may leave and contact *Aemina*?" Nol asked.

"I will, but you may want to make your own. It would seem odd for a couple to walk out of thin air."

Nol and my eyes met. Then we gave Orlaith similar smiles at her assumption. Maybe we'd tell her about our *Muranilde* bond later.

"Leave that to me, Hallë." Nol took my coffee and set it down on Orlaith's table. "Your Majesty, a pleasure." He grabbed my helmet and coat, then guided me to the darkest corner and everything went black. So cold and quiet. Then the rushing sound of cars and the smell of burned rubber, rain, and urine surrounded us. I stepped back and bumped into my bike.

"Holy shit! You took me—you're not allowed—that was freezing!"

"That is for making fun of me." He tapped my nose.

"Oh, come on. You were adorable. Besides, it's not like you don't tease me. It's payback."

"No, that was far different. That embarrassed me. My teasing is only between us."

I held my breath for a few heartbeats, then snagged my coat from him. "Okay, yes, it was mean of me, but that was perfect."

If looks could kill. "How was—"

Shrugging into my coat, I stepped up close. I pressed my hand against his chest and took his hand, squeezing it tightly. "Listen," I whispered.

His mouth shut so fast his teeth clicked.

"That in there was perfect. I know it was at your expense, but now we're in a more comfortable position with her. Did you hear what she said? She's going to enjoy working with us. Because of you, she sees us as more than two *endai* on a mission."

He swallowed, then leaned over me. "Fine," he purred and touched my face. "But you are in trouble for that."

My stomach flipped. What the hell would he do? It had to stop before it went too far. "Am I?" I raised an eyebrow, not as good as Nol's eyebrow raise, but it was at least decent, in my opinion. "I've been nice to you because it's you. You don't want me to treat you like a too-forward asshole, do you?"

"If I were you, I would not try it."

We would not play this flirting war here just to make each other uncomfortable. Nope. The pain-in-the-ass thought my reaction was funny. We weren't used to each other, and it always caught me unprepared. But not this morning. Admittedly, he'd grown up to be a gorgeously handsome *endao,* and the conceited asshole knew it.

"Okay." I patted his chest, raised myself up as high as I could, and kissed his lower cheek, then the other, surprising the hell out of him. I'd never done that with him. My other friends, yeah. Not him. "See ya at home. Oh, and by the way, I'm kicking you out. I'll give you the key to the loft, but you'll need to start paying rent in April."

Nol chuckled. "Right."

"Seriously." I made sure he saw it in my eyes. "Free ride's over, buddy. You wanna stay? Stay. But you'll get the whole experience."

"Come on, Hallë. Be serious."

I put my helmet on, lifted the visor, and started the bike. "I am. That's what you get for acting so entitled."

"Wait—"

I tapped my visor down, revved the engine, and left my pain-in-the-ass *muranildo* in the rain.

5

"You did well, little crow." My grandmother smiled as she sat on a cushion in the house she shared with Tolwe. If I understood correctly, they lived in the *Zayuri* village of *Jinatrau*, near the capital. I sat in front of her, not that anyone could see me but her. I'd weighed the risk and used *Olauvë* to update her—it was that important.

"Are you going to the capital for this?"

Yalu scoffed. "No. Not this time. I'll be speaking to them immediately after this, however."

"But they know? That we're talking?"

Yalu's non-answer answered for her.

"Yalu! I thought you got permission."

"A few senior members know. Your grandfather and the inner circle knew of this meeting with the fairy queen."

"Five people?"

"Your 'involvement' with Aswryn's curse is causing waves."

"But this—"

"More people will need to get involved. I'll push for an answer before your next meeting. I can't guarantee anything."

"So they'll keep their noses high while the Queen of the Fae prepares for inter-realm war. And if I have to go in blind again?"

"Be as graceful as you can while giving away as little as possible. We don't want to go to war. You may tell them we know nothing of their race and that we have no record of any treaty. Ask them for a copy of the treaty for us to read, if they would be so kind. The members—including your grandfather and me—want to know why we have no record of their people. They are skeptical."

"I was, too. It was when she spoke about our family that I believed her."

"It is interesting. I don't know what ancestor that would be. We can trace our line back to the second era."

"Maybe that is where you should start looking."

"Nevie, those papers are fragile. They can't be taken out of the preservation room for fear of deterioration. If your father were well, or if Nolan were here, I'd send them to research in there, but neither is possible."

"Maybe I could convince Nol to go over there. He's bored, anyway."

"They might not let him go back once he's here. Why do you think he hasn't tried to visit Sanae? Tolwe complains about her attitude. I'm sure she feels abandoned, regardless of what Tolwe tells her. But as Nolan is the only one she can communicate with, it's a one-sided conversation."

"Sanae." I shivered. "I can't believe Nol has a dragon. He doesn't talk about her. That's the hardest part to believe about the *Zayuri* thing." I shared the memory of Nol's discomfort in cars.

Yalu laughed. "He's not in charge. I agree with him. Sanae has intelligence."

"Well, with that lightheartedness, I'm going to leave you. Nol got no sleep last night. With Ray and Charlie out for the day, we can sleep. And we can't do that until I'm back."

I would have hugged her if I could, but we were discussing this on a celestial plane connected to *Endae*, and I had no physical body. We'd visit in her dreams later this week. While in reality, we weren't physically touching, a hug felt like a hug in a dream.

Unlike last time, my magic didn't pull me back. I wasn't exhausted. I released my anchor to this realm and was back in my consciousness, in my body, within heartbeats. A head was on my stomach. And I was propped up on pillows. Nol's silky, cinnamon-red hair hid his face, and by the rhythm of his breathing, I knew he was asleep. While that wasn't a good thing—my body was vulnerable in the celestial plane—Nol had admittedly told me he hadn't slept in two days. And I suspected longer still.

We weren't in the family room anymore, either. My bedroom curtains were closed tight, but nothing could block out the city noise. I brushed Nol's hair back and bunched my muscles to sit up. But I paused. It would make his head slide off and wake him up. When would he have another chance to sleep?

I placed my hand on his back and tried not to move too much. The position was awkward, though. He'd obviously thought this through and knew that once I woke up, I'd be too uncomfortable to stay still—and thus wake him up. I tried anyway, scooting down a wiggle at a time until the pillows weren't at the small of my back—that was my aim, anyway.

I got about five centimeters before Nol stirred. I froze and waited. There was another possible way to keep him sleeping. If Nol still slept the same way as when we were kids, he'd roll away. I waited, holding my breath to see if he'd move on his own.

He hadn't slept in my room here, choosing to take the couch in the family room, even though I'd offered the hammock in my room. Maybe a real bed would be the key to him getting more sleep. Another good reason for him to move to the loft. I had an amazingly comfortable king-sized bed there.

This bed wasn't big enough for the both of us. As children, we'd shared oversized beds at both our houses, and we'd swap homes every week or so. Odd to anyone but our families. Our parents had tried to prevent this habit, but ever since I was a baby, Nol had slept beside me. First, because he was weak and my presence strengthened him. His parents had lived with us for the first decade of my life. That was their downfall. We'd been inseparable until the day I killed our friends.

I tried moving again, and Nol shifted. Now was my chance. I scooted down until my head was on my pillow, while Nol rolled over like I'd expected him to. His legs had trapped the blankets, and I couldn't slide into them. Giving up the not-so-well-fought fight, I rolled onto my side, away from him, and fell right to sleep.

※

DARKNESS. WATER LAPPED AT my bare feet.

"You will never be forgiven." A hand pressed on my shoulder, first lightly, then too much weight to bear. My shoulder cracked.

I screamed, but no sound came. I had to keep moving, or the pressure was sure to crack the rest of me. My foot touched something in the water. Bloated fingers splayed out, one finger, then the thumb. I had to keep going. The next hand my foot touched was more bones than flesh.

"Consider everyone dead to you. As Nolan said, you are dead to us." These were the words they had spoken to me the day I was banished.

Light arose in front of me, a sun—but too white for sunrise. The hand touched my other shoulder. I had to keep moving before it—too late. My other shoulder cracked. The snap echoed through the quiet, dead place. I felt no pain because I was dead to them...

My arms flopped as my shoulder bones broke apart. The skin tore. I hated this part. One arm dropped into a puddle of bodies, helmets, guns, knives, and barbed wire.

I knew this place.

A crow cawed as it dropped from the sky, a silhouette against the white. It pecked at a head with red hair—familiar red hair. My other arm plopped into the mud. A hand touched my back.

Hurry!

In my haste, I didn't step high enough, and my bare toes snagged an arm. I fell. The knives, somehow standing upright, pierced my torso as I landed next to a head of light caramel hair—curly like mine. Unable to lift myself without my arms, I rolled onto my side. The knives sliced open my sides—but it didn't hurt. Mud got everywhere: nose, ears, and wounds. I blew mud out of my mouth as I rolled and came face to face with amethyst eyes. Dead, flat, and just beginning to cloud over.

"*Murë*!" I screamed and wiggled around the sharp knives until I wasn't facing my mother's dead face. She hadn't shown up in my dreams in seventy years or more.

Now the sky was white and cold above me. The crow cawed again. I tried to sit up, but the mud suctioned me in. It never sank bodies lower, but glued them there forever. The knives were gone. Another hand touched my hips and pressed down.

"No!" I thrashed around.

The hand let go, and I rolled over to face my mother again—but it wasn't her. I screamed as I stared into my father's sightless light green eyes. Next to him were Yalu and Nol's mom, Wennië. All dead.

The hand found me again. It grabbed me under my armpits and sat me up. The eyeless, noseless creature faced me, but this time, I didn't scream. Was it because I'd seen this thing in almost every nightmare since I could remember? It pulled me to my feet. My heart was racing, and I couldn't look away. I didn't move, just stared at it. It gnashed its sharp black teeth and turned me around.

No Man's Land lay before me, filled with *endai*, not human soldiers. Then, off in the distance, a fire-yellow glow moved about, like a firefly. I stepped forward, but the faceless creature still held me to my spot. The light floated, leaping from one dead *enda* to another. As it came closer, it grew, until it was right next to that familiar red-haired skull.

Sparks spewed out of the light, now as large as my hand. After heartbeats, the head rose, attached to a body. Skin sloughed off once it had stood, but the light stayed on top of the head. The dead thing stood taller than me, a very familiar height. It turned, and Nol's dead, pale blue eyes stared at me.

"This was your fault, Hallë. You broke the treaty." The light from Nol's head reflected off all the eyes of the dead *endai*.

"No!" I screamed and screamed.

The white light of the sky intensified until the yellow glow couldn't compete. Their eyes burned with cold light, until it engulfed the faces, the bodies, the mud. All of No Man's Land was gone. White nothingness surrounded me. I looked over my armless shoulder, but the creature was gone. Hands covered my face—my hands. They were back. The cold grew warmer, the white not as harsh. A fresh breeze played with my hair as a rustling started above me. I looked up to find a deep green forest canopy dancing for the wind.

The natural energies of the forest swirled around me, warming me, slowing my heart. I inhaled the spicy citrus scent of the ancient forest, a place from my youth. My body folded, and my hands touched rough bark, the grooves deep enough to use for handles. I sat down in the palm of the familiar ancient tree. It looked a little different now, grown since I'd left. The walls of the palm were higher, more of a bowl where the three limbs branched out from the trunk. I lay my head against the bark and closed my eyes.

My eyes fluttered open. The familiar lemon scent of Murphy's Oil and the lavender fabric softener assured me I was back at home. My room was shadowed, but I saw light from behind the curtains. Something heavy pressed against my head. The thumb moved, brushing the tip of my ear through my hair.

"Hallë?" Nol whispered, so close I felt his breath against my forehead. "I'm sorry, Hallë. I know you don't want me in, but I couldn't wake you."

"Did you see it?" I whispered back.

"Yes. I can't imagine a place like that. It astounds me the places your mind makes up to torture you."

I scooted back, but I couldn't go too far without falling off the edge. Nol scooted back, too, so we could look at each other. In the twilight of the room, his eyes glowed almost silver.

"It's not made up. I haven't dreamed of that place in a long time. It makes sense that my mind would take me there, though. It was a war zone, and I'm terrified my actions will start one."

"War?"

"Yeah. World War One. It was called No Man's Land. We traveled through it once, after the fighting had left the area. It's stuck with me ever since."

"A nightmare of a place."

"War is a nightmare, Nol. And no one wins."

"You don't mind that I changed it? Our tree was the place that appeared. I'm sorry—"

"You're fine, Nol. Thank you." I rolled carefully onto my side to reach for my phone. "Seriously?"

"What?"

"It's only been three hours since I talked to Yalu."

"Ah, your night terrors aren't very considerate, are they?"

I snorted. "Considerate night terrors. I wonder how that'd work."

"You were supposed to get up after the session. I made sure you would need to in order—"

"You were tired. I didn't have the heart to wake you. Sorry that my nightmare certainly did."

"I've told you before, never apologize for your nightmares."

I went to argue, but when he rose to lean on his elbow, I chose something else. "Can you get back to sleep? I can go sleep in one of the girls' rooms."

"Please stay. I think it helped to be beside you."

"But if I have another one, it'll wake you again. You need to sleep, Nol. Don't give me any BS *Zayuri* excuse."

"Keep the link open," Nol suggested.

I started. That might lead to something he didn't want to share yet. "What?"

"When we kept the link open, your nightmares were never bad enough to wake either of us."

"Nol..." We hadn't tried to open our bond's link to one another, except right after I thought Nol was dead. "Fine. But you're still moving out."

"I'm too tired to argue. I just want to sleep."

A feeling deep in the back of my mind reached out to the part of me that wasn't this me. I found the warmth next to me that wasn't

Nol. We opened the link, and our thoughts settled. Nol opened his eyes once, lifted his head, and looked at me with my eyes closed. He scanned the dark room.

"Nol, close your eyes."

"I'm just checking—"

"I'll make you see nothing," I said, threatening to make him see what I saw, which was behind my eyelids.

"I already see behind your eyes," he grumbled, but gave up and settled back down. I felt the pillow against his cheek as if it were my own. He blew at the hair on my forehead. I saw my hair move through his eyes as I felt his breath.

"Don't do it." I went to cover my nose as I felt the thought form in his mind. His reflexes were faster, and I squeaked as he tapped my nose moments before I covered it. "You are such a pain-in-my-ass!"

His shoulders shook, and again, I felt it from my perspective and his. "Not as much as you are in mine."

"I thought you were tired." I opened my eyes and glared at him, seeing double, as we both saw through our own eyes and through each other's. Disconcerting, but normal for us. "I think we're both annoyed with you," I grumbled. My soul was more amused at our teasing than annoyed, but still. Nol's soul was always more playful.

"When has that not ever been the case?" Nol giggled, but closed his eyes again. Now both our sights were dark and calm.

His breath shuddered. "Thank you."

"*Sajë*," I whispered as I reached out and patted him.

He grabbed my hand and placed it on his chest. He had so much sorrow in there, but I wouldn't pry. That's not what the link was about. Yes, we could invade each other's thoughts. Nol had technically done it when he altered my dream—but that's what he'd always done. How many times had we done this as children? So, so many. But not since Nol had come to find me. Here our lives were more private. We had memories and thoughts we didn't want to share.

"Nol?" I whispered. Too late, though. His mind had drifted off before the last sound left my mouth. I'd tell him later—if I remembered what I'd wanted to say.

6

BY EIGHT THAT EVENING, we hadn't heard a damn thing from *Aemina*. I let my frustration out on the spots on my kitchen counter after I'd done the dinner dishes. Charlie had come home about five minutes ago but hadn't come to say hello yet, taking Ray straight upstairs to bed, I assumed. Ten to one, my little niece was already passed out.

"How am I supposed to find a job?" Nol had been complaining since we'd woken up from our nap.

"Google it."

"Can I work at your shop?" He tapped a card on the peninsula counter. He was learning solitaire.

"No." I rinsed the rag and wrung it out.

"Can I pay rent for here instead?"

"No. You need your own space, and you aren't sleeping enough." And we weren't sleeping together again. We couldn't make a habit of depending on each other.

"And being in the middle of the city is better?"

I looked up from the counter, but his eyes were searching his cards. "I've told you repeatedly, it's soundproofed."

"I'm not ready."

I went back to cleaning. "You shouldn't have challenged me, then."

"I have been thinking."

"Oh, boy."

"You said you loved me."

I stopped wiping around the coffeemaker. "When?"

"In front of the fae. You said you love me, but to leave the politics to you."

"And?"

He stopped and rested his arms on the counter to look at me. "I saw Orlaith's face. She read into that more than you meant."

"Hmm." I started scrubbing again.

"Are we playing at an angle?"

"At an angle? You mean playing an angle." I couldn't keep my lips from curling up a little.

"That is what I said. So are we?"

I looked over to see him watching me, his head tilted as he leaned on the counter. "No. It doesn't matter what they think. I can say I love you, and it does not mean we're...together."

"Lovers? I know the term."

I wrung the rag out a final time and tossed it in the dirty towel basket under the sink. "Right. Is it bothering you?" I folded my arms on the counter and leaned forward, across from Nol.

"That you said it? No. We are linked. That love is endless no matter how we choose to live our lives, but Orlaith's face..." Nol's gaze went distant as he considered how to describe the queen. "She is curious about our relationship."

"Do we tell them we are *muranildi*? Will they know what that is?" I touched one of the king cards and tugged it out from under the stack he'd built up.

"Our bond can be a weakness for our enemies to exploit." Nol gathered the cards, grabbed the card I'd stolen, and tried to shuffle the deck. "We should wait until their intentions are more opaque. Is that the word?"

"Clear. I agree." They could kill me to defeat Nol. My heart raced at the image of Nol's lifeless body lying on the grass, Gileal checking for a pulse. I swallowed. Not going to happen. Absolutely not.

"Are you all right?" Nol noticed my distress and stopped shuffling, but Charlie announced her presence with loud shuffling footsteps through the house.

"Hey, guys," Charlie mumbled, not at all like herself. She went to the freezer and grabbed a pint of ice cream. Neither of us said anything as she pulled the drawer out and grabbed a spoon. I followed her out of the kitchen and stopped next to Nol as we watched her plop down on the couch.

"What is happening?" Nol whispered to me.

"Nothing good," I whispered back.

We hadn't seen her since we'd come back this morning.

"Charlie?" I spoke up. "What is wrong, love? Let Tatie Hally help." I went and sat beside her.

"Doug. He—" She sniffled, talking into her ice cream. "He was cheating on me with his secretary."

"Oh, love, I'm so sorry." After a hug, I guided her through the hallway, up the stairs, and sat her down on the couch. I pulled her larger body close to mine and adjusted our position until I could hold her as she ate her ice cream. Nol sat down on the other side of the couch, grabbed her feet, and started rubbing them. Ah, how cute.

"Have you heard from the council?" Charlie asked.

I would have told her it wasn't important—because for her, it wasn't—but I appeased her to get her mind off Doug. "No."

"What happens if they don't contact you?"

"Yalu said to be graceful and give away as little as possible."

"I hear a 'but' coming." She put the spoon into her mouth.

"I'm going to be honest. If the council won't tell me what not to say, I won't worry about it. It's not like I know government secrets that can cripple our country."

"Hmm, sounds fair. Was the queen cool?"

Define cool... "She wasn't mean or snooty."

"Good." She snuggled in and took another spoonful of ice cream.

Charlie ate half of the container before she fell asleep watching the movie Nol had picked. I didn't remember seeing the end, so I assumed I fell asleep soon after her.

"*Majut*," Nol swore in *Aemirin*, waking me up.

"What time is it?" I stretched, reaching up.

Nol grunted and got up. "We have visitors."

"Holy shit, is it past eight? Is the driver here?"

"No." Nol touched a *meril* on his necklace and paused. "It's Tolwe, but he has someone else with him."

Nol sped out of the house, barely making a sound on the stairs.

"What's wrong?" Charlie croaked and almost smacked my face as she stretched beside me.

"Tolwe is here."

"What time is it?"

"Don't know yet." I reached for my phone, but it wasn't on the table anymore.

"Hallë!" Nol yelled. Footsteps thumped from the back of the house. "Uncle, wait. Keep him out. The girls are asleep."

"What is he saying?" Charlie asked. She didn't speak *Aemirin*.

"There is no way I'm waiting out in this weather. Where is she?" a snotty voice, speaking *Aemirin*, shouted.

"Oh, fuck." I almost shoved Charlie off me as I fell to the floor between the table and the couch. I was off the floor in seconds. Whoever it was, they wanted to come into my house. No. Fucking. Way.

I was on the landing when Nol stopped a step below me. "Council," Nol muttered before Tolwe appeared in the doorway, blocking whoever it was from coming in out of my mudroom. "I'm sorry, Hallë." Nol showed me the anger and worry in his eyes right before he shut down his emotions from years of *Zayuri* training.

I gulped and almost choked on my spit as I stood as tall as my five-two frame allowed and shoved all of my nerves down. They didn't want to stay down.

"*Basean Tolwe, esamia,*" *General Tolwe, greetings*. I'd never gone out to greet him when he visited Nol in the backyard and never attempted to peek out any windows as they'd trained together early in the morning, but Nol had told me that Tolwe had made general decades ago.

Tolwe stared at me, not finding his words. "Hally." He shook himself aware and answered after a few more seconds. "I have escorted *Loret* Estwyn here. Forgive us for intruding on your home—"

"Don't apologize to the *savilë*, *Basean*. We are on official business, and she will hear my words. Get out of my way."

Tolwe didn't move. "May we have permission to enter further?" They didn't have permission to enter at all, but Tolwe was trying.

"Permission, from a *savilë*? Have you lost your mind?"

Oh, this would be fun, and early in the morning to boot.

Tolwe closed his eyes and waited for way more than ten seconds. "As you are *savilë*, you are not required to listen to anything we say. Respectfully, will you allow us access to your home, please?"

"She has no rights!"

I could only picture this stubby, bald guy with big teeth, a robe, and a hat, face going red and sputtering—oh, with a mustache, but *endao* didn't grow facial hair, so scratch that one. Which Disney movie was that from? I stood up straighter in my pajama shorts and oversized shirt. Damn it, why couldn't I have gotten something more appropriate on first? Or coffee. Or, damn it, the world shouldn't revolve until after eight in the morning, at least.

"Thank you, *Basean* Tolwe. I appreciate your recognition of that fact, considering I was stripped of everything—including being *endaen*, which I never understood."

"Get out of my way, Tolwe." Oh, informal names now? Lovely.

Tolwe looked at Nol, emotions down, but I could tell he was annoyed. Nol shook his head, and Tolwe glanced at me. He had no idea what to do. The general, who had held no emotion around me before and who I'd thought couldn't stand me as a child, stared at me, begging for guidance with his eyes.

"Don't let him past the stairs, Nol," I said in English. "I mean it. He has no jurisdiction here, and I am not in the mood for bullshit."

"Understood and agreed," Nol said loud enough for me to hear over the pompous ass yelling at Tolwe. Before I could say anything to Tolwe, the *endao* shoved through, under Tolwe's arm. Nol and Tolwe were about six foot four, whereas the average *endao* stood at around six feet.

"Hallanevaë, I present to you *Loret* Estwyn." Only a junior council member for this trip. They weren't taking this threat as seriously as they should.

The council member, Estwyn, couldn't have been over five hundred. He had wispy, light blond hair and taupe eyes darker than Queen Orlaith's, but they reminded me of hers. Of course, he was taller than me, but he was under average. His face held a permanent sneer. Even as he looked from Tolwe and up the stairs to Charlie listening in at the top with Ray, his expression never wavered.

"*Savilë.*" He tugged on the hem of his uniform, royal blue with embroidery swirls of the capital's official flower. Typical shirts hung lower than the hips, many longer in the back than the front, his included. I could tell the material was the *Endae* silken fiber commonly used for formal occasions and government officials. Nol's mom's least favorite dying material. I loved it.

With my distracted mind wandering into the past, I almost missed what Estwyn said next. "...role as interim diplomat for this encounter and has laid a decent foundation for discussions."

"Pardon me, *Loret*," I tried to explain, but he ignored me.

"I will be taking over as representative immediately. Contact this Queen Orlaith and inform her I am here. Now would be acceptable."

"I can't." I didn't even know what time it was. The sun hadn't come up yet, so well before eight.

Estwyn sputtered, reminding me more of a Disney character, even though he looked nothing like one, to my disappointment.

"What?" He snapped his head around and met my eyes, talking to me, not at me, for the first time.

"Did you even pay attention to the message I sent?"

"Don't talk to me like that, child. I am an *Amura Ore* member. You need to find a way."

"I don't need to do anything. Or do you understand the meaning behind the *Savile* title?"

"Don't sass me."

"First of all, this is my house, and I will not be scolded by anyone, especially an *Amura Ore* who agreed to let his peers banish a child to a place they knew nothing about—an illegal sentencing, I will add. Second of all, I have not been a child since I held my foster mother's severed arm in my hands in the ruins of our home."

I gasped when I realized what I'd blurted out. It pissed me off to no end that he'd brought that out in me. I'd never told anyone about that day, what I'd found there in the rubble.

"I do not need to hear fictitious or dramatized sob stories to make me feel sad for you."

"How—you need to leave my house before I say something I'll regret. *Loret* Estwyn, you may come with us when we go, but you will wait outside. Tolwe, get him out of here."

Tolwe was already pushing the sputtering *endao* out the door, and I heard them arguing and thumping on the stairs as they left.

"I need, um, to go check on them." Nol hesitated for a second longer, looking up the stairs at me on the landing and Charlie at the top.

The hush of the house after the argument felt stifling. I wanted to run out there and yell at Estwyn some more.

Charlie caught my attention when she met me on the steps. "I didn't need to understand the language to see—"

"I know I handled that horribly. This won't be okay."

"Tatie, no. He was an ass. I don't know what any of that was about, but I can tell he's a fucking douchebag."

"I should have kept my cool and not kicked him out."

"You did fantastic listening to him for so long." She scrunched her nose and cocked her head. "But do you wanna give me some details?"

I patted her shoulder and tsked. "Sure, but first, coffee."

"Definitely."

7

"You shouldn't have taken us through the shadows. What if she's pissed and they're not coming?" At eight in the morning, I was pacing my living room and tapping my phone against my palm.

"I'm sure they'll be here soon." Nol adjusted his coat on his lap, lounging on the couch, arm over the back.

"Why is this happening? Why can't everything be simple?" My black booties clicked on the hardwood as I paced, and the slitted legs of my romper flared with every step. I'd found a semi-presentable outfit. On the top was a boy-short bodysuit with a lace-up corset. It had long sheer sleeves, and the legs were loose with slits up to the boy shorts. I'd found it hidden in the back of my closet. Go me.

A knock on the door stopped me. I glanced from Charlie to Nol. Our plan was simple. Charlie stayed upstairs with Ray, and Nol went to get Estwyn while I answered the door. Why was I nervous? I started checking off reasons in my head as I went to the door.

A short, light-brown-haired, brown-skinned man stood at my door. He shoved his hands into the pockets of his black coat as he studied my yard, as if he could see through my laurel and lilac hedge.

"May I help you?"

At that, the guy turned to me, eyebrows high in surprise. "It's me, Quinn."

His uncertainty won me over, and I cocked my hip and smiled. "You don't seem so sure there. Are you lost? You're not selling anything, are you?"

"Huh? No. I'm Quinn from Thursday?"

"What do you mean?" This guy was not the black-haired, browned-eyed man—or fairy—who had leaned against my shop door.

"I'm your ride."

I stared and tried to fit him into the memory I had of the sly, cocky guy who hadn't taken bullshit from Brodrick. It wasn't fitting no matter which way my head turned.

"Oh, shit. Sorry, the glamor. I use two identities." He blinked, and a taller, paler fae, or fairy, or whatever they wanted to be called, stared back at me. The Thursday night identity was much closer to the Quinn standing here now. The same height, six foot two-ish, with shoulder length hair and that sly demeanor. But instead of black hair and brown eyes, they were gray. Mercury gray eyes, and charcoal gray hair that was black until he turned his head a certain way. Pointed, pale ears poked out of his thick hair, and his sharp jawline and high cheekbones screamed inhuman, but totally sexy.

"Holy shit," I whispered. "That's...that's as good as Aswryn's."

His expression and eyes darkened, and I realized I'd insulted him.

"I mean...it's just that's the only—well, actually, no. I've seen it twice. I'm not—oh fuck. I'm sorry. I wasn't comparing you."

"Forgiven, if you don't do it again."

Mouth dry, I nodded and scooted over to let him in, but he stayed on my stoop. His eyes wandered over me from head to toe. He lifted a corner of his mouth and met my eyes. "You look lovely."

I inhaled to thank him, but remembered Orlaith's warning. Quinn's almost-there smile turned sly. I narrowed my eyes. "If I can't thank your people, what do I do when they compliment me?"

"Give one back?" Quinn purred. "Unless I don't have any qualities worth admiring."

"Cocky. All right." I swished my hair back and roamed his outfit. My lips twisted as I thought. "And you have," nice everything. Nothing on him cost less than two hundred dollars, if I were being modest. Tailored black slacks, a black buttoned shirt, and a gray tie.

His pea coat hid most of his blazer, except for the front. I couldn't think of one damn smart-ass remark. "Kind eyes."

His smile dropped. He hadn't expected an honest comment. Quinn licked his lips. "Thank you."

I pursed my lips as he chuckled. "Wait—"

"Are you and your *Zayuri* ready to go?"

I held a finger up. "About that, there's been a development."

"Oh?" The playfulness left him. His eyes flashed farther into the house, where he could see all the way to the back.

The porch door clattered as it opened, and Estwyn sputtered on about who knew what. Nol opened the mudroom door, making Estwyn enter before him. The council member stopped just inside the living room. Nol pushed him closer.

"We've got a tag-along."

"I see that. Does he have to go with us?"

"'Fraid so."

"Damn." Quinn tsked and swung a set of keys I hadn't seen earlier. But then there were so many more interesting things to see on his person.

"Where's Tolwe?" I asked as the two came up to me.

"He's not coming." Nol studied Quinn for a moment. "You are the one the queen was hiding—or trying to."

Quinn took one hand out of his pocket and pointed at Nol. "Guilty—but you know, had to test you. Surprise, you passed. I'm Quinn."

Nol laughed, and Estwyn complained because we weren't including him. We ignored him.

"You were there?" I asked, stepping back. Where?

"Yep, you just weren't looking the right way. Who's the whiner?"

"Quinn..." Nol drew out his name with a sigh. "Meet *Loret* Estwyn—straight from *Atrau* to stir up drama."

Quinn rolled up onto his toes and lifted his face to the ceiling. "I take it he doesn't speak English."

"We can translate." I did a one-shoulder shrug.

"Who is this? Tell me what you're saying." Estwyn kept spouting off demands, not even concerned about our argument earlier. Looked like Tolwe couldn't convince him to change his attitude.

"*Loret*, this is Quinn. He's going to take us to Queen Orlaith."

Estwyn squinted at Quinn, then gave him a barely there bow. "*Esamia*."

"Hello." Quinn bowed about the same angle as Estwyn. "Ready to go?" he asked the rest of us. He nudged Estwyn through the door with a head tilt, and Nol followed. I dashed in and snagged my coat off the chair as the guys walked down my driveway, where a sleek black Porsche waited at the end, just on our side of the sidewalk.

Quinn spun his keys around as he watched the three of us walk up to this car. "I wasn't expecting a third passenger, so it's gonna be tight."

"The only comfortable one will be Hallë."

"Har-har, Nol."

Quinn opened his door and pulled the latch. "Nah, you'll love the front seat."

"I have found I don't like cars and driving." Nol opened the passenger door.

Quinn stopped with his hand on the door frame. He squinted at Nol over the hood. "Don't *Zayuri* ride dragons?"

I snorted, not able to hold in my laugh well enough.

"Yes," Nol bit off at my reaction. "But it's safer."

"How? You're riding a flying dragon."

"One I have a close relationship with. I trust her with my life and she trusts me with hers."

"Okay." Quinn inclined his head, yielding. He let go of the frame and moved to let Estwyn and me get in the car. "Sorry that you'll be in close quarters with the old pompous ass," Quinn muttered.

"Gee—" I stopped that remark. Present a solid front and don't argue in front of the other country. I knew that rule, but did that count when they were kicking me off the team? "Estwyn is overwhelmed. It's his first time here."

Estwyn heard his name. "That's *Loret* to you."

I couldn't stop the eye roll, and Quinn smirked, his eyes roaming my face. Oh boy, Mother, help me. I tipped my chin down and turned away.

"What is this thing?" Estwyn stood behind me, waiting while Quinn and I kinda flirted. I didn't mean to, I swear.

The moment was ruined, and I was sure Nol would give me shit later. I turned back to Estwyn. "It's called a car. A mode of transportation here. Please, get in."

"They don't travel through the trees?"

"No—at least the humans don't. I don't know anything about the fae. If you would, *Loret*?" I waved my hand toward the car, as he wasn't getting my less obvious gesture.

Estwyn's top lip curled before he bravely ducked in and scooted behind Nol—which wasn't far.

"Good luck," Quinn teased as I went in after him.

I gave him a squint of my own, but he saw through my thin attempt to hide my displeasure of Estwyn. We took I-90 to Highway 522. Quinn had the greatest time taking the curves and scaring the shit out of Nol, who was familiar with the oh-shit handle. I couldn't decide which I enjoyed more: the ride or the other *endai's* terrified faces.

For a while, I wondered if we were going all the way into the Cascades, but we turned in Issaquah and drove until a mountain was nearly on top of us, past windy roads in places no houses should ever be built. Then, at the end of the road, Quinn stopped the car and waited. Ahead of us was a little mound of dirt, but a hundred feet or so later was the edge of the small mountain we'd been driving up. The top half of the evergreen trees below swayed in the wind, rain, and fog—or was that technically clouds since we were quite high up?

"What's goin' on?" I half teased. He wouldn't bring us all this way to dump our bodies, right?

Quinn revved his engine, then started driving again, right up and over a little gravel hill. The air in front of us started to waver, like looking through a thick piece of glass. I held my breath as Quinn drove right through it and into…somewhere else. A few more feet and we would have driven off the side of the mountain. The clouds, rain, and trees were gone, replaced with a scene that did not belong in the Cascades of Washington.

As if right out of a Tuscan magazine, acres and acres of grapevines came into view and, in the distance, a waterfall. Quinn sped through the winding road between grape fields and up to a yellow mansion as big as a city block. As we came closer, I realized the building was several smaller mansions contained behind a wall. There was no moat.

Estwyn had gone silent. I checked to see if he was still with us before looking at the gorgeous grounds again. Okay, if we became friends, I was coming here every weekend.

No one said a word while Quinn drove around the front yard's white fountain and parked close to the front doors.

After a minute of us staring at the immaculate grounds, shaped green bushes, and red, white, and pink flowers, Quinn broke the silence. "Ready?"

This Faerie thing was no joke.

Nol opened his door first, letting in cool air filled with the fresh scents of Ponderosa pine and spruce of the Cascade Mountains. Quinn pulled the latch for my side while Nol stretched his long legs. Estwyn pushed on my shoulder but didn't say a word. I looked back and understood why.

Quinn held his hand out to me, and I took it, trying to be quick to let the soon-to-be-sick assembly member out of Quinn's high-scale Porsche. As soon as Estwyn stumbled out, he placed his hand on the car's fender, bent over, and heaved. Luckily, there was nothing in his tummy to throw up. What a whiny-ass baby. Nol did better over on his side as he leaned against the hood of the car and watched Estwyn make a fool of himself.

"If I ever wanted to go that fast, I'd ride a dragon," Estwyn complained after he was all better.

"That is one thing *Loret* Estwyn and I agree on," Nol mumbled, his chin resting on his forearm on the roof.

"You might feel safer driving," I suggested.

"Let's get this over with, shall we?" Quinn asked, holding his arm out for me to take.

I tried to be graceful as I declined. His smile fell. I tipped my head at Estwyn. "Gotta be with the other *endai*. That little thing called politics?"

Estwyn walked around me, butting between us and breaking our stare. Maybe that was a good thing. Nol came to stand beside me.

I looked away from Quinn to take in the landscaped grounds. "I did not expect this," I muttered, still unable to soak in the entire place.

"What did you expect? A pink fairy castle?" Quinn winked a now almost cloud-gray eye at me.

"Maybe." I lifted a shoulder. Had I?

"People leave us alone here under the veil. It's not exactly in Faerie, but it's also not out in the human world. It's confusing for outsiders. Lots of glamor to keep us safe."

Estwyn turned away from the mansion and hissed over his shoulder at the three of us, "What's he saying?"

Nol sighed. "Don't worry, *Loret*. We will translate when it's time."

Estwyn grumbled and seethed.

"Come. The queen is waiting." Quinn walked around Estwyn, now taking on the professional attitude we should have all had at the beginning. Something about Quinn made me want to give in and act casual.

A pair of guards in black suits, black ties, and with swords at their hips met us between the white pillars in the entryway. The bright white front doors, over ten feet tall, opened on their own as we walked up the two front steps. The female guard had her hair pulled back in a bun. Little silver barrettes held braids close to her head, like stars in her raven hair. Her eyes were lilac, and her skin was tiger-striped white and cream.

I picked my jaw up and turned to the other one. He was taller than Nol, upward of seven feet. Dark skin, darker than Lewis's, and white eyes, but when he rolled them to scan our group, a hue of blue caught the light. Their faces were so grave and intimidating, but then again, that was part of the job.

The tall dark one's face broke into a smile, showing off thin white teeth, but his smile was infectious and lovely.

"Welcome to our home, *endai*. It has been too long. If you would please walk this way?"

The other fairy—fae, I needed to figure this out—dipped her head, gave us a quick, shy smile, and cocked her head to have us follow the other fairy.

"What did he say?" Estwyn asked again. Jeez, would the guy just shut up?

"Figure out how to speak English and you'll know," I muttered in English before I could stop myself.

Nol held his breath to keep his laughter contained, but Estwyn watched me, clueless.

"He just welcomed us. I assure you, you won't miss out on the important stuff."

Our shoes, except Nol's, tapped and echoed down the hall as we passed arches to other rooms and down the main hallway. We passed more fairies and a pair of cats chasing each other. No walls with paintings of old fairies on them, but there were sconces and art from numerous generations. I almost stopped at what looked to be an original Van Gogh. No, that couldn't—holy shit. Tables with glass-covered pieces, an ancient-looking dagger, and a sheath. A glass-covered Celtic-style tapestry. I wanted to ask about things so badly, but I couldn't let them know how long I'd been here until I got permission—*if* I got permission.

"Why didn't Tolwe come?" I whispered to Nol after we'd passed a few doors.

"He refused to stay. He handed *Loret* Estwyn off to me, clasped my arm, and walked through the portal. I don't blame him."

I looked past him to the junior assembly member sporting a sneer. "What? And miss his appealing attitude? Tolwe doesn't know what he's missing."

Nol grunted. "I would have liked his company. We don't know what we're headed into."

"Stop pouting. You've got me. I may not do fun sword tricks or flaunt my magic, but I have moments of genius."

Nol started to laugh, but he turned it into a cough as we stopped at the double doors. The female guard knocked. Another pair of guards on the inside of the meeting room opened them for us. I didn't notice them much, taking in the room instead.

A long window took up the left wall, displaying a beautiful English garden that I was sure would smell divine later in the year. Three groups of furniture sets, divided the room into sections. Orlaith was at the end, sitting in a wingback chair, ankles crossed, and wearing a plum suit and cream pumps. She wore a silk sash, a different shade of purple, with a fist-sized amethyst and diamond broach placed at her left shoulder above her heart, similar to Queen Elizabeth's blue one.

Quinn went in first, then me, followed by Estwyn and Nol at our backs.

"Hally, Nolan, I—" Orlaith's face fell as Estwyn came around from behind me and stood by Nol's side. "You've brought a visitor."

"I apologize, Your Majesty. He insisted."

"Well, introduce me!" Estwyn hissed.

The queen's glare sliced to Quinn. She said something in a language I didn't recognize and instantly wanted to learn. Quinn bowed low, arms at his sides, and said something back. Orlaith snapped a quick word and looked back at me.

"Hally, you are already on precarious terms with me and you bring yet another *enda* here? Are you hoping for war?"

"That isn't our intention. Please allow me to introduce my replacement." I gestured to Estwyn. "He will explain everything."

Orlaith nodded, her jaw working as her eyes darted between us.

"Um...do you, by chance, speak *Aemirin*? I don't want to assume either way."

"Not anymore, no."

Estwyn hissed at us and tugged on Nol's sleeve.

"Your Majesty, allow me to introduce you to *Amura Ore* assembly member, *Loret* Estwyn."

She blinked at me, and we waited, staring at Estwyn. He gave the queen a barely fifteen-degree bow. Holy shit, how rude.

"*Loret* Estwyn," I said. "Her Majesty, Ruler of the Fae, Queen Orlaith. Address her as Your Majesty." I helped him out, using the English term instead of *Aemirin* royal terms.

"Your Majesty, it is an honor to meet you. *Hasin* Twynolan, translate."

"Hallë is doing a decent job of that already, *Loret*."

"I told *you* to." What was with him, thinking he could order the *Zayuri* around? They did not answer to the council. They only followed direct orders from the royal family. What the hell was going on in *Aemina* that he thought he could get away with this bullshit?

"And I refuse. Hallë is better at this language."

Estwyn grumbled for a second as Orlaith watched, her hands resting on her knees, tea on the table, and her chin high.

"Is something wrong?" Orlaith asked.

"Um...no, not really."

"Your Majesty, on behalf of the *Amura Ore*, I do solemnly apologize for intruding upon your land," Estwyn said. "Had we known, we would have brought a representative along with *Hasin* Nolan when we permitted him to hunt down Aswryn." Estwyn paused, allowing me to catch up.

Orlaith watched me as I translated, brow furrowed, but then she met Estwyn's eyes when he began again.

"I am authorized to answer any misunderstandings," Estwyn explained. "*Hasin* Nolan's mission, whether it be in *Rosava* or *Endae*, was to assassinate Aswryn and end the curse that Nolan has explained previously. While...ehm...Hally has done an adequate job of representing our country and our realm, in general, she will no longer be in that position. I will be the representative from now on."

Orlaith cleared her throat to speak, but Estwyn didn't stop and listen.

"It is true, we did not know how or who to contact." Estwyn looked around the room, sneering as if they weren't worthy of being contacted anyway. "We have sent word to the other countries for their records; however, it seems no one can find any evidence that our species once co-existed, let alone created a treaty. Although, not an excuse, we claim ignorance for our actions. We apologize sincerely. We also respectfully request access to this treaty for us to review—all three countries so this may never happen again."

No one said a word after I was done translating Estwyn's long speech. We all stared at Orlaith, waiting for her response. Even I knew all representatives were supposed to listen more than talk. Why had they chosen this idiot? Or perhaps there weren't many more left to choose from, and of course, they never would have chosen my grandmother.

Orlaith took a deep breath through her nose. "What a wonderful job of translating you did, Hally. What do you know of this council member?"

"Erm...I don't—"

"I answer her questions," Estwyn interrupted me with a louder-than-normal hiss. "What is she saying?"

"Excuse me, Your Majesty." I switched to *Aemirin*. "She asked me if I know anything about you."

Estwyn scoffed. "How would you know anything about me?"

"Please forgive me, Your Majesty. He's asking what you said, and I forgot to include him."

"But I asked you, not him."

"He still wants to know."

"Fine, translate this."

I licked my lips and prayed I could keep up.

"I will not play this back-and-forth game. Either take Hally and Nolan home now and all will be done, or I will speak with Hally and Nolan only. At least she knows how to listen and has manors."

"She can't represent our realm," Estwyn snapped.

"Why?" I translated for Orlaith.

He gaped at the queen, shocked she would dare question him. "She is *savilë*."

I didn't have a chance to translate before Orlaith responded. "Come again?" Orlaith stood. "What is a *savilë* doing in my realm?"

"As I've said—" Estwyn began.

But I didn't get a chance to translate for him.

"You have a *savilë* helping a baby *Zayuri* hunt a mastermind mass murderer in my realm. You should have sent several *Zayuri* years ago to hunt Aswryn down. Did you ever question what she was doing when she was in my realm?"

Orlaith was talking so fast that I fumbled the dialogue. Orlaith's attention focused on me. "Enough of this. You will stay and answer my questions and whether your answers are sufficient will determine whether I send you back to them. Quinn, take *Loret* Estwyn back. See that he leaves this realm immediately."

Quinn held a sputtering council member by the arm, dragging him backward as I translated for Orlaith. Nol glanced between him and me, not knowing who to stay with.

"*Zayuri*, go with them to the car. Explain to this second-rate assembly member what I've said and come back for your *savilë* friend so you may take her back if I do not like her answers."

Nol bowed and hot-footed it backward and out the door. The door closed, muting Estwyn's complaining, and then there was silence.

"*Savilë* Hally, you have five minutes to convince me not to go to war with *Endae*."

I gulped and turned around to face the queen. My mind went blank.

8

A minute passed in silence while I pieced my thoughts together. If I couldn't convince her not to go to war, my life would be forfeited once I stepped into *Endae*. My mind went back to my night terror yesterday. I squeezed my eyes shut to get the image of my mother's dead eyes out of my head.

When I opened my eyes seconds later, Orlaith had sat down. "Hally? You need to explain yourself."

Which part? She'd asked so many questions between Estwyn and me, and they were jumbled up in my mind. I opened my mouth to speak, but I couldn't manage a squeak.

"Is Nolan *savilo*?" Her tone and her eyes had softened.

Nol? I shook my head.

"Why are you *savilë*? You're barely an adult, you and Nolan both."

"I—they sent me to Earth after—" I held my breath for a moment. "—I lost control of a spell and killed two of my friends."

Orlaith's taupe eyes widened, and she sat straighter in her chair. "You lost control of your spell?"

I shifted from foot to foot as we got on this very uncomfortable ground. "Not exactly. It wasn't *my* spell. I found a traditional spell, and those were difficult for me. I thought it was simple, even though I was told it was too advanced for me." One of those people was Nol.

"How old were you?"

I took a deep breath to calm down before answering. "One hundred twenty-seven."

"Of course, you couldn't do those spells. You were still learning the balance between your magic and traditional magic. *Endai* are still just as ignorant as when they left this realm. You're clearly over two hundred. How long have you been here? Why haven't my people sensed you?"

I couldn't help but play with my bracelet, the one thing I still had left of my sister, Emma. Her closeness gave me strength. "I blocked my magic when I got here, so my cells couldn't release that energy. When Aswryn found me, she overloaded my system with magical energy and broke my spell. That's what you felt."

She didn't say anything for a minute, digesting the horror of what I'd done to myself. Even Aswryn, when she found out, had said it was blasphemy—and that's coming from someone who was performing genocide.

"Why did you agree to save *Endae* if they exiled you?"

"*Zayuri* are immune to the curse that Aswryn cast upon *Aemina,* and she wanted me to help her overcome that. It was either help Nol voluntarily to bring her in or be an unwilling victim while Nol did it by himself. She also threatened the humans close to me."

"You did it to help Nolan, not *Aemina*."

"Aswryn couldn't be left to carry out her plans." I looked at my shoes. "I've seen tragedy. If I could help stop another one, I'd do it."

"If we couldn't sense you, how did Aswryn find you?"

"I don't know, Your Majesty."

"Perhaps she came here before you blocked yourself and sensed you. She's been coming since the nineteen seventies."

"The nineteen seventies? Nol discovered she was coming to this realm recently. No one in *Aemina* knew where she went. He tracked her *imolegin* just last year, and he found me. Even though she's gone, her curse is still terrorizing *Aemina,* and people are still sick."

"That doesn't surprise me. Nor would it surprise me if others helped her cast it, which would be why the curse didn't end."

"Nol thought she was working with someone else, but the *Amura Ore* disagreed."

"Aswryn's allies are everywhere. Their agenda is bigger than crippling *Aemina*."

Queen Orlaith glanced behind me and nodded. The doors thunked, and I turned around to watch Nol walking in next to the tall, muscled guard from the front door. They stood close, and Nol's face held a hint of a smile.

"Forgive me, please. Estwyn was a bit frustrated, and it took some persuading to get him to leave."

"And I'm sure you enjoyed talking shop with my guards."

"Talking shop?"

"Sharing ideas and experiences with other fighters."

He ducked his head a fraction. "Oh. Yes. We did take some time to talk."

Orlaith's lips curled as if amused with his answer. His mood had improved. Whether that was from talking shop or getting Estwyn out of here didn't matter. He amused the queen. "Nolan. I believe I owe you an explanation."

Nol clasped his hands behind his back and tamped down his emotions.

"You've said Aswryn's curse is still affecting your people. Hally has told me the *Zayuri* are immune to it. Even in death, Aswryn poses a problem in both our worlds. She may have created a curse for your people, but she used our people to make it. She has been taking our children for decades, using them as test subjects."

I glanced at Nol to see if he was as surprised as I was, but all I got was his emotionless *Zayuri* expression.

"Here's my offer. Find our children and I will consider not declaring war on *Endae,* and I *might* grant you asylum, Hally."

Zayuri were known widely as assassins, but with a *Zayuri* as my *muranildo*, I was learning there were depths to their organization. They just never corrected the rumors, which in turn gave the *Zayuri* an air of mystery.

"Do you think you can do this?" Orlaith asked.

"There is no hesitation in my mind," Nol answered without missing a beat. "Children are precious. I have worked on a few abduction missions, as horrible as that crime is."

"Tell me about them."

Nol released his arms from behind his back and shifted his weight. "All four of them were found. With the curse, people became desperate. They missed their children. That happened in two cases. The other two children…I found them, but it was too late. They'd died before I was assigned the case. I must warn you that even if we are successful, the outcome may not be a joyful one. Finding children is always bittersweet. When they are found alive, there is trauma and fear of it happening again, even if the kidnapper is caught. The death of a child is …" Nol paused. "It changes you."

"Agreed. I am a mother and I know the pain of losing a child. But it is my nephew's son I am concerned about. Aswryn took him when she killed his mother. He is only three."

Nol nodded curtly and swallowed hard.

"You will work alongside my top agent. He will share everything with you." The queen rose from her seat and turned to a door at the other side of the room. She nodded to one of the guards, who I recognized. Brodrick bowed to his queen without her saying a word and left the room."

A minute later, a dark, shorter man came into the conference room behind Brodrick. Oh, no fucking way.

One rule, no one talked about Drake. He even scared Ian. While my tattoo mentor had been an idiot, Ian had known the rule and followed it. I didn't know how to react. He'd helped Katie, her infant son, and me get up to Washington and out from under Ian and his buddies' thumbs. What did this mean that Drake was walking in and standing six feet away from the Queen of the Fae?

While he'd always given off the vibe of being a slim, fit, five-foot-ten-inches African American before, that was not the vibe he gave off now. He still had the same coloring and height, with black, close-cut hair, but Drake's eyes were dark aquamarine with gold flecks, and he had the sharp fairy angles. And we couldn't forget the pointy ears. If none of that confirmed it was Drake, the tribal tattoo on his neck solidified it. I'd done that piece five years ago. He met my eyes with no bit of recognition in them. Oh, now I had questions and a suspicion.

"Hallë," Nol called my name, bringing me back to the here and now. "Hallë?"

I forced myself to focus on Nol instead of Drake.

Nol sidestepped until his side touched mine and whispered, "Are you okay?"

It took a few tries, but I swallowed. The day was getting worse and worse, and it wasn't even ten in the morning.

"Drake," Orlaith said, "this is *Hasin Zayuri* Nolan, who I promised you would meet. And Hally, his friend and our unofficial representative to *Aemina*."

"Unofficial, Your Majesty?"

"Technically, she's *savilë*, but I want her, not the pompous elf they sent."

Drake's eyebrows shot up as he stared at me like this was the first time he'd ever met me. "Intriguing."

"Take them back to Seattle and share all of your findings."

"As you wish, Your Majesty. Hally and Nolan, care to follow me?"

Nol and I bowed to Orlaith.

"And see to it that they get a contact number."

"Of course, Your Majesty."

The guard led Nol, Drake, and me through the mansion, while Drake narrated the entire way about unimportant crap. I couldn't think of anything besides how the hell this was the same guy who had helped us to Seattle. The same person who had dealt in shady deals with Ian and other drug dealers. But I couldn't say anything with the guard there—or in this mansion. I'd get answers, though, and soon.

"I'm sure you have many questions about Aswryn, but would you like to start right away or get a few hours of sleep first? I heard you've both had a busy last twenty-four hours."

"We're fine. The children come first. Tell me, where were these labs you found? Which regions were they in?"

"One was in LA and the other was in London."

"I do not know these." Nol hesitated. "Perhaps I'm not using the right word. Are they cities?"

"Large metropolitan areas."

While the mansion looked big from the outside, I could not have fathomed the size of this place from the front. We followed the guard around and turned left at the base of a wide staircase and into a great room bigger than the main floor of my house. The ceilings rose three stories up. A massive fireplace took up most of the left wall, and if I ducked, I could walk right into it. We stepped off the cushy rug as we passed the breakfast nook—if a living room-sized rotunda could be called a nook. The guard walked ahead, straight through the kitchen, opened the farthest door, and waited for us.

"Was there anything else similar in the labs? For instance, the one in Seattle was found near medical research businesses."

"I'm not sure if they were close to any medical facilities. I'll have to look again."

Drake and Nol walked through the door first, but I paused as I went through. The enormous thing reminded me of Bruce Wayne's or Tony Stark's "garage" full of fancy cars—wait, nope. Four everyday cars were in the corner next to the entrance. Drake led us to a pearl-white Tesla while the guard stayed at the door.

With a scowl, Nol tapped the door where the handle normally would be.

"Problem?" Drake asked above the hood of the car.

"He doesn't like riding in cars," I said.

Drake narrowed his eyes. "*Zayuri* ride dragons—"

"I know." Nol clenched his jaw as he pulled on the door. "Where is the handle?"

Drake let out a bark of laughter. "Ah, that. Push on the back and it pops out."

"There, there." I patted his shoulder before I got in the back, not having any problems with my door.

He gave me a seething look that from any other *Zayuri* might have been intimidating. I winked before ducking in. We settled into the black interior as Drake pressed the button, and the dash lights came to life. He pushed another button on the ceiling and the garage door opened.

"Okay, Drake," I finally said. "What the fuck is going on?"

He looked at me in the rearview mirror. Nol turned around after securing his seatbelt, his eyes wide with surprise.

"I could say the same. I thought you were some magicless elf, runaway kid."

"I'm not a kid, and don't you think you could have filled me in?"

We left under the rolled gate into the morning sunlight.

"It's not like you mentioned anything, either. I even let down my glamor several times and you said nothing."

"I didn't know fairies existed!"

He glanced around his seat, but had to turn his attention back to where he was going as we got on the dirt road. "You didn't?"

"How do you know each other?" Nol asked.

Drake fidgeted in his seat.

"Ian," I blurted.

"Ah." Nol turned and settled himself in his seat.

"Shit, you're serious," Drake said.

"Were Katie and Ian fairies?"

"Ian was half-fae, and Katie was full fae."

"Aswryn took Seamus. He's the queen's nephew isn't he?" I voiced my suspicion.

Drake's expression said it all.

"Fuck. Tell me about Katie."

Drake sighed, and I thought he would refuse to answer me. "Princess Catrina left her home in Seattle over two decades ago to work undercover to find the kidnapped fae children. You met her after she, along with Ian, got hooked on cocaine, although he was stupid before the drugs fried his brain.

"As you know, I helped Katie get home before Ian's sentencing, but what you don't know is that Aswryn's fairy trafficking ring was gunning for her and Seamus as a punishment for Ian. I didn't want her to find you either, and your situation in France gave me the perfect cover to get you away."

While I'd been a witness and turned Ian in, Drake had helped me get out of the trial so I could go get Charlie and Ray in France three years ago. Drake put me in touch with Lewis through his old tattoo shop in Tacoma once I'd brought Charlie to Seattle.

I kept my eyes on Drake as he drove through the winding roads down the mountain. "Agent Zack-ass thought Seamus was safe and living with his grandfather."

"I know." Drake frowned but didn't say any more. They'd lied to Zack, and I thought Seamus had been safe with some fictional grandfather. I'd been waiting for a call to make a playdate with Ray.

"Katie went to him for help after she found a boy named Derrick."

Drake's aquamarine eyes darted to mine in the rearview mirror. He hadn't known? "Does Zack know the truth?"

I sighed and looked straight ahead, focusing on Nol's hair. "I don't know if Katie told him anything. He never mentioned it to me when he harassed me about Derrick." But Zack had experienced Aswryn throwing Ian around Yula's Quill and killing him. Kinda hard to be in the dark after that demonstration. Not that Drake needed to know that.

"What did you tell him?" Drake stopped at a light and turned in his seat, making eye contact with me as if that assured him I wouldn't lie.

"The truth. That I'd never seen the kid. I didn't even know they were involved in anything besides drugs. Zack hadn't either until Katie came to him." I tipped my chin at Drake as the light turned green. "Of course, he didn't believe me, but he left me alone after Ian killed Katie."

Drake turned onto the on-ramp lane without using his blinker. "I think Aswryn killed Katie."

"Why?" I asked. Could that be true? If Aswryn took Seamus...were they sure it was Aswryn? It was her MO, but how did they know for certain?

"I felt Aswryn's *imolegin* when I went to her house after the police were done."

"Ian came into my shop covered in blood right after Aswryn showed up, though. Aswryn, disguised as a human, made an appointment and tried to kidnap me. I don't think she planned to break my block before she took me with her. When she started fighting Gileal, things got heated and, poof, block broken."

"Tell me about this block. How the hell can you block your magic?"

"Um...do you know about my family's history?"

Drake shot me a look in the rearview mirror.

I gave him a quick rundown of how my magic worked and my inability to use traditional spells without screwing them up. "So I tried to close off those cells and it worked."

"That's...I don't know what I'd do if I lost my magic."

"It took some getting used to, I'll clue ya," I muttered.

Neither of them said anything. Yes, it had been a horrible thing to do to myself, which was the main reason I'd been too ashamed to tell Nol in the beginning. When he found out, he'd blown up and walked out on me.

"Hally?" Drake asked after merging onto I-90. "Humans can't know about us."

I scowled. "Do you think I want them to know? I lived in France through both wars, Drake. Humans are fucked up."

"Humans aren't the only ones," he muttered, almost too quietly.

"I know," I muttered back. Not wanting to talk anymore, I rested my forehead against the window and closed my eyes.

A light touch on my knee brought my head around. Nol's light blue eyes crinkled as he smiled sympathetically. Witnessing and fighting against Aswryn's distractions must have come with its own evils. I touched his fingers and leaned back against the window again.

9

"I'm sure your portals don't extend that far." Nol tapped Drake's tablet lying on my peninsula counter, where a map showed Nol how far London was from Washington.

"We don't have portals." We gave Drake matching shocked looks. They had to have portals. "We travel through Faerie."

"Like at the mansion?"

"Yes, but Faerie goes beyond that. It's not a different realm. Faerie is…an entity of this realm that can think for itself."

"I read about this," Nol spoke up. "I assume there is some truth and accuracy in these stories."

Drake dipped his head. "That's true, but unless you're fae, you'll never fully understand it."

"And it's faster?"

"It can be, if you know the way." Drake tapped on the counter, standing beside Nol at the peninsula. "Faerie can fuck with you when it feels like it."

"So don't use Faerie to get to London?"

"It wouldn't be wise. The place where you killed Aswryn? Let's start there. We can travel to Los Angeles tomorrow. You've been back there, right?" If Drake knew so much, if the fae had been spying on us, wouldn't they know?

"We haven't—"

"I have gone back there a few times," Nol interrupted me. "But I assume you know that already."

My jaw dropped, and I rocked back on my heels. Nol had never mentioned going back there. Where she'd brought Nol and Ray to that horrible night.

"Anything you can gather?" Drake ignored Nol's assumption and leaned his forearm on the counter to face him.

"Gather?" Nol popped his last apple slice into his mouth. "I'm certain I can take things to Hallë's house, but I would rather not. It was quite traumatizing for all—"

"All?" Drake assessed us.

I glared at Nol from across the counter. Oh, he had some explaining to do.

"Who else was there?" Drake's voice lowered.

My shoulders dropped in defeat. "After Aswryn took Nol—"

"She *took* Nolan?"

"How much do you know about the whole thing?" I squinted at him.

"Assume I know nothing."

Nol's *Zayuri*-trained expressionless face gave nothing away, but his damn words had. He'd never been skilled in politics. What would Queen Orlaith do to the girls? I had to protect them. Perhaps Drake wouldn't tell his queen like he hadn't told her about me. There was no telling what he'd do.

"I went there to face Aswryn on my own," I admitted.

Drake's eyebrows shot up. "With no magic."

"It was stupid. I know."

Drake assessed me with his aquamarine eyes, not swayed in the least. "Who's all, Hally?"

Shit. "If I or others were doing something illegal in the eyes of the fae, what would happen to those people and me?"

"If I tell Her Majesty, as a loyal subject should, she would look over the circumstances and determine the punishment."

"How much trouble would a subject get into if they'd neglected to report an *endaë* living here illegally?"

Drake straightened, puffing out his chest. He must have known I would use it. "Probably in even more trouble. But again, the queen would consider the situation. She's a fair ruler, much better than her father in Europe."

Interesting. I filed that away for later.

"Would you risk that and tell her if I'd happened to break that particular law we're skirting around?"

"Hally, just tell me, 'cause I might have something you'd be interested in knowing."

The coffee alarm went off. "But first, coffee?" Maybe with a shot of whiskey? Sure it was ten in the morning, but as a famous singer had wisely said, "It's five o'clock somewhere."

"You can talk and make coffee at the same time. I've seen you do a hella lot more." Drake touched his neck tattoo.

Nol opened the fridge and pulled out the pizza. He was always hungry.

"Use a plate, Nol."

He scoffed, but opened the cabinet.

"Pain-in-my-ass," I grumbled.

"Not as much as you are in mine," Nol chimed back.

Drake waited while I got my mug out and poured my coffee. He cleared his throat three times, though. Unable to procrastinate anymore, I faced him and leaned my elbows on the counter.

Drake watched me, deadpan.

"Aswryn attacked us twice. Once at my shop and once again at my house. I blocked her magic after I thought she killed Nol. Gileal took her and Nol's body home that night. Like I said, I thought he was dead and that Aswryn was in custody."

Nol came to stand next to me and took a big bite of his pizza. I'd glossed over this part with Nol.

"Two nights later, Aswryn took Ray right out from under Charlie and me. She left me a note with a clue, and I snuck out to get Ray. I know it was stupid to go alone, but I didn't know what else to do."

"Thinking Nolan was dead? What did you plan to do to get her back?"

"There was no plan. I told you it was stupid, but I...didn't want to kill Aswryn."

Drake made a sound to interrupt, but Nol got there first.

"Ray helped untie me where she had us caged." Nol's eyes darted to me. He'd never told me that before. "I came out before Aswryn could subdue Hallë. She would likely have caged her as well if I hadn't."

"Did Ray see anything?" Drake knew the answer.

I bit my lip ring and looked down at my black coffee—alcohol free. "She's three, Drake. She..."

Drake reached over and touched my hand. "She did, didn't she?"

"I don't know if she saw what happened there. She has nightmares about her time with Aswryn, but nothing about the fight."

"Ray knows," Drake answered his own question. He dropped his head back and paused before explaining, "You need to keep this to yourself, Hally. I'm sure Queen Orlaith will tell you, but you gotta let her admit it. Swear?"

My throat hurt as I swallowed. What was he talking about?

"Haven't you wondered how we know so much? Now, I don't think it was supposed to happen. I think the goblin was only supposed to spy from your backyard, but she didn't expect Ray to see her."

My blood went cold. "Feya."

"That would explain things," Nol said around a mouthful of pizza. "Since we only recently found out about the existence of fairies, I haven't stopped to consider it."

"Don't talk with your mouth full," I snapped.

All he did was smile at me as he chewed. Ugh.

Drake stayed quiet as he let me mull over this information and calm down. Feya was Ray's imaginary friend who'd appeared a few days after Aswryn had taken her. Three-year-olds have imaginary friends and being kidnapped has lasting effects. We'd figured it was a coping mechanism. Why would we suspect fairies? They hadn't been real four days ago.

"She's been careful with Ray, but Queen Orlaith had Feya ask her some questions. Ray never said much about you."

"She knows not to." My control of my temper kept my voice flat. "The visits end immediately or I'll end them."

Drake pressed his lips together. "I'll see what I can do."

"No, Drake. No more. She's three, and she loves her friend, trusts her friend, and wants to spend time with her rather than with her human friends."

"Then perhaps Feya should continue to visit," Drake suggested.

"No."

"Hallë—"

"*Sae, Twynolan. Ni fula. Lasi,*" I said in *Aemirin*. *No, Twynolan. It stops. Now.*

Why wasn't Nol as angry about this as I was?

"Think of this from Ray's perspective," Nol said in English.

"They manipulated her," I continued in *Aemirin*.

"And it would break her heart to lose her friend who has been there for her like none of us have been able to," he spoke softly in English. "For now, let it be. Ray already says her friend is a fairy. Is it really a betrayal?"

"They used her." Too angry to stand there and drink coffee, I crossed my arms and walked away from the two of them. I glared at the refrigerator with alphabet magnets and pictures. Sunday dinner with Lewis, Yumi, Mateo, and Sam. Ray, Charlie, and me on the ferry. And more.

"I won't let anything happen to them."

Nol grabbed my right hand, the one in the cast and touched my fingers. "Neither will I. *Idorem'a*, remember?" he said, reminding me of his promise he gave to me, a *Zayuri* oath of protection, when he learned how special these humans were to me. I nodded, before shuffling around to face the kitchen peninsula, where Drake stood, waiting and paying really close attention to his phone.

Nol reached around Drake and dragged the tablet over with one finger. "Let's go to the Seattle lab. Hallë, put your coffee in one of your travel mugs." Nol pinched the tablet screen and zoomed out of London. "Then we will visit the Los Angeles places."

Drake shoved his phone into his back pocket and checked his tablet again. "The LA trips has to wait until tomorrow. I've got other work to clear up first."

I blinked, staring at them. The two collected their crap in seconds flat without even looking at me. Drake headed to the back while I grabbed a travel cup.

"Hallë?" Nol touched my cast. "You don't need to go."

"Go? I can't believe you didn't tell me you went in the first place."

"I know it was traumatizing—"

"So you decided for me. I'm not a child, damn it."

"I know."

"Then stop treating me like one. That place you saw in my dream? It's real. I walked through it. If I can handle No Man's Land, I can handle Aswryn."

"You've had so many night terrors lately."

"I can't let those dictate my life. They don't define me, and I won't adjust my life to keep them from happening. You know it wouldn't prevent them, anyway."

Nol took a deep, steadying breath. "You're right. It was selfish."

I screwed on the lid to the travel mug, set my jaw, and studied his face. "Damn straight, it was. Let's go."

10

Charlie called on our way to the lab. That's how I found out Nol had taken her there. Every time he went. Right now, Nol was at the top of my shit list. It felt more like he didn't trust me rather than an attempt to protect me after learning about Charlie. Perhaps that wasn't the case, and it was my insecurity rearing its head. What if I couldn't control my magic? Nol kept reassuring me that my magic wasn't the reason the prank had gone wrong, but we'd never know for sure.

Queen Orlaith had said I would have found a balance. I wouldn't have been a threat if they'd let me learn instead of calling it a disability. Still, I'd watched my friends burn from the inside out. And I hadn't been able to stop it. What I'd needed was to learn some damn humility. Not that they hadn't tried to teach me, I'd just been to damn stubborn.

Drake's whistle grabbed my attention. "There's a lot more lab equipment here than the other labs."

I barely recognized the place in the daylight. I didn't even recognize the main floor. Aswryn hadn't taken me as far as this. I'd fought her off as soon as she'd carried me through the third-story stairwell. The place had been so dark that I'd never seen the spot where Aswryn had died—where Nol had killed her.

Overcast March light filled the room through the lab's floor-to-ceiling windows. A long rectangular island divided the space, and empty black counters lined the walls. Flasks, containers, and lab stuff filled the glass cabinets above one wall. A desk with bookshelves behind it occupied one corner next to the window.

"Charlie is going through Aswryn's work to find a cure," I told Drake.

I headed to the desk and all the books behind it while they talked about...whatever.

"You said the curse isn't an illness, though," Drake said.

"Aswryn cursed a virus, which is still spreading throughout *Aemina* even after Nol killed her. If there is a cure for the virus, the curse will be rendered useless."

"And Charlie knows this because...?"

"Charlie is an epidemiologist, and she's been researching me for years," I said almost absently as I opened a lab notebook written in Spanish. "*Dominar el stema inmunitario.* Charlie doesn't speak Spanish. Nol, you should have brought me here from the beginning. This one's about something taking over the immune system. What if the answer was right here the entire time?"

Both of them came over to see what I had. Drake grabbed one of the many journals like the one I was holding. "Aswryn knew Spanish. Her lab in LA had Spanish textbooks. All her journals there were in English, though."

"Do you have them? Charlie might be able to use them." Nol came to look at the journal over my shoulder. Feeling petty over him hiding their visits from me, I hid the journal's contents from him. I pointed my chin toward the shelf of other journals for him to look at. Nol's expression went flat, but he didn't fight me on it. He should have told me.

"I turned them over to The Queen's Guard." The paper snapped as Drake flipped through the pages. "She'll probably give you access, but she won't let you take them out of the vault."

Nol cussed in *Aemirin*.

"Why? They're notebooks," I asked.

Drake scowled as he scanned the contents of one page. "We can't let this research get into the hands of her conspirators."

I pursed my lips and turned the pages. Charlie wrote in notebooks like these to document her work. I flipped to the conclusions page. Whatever this was, it didn't appear successful. The technical words, English or Spanish, were above me, but I could translate them for Charlie as best I could. "Have you looked for any address books or ledgers?"

"I don't think nefarious elves worry about taxes." Drake leveled his aquamarine eyes at me like that was the dumbest thing I'd ever said.

I shook a finger at him. This old fairy needed to think outside the box—I mean, it wasn't that far out. "Not if they have labs in abandoned buildings. Didn't you say you found some kids in a house?"

"Abandoned house."

Grunting at his answer, I snapped the book shut and grabbed a different journal on another shelf. "Looks like she spoke German, too." I put it on the desk to translate later. Fuck, this was going to be a bit. At least it gave me something to do while my wrist healed.

Drake picked up the book I'd set down. "Do you speak German?"

"*Ja wol, ich spreche deutch. Of course I speak German.* "It was the second human language I learned." I continued in German.

"That sounds like a southern German accent." Drake tapped the book on my shoulder, smiling.

"Good ear. *Ich have in Stuttgart gelebt.*" *I lived in Stuttgart.*

"Shockingly, I've never been to Stuttgart."

"Eh, you're only seven hundred. You'll get there."

Drake snorted and went back to looking at a journal.

"There has to be something in here. I'm going to collect a bunch of them and bring them back to the house where there's coffee and heat. There's so many journals." I'd never questioned Charlie's findings and had pictured her finding the little critter under a microscope floating around some solution she'd prepared. Nope. This made more sense. I shut the journal and placed it on the take-home pile I was making, all while glaring at Nol.

Nol huffed as if I was being ridiculous. "She believes she'll find the antiviral in one of them or at least the path to create one."

"We have some of those." Drake's voice perked up, and he set his journal down. "Living forever, you have time to develop cures."

My jaw dropped. "Forever, as in immortal? Holy shit." Then I remembered Mateo's question. "Are there such things as vampires and werewolves?"

Drake's eyebrows shot up. Worried for my sanity, maybe? "No."

"Mermaids?" So he thought I was a nut. What was the use in stopping, then?

"There are merpeople, yes."

I jumped up and down a few times. "Nol, there're mermaids!" They looked at me like I'd grown another head or two. "I'm sorry—" I tucked my hair back, brushing the dragon ear cuffs. "Those are my favorite fairytales."

Drake laughed. "I'm sure they're not what you imagine. No Disney princesses or anything. They're snooty and think land-bound people are gross and savage. Our laws are ridiculous in their eyes. Oh, and we are also out of control."

"I've found endless references to merpeople, and they're all vastly different. Are any of them accurate?" Nol was scrolling on his phone, most likely Googling the word. That smartphone and him...

"Uh." Drake went to Nol and looked over his shoulder. "Here..." He tapped something on Nol's phone.

For Pete's sake. I went back to looking through the journals, separating them by language.

"They're not mammals, so no boobs like any of these," Drake said, as if that was the most important thing. "And they can change colors. Kinda like...this one, but their tail fin is vertical, so they move like a fish."

"Interesting."

My eyes kept darting over to them, not working and looking at my favorite mythical creature. I'd get Nol's phone from him later and check out his history. We needed to get working. I pulled open a drawer in a cabinet behind the desk and found a few canvas grocery bags. It boggled my mind that Aswryn had lived here off and on for decades, and no one had considered it before. I shook a bag open, and a receipt fluttered to the floor. I dropped the bag on the desk and reached under the chair to grab it. She hadn't bought much: bread, orange juice, apples, and Lysol wipes. "You guys. Here's an Albertsons receipt on…East Harrison Street. That's on Capitol Hill, right?"

"I think so." Drake came to look, and I handed him the receipt to hunt for more unexpected treasures.

Of the six canvas and reusable grocery bags she had, three had receipts. Another from Albertsons, one from a hardware store, and one from a gas station. All three were in the same vicinity. We started looking in the drawers for more paperwork. While my guess was that she'd been squatting at the Steam Plant—could we call this squatting if she was just working out of here?—the paperwork could lead us to where she was holding the kids.

Nol got on his phone again after going through the drawers under the desk. "There must be thousands of residential houses in this Capitol Hill area alone. *C'yo*, these streets are so confusing."

"That's why we need to find more paperwork," I said as I continued to looking. "I assume you've checked the rest of the building."

"For what? Children? I believe I would have mentioned that, Hallë."

"For anything related to Aswryn, Nolan," I snapped at his irritated tone. I'd just asked a question. Jeez. "Was she using any other rooms?"

"Yes, actually." Nol took his eyes off the screen and waved toward the front of the room. "The closet she kept Ray and me in and the bathroom."

I set my hands on my hips and cocked my hip. "Really? Who would have ever thought she would use the bathroom?" Smart ass.

Nol went back to his phone.

"Lookie here." With both hands, Drake reached into the bottom of the left cabinet. He pulled out a small safe, no bigger than a shoe box. "There's a spell locking it."

"She's dead. How are her spells staying around after she's dead?" I asked.

"It's not her magical signature. Probably an amulet." Drake pulled it onto his lap. He pressed his palm against the front and mumbled a spell under his breath. A second later, he pulled his hand back, hissing at whatever was protecting it.

"Fuck that." I leaned back to see the front of the safe. Not only did the case have a keypad but also a lock. It didn't matter. I sent my magic into the electronics behind it and the locking mechanism. Drake was right. A *meril* held it closed. "I feel the *meril*. It isn't complicated, though." The *meril* cracked as my magic broke the spell. Five seconds later, the door popped open. "There."

"Fuck." Drake opened the door and pulled out the broken *meril*. "You broke it."

"I'm tired of her bullshit. Whoever was making her *merili* better hope I never meet them." Perhaps it was the same person who had made the slave band. At the thought, I itched my arm over the band.

Drake placed the cracked casting in his palm. "What kind of amulet is this?"

"That one was made from a water sprite casting," Nol explained as he plucked it from Drake's palm.

"Is the *imolegin* familiar?" I asked. A long shot, but as a *Zayuri*, I'd bet Nol had met some shady magic casters.

Nol pinched it between his thumb and index finger. "No."

Drake rose off the floor with the safe and pulled out a folder. "This looks promising and...disturbing." He flipped through a few pages and handed it to Nol. Drake reached in again and pulled out more paperwork. "Here." He gave me several pages.

Addresses and lease agreements. "These are in German." I pulled my phone out and checked the time. "Crap, it's eight at night there. I can call them in the morning and see what's happening. Luckily, Germany is nine hours ahead of us." I added it to the already full bag. "In the meantime, I can translate some of these."

We jumped when Drake's pocket started ringing. He yanked the phone out and answered it. "I'm busy."

The person on the other end began yelling.

"Fine, fine. I'll be over soon." Drake sighed as he listened. "No, don't touch anything else until I'm there." He shoved his phone back into his pocket and frowned at Nol. "I've got another case I'm supervising. They're pretty green. I'll be over tomorrow to take you to LA. Call me if you find anything interesting."

"Hallë and I can search for these businesses without you, but if I find something I will call you."

"That's not the best idea. You might be some amazing warrior the queen believes can get results faster than us, but you don't know fae. You're in unfamiliar territory, and you'll need backup. We'll do it together."

"The children cannot wait." Nol seethed. Whether from frustration that he couldn't go immediately or Drake's comment, I wasn't sure.

Drake's jaw tightened, and his eyes got hard as he stared at the taller *endai*. "Fighting Aswryn's allies alone will put the children in danger."

"Agreed." Nol waved his hand toward the door, for Drake's green...agents. The Queen's Agents? That sounded stupid. Whatever they were called, he waved to dismiss them. "Find someone else to supervise your green people and let's go."

Drake and Nol glared at each other from three feet apart while I stared from behind the desk.

"I've been looking for these children for years. Katie and I were working to find Aswryn's network. You won't find children up there, just more clues. I was right in the middle of another case when Her Majesty called me home this morning. Let me tie this up, and I'll show you where I found the kids in LA. You'll understand once you see it. I'm sure all that's up on Capitol Hill is Aswryn's flat. Hell, it might even be a hotel. I don't fucking know where she slept. Just trust me on this. We'll leave tomorrow. Research what you have here. Maybe Hally's Germany contacts pan out. If we need to, I'll take you there, too. But please, wait for me."

Nol lifted his chin and looked away. "We can wait, for now."

"Glad to hear you say that. My team is over an hour away, so—"

"I will take Hallë through the shadows."

Drake stopped and frowned at Nol. "What?"

"It's a *Zayuri* thing. Go on."

Nodding, Drake pressed his fist against his chest before he left the room.

"I don't like your shadow walking," I said once Drake was gone.

"Shadow walking?" Nol's mouth curved into a smile as he turned back to me.

"Whatever you want to call it. Shadow traveling? It was cold, and I couldn't breathe, and It left me a little dizzy."

"It is awkward the first few times, but you get used to it. Are you taking all of that?"

I glanced at the bag on the desk. "Yeah. Why?"

"That is as heavy as you are."

"It is not. What, you can't shadow travel with heavy books?"

"Yes, but I doubt you can carry it."

"Can, too." I jutted my chin out.

Nol lifted an eyebrow in challenge.

Setting my jaw, I lifted the heavy thing and slid it off the edge. And I did not drop it! It might have hurt my fingers to hold on to it, but I managed.

"*Ai*, let me see it." Nol reached for it.

"No." I stepped back and swung it away from him. "I've got it."

He gave me a doubtful stare.

"I do! Let's take the bus, though."

Nol held his hand out, waiting for me to leave first. What? Was he going to lock up? Whatever. There was no way he was getting this bag. The door clicked shut behind me, and the hall—the one where Aswryn and I had fought and the place where Nol had killed her—stretched before me. It hadn't bothered me on the way in, but the brain was a funny thing. I swallowed and refused to let it bother me. Yeah, like that told my subconscious who was boss.

Nol's arms came around me. I jumped and shouted out, but the room faded. "Close your eyes," he whispered in my ear before we were in utter darkness, the surrounding air rushing by in absolute silence, until it wasn't, and we were in my house, in the hall under the stairs, to be precise.

"I told you I didn't want to go through the shadows."

Nol let me go, and I wobbled. I dropped the bag and reached for his arm or the wall or something.

"And I didn't listen." He grabbed my arm and waited until I was steady before he let go. "I hate the buses. They smell and the people stare and judge."

"You're such a baby."

Nol tapped my nose and walked off toward the front. Probably to the kitchen to find something else to eat.

11

"This isn't a good idea," Nol told me for the fifth time. He flopped down on the couch in the living room, holding one of Aswryn's journals.

I tapped my fingers on the fireplace mantle in my living room as I listened to the phone ring and didn't answer him. Zack needed to know. I hated the poor excuse for a DEA agent. Since the fight with Aswryn, I had warmed up to the idea that he wasn't as deplorable as I'd once believed.

"Hally?" Zack answered in his weaselly voice.

I slide my arm off the mantle and settled my fist on my hip. "Gee, nice to hear from you, too."

"I told you not to contact me. It keeps you and your buddy safer."

"You're gonna want to know what I need to tell you."

"Is this pertaining to Ian's attack at your shop?"

"Sort of."

The phone picked up some of the air from his sigh. "I can't today."

"Neither can I. How about tomorrow?"

"I'm off tomorrow, too," he griped.

"Perfect."

Zack groaned. "I've got shit to do in the afternoon. I'll meet you before nine."

I wrinkled my nose. Nine? That meant I had to get up before eight. Yuck. "Fine. There's a tattoo supply shop in Tukwila that I go to sometimes. It has an artist's lounge. Tell them you're there for me, and they'll bring you back. This is serious, Agent Thomas." The owner, Tiger, would be there, but the shop wouldn't be open. I'd have to do her a solid. I hated owing that woman. She made sure she got her pound.

"What's it called?" Zack asked.

"Tiger's Tattoo Emporium."

"Right." Zack hung up.

"I assume I'm supposed to tell Drake you're getting tattoo supplies that aren't important right now?" Nol asked.

"No. It's none of his damn business where I am. Besides, I'm not going with you. I doubt he'll care much where I am. Don't give me that look. I hate the guy, but Zack deserves to know. He is still looking for these kids. Plus, sometime in the future, DHS or the DEA might come knocking on my door again when they can't find them."

"Uh-huh." Nol flipped the pages in one of Aswryn's journals.

"Do you understand any of that?"

"Sort of." He wrote something down on a notepad beside him on the couch. "I can look up phrases I do not know and get answers. Aswryn was thorough. I have always known that."

He should have brought me there sooner, but I wouldn't reiterate that point. He hadn't. It was in the past. We needed to move forward. If only life were that simple.

Nol tossed the journal onto the table and puffed his cheeks out. "What time does Charlie come home again?"

"Five-ish. Wait, no. It's Saturday."

"That evening class she promised to teach." Nol scowled. "That professor is as pompous as ours ever were."

"Technically, Charlie is a prof, too. She does more research for the team than teaching."

Nol grumbled.

"And your father is a professor."

"We've established he is an exception. I suppose we need to extend that to her, as well. I've met Charlie's boss. He is inappropriate with her."

"Stan? Really? What'd he do?"

"I saw him looking at her butt one day."

"You look at her ass all the time."

Nol jerked and sat up straight. "Excuse me?"

"I'm not blind, Nol. You have. Charlie is pretty and flirty and intelligent."

"She's very young."

"So are you, for an *endao*. Don't hold it against her."

"What are you suggesting?" Nol narrowed his eyes at me. "She's your niece."

"So...if you do choose to—"

"Never." Were his cheeks getting rosy?

"Don't break her fucking heart."

Nol and I stared at each other for a moment. I fought a smile as I watched his cheeks flush.

"I won't, Hallë. I swear."

"I'll hold you to it." After an awkward silence, I grabbed a few of the journals and took them to the dining room. "Let's sort these. Maybe we can start a catalog—or come up with a system." I set the loose papers at the end of the table and spread them out. Four folders in total. I shook one. "These are the bane of every adult's existence."

Nol stood at the opposite side of the table, nearest the living room, holding the notebook from earlier. He raised an eyebrow at me.

"Junk mail. I was hoping to find bills or statements in the mail pile I grabbed, but it's all crap."

"The books you want to translate, I left alone. These"—he set the notebook down on top of two others—"are lab books. Charlie will be pleased to have more."

"These five are not lab books." I pointed to the thin, handwritten journals in the middle of the table—usually where Mateo sat. "We should start looking for clues in those."

"What is the pouch of papers near you?" Nol pointed to the manilla envelope.

"That's stuff from the safe. Some passports and credit cards."

Nol came over and emptied the contents onto the table. He opened each passport. "Dana Miller and Dana Rodriguez. The credit cards, this is how I've seen you pay for things."

I grabbed her Rodriguez passport, and her frowning human identity stared back at me. That she'd tricked me, come into my shop disguised as a human, and bespelled me to like her creeped me out. How had I not seen it? The signs had been there. Any magic made me nauseous with my magic blocked, and every time she'd been around me, I'd gotten sick. And she'd kept touching me and insisting on meeting alone. Ray had even seen through it and tried to tell me.

"Hallë? Did you hear me?" Nol placed his hand inside the passport book and covered the photo.

I started and took a deep breath. My face flamed. While Nol had never shamed me for not seeing through Dana/Aswryn's disguise, it disgusted me that I'd let it happen.

"Is there a way to track what is bought on these cards?" he asked gently as he took the passport and covered both of them with the envelope.

"Yeah, but we'd need access to her bank account." I tried to shake the feeling of Dana. "If you're up for it, we can take my bike up there and look. Sense for her *imolegin*."

Nol shook his head as he looked through the junk mail in his hands. "Not alone. I am angry that Drake left and Queen Orlaith didn't supply us with another guide. That is all. I won't do anything reckless." His eyes darted to me, but I saw the flash of a grin.

"Do you think Drake is right? About what's up on Capitol Hill?"

"Even if he is, I don't trust Drake. The disloyalty to his queen by not reporting you still bothers me."

"He's trustworthy. I'd tell you to ask Lewis, but he wouldn't say anything over the phone. You don't talk about Drake."

"Lewis knows him?"

"Yeah. His whole old tattoo shop does. Lewis has a complicated past, but that's his story to tell. Drake told me to find Lewis once I was here, that he'd be waiting for me."

Nol pursed his lips, still not sure. "If he had revealed himself, you wouldn't have been alone here." Nol touched my cheek. "I see the pain this banishment has brought you."

"No." He knew nothing about it. Not that I felt any anger or resentment toward him, but he would never understand what I'd been through.

He opened his mouth, closed it, and looked away. "How many family members have you buried? How many have you watched grow old?"

"Don't." I refused to cry. Even though Nol didn't believe I deserved this banishment, I knew I did. Accident or not, I'd killed our friends with magic to prove them all wrong.

"I searched No Man's Land on my phone after we woke up. And both wars. To have gone through that—caring for children through it all? I can't imagine."

"Then don't try. It was a long time ago. many good things came after that. I miss my sister, but I survived. What transpired back then, I've come to terms with."

"Drake should have told you about himself is my point."

"Yeah, well, you have a crappy way of making your point."

"I'm sorry you've been alone," Nol whispered, not letting me go. "Hopefully, meeting these people, you can make some friends. I still want to win an appeal, but when I go back, you won't be alone."

I bit the inside of my cheek. "I don't want to go home."

"I know. I suspected that before you told the queen. Still, I want you to have the option to come. To visit your family. I have an idea, but I won't...what is the phrase? Raise your hopes?"

"Get your hopes high."

Nol smiled, his eyes crinkling. "That one."

I wiggled to get him to let go of my face, but he kept me there. "You're still moving out."

"*C'yo*," he cussed and let me go. "Am I not being sincere? I haven't teased you at all."

"Quit whining. It'll be good for you.

My doorbell's ringing brought his head up, searching for the source. I smiled at Nol's bewilderment as I went to answer it. For a second time that day, Quinn stood on my stoop.

I leaned against the door frame and crossed my arms. "Are you lost?" I couldn't keep the smirk off my face, and neither could he as he pushed his hair out of his eyes.

"Maybe?" He didn't look past me or say anything else, just stared with that smirk and the changing gray eyes.

"What can I help you with now?"

Quinn took a step closer and leaned against the other side of the frame. "I wanted to apologize about Brodrick."

"Brodrick?"

"Yeah, at your shop. He's a jerk."

"I gather he's not very bright, either."

His eyes flashed light gray for a moment, almost mercury gray. "He's the queen's cousin—one of them. She kinda had to hire him."

"Really?" I bit my lip, and my tooth hooked my lip ring.

"Mm-hmm. Honest." He held up three fingers in the Scout's honor sign, and I rolled my eyes at him.

"Is that why she had to hired you, too?"

"Anyway, I wanted to apologize." He ignored my question. "We didn't have time this morning to really talk. I was running late, and we had to leave."

"And the Estwyn thing."

"How do you deal with him?" His eyes bulged.

"Wouldn't know. I've kinda been stuck on this side for a while."

"One encounter is enough, for sure."

I pushed off the frame and moved so he could come in. "You want coffee or something?"

"That would be lovely." He followed me in.

Nol was leaning against the wall opposite the doorway. One of his eyebrows shot up, but his eyes held no humor. I nodded at his unasked question. This wasn't a problem. I had this.

"Nolan—nice to see you again."

"You as well."

Quinn hesitated at Nol's flat tone. "Am I intruding?"

"No." I waved him through. "It's all fine. We just haven't had a lot of sleep, and we've got a lot of work ahead of us. Come pick out your mug."

"Oh, I get to pick, do I?" He shuffled over and stood by me. His height allowed him to see the higher shelves. We owned a lot of mugs.

"That's right. Mugs are a fantastic indicator of one's intentions."

I caught Nol moving into view, standing in the dining room, his arms crossed as he watched Quinn. *Please don't tell me he doesn't trust Quinn, either.* He'd said I might be able to make friends, and he didn't want me to be alone. I gritted my teeth and tried to ignore Nol's stare.

"This one, I think." Quinn pulled out an old Care Bear mug with a rainbow and three characters. Ray usually picked that one for cocoa. "What? Is it not me? You don't have any Seahawks ones."

"Seahawks? Nope, we're Sounders fans in this house."

"I see that. And a few others...*Les Rouge-et-Bleu*?" Quinn pulled out my Paris Saint-Germain Football Club mug, white with their blue and red logo.

"That's right. Have you seen them play?"

"I have not. I'm not much of a football fan."

I laughed and bit my lip again like a fool. Ugh, I needed to stop that. "At least you call it football."

"Of course. Have you seen an American football game?"

"I tried." I winced. "It's almost as boring as baseball."

Quinn's jaw dropped. "How can you say that? Do you not know the history of that beautiful sport?"

I squinted, unsure if he was teasing. "How long have you been in America?"

"Long enough to witness the invention of baseball."

"Now that's a long time."

"Is it though?"

I reached around Quinn, grabbed the PSG mug, and poured coffee into it. "A much more grown-up choice."

Nol scoffed. I looked over in time to see the stiff set in his shoulders and that hint of hurt in his expression before he left the room. Shit.

"Was I...are you two involved?"

My shoulders dropped. To anyone else, Nol's body language might have been perceived differently, but I knew.

I kept my voice low, hoping Nol wouldn't hear me explain. "We just lost a very close friend of ours. Finding new ones is going to be hard."

"I take it you and Nolan were best friends, too?"

"Until the day I was banished, we never spent more than a day apart."

"A day? Ever?"

"Ever. And this friend came in..." My throat choked up. Mother, help me, but I missed Gil. Even though we'd been apart for one hundred and nineteen years, I'd known they were all right—I'd thought they were anyway. I'd gone on living my exiled life, knowing they were living theirs. Now Gil was truly gone.

"I'm sorry. I should go so you can see how he's doing."

"No, don't."

Quinn set the mug next to the sink and gave me a soft, understanding smile. "I've recently lost someone, too. I understand. Go comfort him." He brushed the back of his fingertips under my jaw. "I admit, I came here for another reason."

"Oh?"

"I wanted to find out if you two were...a thing. And if you weren't, I wanted to invite you out tonight—if you're not doing something."

"Something?"

"Yeah, for St. Patty's?"

"It's St. Pa—it is!" I glanced at the dining room table, the papers and journals scattered across it. Everything was happening tomorrow. The research would take days. "Yeah. It'd be fun to go out and do something."

"Yeah?" His eyes lit up, flashing silver. "Wonderful. I'll be here around nine. You don't need to wear anything fancy. I hate stuck-up, fancy first dates."

My insides fluttered. First date? When was the last time I'd done that? Kenny was my last boyfriend, and he'd rarely taken me out.

"Is that okay?" Quinn hedged as we walked back to the front door.

"Oh, yeah." I waved my hand to dismiss my pause. "I was just...it doesn't matter. All good. I'll see you at nine."

He tilted his head and chuckled.

"What?"

"It's cute how you say 'all good' like you're from here."

I pursed my lips at his teasing. "Watch it or I'll cancel."

With a quick move, Quinn grabbed my hand and kissed my knuckles. "*Jusqu'à ce soir, ma dame.*" *Until tonight, my lady.*

My jaw dropped. I had not expected French. "Oh, *tu parles français?*" *Do you speak French?*

"*Oui.*" Quinn backed out and waved as he closed the door.

The entire time, I couldn't stop smiling. Jeez, I was in trouble.

"Our best friend just died." Nol's words were thick as he walked out of the hallway and into the living room. "And you're flirting with someone. Did Gileal not mean anything to you?"

I rocked back, but steadied myself. This conversation needed to happen. "Of course, he meant something to me. We must continue on, Nol."

"You continue on fast. He's been dead three weeks, Hallë."

"Yes." I reached for my bracelet and took a deep breath, my heart racing.

"As you said before, he was there for you in the end, yet you have barely mourned him."

"I've mourned him—I still mourn him. That doesn't mean I'm going to crawl into a cave and hide from the world."

"Is that what I am doing?" He looked down at me, deadpan, his voice holding no emotion.

I couldn't keep the frustration out of my voice. "Practically."

Nol scoffed and stormed back the way he'd come.

"Stop. Let's talk."

"What is there to talk about? You are done mourning our closest friend while I am hiding in a cave."

"I am mourning him. Damn it! Stop." I ran through the house and caught his arm before he reached the stairs. He stopped but didn't turn to me. Change was hard for Nol, and I liked to think that staying here was helping him deal with losing Gil. If he'd gone home right after Gil died, he would have had neither of his best friends. "I have lost many people and…it's easier to—to keep going. It helps you not think about it so that when you think of them, you remember how they used to be, not that they're gone. It hurts when a reminder that they're gone hits, but I have to believe that Gil would want us to continue."

"So you want to keep going like he's still here? Forget he is dead? That isn't healthy, Hallë."

"That's not what I said."

Nol turned to me, the tears in his eyes catching the light from the living room behind me. He clenched his jaw. "He never stopped loving you."

"I know." Sometimes I wondered if it had been too much. From an early age, Gil had always said he loved me, never hid it or expected me to say it back. He knew my feelings for him were different. "But you know I was never in love with him, and he knew that, too. I've been gone for a century. Did you expect me to love him forever? Never have any relationships and pine for him until the day I died? I mourned you all when I left. I had to learn to love other people and find a reason to—to keep going. I had to let everyone go to find some sort of peace."

Nol ripped his arm away from my fingers. "You let us go?"

"I had to stop crying over you some time! I had to figure out a way to function without you, Gileal, my parents, Yalu. Tell me, how was I supposed to continue living if I didn't let you all go?"

Nol looked over my head toward the living room windows. A tear escaped as he shook his head. "I don't understand how..." He raised his hand and let it drop again. "How do I..."

"Continue?"

He nodded, still staring off, his face partially in shadow.

"I know you've lost people, too. You saw them suffer from the curse. It couldn't have been easy. And now, you know they're still sick—"

"And there's nothing I can do until we figure out why the curse remains."

"Yeah." I grabbed his arm and pulled. He came to me willingly, because, well...I couldn't force him to move anywhere.

Nol leaned over and let me hug him while resting his cheek on my head.

"It's gonna be okay, Nol."

"I miss them so much," he whispered.

I nodded and wished he'd talk to me about what had happened. Yalu had told me he'd lost people and that I wouldn't have recognized him after I'd left. She'd said Gileal and my friend, Rajamë, had convinced him to continue. I had a feeling Rajamë had died from the curse as well, but Nol never wanted to talk about the people at home—especially our friends—shutting me down whenever I asked about any of our peers. I didn't want to shut him down now by mentioning anything or offering to talk or listen.

"You wanna go get ice cream?"

He huffed a laugh. "We have to work." He tried to move away, but I tightened my grip around him. He relaxed again.

"We will, but if you want, I can take you down to Jackson Street and buy you an ice cream cone."

"I'm not a child, Hallë."

"Isn't that my line?"

He stood up so fast that my arms flew wide. "I don't treat you like a child."

"So you've said—"

"I worry about you, and I care. You are my *muranildë*, and sometimes you do crazy, stupid stuff. Like jump in the middle of two powerful spells."

"This again?" I rolled my eyes.

"Or..."

"Here we go."

"Not tell me you blocked your magic. I left you all vulnerable and unprotected while I searched for Aswryn." He grabbed my face and squished my cheeks. "Do you know how much that scared me? I can't lose you, too."

"Well, duh." I pushed his hands away so my words didn't slur. "You'd die, too."

Nol raised an eyebrow and glared at me. "I love you differently than everyone. No one understands it." He swallowed until he could talk. "But Gil did."

He wiped a hand down his face, tears welling up again.

"Hey? You're a pain-in-my-ass, you know that?"

He laughed, picked me up, and threw me over his shoulder.

I started smacking his back as he carried me out the front door. "Put me down! Where are you taking me?"

The door closed on its own as we stepped out. He wrapped an arm around my legs to keep them from kicking him as we left the front porch.

"Twynolan! I'm not kidding. Don't make me hex you! You'll itch for a week."

Nol chuckled.

"Are you serious? Where are we going?"

He walked down the driveway where anyone could see us. "You said you were going to buy me ice cream."

"I need my wallet for that!" I beat against his back again.

"Nah, I'll buy it, then."

He didn't put me down until we were at the corner of our block. Several of our neighbors had seen Nol by now. He took Ray out to ride her bike down the sidewalk every other day and went for a walk in the evenings, dragging one of us along with him. Mostly me, because Charlie was either putting Ray to bed or out with Doug—the cheating asshole. Since he'd decided to stay, Nol had made a point to greet the neighbors and get to know the nosy ones. He even flirted with eighty-year-old Mrs. Rosenberg across the street. Apparently, Nol was a strapping young man. Along with his "badass" title, his head was way too huge.

12

"You look fine, Tatie," Charlie said around a piece of licorice. She watched me smooth down my shirt again and check my makeup for the hundredth time.

"He said not fancy, but are you sure this isn't too...I don't know." I wore an off-the-shoulder sweater that went down past my hips and black leggings. I'd wear black booties to go with it before I left.

"It's fine."

"But—"

Charlie squeezed my arms, her eyes wide as she met my eyes from inches away. "You love that sweater."

I nodded. But like all my sweaters, the knitting was loose, and I wore only a black halter top bra. "Maybe I shouldn't go."

"You're worrying too much."

"I'm not worried. I feel guilty. I told myself this was all right to do, but I haven't made much progress in those journals—"

"What you've already done has helped immensely."

Charlie had done a happy-dance-squeal combo after she'd come home and I'd given her fifteen translated pages. Not that I understood it all.

The bathroom door moved, and she adjusted her weight as she leaned on the doorframe. "Now that Nolan finally told you about going to the lab."

"He's not your boss. You could have told me any time." I wiped at a smudge of mascara, too stubborn for its own good.

"I know," Charlie muttered under her breath. She picked at the licorice in her hand, stripping it in two.

Giving up with the tiny brush, I pictured my lashes without lumps of mascara and called my magic to change it. Yes, I was using magic more often, and I had mixed feelings on the matter.

The doorbell rang for the second time today.

"I'll get it!" Ray yelled in her high, three-year-old voice.

Charlie's rich brown eyes widened before she bolted away from the bathroom, around the corners of the upstairs hall, and down the steps.

"Charlie! It's okay." I leaned over the railing.

She stopped at the landing and looked up at me. "She'll let something slip, and he'll know—"

"She can't open it."

"She knows how to unlock it."

"Release the door, Hallë. I have her," Nol called up. His voice traveled with magic rather than volume, so Quinn couldn't hear.

I released the door so Nol could open it. "I had the door, love," I told Charlie.

She harrumphed. "Elven magic, of course."

"Are you complaining?" She was against me blocking my magic again, so complaining made no sense.

"No—" She grimaced as Quinn's voice drifted up the stairs from the living room. "Go have fun. We'll talk later."

One more check in the mirror. My mascara was fine, but I checked my back. A few of my shrapnel scars showed, but I wouldn't need to make up a lame excuse for them with Quinn.

I shuffled out of the bathroom, my socks shushing over the wood floor.

Charlie waited for me on the stairs and reached for my hand when I got close. "You'll do fine, old lady."

With a laugh, I leaned into her as she giggled. With her hands on my shoulders, she followed me down the stairs.

"Hello," Quinn said as I made it into the living room. He stood in the small foyer, his hands in his black peacoat jacket. Black trousers—apparently my idea of "not fancy" was different from his idea of fancy. Shit.

I waved, nervous. When the hell did trousers mean non-fancy? This wasn't a good idea.

"Hey." He frowned. "Where's your green?"

I stopped in my tracks.

"I mean, your eyes are beautiful, but they don't count."

My green? I racked my jumbled brain.

"St. Patrick's Day?"

Crap, that was the second time he'd reminded me today. "Right. Um..." Did I have anything green?

"Oh, Ta—Hally, I've got something," Charlie slipped, almost calling me Tatie. Usually, it didn't matter. We blamed it on Ray referring to me as an aunt. She called Mateo and Sam her uncles, as well.

Everyone watched Charlie shuffle back into the hallway. She came out ten seconds later with a sage-green silk shawl. She draped it over my shoulders, kissed my cheek, and shooed us out.

"Have fun! Go."

"That was abrupt," Quinn said as Charlie shut the door on us.

"She...um." I looked up at the night's cloud cover, orange and stormy gray. "Charlie just found out her boyfriend was cheating on her. She's one of those helper people, you know?"

"Ah. The girls seem to like you and Nolan." Quinn's arm bumped my shoulder, but he didn't touch me otherwise. None of that overbearing guy, arm-at-my-waist crap like most American dates I'd gone on. But he wasn't human. This was going to be weird.

"As you'll see, Nol can be likable—annoyingly so when you've known him as long as I have and you see people's reactions. Ugh." I rolled my eyes, and Quinn laughed.

"I know one of those types." Quinn opened the door for me to the same Porsche as this morning.

"He doesn't exploit it." I pointed my finger for emphasis as I slid into the soft, black leather interior. My mind went back to the night

Nol first found me in Seattle. How he'd been worried about whether my friends would like him.

Quinn smiled and shut the door. The hush and smell of fine leather surrounded us.

"So where are we going?" I asked.

He turned in his seat to face me. "That depends..."

"Uh-oh."

"It's not bad." He laughed. "Have you eaten?" In the light from my house, dim through his dark tinted windows, I could make out the outline of his face.

"Um...yes." Cucumbers and carrots with Ray counted. We had a lot of cucumbers.

He eyed me for a second. "We're getting something to eat."

Fantastic. Quinn's "not fancy" was different from mine. Vastly different. I'd taken Charlie and Ray to the French restaurant for some Sunday brunches, dressed up in pretty dresses. Now, tonight, the lights were dim. I hoped dim enough that the patrons and staff couldn't see my leggings. At least the shawl hid the sweater.

"What's wrong?" Quinn murmured to me as the waitress guided us to our seats.

"Nothing."

"You're fidgeting. I'm screwing this up, aren't I?"

"You're fine." I hooked my arm on his, the peacoat rough against my hand. "I'm just...I'm fine."

The lady gestured for us to follow her to a darker corner booth, where we could see the other patrons, especially at the bar. I ordered my drink right a way. Quinn helped me with my coat and waited to take off his jacket until I was seated.

Yeah, our fancies didn't line up. But hell, his causal look was not bad, I'll clue ya. Black slim-cut dress shirt—or was that dark green? I couldn't tell in this light. Black trousers creased down the front.

What was dressed up for him? The only thing casual about him was his black-on-black Chucks, which I found adorable.

"I thought we weren't doing fancy, is all," I explained as he kept glancing at me and out into the room. "I don't usually wear leggings here."

His face fell. "You've been here." He made it a statement.

I chuckled. "It's a French restaurant and France is where I've spent the majority of my time. The first human language I learned was French. I like this place."

"I am screwing this up. Dating in this day and age is nerve-racking."

"Are you kidding me?"

Quinn held his breath, his gray eyes stunned.

"This is fine."

"That's the third time you've said *fine* since we've been in here."

"How are you nervous? We're out for St. Patrick's, at a nice place, just two old geezers out for the night."

"Who are you calling old? I'm only thirty-two." He paused, his eyes sparkling. "Hundred," he whispered.

I sat back and stared while he continued to beam as he picked up his ice water. Thirty-two hundred years old? Maybe being around fairies wasn't a good thing. Were there any fairies my age? Was I going to be the baby again?

"Hey? It's okay—" Quinn lifted his hand and brushed away something on my cheek. "Am I too old for you?" He winked, but I didn't smile back.

Three swallows of ice water later, the pulse in my ears slowed and went away. "You're older than my grandmother. Of course, you're too old for me."

He snorted and leaned back, laughing at the ceiling. "You do know we're immortal, right?" Quinn grabbed his glass and swirled the ice around. "The truth is, I wasn't sure if I was going to ask you to come out. We've had similar losses as of late."

I homed in on him, our surroundings gone.

"Aswryn killed my fiancée three weeks ago. Her son is the boy Aswryn stole."

This couldn't be a coincidence. I said nothing, conflicted about whether to admit I knew her.

"She..." He bit his lip and tapped the glass of water. "Katie had a past, and Aswryn has followers—Fae followers, as well as elven ones."

That threw me. How did he know? Focus, Hally.

"But I am positive she wasn't part of Aswryn's group."

"Aswryn told me they would have accepted me if I hadn't blocked my magic or had too high of morals?" I squinted as I made it a question, like having too high of morals was a bad thing. "She was ranting about it when I was trying to—" I bit my tongue when I almost mentioned Ray.

"Ah, your fight at the steam plant. Yours and Nolan's magical signatures saturated the entire building."

"You've been there?"

"Me personally? No. I'm...Queen Orlaith's foreign relations officer. Sort of."

"Sort of?"

He winced. "It's complicated."

"Is it?"

He sipped his drink, and then his eyes rose to the young waitress who had appeared out of nowhere. Or maybe I hadn't been paying attention.

"Hello, are you ready to order?"

Movement from the entrance caught my eye. A tall, stocky gentleman in a dark coat ignored the greeter and wove his way around the tables, hyper-focused on us. I couldn't tell if he was fae or human from this distance.

"Um, Quinn?"

Quinn stopped explaining that we needed more time, and they both turned to me.

"I think that guy is coming to our table." I pointed with my chin.

Quinn turned, then groaned. "Would you excuse us, miss?" he asked the brown-eyed waitress.

She nodded and was leaving as the man came to stand in front of Quinn.

"Your H—Quinn." His eyes darted to me. "I know you said not to disturb you, but there's a problem." He glanced toward the doors, then back at Quinn. Another man entered the restaurant, leaner with lighter hair and skin, his jaw set and chin lifted high. He took a moment to locate our table, unlike the darker-haired, more muscled fae who'd known exactly where to go.

"What could possibly—"

"Um, probably that guy?" I pointed out.

Both looked over at Mr. Snotty Pants.

"Fuck," Quinn whispered.

"We knew nothing of his arrival until he got here, sir."

"He isn't supposed to be here until next month." Quinn sat up straighter and brushed down his shirt. "Hally—this might not go well. Bear with me, please. Wes, stand near Hally." He shooed who I figured was his bodyguard.

"Prince Cuán." Mr. Snotty Pants lifted his nose even higher.

Prince?

"Lord Gavin," Quinn greeted.

Gavin's sneer turned to me. How he could see that far down with his head so high, I had no clue. His lips puckered. "So it's true. She allowed an elf into her kingdom. Is Queen Orlaith forming an alliance? Have your loyalties changed?"

"My loyalties aren't yours to discern, Lord Gavin." Quinn turned and rested one elbow on the table and the other on top of the bench. "Who told you about this?"

Gavin raised his upper lip. "Rumors spread."

"That fast? I don't think so. Are you here to see for yourself, or are you here in an official capacity?"

"Withholding this breach of the treaty isolates Queen Orlaith. King Lorcan knows of the rumor and sent me to investigate. Why didn't you report this violation? The kingdoms must know about this."

"I advise you to go to Queen Orlaith with this, otherwise it appears suspicious."

Gavin scoffed. "You are her foreign relations officer, are you not?"

Quinn set his jaw. "Go discuss this with Orlaith. Wes can take you."

"I have a car."

"Weston will take you. Your car will stay here."

"Your Highness, I'm assigned to you," Wes argued.

"Then assign someone to take him to the manor. I'm off duty and enjoying a night out. Weston?" Quinn jerked his head to the side, and Weston grabbed Gavin's elbow.

"Lord Gavin, if you'd come with me, please," Wes mumbled.

"Prince Cuán, the king wants answers from you."

"The king can wait," Quinn muttered as he turned back to me.

"Prince Cuán?" I asked as soon as they'd left.

"Hally."

"Complicated? Are you a spy?"

"No."

"Did you ask me out to get information? For who? Queen Orlaith or King...Loren?"

"Lorcan. He's my older brother. Orlaith is my niece. Older by thousands of years, but lineage-wise, she's my niece. I'm not gathering information on you." He rubbed his temples. "I told you it's complicated, and I had hoped to get to know you more before we got into the bureaucracy of it all."

"You're a prince, not a foreign relations officer."

"I'm both. For both of them. Sort of. Can we not talk about this? At least until the second date?"

"There's going to be a second one? I doubt that."

"Because I'm a prince, or because you question where my loyalties lie?" Quinn tensed.

"I respect honesty, and I thought this was a date. But that isn't possible, is it? Not when..." I dropped my napkin. "Take me home, please."

"Hally, I'm sorry. I just wanted...I kept it from you because you didn't know. Everyone knows who I am, and for one night, with one person, I wanted to be normal. A commoner, if you will."

"So you're using me to be normal for a night?"

Quinn gaped. "No—well, I guess it could be conveyed that way." He licked his lips and fidgeted. "Hally, I really like you."

"Why? Because I'm an *endaë*?"

"You didn't back down from Brodrick. No one does that."

"You were pretty defiant yourself."

"I outrank him." He smirked. "Don't underestimate him, though. He's smarter than you think and catches on to things."

"Good to know." I scooted out of my seat and grabbed my coat.

"Hally, I'm—"

At my glare, he deflated and slid out after me.

It wasn't until we were in his car that I spoke again. "Do I need to worry about um...Lord Gavin?"

He started the Porsche and pulled out of his spot in front of the restaurant. "Possibly. He's King Lorcan's foreign relations officer...and my friend."

"You don't act like friends."

"Our relationship is rocky right now. If you want honesty—I'm not sure how much I can tell you about our relationship with them."

"Sounds like that's rocky, too."

Quinn didn't respond. Instead, he focused on driving back to my house. Our St. Patrick's Day first date was ruined. Damn fairies. Or maybe not. If not for this, when would Quinn have told me? When would the queen tell us about Ray? Too many complications.

13

My night vision let me see more than a human, but was it my imagination, or did the darkness above me appear lighter? I adjusted my head on the pillow again. If I didn't fall asleep soon, my grandmother would wake for the day and I'd miss my window. Not that I looked forward to what she had to say. But I needed to know what Estwyn had told the *Amura Ore* and what the *Amura Ore* had said back.

My eyes fluttered shut for the thousandth time. With *Olauvë*, my mind needed to cross from one realm to another, but dream-walking eliminated barriers and distances. The dreams of those I knew were easiest to invade and had to be avoided at all costs.

Finding the way through the fog that divided the realms felt like walking through waist-deep water, but after that, my grandmother's mind became clear and vivid.

My grandmother was dreaming, like normal people do in dreams. I tried not to see more than glimpses. Towle stood behind her as she gardened. They were at her home in *Rudairn* and not in the *Zayuri* village where they lived now.

"Yalu?" I kept my tone light.

As with all dreams, it took her a moment to recognize me as an outsider and not part of the dream. "Nevie." She walked over and hugged me. I needed that hug. When she leaned back again, her stern expression sent a ribbon of dread through me. "Things aren't good here. For you."

The dream wavered, and Tolwe was gone. Like many dreams, things shifted in a blink, and we were walking through a garden, which wasn't hers anymore. For a moment, her mind wandered from dream to semi-reality.

"I assume Estwyn blamed me? Are the fairies and I working together? Or did my evil guile entice the queen to choose me?"

"Estwyn said that neither of you let him finish any sentences—he barely got to talk. Um, because there was a language barrier, you told the queen she didn't have to keep Estwyn." She gave me a pointed look to make sure I knew that. "You didn't explain that he was there as an official representative, but a messenger. He said the entire meeting appeared staged. He offered two alternative explanations. One, you're both lying and working together to sustain the curse after Aswryn's death, or two, if you truly have just met this race, you are responsible for the continuation of the curse and he is concerned about the fae's safety around you. Since you are *savilë*, we should never trust you."

"You know all of that is a load of shit."

"The *Amura Ore* trusts him, and as they chose only one person to come, he is their only source."

"Why didn't they bring more people, then? There should have been an entourage, at least a scribe. They did it on purpose. Estwyn interrupted the queen regularly and wouldn't let her talk. Why are they willing to believe I was involved rather than figure out why the curse is still there? If they kill me, the curse will continue. Perhaps if you suggested *Olauvë*?" But we both knew the council would never agree to hear my side.

"The only way to clear your name is for someone else to end the curse. Gileal embedded himself amongst Aswryn's known *endaen* associates. Most of the intelligence *Aemina* gained about Aswryn originated from Gil's and Nolan's experience and research. After Gileal's first encounter with Aswryn, he reported the extent of her power. Now rumors are circulating that Nolan and you are to blame for Gileal's death. That you were both working with Aswryn."

I stopped walking, the long grass tickling my bare feet. "How—how could they even—" I paused and turned away, staring into a vast valley of red, purple, and yellow wildflowers.

Yalu tugged on me until we were walking again. Past the valley, a forest awaited us, one more ancient than any of Earth's. The massive *Coyana* trees of *Endae*, twice as tall as the California Redwoods, towered over our path, teeming with life.

Yalu patted my arm as she led me under the trees. "It was someone's suggestion, not what they all think. Some are getting desperate as more people die."

Then ahead of us, the scene changed again. Mists shifted, and instead of trees, there was the angled slope of a building. I didn't know where we were or even if a city existed, hidden in the mist of the forest.

"Hallenaevë, as those few fanatics get louder and their delusions gain traction, others will start to believe. Some have suggested bringing you both back and forcing you to break the curse."

I stared straight ahead toward the building.

"Nevie?"

"I'm listening, Yalu. I think you should know what really happened. She kicked him out after he told her I was *savilë*." And I explained the entire conversation as best as my memory served me.

"The only thing I think you could have done differently was to tell Orlaith the truth from the beginning—but you did everything right to the best of your training. I'm proud of you. We will stall, but Tolwe and I can't do it for much longer."

The slope I saw earlier was only a small fraction of the building it belonged to. What buildings in *Aemina* were this big?

"Yalu, where are we?"

She took in a deep breath and held it as she peered around. "Oh. I hadn't noticed our stroll. *Atrau*, it seems."

"*Atrau*? I didn't realize how deep in the forest it is." I'd never been to the capital but would have gone for my apprenticeship.

"Oh, it's not. That's the dream, but the buildings are *Atrau*. All this talk of the *Amura Ore*, I'm surprised my mind didn't take us straight to the floor." She snaked her arm around me and held me close. "I feel myself waking. Be safe and work quickly, my granddaughter." With that, she faded out of existence along with her dream.

14

Sunday morning, the Volvo engine's ping vied with the white noise of the rain as I watched the road outside Tiger's Tattoo Emporium in Tukwila. Sure enough, the nose of a Honda—or was that a Toyota?—rolled up into a parking spot across the road. The people in the car didn't look my way, but I knew they had followed me. They'd kept their distance on the highway. Four exits back, I'd lost them, but they'd popped up in Tukwila and made every turn I took, even the extra turns around the mall, and they'd waited down the street while I bought a latte at Starbucks—a place I rarely visited.

I was sure they'd gotten on at my on-ramp, too. He was the same weirdo with a surfer's cut and black sunglasses that I saw on the I-5. The man beside him was just as ridiculous looking, with a beanie and sunglasses. Still, there was no doubt in my mind. They were following me. But who were they? Not men in black, that's for sure. No government official could be allowed to have that haircut. Fairies sent from Orlaith? She could still be watching us. They appeared human, but I had no way of knowing if they were fae under glamor.

I took my last sip of coffee and got out of the car into the pouring rain. Agent Thomas would be here soon, but I'd get a few items to keep up the appearance of a simple supply run. I bolted, puddles splashing, but I dodged the deep one near the curb.

The hush of the store replaced the downpour outside. The familiar scents of tattoo ink mixed with the rich incense of dragon's blood and lavender permeated the air. Tiger's supply store settled me, reminding me of days before fairies, before *endai,* when I was plain old Hally Dubois, tattoo artist. But did I want that back? I had Nol—for however long he wanted to stay—but we'd made a communication *meril* that we were determined to keep, regardless of my exile. And the fairies? That remained to be seen, but maybe I would have friends I wouldn't outlive in my exile, and that was worth exploring.

"Hey, girl!" a husky smoker's voice came from the back as I walked down one of the aisles of tattoo supplies.

"Hi Tiger. Hey Mitch." I waved at the two artists in the back behind the counter.

Mitch had more piercings than I could count, dark wavy hair down to his back, and a bushy black-and-gray beard. He stood next to the counter, his eyes level with the top.

"Still workin' on that beard, huh? It's gonna be taller than you are soon." I winked as I came up next to him, bent down, and kissed his scruffy cheeks.

Mitch stroked said beard when I straightened. "That's the plan."

"You get your first tat, yet?" Tiger asked as I gave her an elbow bump. As her name suggested, Tiger had tattooed seventy-five percent of her body in tiger orange, black, and white. Her whisker piercings—white today—twitched as she smiled. Her long incisor-capped teeth glinted in the fluorescent lights of their shop.

"As soon as you find an ink I'm not allergic to."

"You gonna let me give it to you?" Tiger winked, knowing my answer, yet they always teased. We went through this a lot. My colleagues had a bet going on who'd be the first to tattoo me once they found a safe ink, which they'd never do, considering the ink had never been the real problem. Tattoos were too identifiable, so I couldn't get any. But I had a list in my mind of the ones I wanted to get. The problem I ran into was which one I'd get first.

"Hell no, girl. I'm doing it," Mitch argued.

"Guys, you're both wrong. I will give myself my first tattoo."

They scoffed and snorted.

I leaned my forearms on the counter. "Thanks for letting me use the back."

"Not a problem. He's back there waiting for you."

"Of course he is. Let me guess, he was waiting for you to open the door this morning."

Mitch pointed at me and tsked. "Sure was."

"I set him up with some coffee in the back. He's the DEA agent who was hot on down in California?"

"Hot on?"

"You know, hot on your tail?" Tiger smirked at her own joke.

"Ha-ha. Yes, he's the one. Thanks for taking care of him." I clapped Mitch on the shoulder as I walked through the beaded curtains to the break room, where the artists hung out when they visited. Many local tattoo artists frequented Tiger's place. While online stores were getting popular, Lewis and I wanted to keep our supplies local, and from what I could tell, many of these other tattoo shops felt the same way.

The back smelled more of ozone from the computers and various tattoo books Tiger kept in her office. Rain beat down on the clear, corrugated plastic that covered the patio out back, creating the perfect soundproofing from curious ears. The small place had comfy chairs and couches, all vintage of the mid-nineteen hundreds or earlier, arranged on fake grass. Terrycloth quilts and mint-colored wood tables completed the decor. Agent Zack Thomas was perched on the edge of a well-kept nineteen-fifties floral-patterned couch. His coffee cup, complete with a small plate, rested on the table in front of him, while he sat as close to the outside heater without curling up to it. I didn't blame him.

"Agent Thomas, thank you for coming. Although, I thought we'd agreed to nine o'clock."

"It took less time than I thought to get here." And he didn't even sneer when he said it. Shocking.

"Lucky you."

"Why? Did you drive?" There was the bit of hoity-toity I was familiar with.

"Yep, took the Volvo." I grabbed one of the coffee pods Tiger had here in the back and pulled out a mug from her cute vintage set. While I waited for the single serving of my favorite drink, I watched Zack fidget, impatient to know why I'd asked him here. He did have kids to find, and so did we. I sat on the opposite side of the couch and angled myself to face him. I licked my lips, paused, remembering the two possible fairies out front, and scooted closer—as close as I'd ever willingly come to him before—to be heard over the rain and out of magical hearing.

"I know who's behind the kidnappings."

Zack jolted back, his eyes wide with shock.

"And you won't find them, no matter how many agencies help you."

"Hally, is this a threat?"

I closed my eyes and shook my head. "Nol and I are assisting in the search now. You'll never find them, because Aswryn took them." I let that sink in. "And none of them are human—at least fully."

"You said you and your friends were the only elves."

"I was wrong." I went on to explain how long Aswryn had been here and who these children were. That Agent Thomas took this without disbelief baffled me. He'd witnessed Aswryn's handiwork up close in Yula's Quill, but he'd taken it all in stride. Such an odd human reaction.

"I want to help."

"You can't. They know you're involved in a small capacity, but they keep feeding you small insignificant information to keep you looking."

"It's not insignificant. I've met these parents and pulled together first-hand witnesses."

"Do you think you could bring this to me without your agent buddies knowing?"

"Not without me—"

"There are rules. Humans can't know. I can't tell them about the girls, my family, or my friends. I don't know what those repercussions would be, and I imagine they're watching you like a hawk." He tried to interrupt. "What is more important? Finding the kids at all costs or you being the hero?"

Zack pressed his lips together hard. His beady brown eyes were about to explode with frustration and anger. We hated each other, not as much now since we'd come to an understanding and he'd stopped trying to pin me for conspiring with Ian.

"Any information you can give us will help. You wanted me to tell you what I know, and now I have. I'll tell you what I can, when I can. Nol is looking at a place on Capitol Hill to check out when we get a fairy to escort us."

"You need one of those?"

"He's our liaison and the agent in charge of the mission."

Zack scowled. "He's done a swell job of it so far."

"Don't pout—"

"You said Capitol Hill?"

"Yeah, I found receipts in Aswryn's lab from a mini-mart and a grocery store. They're relatively close to one another."

"What about Westport?"

My turn to scowl. What on earth could he have found in Westport?

"It's where Katie saw Derrick. She was out there with her boyfriend."

Quinn? My stomach dropped. "Did the boyfriend see him too?"

"All I know is that she ran into some old druggie friends. They went back to the shack of a house, and Katie saw Derrick. I think her boyfriend stayed in the car. She was adamant that she did not take any drugs, but the boyfriend refused to let her report the house. Now I know why—wouldn't want the locals finding out about fairies running drugs and trafficking kids."

"It could be why she recognized Derrick. Fairies don't age as fast as humans, so he could appear similar to when they took him."

"Katie said she thought he'd gotten out. That's why she called me."

"Do you have the address of this shack? Have you been there?" I asked.

"I went there before I came to you in February. There was nothing. The back side of an old half-torn-down house."

But fairies used glamour. Even their vineyard was cloaked, shielded, or whatever. So it could have easily been hidden from Zack's human eyes.

"I need your evidence and that address. Please, Agent Thomas. I've told you Nol tracks people down like a sword-wielding bounty hunter."

"It might take some time. I can't just walk in and make copies at any old time. And I want to be in the loop on everything."

"I'll try to keep you in the loop as much as I can. At the very least, you'll know when we find the kids."

We stood and actually shook hands. "I'll be in touch."

"Agent Thomas, I believe this is the first time we've come together and not walked away angry at each other."

"Besides the Aswryn incident? When I rescued you and your buddy from the steam plant?"

"I so didn't want you there. Anyone but you."

Zack snorted and shoved his hands into the pockets of his brown pleather coat. "I don't look forward to dealing with you either, but if this is successful…god, Hally, it would be worth butting heads with you all these years."

The petty part of me wanted to disagree, but the big mature girl I had to be agreed. We'd get information soon—Katie's information—and we'd find Seamus and the others. My phone buzzed in my pocket. I jumped but recovered.

"Charlie?"

"I think you need to come home soon," Charlie said quietly in French.

"*Pourquoi?*" *Why*? I asked.

"Nolan. He's agitated and left another message on Drake's phone. I think he might go out on his own."

"*D'accord, je viens,*" *Okay, I'm coming*. I moved my mouth away from the phone to speak to Zack. "I have to go, but wait until I'm gone before you leave. There might be fairies following me."

Zack gave me a confused frown.

"Just trust me." I sped out, buying a few tips and purple ink. With a hurried goodbye and apologies to my friends, I was out the door.

15

An hour later, I walked in through my back door to find Nol shoving on his boots in the mudroom. When I'd left this morning, Nol had been following his normal routine: training, albeit without his uncle, then food, coffee, and a newspaper. I'd made the mistake of introducing him to the local newspapers, and now we had three different subscriptions. Paper ones. Digital was becoming an actual thing now, but clearly, we had to have the paper versions for Nol's happiness. One more thing for Nol to take with him when I kicked him out next month.

"What's up?" I asked.

Nol's booted foot dropped to the floor, and he turned to face me, all emotions hidden. Oh dear. "I'm done waiting for Drake."

"You said yesterday you wouldn't go alone. That you wouldn't do anything reckless."

"I won't. He said he'd be back today—he isn't here and he hasn't called. I plan to take a walk around those businesses. If I sense something serious, I'll call Drake—again. I'm tired of getting his voicemail."

"We could call the mansion. Drake gave me that number, too."

"This will help clear my head, Hallë. The queen asked me to find the children, yet I am...*ai, metaen esye laväero.*"

"Okay, no need to call ourselves names you are not...*that.*" English didn't have such a harsh name for a such a useless person as *laväero*. Worse than the c word or n word. *Zayuri* soldiers cussed a lot.

"He said he'd be here today—"

"I know. There could be fae working for Aswryn up there."

"What is the phrase about crossing paths? I'm used to working alone, and if there are fae, they won't be prepared for me."

"Nol!" I groaned.

"Come with me, then? Mother knows the car is big enough to hold everyone." It wasn't as big as *that*.

"You'll sit in the passenger seat while I drive? You must be desperate."

"No, I'm thinking above my own comforts."

Was he, though? "Do you really think you could take out fairies on your own?"

"We can together."

"You've said before I don't know any fighting spells. What kind of help would I be?"

"Stay behind me while I defeat them. If you must, use an orb or two until I can make it to you. It worked with Aswryn."

I blinked at him, recalling his lifeless body in the grass. "Um...you almost *died*."

"Before that. I recovered and fought her. You weakened her hold on us, and Gil and I broke free. Your orbs worked."

I harrumphed. He had an answer for everything—like normal. Nine times out of ten, Nol was right, though. "Fine." I yanked off my red swallow-tail coat and grabbed a raincoat instead. Pausing, my new coat half on, I looked down at my outfit: extra long-sleeved gray sweater, black jeans with zippers and tears, and black Doc Martens boots with red roses. This'd be fine, right? "Whatever," I muttered as I yanked my coat on. "Charlie, I'm driving Nol around Capitol Hill! We'll be home for dinner." I glared at Nol as I said the last. We were always home for Sunday dinner, even if it was just going to be us tonight. We couldn't risk the fae meeting Mateo, Sam, or Yumi. The fae encounter with Lewis was as much as I could handle. I wouldn't put them in any more danger. They didn't like it, but Yumi had gotten through to them.

"Okay, Tatie," came her reply from upstairs. "Be careful, both of you."

"Bye Tatie! Bye Nolan!" Ray yelled right after her mother.

THE ELDERLY MAN COMING into the hardware store held the door open for me as Nol and I left. We hadn't felt Aswryn's magical signature, but when Nol tried to cast a *Zayuri* spell close to the bathrooms, I'd elbowed him. Now he was pouting.

"No one would have seen it."

"I'm sure we can pick Aswryn's *imolegin* up outside somewhere." I got it, really, but no matter how desperate, we would not do any magic around humans. *Zayuri* or any other. Nol stormed ahead of me and down the sidewalk. He'd slept some, so his grumpiness was pure frustration.

I thought we'd go back to the parking lot, but Nol kept walking. "We're not going to walk, are we?" We'd already visited the grocery store, the mini-mart, and the dollar store next to it. "It'll take forever to search this whole place. Do you know how big of an area Capitol Hill is?"

"We may not sense it if we're going too fast."

"Uh-huh. We're not walking for hours. In the rain."

Nol gave me a stubborn, emotionless stare.

"No." I stomped my foot, then regretted the old childish habit. "If we can't sense anything, we can go back and walk around. But we're driving first."

Nol shrugged and kept walking.

"Nol!"

"You can go driving around."

"Fine!" I called after him from half a block away. "Maybe I won't call you if I find something. I'll just check it out by myself."

Nol turned and gave me that stare again.

"It will literally take all day to walk around here." I spun my keys on my finger before unlocking the Volvo's door.

Nol kept staring at me as I yanked the heavy door open and got in. He stayed there as I drove past all the parked cars, out of the lot, and stopped next to him on the street. I reached over and unlocked the door, but I would not roll down the damn window. Finally, he dropped his shoulders and walked over.

"You are a pain-in-my-ass, you know that?" I informed him as he yanked his seatbelt on.

"Drive slow or we won't sense it."

Whatever. So time was too precious for our normal retort, too?

"What is with you? I know you're frustrated, but you know the way to finding these kids won't be laid out for us."

He rolled his shoulders to adjust his hidden sword straps as he looked straight ahead, shoulders tense and *Zayuri* mask set. Pouting wouldn't help the situation. He was two hundred and fifty-five years old—not eighty! I nudged him, then nudged him again.

"We'll find them." I patted his knee while I drove like some old granny, ten miles under the speed limit.

"I hadn't planned on you coming."

"Yeah. Or taking a car." I kept the speed at about fifteen miles an hour, pissing the guy behind me off. Oh well. The old houses were beautiful, sprinkled with modern apartments. I'd never understood the reason all the houses were built on mounds. Almost every yard was raised at least three feet above the sidewalk. Large trees lined the sidewalk, blocking some views of the homes. The car behind me honked as I stopped at the stop sign.

Nol tapped his fingers on the door as he scanned the street ahead.

"What if I tried using *Olauvë*? I picked up the curse's signature in *Endae*. What if I felt *imolegin* here, too?"

"That was the curse's signature inside live bodies, not residual magic. Let's try this way first. If we find nothing, We'll try your way. Don't scowl at me. You're driving, and I don't feel comfortable sitting in a car with your unconscious body while you search in a different plane of reality."

I huffed and drove off, every once in a while pulling over to let the other drivers pass. Ahead of us at the next intersection, we had to choose to go left or right as a multistory building stood in front of us, with stores on the first floor and apartments above them. My stomach rumbled as I caught sight of the cafe across from us.

"Wanna take a break? I'm sure you're hungry, and I forgot to eat breakfast."

Nol wrinkled his nose at the cafe. "Do you truly want food, or is it coffee you're interested in?"

"Can't I want both?"

Nol groaned, and I found a parking spot. A fine drizzle engulfed us as we stepped out, and I hurried to get under the canopy before it ruined my makeup. Then I realized I'd forgotten to lock the car, and 1984 Volvos don't have fobs. Nol smirked at me when I locked the door with a flick of my magic.

"Shut up," I mumbled.

He grabbed the door, still smiling. "What happened to no magic in front of humans?"

"It's not like anyone can see that."

Nol elbowed me as we walked over to the host table and the "wait to be seated" sign.

"This will not be quick," he muttered.

In the lobby, three middle-aged women, all wearing purses bigger than their heads, sat on the bench to our left, and an elderly couple sat to our right. I gave the host my name and sat next to the elderly man, but Nol stayed standing, looking around as if scouting the place. I almost kicked him.

"I'll be back." His eyes narrowed, and he walked toward the kitchens and restrooms.

A hostess called the couple over. Nol came around the corner a moment later, weaving between the three people and straight at me.

"Come with me," he murmured. He held his hand out as the ladies smiled, admiring his backside. What would they say if they could see the sword sheath attached to the jacket? One lady, who looked to be the youngest, fanned herself and the other two giggled.

I frowned. "Why?"

He shook his head and left me to chase after him. His pace didn't slow, and I had to do a jog-walk to keep up. We got to the hallway near the restrooms before I came even with him.

"Is there an issue with the bathroom or something? You know how to work the faucets."

I expected a glare or an eye roll, but his expression remained blank. He pushed the employee-only door open, poked his head in, looked both ways, and was off again. The door swung open into the kitchen. The kid doing dishes did a double take as Nol walked through like he owned the place. I hurried after Nol and grabbed his arm as I caught up.

"What is going on?" I asked, only loud enough to be heard above the water and grills.

"I can sense Aswryn's *imolegin*." He opened the door out into the sour-smelling back alley. A dirty, rusty dumpster was pushed up against the building, with five trash bags next to it. Nol marched on to the right, his strides almost twice as long as mine.

"I can't."

"You're not *Zayuri*. It's faint, but it is coming from behind this building."

"Hold up, Nol. We can drive around and follow it on the street."

Almost at the end of the alley, Nol turned and glared. "What is your aversion to walking? You run almost every day."

Gritting my teeth, I tried not to take it personally. "Your legs are longer than mine and you're on a mission. I'm not jogging after you the entire time."

Nol's face lit up, surprise rushing into his eyes. "Sorry." His eyebrows knit together as we headed back into the cafe. "I should have considered you."

I wrapped my arm around his middle and gave him a side hug. Nol always matched my pace when we walked, without fail. Nol yanked on the door, but it didn't open until he cast a small spell to switch the lock.

He lifted a shoulder with the same kind of smirk from before. "There was no one around." But then he got serious as we retraced our route out to the car.

"It has to be close, right? The other traces weren't this strong."

"Yes." He looked up before he slid his seatbelt on. "Judging by all the surrounding houses, this could have been her Seattle home."

My shoulders shook as I inhaled. "So maybe not a place she kept kids?" Disappointment and relief wrapped into one. Wherever they were, I hated to think about what Aswryn had done to them. "*Please, Mother…*" I paused in my internal prayer paused as I realized I didn't know what to pray for. These children, when we found them, would be in some degree of distress no matter what. "*Give me the strength to help them.*"

Nol reached for my hand on the steering wheel, pulled it close, and squeezed. He said nothing because I knew he thought the same thing. We went around the block, not as slow as before since we had a specific destination. Nol stopped me as I turned left and past the cafe. The house on the left after the shops was a two-story with garden gnomes and roses.

"This one." Nol pointed to the smaller home, one without a raised yard. "I sense Aswryn's and others."

"Others?"

"I don't recognize them. It's…"

"Fae?"

"Possibly, but I won't make any accusations. Never assume, Hallë."

A tall human male, with a dirty blue T-shirt, was repairing the chain-link fence in the front yard. No—he was attaching a "for rent" sign to the gate. Holy shit.

"Park and wait here. I'll talk to him."

I parked two houses down, but like hell I'd wait in the car. "It's better if we both go over."

Instead of arguing, Nol jumped out and stormed to the house before I even shut my door. Shoving my keys and wallet into my pockets, I jogged to make it over before Nol started a conversation.

"I just put it up for rent online today," the man said as he clipped the extra wire off the sign.

"Hey, honey, wait for me." As I came up, I grabbed Nol's arm and stood close. Just a young couple interested in the house. "How much is it? We just saw the sign—didn't check any apps."

Nol looked down at me, and I smiled a huge, pretend smile.

The man, who I assumed was the owner, glanced at the small house with peeling white paint and blue trim. He brushed his fingers through his short graying hair as his eyes came back to us, rather to Nol. "Forty-two hundred a month."

I coughed. Holy shit. I knew housing prices were skyrocketing, but damn. This thing was tiny and run down. Clean, but run down. "Does that include water, sewer, and garbage?"

He glanced down at me. "No." Then back to Nol. "But I installed solar panels, and we have fiberoptic internet, so that'll keep prices down."

"Yeah..." I swallowed. Oh so far down. Was this guy for real? "What do you think, hun? Should we check it out?" I asked Nol.

"Solar panels?"

"The...um..." Nol looked at the house, then me. So lost. I refrained from laughing. Barely. "Fiberoptic..." A quirk of his lip as he tried to keep a straight face. "...would be better."

"I guess. Can we see it?" I asked Mr. Sexist.

"You're seriously interested?" again asking Nol.

"Why not? Sweetie?" Nol leaned over, tilting his head so the guy couldn't see his amused face. Finally, a smile.

"Forty-two is more reasonable than what we're paying now." I leaned around Nol and looked at the guy.

"I require first, last, and a two thousand dollar deposit. Can you afford that?"

Fuck. Ninety-four hundred dollars? They expected people to pay that?

"Been saving up for six months," I lied through my teeth. I didn't know how far I'd take this ruse, but if we had to rent the house to get inside, I'd do it. Then do a sub-rent—charge half of what he was asking, and tell him we had roommates.

"Okay, follow me."

The yard featured grass and crappy, invasive Yellow Archangel and Herb Robert in the garden under the window. Paint peeled off the trim bordering the old metal one-paned windows. Was that lead-based paint? The owner struggled with the knob, and the whole thing shook as he shoved. The inside smelled—not of mildew, thank the Mother, but stale air that needed a good airing out. Baseboard heating—the solar energy would be used up on heat alone. The hollow sound of our steps assured me of a basement. We needed to check that out, too.

I opened my senses in hopes of feeling Aswryn's signature. We were close enough that if spells were performed here I'd feel it. My attempted panned out—and I felt those other signatures Nol mentioned. Aswryn's was the dominant magic, but a stew of others crept into my awareness like spices. I doubted if I could single them out if I felt them again somewhere else. I wouldn't be surprised if Nol could, though with is special *Zayuri* magic.

Nol followed the owner through the living room toward the kitchen as they talked about attics and the postage stamp yard. Don't forget the gated, paved driveway! Nol turned back to me when I stayed in the hallway. I tipped my head. I'd go exploring by myself. The corners of this mouth dipped down, but he couldn't do a thing to stop me.

My steps were lighter than the two heavier males, but I doubted the owner even noticed I'd left. Potential renters didn't need to explain themselves if they wanted to go off on their own, right? The guys' voices carried through the house, not that Nol said much. A question here and there. The small hall bathroom stank of bleach and mildew.

Both bedrooms were as small as the bathroom. I found the attic access in the right room, but where was the basement entrance? I stepped into the primary bedroom, where a dark stain covered a six-foot circle in the old wooden flooring.

An unfamiliar ring of a cell phone echoed through the house. The owner's gruff tone answered, and as he talked, Nol spoke over him to tell him he was going to go find me. I sent my magic out, testing the room for anything I couldn't see with my eyes. Where Aswryn was concerned, we needed to be prepared for the worst. Before my magic made it across the floor I felt it. A snag, as if my spell was caught on something. I pushed forward as it tried to hold me back. The floor groaned, then a splintering sound just before the floor gave way.

I let out a yip of surprise as my legs went through the Hally-sized hole in the floor. The wood scraped my calves and shins. I reached for the edge but couldn't hold on. Instinct took over, and my body slowed down, my magic controlling the descent. The wood fell faster, creating a pile of splinters to land on. It wasn't comfy.

"Hallë, don't move!" Nol called out from above. His head poked over to check on me, then left again.

Dirt floated all around me and into my lungs and eyes. The light from the window above revealed a tool bench and the staircase ten feet to my right.

A loud clattering came from above. A pulse of magic shook the door at the top of the steps on its hinges. I felt Nol's *imolegin*. Another pulse, this time not Nol's magic, shook the flooring, raining down more dirt around me. The owner yelled, and Nol cast another spell. Glass shattered as the house shook. What the hell was going on up there? As spells shook the house and more dirt dropped on my head, I pictured the rubble against one wall and swept everything at once to the far side of the basement. How much dirt could there be up there?

"Nol!" I yelled. "What's going on up there?"

He didn't answer, but his opponent cast another spell.

"Who is up there with you?"

Nothing.

A voice from the front called out a word. A name? Heavy steps ran toward the kitchen and Nol. A surge of foreign magic. These had to be fairies. I'd never felt *imolegin* like this. The owner yelled, and the other fairy responded.

"She's in the basement," the owner said.

"He's *Zayuri*. You can't take him on your own! We can deal with her later." The new guy cast something to make the walls shake.

Nol's signature engulfed the kitchen. Both fairies hit the floor, and I thought that was the end of it, but no. The owner yelled a word right before Nol threw another spell his way. I gritted my teeth and pulled down the floor from the end of the kitchen to the front of the house. The left part, not the whole thing. The floor rattled at first, but then after some moaning, the floor collapsed. Two seconds later, I had a visitor down here with me, falling on the tool bench. The range slid down after that, narrowly missing him. He screamed, then shoved the flooring away from him.

Nol called my name, but I couldn't focus on him and their fight. My opponent's eyes locked with mine. The basement held little light, but I caught the fairy's sneer from across the room. Before he could catch his balance and get the upper hand, I created a ball of air and added a considerable amount of raw magical energy to it, like a storm in a bowling ball.

The fairy's mouth dropped open, and his eyes widened in surprise as my magic slammed him into the wall. After a moment, he tore himself out of the dent his body had made. He snarled at me and raised his arms. I gathered the rubble at his feet and covered him with it. He screamed. I squeezed my eyes shut, praying I hadn't fatally wounded him. As I released the spell, he helped it along. Splinters and debris exploded. Wood and metal scratched all of my exposed skin and would have shot into my eyes if I hadn't turned my face away in time.

A thumping from the stairs behind me registered in my mind, but I couldn't look away from my fight. Not knowing what else to do, I tried the same thing, gathering magic again. As my energy gathered, the slave band warmed. Damn it. A portion of my magic flowed to the band as I conjured my mini storm. It was the creepiest feeling I'd ever experienced, like a trail of insects crawling from the core of my magic in the pit of my stomach and into my arm. I managed not to scream and tug at the band like the first time.

I threw the magic I'd gathered, although it didn't feel as strong. He staggered backward, but he'd been prepared for it and didn't fall again. The fairy held his arm out at the same time Nol called out from beside me, "Back up, Hallë! Hide yourself."

I took my eyes off the fight to look at Nol. He swung his sword, the blade emanating a black-blue light, toward my opponent as the blast of his spell hit me. Nol's appearance had cost me time and concentration. Fire ripped through me and over my skin. Nol jumped forward, a *Zayuri* spell cast from him and through his sword. My opponent screamed, but then the noise cut off.

Nol came to my side. He held my face for a moment, then released me. A black light, radiating from my torso, grew stronger until it covered the entire room. The burning sensation from the guy's spell faded. Nol said nothing as I got my breathing under control and he ended his spell.

"Better?" he asked, his voice devoid of emotion. The last time Nol had needed to save me with one of his spells, I'd passed out in the middle of it.

"Nifty trick. Too bad it can't heal scratches, as well." I pointed at the cuts on my face.

He glanced but didn't comment on my injuries. Maybe they weren't as bad as they felt. "Can you stand?"

"You're not mad at me, are you? I didn't step in the middle of two spells this time."

"No, you just tore the floor out from under one of them. I understand your decision, but I was scared for you. You're lucky my training helps me keep a level head."

I squinted. "Is a level head really devoid of all emotion, though?" I grabbed Nol's hand and let him help me off the pile I'd fallen back into. We maneuvered over the planks to the dirt-covered cement.

"Our tour guide caught me off guard, otherwise I would have finished with him quicker and come down here. You did well." Nol went over to the fairy's side, checked his pulse, and stood back up. "I'm impressed with your spells. Not just the orbs from before."

"What's wrong with my orbs?"

He itched his chin as he inspected the fairy-sized dent in the wall. "Nothing. You are—what do humans call it? Branching out?"

"That's it."

He touched the shelves within the radius of the blast. "I think we should get you a focusing object. Your attacks would be more concentrated."

"Like what?"

"A weapon, perhaps?"

I scoffed. "Like my life is so fraught with enemies that I need to use a sword like yours? This is atypical."

"You would not carry around a sword. Something much smaller that you can grab quickly."

"I'm not carrying around a dagger, either."

"Hmm." Nol walked off, checking out the adjacent walls. "Aswryn's *imolegin* isn't as strong down here. I believe her fae friends spent more time in the basement."

"Or she didn't use magic down here. But what could the others possibly need to use magic down here for? There's nothing besides ordinary basement supplies, a washer, and a dryer. What's over there on the other side of the utility sink?" I could make out the top of a dark square, like a crawlspace door.

"Stay back." Nol took five long strides to get from one side of the basement to the other. "Please." He held my eyes for a full five seconds, determined to convey how serious he was.

I dipped my chin in agreement. "I won't wait forever, though."

"Long enough for me to determine the danger." He'd agreed...ish?

As the silence grew around me, I shifted from foot to foot. I lifted my hand to brush debris out of my hair and caught sight of a palm-sized spot of blood staining my coat. I moved the rip around and pulled out the pinky-sized splinter. Lovely. We had nothing clean to stanch wounds.

Still nothing from Nol. I checked on my opponent. Still out. Was he tied up? I stooped and checked his wrists. Holy shit, his wrists were bound with the same cuffs Nol had used on Aswryn. I'd seen them then but hadn't paid too much attention, believing Nol was dying at the time. Yeah, priorities. The cuffs were made of the same metal as Nol's sword and dagger. They pulsed with Nol's magic.

"Hallë."

I jumped, my heart in my throat.

"Didn't you hear me? You should come see this." The grave look on his face twisted my gut. Shit. I hurried over, curious but terrified of the unknown.

"Be warned, you won't like this." He took my hand and squeezed as I ducked to follow him.

Magical energy lingered in the earthen tunnel they'd dug out. The tunnel stank of urine, feces, and damp soil. Roots poked out of the walls, and above us, roots brushed my hair and slid against the back of my raincoat. Nol had to crouch and almost crawl. He let go of my hand and went deeper into the foul-smelling hole ahead of me.

I gulped, my mind split between visions of the tunnel caving in and the image of dozens of mutilated little bodies on the floor. Did I really want to see this? I almost stopped, but too late. Two steps ahead, the tunnel opened into a little eight-by-eight room, brightened by a light orb Nol had conjured when he first came in.

In the far left corner, a pile of blankets caught my eye. On the opposite side, someone had dug a hole for a latrine. I was going to throw up. Nol touched my back and rubbed my neck, his face inches away from mine.

"Breathe slow and shallow. You can do this," Nol whispered, as if someone might hear us. "I know it's hard. Look over here." He pointed to the right corner next to the tunnel. Rope, dirty towels, jugs of water, and plastic cups littered the area.

Shoes were in the last corner. Ray could have fit into the smallest ones. I shuddered at the sight of the small black sneakers. I turned one so I could see the design in Nol's light. Red stripes along the sole and on the tongue. Were they Seamus's? I tried to remember what shoes he'd been wearing the last time I saw him, but I couldn't envision them.

"Nol," I said, my voice barely a shaking whisper. "I need to get out of here." There was nothing I could help with. Nol could do some *Zayuri* finding spell without me. We'd found the place where the fae children had been kept. That's all I could handle at the moment.

I hurried back the way I'd come, without dry-heaving, and thanking the Mother I hadn't eaten at the cafe earlier. Nol came out right after me, breathing deep breaths like mine.

"We need to call Drake," I said after my tenth breath of dust-filled air—free of bodily excrement.

Nol frowned. "I still don't trust him."

"Then who? Orlaith? She assigned Drake to us. Until he does something to make us doubt his loyalty, we need to trust him. You can keep your guard up and be suspicious, but he's all we have."

Nol frowned. "Other than keeping your identity from his queen, betraying her trust, he isn't answering my calls."

"How many times have you called him?"

"Several...perhaps five."

I pulled out my phone. "Tell you what. I'll call Drake, and if he doesn't answer, I'll call the mansion."

Nol waved his hand. "Fine. I'll check on our prisoners."

"You go do that," I muttered as Drake's phone rang. And rang. I hung up and texted. I had to concede and call the other damn number.

"Avalon Vineyard, this is Sasha. How may I help you?"

"Um." I hadn't expected there to be an actual business or that Drake would give me that line. "This is Hally Dubois. May I please speak with Orlaith?"

"Orlaith? I'm sorry, there's no one here by that name." Her bubbly, professional voice was going to give me a headache.

"Is the owner there?"

"Yes, but she's in a meeting. I can connect you to our manager?"

"Wonderful."

"One moment." The hold line music started playing the Firework song that was in one of Ray's animated movies.

"Good afternoon, this is Keith."

"Keith. My name is Hally Dubois."

"What can I do for you, Ms. Dubois?" Again with the professional, polite voice.

"Listen, I don't have time for this. Drake gave me this phone number to contact Queen Orlaith and I really need to get a hold of her since I can't get a hold of Drake. We found evidence of the children."

Keith didn't say anything for a while.

"Hello?"

"One second, Ms. Dubois." He put me on hold again.

"Hally?" Yet another person, but at least this one wasn't fake. "This is Finn, the guard you met at the front door."

"Good. Your front desk lady refused to let me talk to Orlaith."

"I don't know how you wound up with that number. That's the public winery line. Tell me what's going on."

"We found some fairies. They attacked us."

"Attacked you?" Finn swallowed. "Who?"

"Good question."

"We're bringing them to the queen," Nol called out from above. "I'm not waiting around."

"Just a second, Finn," I said in a sweet voice before I muted the phone. "How the hell do you think we're getting them into the Volvo?"

"I'm walking them out of here."

"Walk? They're awake?"

"No, but I'll wake them soon. Trust me, Hallë."

How the hell? Fine, we'd try. I pressed the unmute button. "Be prepared to open that veil-door thingy of yours. We're making a special delivery."

"Wait, what?"

"We're bringing them to you, Finn."

16

Z*AYURI* MAGIC IS VERSATILE, to say the least. Nol woke them both up and marched them out the door and into the back of the Volvo like silent puppets. His magic kept them from moving or saying anything he didn't want them to. I did make sure they could blink, though. Wouldn't want their eyes getting dry. The fairies stared forward like statues, while Nol gripped the armrest on the door. The last hour passed slowly as we went over narrow roads and up and around mountains. No need to scare Nol and make him look bad in front of our company.

The guards indeed had their veil down for us to drive in, and four guards waited for us at the front, including Drake. As soon as I cut the engine, Drake was on my side, opening the rear door to drag one captive out.

"Where did you find them?" Drake demanded of Nol as he shoved the "owner" fairy prisoner against the car.

"In a house on Capitol Hill. I left several messages."

"And you brought Hally with you. She isn't a warrior." But he said it staring into the prisoner in front of him.

"She is not," Nol agreed.

Drake glared across the roof of the car and waited while Nol opened the rear passenger door and made the other fairy step out. All the guards drew their weapons, ready for an attack, while the fairy stepped to the side for Nol to shut the door.

"There is no need to hold that one, Drake. I have them under my control." Nol looked around at all the guards. "Please, if you will guide us?" Nol waved his arm for the guards to go first.

My fairy opponent stood there, unable to move away from Drake's grasp.

"Drake, let him go," Nol said in a warning tone. "They are detained by me. I won't have you abusing him while he's under my control."

"Under...?" Drake frowned, then looked at me for clarification.

"Just let him go. This is the reason the queen wanted Nol to work for her."

My opponent tried to say something, but his vocal cords didn't work, so all he did was snap his teeth. The second Drake let go, the prisoner hustled toward the group, trailing everyone ahead of us.

"Where have you been?" I hissed to Drake as we took up the rear.

"I told you I have another case, but I found someone to take it over. These kids are important, Hally. Our first priority."

"You said you were coming back today. You could have called."

"There were complications."

I waited for him to elaborate, but he didn't.

"That prevented you from sending off a short text?"

"Yes." Drake pressed his lips together as his aquamarine eyes bulged. "I can't discuss it."

We passed the guards at the front door. They looked into the distance like someone would appear out of nowhere and encroach upon their territory. We weren't taken to the conference room like before. This time we turned left and met the queen in the huge living room. Our entourage, minus a few guards, was already in the room as Drake and I entered.

"The tunnel we found contained personal items, and I sensed multiple signatures throughout the house." Nol stood two steps to the side of one prisoner, his hands behind his back as he reported. "Any of them could have belonged to the children."

"They were alive?" Orlaith asked Nol while Drake and I had caught up to the group.

"Yes. Tracking them, however…the trail is at least a week old. With those two fae now in custody, I will study the site more while Hallë studies the books we found."

"Drake reported those notebooks to me. Drake, is Connor prepared to take over?"

"Almost. A few more things to take care of, Your Majesty. I should be fully available by tonight, at the latest in the morning."

The queen looked at the closest guard. "Take the prisoners to their cells. Excellent, Nolan. Hally, I didn't expect you to follow him into battle. Your family's magic isn't meant for fighting."

"I was Nol's chauffeur," I said.

"I didn't realize chauffeurs suffered injuries." She pointed to my legs, then my arm.

I lifted my jeans, revealing cuts I hadn't paid attention to or felt from all the adrenaline and action. Trails of dried blood leaked out of cuts I'd sustained from falling through the floor and landing in the rubble.

"Oh. That's, um…yeah. It'll be fine."

"Drake, take her to get cleaned up. Nolan, what about you?"

"I didn't fall through the floor or have pieces of it magically thrown at me. You'll come to understand how stubborn Hallë is. I can update you while she gets bandaged, if you wish?"

Orlaith fluttered her hand for Drake to leave before she turned and perched herself on a chair near the cold fireplace.

I followed Drake into the hall and around the corner. A familiar figure rounded another corner, heading our way.

"Hally?" Quinn frowned as he took in my injuries. "What happened?"

"We—"

Lord Gavin walked around the corner behind Quinn and almost ran into his back. "Why is the elf here?" he snapped. "Quinn, you told me they were searching Seattle for the fae children."

Quinn tipped his head back and stared at the ceiling for ten seconds. "Let's shut up and let her talk, and maybe we'll find out, Gavin."

Gavin closed his mouth and pressed his lips into a thin white line.

"Um, the queen is listening to Nol's report. You can see if she'll let you listen. I'm not at liberty to discuss—"

"You will answer our questions, elf," Gavin sneered.

My eyebrows shot up, and I stared at him. I wouldn't give him shit now.

"You can ask Queen Orlaith. Drake? May we continue?"

"Certainly, Madam Ambassador," Drake murmured.

I managed not to freeze at the title. I wasn't an ambassador, but that should shut Gavin up. Ambassadors didn't have to kneel and obey peons. Drake continued walking.

"Ambassador? What is the meaning of this, Quinn? Take me to Queen Orlaith at once. I demand to know—"

"Shut up, Gavin," Quinn snapped back. "You'll wait until your scheduled meeting. You're only embarrassing yourself."

Gavin gasped. I stopped listening as I came up to Drake, who'd slowed down for me.

"I'm not an ambassador. I'm *savilë*."

"Her Majesty chose you to represent the elves. That's close enough, and she can correct your title for Gavin. Or not. He barged in here, unannounced. I'm not sure if he has any jurisdiction. I keep out of politics."

"Smart. Avoid it at all costs."

Drake took me across the manor to an actual medical wing.

"It's weird to think you guys don't heal everything like fairytales say you can." I followed him into one of the small examination rooms, the same blah beige and green as most other patient rooms. The floors, unlike the wood and carpet of the rest of the house, were the typical medical room tile—easier to clean bodily fluids off of. I went to climb up onto the examination chair, but the thing moved so all I had to do was slide.

"Shit."

Drake grinned. "Magic." He pulled open the cupboards and looked through the drawers. "They adjust to the patient. Fae come in all shapes and sizes." He pulled out a box from a cabinet above the sink and came over. "We do heal faster, but if someone chops our head off, we're as dead as any other living thing. We get sick and can even get cancer." He opened a drawer and pulled out a waxed paper pouch that could fit in my fist. "This is a healing amulet. It'll aid in the mending of your cuts. It keeps the wound clean, helps clot the blood, and increases skin regeneration."

"Hmm, we have magical teas for that." I pulled the little thing out of his hand. Inside was a thumb-pad-sized red disk. "What's this made out of? For curiosity's sake. Nol and I didn't think there was anything here that held magic like *merili*."

Drake took the amulet from me and focused on threading it on a long piece of twine. "Redwood amber." He held it out, and I turned so he could tie it around my neck. "I think any kind of amber will work, but redwoods hold magic the best."

"Huh, makes sense." I picked the little amulet up off my chest. "We use amber from our sacred trees, as well, but its natural color is green. I am almost positive that our trees are related to the redwoods here, but ours are much bigger."

"It'd be cool to see that."

I let the amulet fall and looked up at the wistful dark fairy. "Maybe you can."

"I don't think you'll heal the gouges carved between our races, Hally. Orlaith likes you, but we haven't forgiven them for what they did."

"I'll have to learn the history of that sometime. Definitely after we find the kids, though."

Drake frowned, giving me a worried look.

I patted him on the shoulder and jumped off the chair, the paper ripping as I did so. I winced, but Drake shook his head. He reset the paper and threw the used piece away.

"Let's get going. I want to get back to those notebooks." My thoughts sobered. "And you need to see what we found. It might be a promising lead. I heard Nol say the kids were taken out of there alive. I'm not *Zayuri,* and I don't have his training, so I couldn't tell.

Drake, it was horrible. To think Seamus—" My throat constricted, and tears came to my eyes.

Drake settled a hand on my shoulder. "We'll find him, Hally. There's one thing I didn't think to mention. I don't know if you've gotten to know Quinn, but Katie and him, they were engaged. He loves that little guy—Seamus even calls him dad. It wouldn't be good for him to get too close to this case. I don't know what I would have done if my kids had been taken when they were little."

"I didn't know you were a father."

"It was some time back. They're older than you. I told them they're not allowed to make me a grandfather until I'm at least a thousand."

"So, in three hundred years?" He thought he could restrict them for that long. Fat chance.

"Don't remind me," Drake growled in frustration. "Maybe I should amend that to eight thousand."

"You couldn't have been much older than them when you had kids. Don't you think that's a little hypocritical?"

Drake mumbled something and gave me a weak, seething look. Or maybe more of a cry for help. Children drove us all crazy. I gave him a wide grin.

As we came through the mansion, Gavin's whining voice reached us near the foyer, echoing down from the living room.

"Jeez, how old is this guy?"

"I dunno anymore. We lose count. Older than Queen Orlaith."

"So, too old to throw a tantrum."

Drake snorted as he stepped in the room.

Gavin took one look at me and got three steps closer to us before Nol got in his way.

"The *Zayuri* is already threatening me. I demand the elves be arrested. King Lorcan is ready to declare war on *Endae* at this very moment."

Gavin kept trying to shove Nol out of the way, while Nol's body blocked the uppity prick. Orlaith stood in the middle of the room, bodyguards flanking her. The queen's mouth stayed shut, her posture neutral, but her expression said it all. Her eyes radiated annoyance and anger, but when Gavin turned back to her, her expression shifted—concerned for Gavin's plight, yet unmoving in her decision. Like a parent of a preschooler. A master of diplomacy.

"Lord Gavin, if you cannot control yourself, I will have you detained." And take away time at the park.

"Control myself?" he screeched. "This is an outrage. Our treaty clearly states that if they enter our realm, they break—"

"Lord Gavin." She didn't yell, but her voice held magic to amplify her words. "That is enough. You do not have the authority to demand anything of me, nor do I need to be told what our treaty contains. If you'd shut your mouth for two seconds to comprehend what I have explained to you, perhaps you would see my point of view. However, I don't need you to understand anything, nor do I need your permission. You won't discuss anything with my father before I speak to him."

"He is my sovereign. I have the right as foreign—"

"And he's my father. You can't act reasonably, thus you will be confined to your rooms until I allow you out, after I've spoken to my father." She nodded to her guards.

Gavin tried to back away as if to avoid the guards, but Nol turned faster than I could see to block whichever direction Gavin tried to turn until the guards grabbed him.

"You have allied yourself with the elves, Orlaith. The fae will all hear about this." Gavin continued his rant as they dragged him out of the room, to be heard and ignored until he was finally out of earshot.

"Your Majesty?" I walked closer at a leisurely, unthreatening pace. "Have you been thoroughly updated? Perhaps Nol and I can be on our way and back on the hunt. We understand you are extremely busy."

"Even more so now," she said, exasperated.

"Yes, because of us. I apologize for the trouble our presence has caused, yet, hopefully, it will turn out peacefully and joyfully in the end."

"Hopefully, yes. I was hoping to keep—" Orlaith pursed her lips and shook her head. "Never mind. Please, do carry on. I am pleased you found such a promising yet disturbing lead. Drake, once he's done with his other duties, will join you. You said by tomorrow morning, Drake?"

Drake bowed, arms behind his back. "Yes, Your Majesty."

"Good. See them out. Quinn, stay. We must talk."

Quinn met my eyes from across the room, and I knew he'd rather be walking us out instead. I still didn't know what to say to him. Our passing in the hall was brief and remained polite, especially in front of Gavin. I nodded, recognizing his look before Nol and I left the room.

17

My hand touched the cold railing as the deep horn of the Bainbridge ferry blew, announcing our arrival in Winslow. The seagulls screeched overhead, some arguing over who got to settle on the pilings that guided the ferry to the dock. A little girl on her father's shoulder threw a French fry for them to fight over. She laughed while her father stared at his smartphone.

Zack was waiting with documents that he had copied late last night. He'd called me at one o'clock in the morning with the good news. I wrapped my favorite swallowtail coat tighter around me and fastened the two buttons. A gust of wind loosened my black and pearl flapper hat, and I hurried inside before I lost the old thing.

With the two fairies who had followed me to Tiger's yesterday, I wanted to make sure no one could find me today—other than Nol, who knew where I was going. I hadn't noticed anyone as I'd taken the bus from my house to the UW, walked through Pike Place Market, down the stairs and to the terminal. No one odd had looked my way as I'd sat in the back corner of the Starbucks, waiting for the boat to dock, either.

I planned to stay for a few hours and do some shopping. Ray's and Sam's birthdays were coming up, and I had no clue what to get them. Once I found a nice quiet spot at a coffee shop or the library, I'd continue translating the few lab books I'd brought.

Westport still hadn't come up in the notes, but Seattle and California had—places Drake had said he'd discovered and raided. Zack could have more information on the Westport place he'd mentioned yesterday. One could hope and pray. Neither hurt.

I almost fell into my seat in the back of the bus as the bus driver gunned it out of the terminal. The island went by in a whirl of Douglas firs and cedars, grocery stores, and a vineyard that reminded me of my little fae problem. The bus went over Agate Pass and stopped in front of the Clearwater Casino Resort in Suquamish. Behind the bus, a van full of seniors from a retirement home was also unloading. No one noticed a small lady in a flapper hat and red coat blend in with the group of people walking in, although I got carded.

I texted Zack that I'd made it. He wasn't hard to find over in the casino's Beach Glass Café, the only person out on the patio. He wore a Hawaiian shirt with green and blue flowers and—were those sailboats? Whatever. He also wore a cream fedora hat, cream linen slacks, and loafers. He'd fit in with the retirement community crowd. I knew he was over thirty-five, but he might have been closer to retirement age than I'd realized. Like I ever gave it any thought.

His arms rested over the railing as he looked into the parking lot and highway. I came up and leaned against the railing next to him. A tag hung out of his paper cup, and I immediately wanted to know what kind of tea an asshole DEA agent drank.

I dropped my courier bag with the lab books and journals onto the floor beside my feet. We wouldn't want to linger here, or at least I didn't, so I got right to it.

"Thanks for getting this so quickly. As promised, I have an update."

Zack's back straightened, but he kept looking out at the cars. I told him what we'd found on Capitol Hill. All of it.

"This morning, they're picking up where Nol and I left off. Hopefully, they'll find something that will bring us closer to the kids."

Zack pushed off the railing and walked to the nearest table, knocking on the glass top. "Fuck."

"Yeah. But there's good news."

He looked at me for the first time.

"The kids were alive when they transported them."

"Can you tell how many kids were there?" I almost couldn't hear him over the rush of the cars from the six feet between us.

I shook my head. "It's not that specific."

Zack lifted a duffle bag from the chair closest to him. "This is mostly everything we have on the case. Derrick isn't the only one we know Ian and Katie took. She isn't—wasn't as knowledgeable about the times Ian went on jobs without her, but she went with him the majority of the time. She told me she got many of them home again."

I knew nothing about that, so I didn't comment. Maybe I'd ask Orlaith, bring it up in conversation somehow.

Zack handed me the bag, and I almost dropped the damn thing.

"A warning would have been nice, asshole."

He smiled his asshole smile, shoved his hands into his pockets, and shrugged. "Thanks for the update. I want those kids found, Hally. I'm willing to help however I can."

"Even put up with me."

"Even that."

We didn't shake hands, but Zack tipped his fedora to me.

"Your outfit makes you look old."

He waved behind him toward me as he kept walking away, past the waitstaff and into the casino. How the hell was I going to lug this damn thing through Winslow to go shopping? Answer: I wasn't. I had to go home.

MY COURIER BAG THUMPED against my hip as the duffle bumped against my butt. The nylon handle dug into my collarbone and neck, and I couldn't shift it to the other side, because I'd broken that collarbone two years ago, and it still ached if I applied too much weight on it.

The next ferry came at one o'clock. That was the thing about transit—it took forever to get from point A to point B. I opted for coffee and lunch while I waited. Maybe I'd find an awesome art piece at the cute local coffee shop for Sam's birthday.

I set my quiche down at the stand-up table and took my first sip of too-hot coffee. A familiar dark-haired man walked past the window, the collar of the peacoat flipped up in the rain. Fuck.

Quinn walked right up, grabbed my plate, and walked right back out. Either I followed him or he got my lunch. I hitched the courier bag over my shoulder and grabbed the handles of the duffle. I had no idea how to play this. Admit everything? A half lie? A full lie? Shit. I'd been so careful!

Quinn walked ahead, off the curb, and across the street to his Porsche. Were we going to discuss this in the car? Um, no. I cut across the street, but I kept a wide berth, walked under the covered storefronts, and stopped next to his car. The wonderful thing about a downpour—people usually avoided them. Thus, we had the sidewalk to ourselves. Quinn stood in the rain, his hair sopping wet, but the water beaded and rolled down his coat. His Chucks were navy blue today to match his dark blue jeans. I found my courage and lifted my eyes to meet his. Charcoal gray and angry. So angry.

"You told a human."

"I know." No sense in denying it.

"And Agent Zack Thomas no less? He's a fucking asshole."

"I know."

"Christ!" He pushed his wet hair out of his eyes. "At least when Katie asked for Zack's help, she didn't tell him about us."

"You knew?"

"Which part? That you and Katie were friends in LA? That Ian was a dead-beat dad? That Drake helped you get established in the local tattoo community? Yeah."

"How long?"

He raised his shoulders and looked skyward into the rain. "For forever. But I didn't know who you were. I just knew you as the kid Ian had scammed into working for him."

"Does Drake know you know?"

Quinn leaned back and straightened his shoulders. That's a big fat no.

"When did you learn that Hally, Katie's friend, was the same as Hally the elf?"

Quinn's eyes narrowed. "After the queen told me there was an elf in Seattle named Hally Dubois."

"So you're saying Katie didn't tell you, her fiancé who knew everything else, about me?"

"Katie didn't know." Quinn held his breath and tilted his head in doubt. "Did she?"

I shook my head. "Did you know Katie came to see me after she'd talked to Agent Thomas?"

Quinn watched me, eyes darting from my eyes to my face to my shoulders. Looking for signs of deception, perhaps? "No."

"When did you last see Katie and Seamus, Quinn?"

Quinn frowned, knowing where I was taking this line of questioning. "We had dinner Monday night. There was an emergency at the manor late in the night. Drake told me about Katie when he found out late the next morning."

So he couldn't have been involved. "Agent Thomas learned what I was when Aswryn came in and destroyed my shop. He, Ian, and Gileal were all there."

"Gileal, the friend you lost?"

I nodded, chewing on my lip ring. "After Agent Thomas found out, he left me alone. I hate the asshole, but he won't tell anyone."

He took a deep breath and stepped under the storefront canopy with me.

"You can't guarantee that."

"Nothing is guaranteed. Even though we don't get along, he supported me." I raised my arms and let them drop. "He came and got Nol and me at the plant that night. He took me to the hospital, even though I didn't want to go."

"Why did you meet with him today?"

Should I trust him? I had no way of knowing he was telling the truth. Anyone could be Aswryn's ally. Orlaith had flat out said that fae were involved in the kidnappings.

"I asked him for the evidence from the joint kidnapping investigation. I want to see if all the kids are fae."

"Do you know how to tell a fae kid from a human kid?"

"No. Is there a way to know?" I asked, trying to keep my voice from sounding hopeful.

"Sometimes. They're just learning how to hide themselves. Is he going to get you any evidence?"

I stayed silent for a while, remembering what Drake had told me about Quinn.

"Are you going to tell the queen about Agent Thomas?"

"Yes. She already knows about Zack's poking around. He asked if Seamus was safe after Katie—after he found Katie."

"I know about that. You guys told him Seamus was with his grandfather."

Quinn turned to look out into the street. The rain had stopped without us noticing. That happened in Washington. It's a thing.

He filled his lungs and let the breath out slowly. "I don't have to tell her right away. You'll get in trouble."

"Why would you do that?"

"I sure would like to look over that evidence you have stashed away in that duffle bag."

Yeah, the damn bag was pretty obvious. "Drake told me not to involve you. He said you're too close."

Quinn's eyes hardened. "He's mentioned something like that to me once. I don't agree."

"And you outrank him."

"Yes, I do. I'm glad you understand the situation."

Damn.

My phone buzzed in my coat, and because my cast was too large to fit in any pocket, I had to set the duffle down. I expected Quinn to grab it and run off, but he only looked down at it.

"Tatie," Charlie went off before I could say a word. "Drake and Nolan took off to the Capitol Hill place."

The problem was, Quinn knew French, and he had a keen ear. His eyebrows shot up to his hairline. Fucking-A, couldn't I catch a break?

"Tatie? Did you hear me? Nolan forgot his phone."

"He forgot his phone?" I asked.

"It was on the charger when Drake got here."

That was odd. The thing was damn near glued to his hip. While I sometimes cursed the day I'd given him one, it had its benefits. Like knowing his location. But at least Nol and I had the communication *meril* we'd made two weeks ago. I was about to remind her of that when I caught movement beside me. I'd forgotten where I was for a moment. Quinn grabbed the duffle and tossed it into his tiny trunk. Shit.

"Quinn! No."

"Quinn?" Charlie asked. "Oh, fuck. He heard all of that, didn't he?"

I thought he'd jump into the driver's seat and take off before I could stop him, but he surprised me and reached for my hand, thought better of it because of the cast, and hooked my arm. He opened my door and waited until I got in. I was so screwed. There was no place I could go, and I wasn't willing to use my magic against him.

"What's happening? Where are you, Tatie?"

"Bainbridge still." I watched as Quinn walked across to the driver's side. His body was stiff with anger. "You're right, Quinn heard you. I'm in his car with Zack's evidence. If I try to make a run for it, I'll have to leave everything he gave me."

He slid in and pressed the ignition button. The Porsche purred as he revved it.

"He won't harm you, will he?"

"I don't know."

Quinn's head swiveled. He looked at me, then at my phone, then at me again. "I won't hurt you." His face fell, and he tried to relax. It didn't work. "I'm pissed, but I should have expected this. Hang up. Please." Oh, that "please" made it all better.

"No, Tatie. Don't hang up!"

Quinn snatched the phone, hung up, and threw it in the back. The phone buzzed, but I couldn't reach it.

"Start talking. Who knows?"

I pressed my lips together tightly and looked out the window. No way, no how, would I tell him anything more.

Quinn downshifted and pressed the pedal to the floor. Did he think that would scare me? He passed three cars at once, just before we would've hit the oncoming car. I was sure he'd scared the driver shitless. He passed more cars. The light at the Safeway intersection was coming up. He didn't have time to stop. High schoolers were on the curb on the corner with their backpacks, laughing and goofing off.

"Tell me, Hally."

I closed my eyes, envisioning the entire intersection, cars, lights, and pedestrians in my mind's eye. They needed to stop and let us pass. I opened my eyes. The brakes of the waiting cars needed to engage. The one crossing the intersection needed to move. While the pedestrians were on the sidewalk, I envisioned a wall keeping them on the sidewalk.

Tires screeched and horns blew, but everyone stayed back. The slave band siphoned energy as I used such a large amount of magic. Not now! I concentrated on the people, feeling the magic trickling away like a sink full of water with a leak.

Quinn shot through, but he noticed the car in the middle of the road sliding out of his way. Yes, I slid a fucking car out of the way. I released my hold, and my head dropped back against the headrest, limp. I didn't practice magic much, so I wasn't magically in shape, to simplify it.

Quinn slammed on the brakes, drifting onto a side street at a speed I did not want to know. "Did you just force an entire intersection out of the way?"

I was too tired to answer.

"What the fuck?"

I rolled my head to the side. Did he not know about me? Surely, Orlaith had told him. I frowned at him, rolled my head to look out the windshield, and passed out.

18

"There she is." Charlie's blurry form moved within my dim room. "Hello, sunshine."

I blinked until the world came into focus. Charlie said nothing more, waiting for me to wake up. I searched my brain and came up with the lovely events that had led to this. Quinn had taken me home?

"What am I doing in my room?"

"Quinn carried you in. You scared the shit out of him with your demonstration of magic and fainting."

"I didn't faint. I passed out from drastic magic depletion. There's a difference."

"Sure, there is." She patted my shoulder. "Anyway, Quinn has some mixed feelings. I think he wanted to take you in, but he promised you he'd wait or something?"

Bracing myself, I sat up. Oddly, I didn't have a headache. I swallowed. Charlie stuck a straw into my mouth. A few swallows of water helped. "He did. So honorable."

"Very." She set the cup on my side table and plopped down on the bed in front of me. "I think he wants to talk to both of us after you've recovered. How long do you think that'll take you? A day, two?"

I scoffed. "A week, at least. But no. Before Quinn interrupted, I wanted to remind you about the *merili* Nol and I made."

"He left his phone, though. That's not like him." Charlie shoved her hair back and tucked it behind her ears. "Have you tried contacting him?"

"Since our phone call? I've been unconscious, Charlie." She was way too worried about Nol losing his phone. "He can reach me if he needs to."

"Not if he's unconscious." Charlie's brown eyes bulged. "He doesn't trust this guy, Tatie. I trust his instincts. Don't you?"

"Normally, but Drake will prove to him that he's trustworthy. You'll see. They'll come back this afternoon and it'll be better."

"Hmm." She didn't look reassured. "The phone thing is still bothering me. Like I said, it's just not like him."

"Then think of something else. Tell me what's going on with Quinn."

"Did you know Quinn is fluent in Spanish?" She had an eerie gleam in her big brown eyes.

"Um, no, but it makes sense. He speaks French, too. He's quite a bit older than me." Where was she going with this? "You're in a good mood."

"Yes. Ask me why."

"Why?"

Charlie laid a hand on my knee. "We have acquired an assistant."

"Quinn?"

"Yes." She drew out the "s" while her eyes got sparkly. "He just doesn't know it yet. Hungry?"

Actually, I was, but I stared at her. "Are you serious?"

"As a heart attack. Let's get some sandwiches and tell him the good news."

"But—"

"We need the help, and this will keep him from going to Orlaith."

"True, but..." But what? It worked. My niece was so smart. "Okay, let's get him helping, then."

Quinn was at my bedroom door when we opened it, looking a bit frazzled. His hair was a mess, and his shirtsleeves were rolled up to his elbows. He swallowed and licked his lips. "How are you?"

"Hungry and not happy with you. You don't endanger innocent lives when you aren't getting your way."

He didn't defend himself, just stood there blocking us in. Ugh, men! Did they ever grow up?

"Excuse us. We're headed downstairs for a late lunch since you rudely stole my quiche. Ray, do you want some cookies?"

A second passed, and Ray ran out of her room. "Yeah!"

"Cookies?" Quinn asked.

I didn't acknowledge him. Instead, I reached for Ray's hand, and we descended the stairs together.

"But you're okay, right?" he asked from behind the three of us in the hall.

I winked at Ray and let go of her hand as she ran to her stool to watch us in the kitchen.

Quinn squirmed as he stood next to the peninsula counter, watching the three of us pull out lunch supplies. "How did you stop that traffic?"

"*Columbe*, do you want a PB&J?"

"Yes," she hissed.

"What?" I raised an eyebrow and waited for her to give me the magic word.

Quinn looked from one of us to the other as we ignored him. Ray rolled her eyes. "Please."

I took the win. Charlie pulled out the cheese and sourdough—that yummy round kind with the huge slices. The best. Charlie made Quinn's grilled cheese first, with two slices of sourdough. He eyed it as I slid it in front of him but didn't move from his spot.

I took my first bite, standing in my kitchen as I stared at Quinn.

"Well?" Charlie flicked her hand at Quinn's untouched food as she leaned against the counter beside me. "Eat your food. It's getting cold."

"How did you manage to move an entire busy intersection?" Quinn asked again. "Are all elves that powerful?"

I cringed. "It's a long, boring explanation. Let's just leave at: I'm a powerful *endaë* and *savilë*. Don't cross me." I took another bite. "Eat."

He grabbed his sandwich. I doubted he even tasted his first bite.

"Your reckless actions endangered everyone at that intersection, and I couldn't sit by and hope that the cars stopped and the kids stayed on the sidewalk." He didn't even look the slightest bit guilty. "One day, I might rely on my magic too much, get too cocky, and make another horrible mistake. Mistakes with my magic aren't good."

"I can imagine." Quinn nodded then took his second bite, chewing slower now.

"No, you can't." I swallowed my bite before I continued. "Something could have gone terribly wrong today. I knew the risk and did it anyway. Why didn't you take me straight to Orlaith and have me detained in an anti-magic cell?"

"We have nothing like that."

"Sure you don't."

"I wanted to get the full story. And I told you I wouldn't tell her right away."

Ray skipped around us to put her plate in the sink.

"Will you tell me how these two learned the truth?" Quinn pointed at Ray as she ran around the corner and out of sight.

"Frankly, I can't trust any of you. Until I know they'll be safe, you won't get squat. I'm supposed to be a diplomat. Exiled or not, I can't mess this up. Every encounter is political. You know this."

"Even our date?"

"Yes. Though I admit I let my guard down somewhat."

Quinn picked the crumbs off his plate after his last bite. "Charlie explained she can sense that we're not human."

I turned to Charlie. "You can tell the difference in them, too?"

She looked up from picking at her food. "When they aren't under their glamor. I haven't encountered one under its influence, at least to my knowledge."

"I think I know why."

We both looked over at Quinn, waiting for him to continue.

"Okay," I prompted.

He leaned back to look around the corner where Ray was playing in the living room. "I think they're part fae."

"You can reproduce with humans?" Charlie's voice rose a few octaves in her excitement. "How? I mean, because you're a different species, or are you a related species? We look similar. But humans don't have ME cells or an ME organ. Is fae anatomy more like humans or elves? You must have an ME organ, right? How else could you produce magic?"

Quinn's eyes glazed over as she fired off her questions, asking more about related magical energy cells and other biology, science-y stuff.

"Charlie, love, I don't think he's following."

"No, not really, but humans and fae are close enough to reproduce. Not all fae can, though. Brownies and goblins, no. Merrow, obvious, right? Sasquatch...I've never heard of anyone considering that pairing."

"There're other kinds of fae?" Charlie gasped. "Sasquatch is real?"

"Charlie, focus." I finished the last of my sandwich and put my plate and Quinn's in the dishwasher.

She backed up a step, grumbling, but remained energized. She reminded me so much of Emma.

"I was about to say." Quinn smirked at Charlie's pouty grumble. "Humans and fae have a far-back related ancestral clan. If that's the case with your family, Charlie, I don't think there will be any issues with you knowing."

"Um." This wasn't how I thought the conversation would go.

"Have you met any of Charlie's other family members?"

Charlie and I looked at each other and back at Quinn. The whole not trusting him thing still stood, especially after the stunt in the Porsche.

Charlie ate the last of her sandwich. "What happens when a human learns the truth? Are they killed? Are their memories wiped?"

"No one is killed, but their memories might be altered, depending on various things."

"What about Agent Thomas?"

"I can't speak for Her Majesty. He's cooperated, given you all this information, and kept your secret. It's only been three weeks, though. If Her Majesty does not approve, his memories of our interactions will be altered so he believes he was talking to humans. The sooner the queen knows, the better off we'll be."

"Okay," Charlie said nonchalantly, nodding like this was no big deal. It was a big deal.

"Just like that?"

"Well," she hedged, then smiled at me. "We have a few things to do first."

"Now hold on—" Quinn held his hand out toward Charlie.

"You wanted to see Agent Thomas's evidence, didn't you?" I asked.

He stopped, lips pursed. We had him.

My phone rang from somewhere in the family room. Crap. On the fish tank stand. My ribs were sore as I pushed up. Quinn watched from his spot on the small couch. Three journals were spread out on the cushions around him while he had one in his lap.

"Hey, Charlie." I slid the phone against my ear as I greeted her.

"I'm on my way back. They're trying to convince Mateo's sister to bring over his niece so Ray will have someone to play with. Gotten any further?"

"It's been—" I looked at my phone "—an hour."

"Sure, sure. Be back soon."

Quinn dropped the journal on the couch and stretched. "We've been here all afternoon. Wanna take a break?"

Yeah, and we hadn't heard a thing from Nol and Drake. How much longer did we wait? I didn't want to distract them. A mental connection could be just as problematic as a phone if they were in an intense situation. What kind of intense situation could they have gotten into at an empty house? None. Which meant they'd gone somewhere else. I looked away from the bay window and focused on Quinn standing in front of me.

"Are you okay?" He rested his hand on my shoulder, and leaned over.

I let go of my bracelet and set my hands on my hips, but with the cast, it never worked. Instead, I clasped my right arm with my left hand behind my back. I needed to stop fidgeting. "Just tired. Eye strain." Worried. What if Nol was right?

Quinn, who'd watched me fidget, smiled softly. "Break time, then. Just until Charlie gets back?"

I looked around the family room, Aswryn's notebooks and documents from Zack's investigation were strewn on the floor and couch. We still had so much to go through. I rubbed my eyes and slapped myself with the cast.

"Okay," I said behind my hand as I rubbed my nose.

Quinn scoffed and walked toward the stairs. "Let's get away from it so we're not tempted."

I'd have said something snarky if it hadn't been true. We had found nothing much about locations, but we had found stuff that Charlie could use.

"Her notes make me sick," Quinn said.

Aswryn's notes were detailed, and some of them discussed test subjects and samples. We knew what those were—who they were. "I told you if it bothers you, stop. You're too close to this."

"It's not Seamus. That Aswryn died before Seamus could become a victim is what keeps me working."

"I don't understand any of what's in there. Hopefully, it'll help with both finding the kids and a cure. Finding a cure might be the only way to save *Aemina*."

"I don't get why *Aemina* hasn't been looking for a cure."

"They were—until Aswryn took out most of their healers. Then they focused more on finding Aswryn and breaking the curse."

Quinn stopped walking, his face hidden in the darkness of the main hallway downstairs. "We knew of the atrocities here, the kidnapping and torture, but we didn't know about the curse. Or about what she was doing over there. Why would she do that? It makes no sense."

"Gil found evidence that she was the daughter of a *Mellorian* diplomat. Her mother had an affair with an *Aeminan* council member, and they were targeted when she was still a child. It would have been an embarrassment to the *Amura Ore* if the assembly member had acknowledged them, and it could have angered *Mellori*, with whom we are on precarious terms as it is. More so now."

"Revenge? A curse to kill an entire population because her mother was killed." While Quinn didn't shoot the idea down, he didn't seem to have much faith in it either.

"She was quite unstable when I met her." I got him walking again, out into the light of the living room. "Have you ever heard of *Asaidaë'a Metaela*?" I asked as I veered toward the kitchen for a drink.

"I haven't."

"It means '*Metaela's* revenge,' our first royal family. Aswryn referred to it like it was a group of some sort, and Orlaith said she was working for people with an agenda."

"An agenda. Hally?"

"Hmm?" I opened the fridge and got a soda.

"Are you sure she said *Asaidaë'a Metaela*?" He didn't even butcher the name.

"I suppose it could have been something else." I popped the top and went back to the living room. "The circumstances were a tad hostile, but even if it was something that sounded like that—"

"Does *asaidaë* sound similar to *aiséiri*?"

"I've never heard the word. What is it?"

"It's Gaelic."

"Anything's possible. What would *Metaela* be, then?"

"*Meabhlaire*, the Deceiver, an ancient god we do not speak of. He is only known as Deceiver—his name was stricken from any Gaelic record and never mentioned in fables. Hally, *Aiséirí an Meabhlaire* means 'the resurrection of the Deceiver.'"

The diet soda went sour on my tongue. "Do you think Aswryn was worshiping a Celtic god? She referred to our Mother when talking to me. Reverently."

"What is the name of your goddess?"

"Anara, Mother of All Creation."

"That could be changed from Anu easily. She's also referred to as Danu, the Mother of the Gods."

"There's nothing in our history that refers to any other gods."

"That's because someone buried your past. You never heard about us. Why would you have heard about our gods?"

I groped for the back of the chair closest to me. Our Mother was real. The proof of her existence was all around us. She'd created us. "That's not—She is real. I have accepted the existence of other gods, and I never denied the religions of the humans, but ours is real."

"Of course. Gods take many forms. I can't believe this has been kept from your people."

"Lost to history. I can't accept that someone knew and kept that secret." Would Gil's father know? His father was a cleric dedicated to Her and Her moon. "I know Her to be the truth. I have lived countless lives—" I didn't finish that sentence. I needed to talk to Nol before we told them about our *Muranilde* bond.

Quinn set his hand on my shoulder. "I'm not saying She isn't real, or that She is less than you know Her to be. We have more gods than just Anu. If our Anu is the same mother as your Anara, I think you need to know the rest of the history. So do your people."

"She created us."

"Which is why She is Anu, the Mother of the Gods. There are some things I think you should see at my apartment. You can also read up on Anu and Meabhlaire's ancient war."

"War?"

"The one where she trapped him in a world between the realms so he could never hurt her children again."

"Fuck me."

From the laundry room, we heard the back door hit the washer—it happened often. "I'm back!" Charlie called. Then we heard two thunks as her boots dropped.

"We're in here, love," I said before she started up the stairs.

Her quick socked feet thumped down the hall. "Taking a break?" Quinn moved over so I could see Charlie.

"Help us pack up. We have to go to Quinn's."

Her eager face dropped as she saw mine. "O—kay."

I could only imagine what she saw, with all my hope in everything I believed in crashing down around me.

19

"Now, will one of you please tell me why Hally is as white as a ghost?" Charlie dropped the box of lab books onto Quinn's coffee table. Quinn set the duffle on the floor, then turned on some lamps and pressed the remote to lower the blinds. Even though he was right in the middle of Bellevue, we couldn't hear a thing. His house smelled like a guy's place—that woodsy fireplace smoke of candles and wall plug-ins, plus the cologne he wore. Dark furniture, soft cushy carpet, and silence.

"I think I broke your tatie."

Arms around my stomach, my world falling around me, I walked around Quinn's expensive furniture and looked out at the planes flying in and out of Seatac. The lights on the tails and wings blinked red, green, white, and blue. Quinn's condo boasted a large, landscaped balcony with soft lighting and a view of Seattle and Elliot Bay. We were on a higher floor, but I couldn't remember how high.

Not all religions' myths were accurate. Anu could be Anara. She was our Mother, the creator of all of us, but my ancestors didn't consider the other Celtic gods as meaningful? Gil's family held the moon in high regard and worshiped it and its cycles along with the Mother. But why didn't our histories mention anything about these other gods if Anu and Anara were the same goddess?

Charlie came to stand next to me and rubbed my back. Her thin, warm fingers kneading my shoulders calmed my racing heart. "No one can break you. What'd he do?" She set her chin on my shoulder.

"My people's entire religious ideology might be a lie."

"Oh." Charlie paused. "Um, well, you—" She gave up and turned away. "What the fuck, Quinn?"

A stir of magic turned my attention back into his apartment. He entered, his sly expression replaced by a more sheepish demeanor. "I don't think it's a lie, Hally. The elves are part of Faerie—tell anyone outside this room that, and I'll deny it. My people still haven't forgiven the elves, but it's true. *Endaen* is a race of fae. It is very plausible Anu and Anara are indeed the same. Why your people chose not to include the other gods, I bet, has something to do with your lack of knowledge of the war and Earth." He held out a dark cloth-bound book to me. "Here. It's a personal copy." He rolled his eyes. "Only royalty keep these."

"Huh, I think being royalty has more perks than fancy old books," Charlie muttered, lifting a slat of the blinds and giving the outside world another look.

The book, very thick but about as long as my hand, opened to a page somewhere near the middle. The scent of old paper and ink flowed over it. While the book looked around fifty years old—it didn't have a copyright page—it was in good condition.

Quinn, from over my shoulder, flipped toward the back. "Here. The First War."

"We're researching the First World War?" Charlie dropped the slat and walked back to us. "Does this have to do with Emmaline or the Dubois family?"

"Um, a bit farther than that." Quinn left again and returned with a file folder box. "This is what Katie and I found after she came home. Hally?" Quinn waited until I looked at him so he knew he had my attention. "If Aswryn really meant the resurrection of Meabhlaire, we may have a much, much deeper agenda than Orlaith thinks we do. Charlie, if you would, please start looking at Zack's files?"

"Is there something in particular that will stand out to me?" While Charlie cared about the missing children, her focus was on the virus. Quinn's focus stayed on the children, and I was trying to appease both sides. "Here's his interview notes—god, his writing is atrocious."

I sat on the edge of the couch, soaking in the words in Quinn's book. "This is the war between Anu and Meabhlaire. Did they create the gods or everything?"

"Anu and Meabhlaire created things."

"Their children were things of the Earth—water, fire, rocks, etc.—but Anu wanted living children to cherish and nurture. Anu explained that Meabhlaire couldn't produce children, and she found another consort, one that gave her...us."

"Excuse me?" Charlie looked up from the binder she had her nose in. "You think your people are gods?"

"Descendants from—just like the Christian god. He made man in His image. Same idea. The main idea is that Meabhlaire was mortified, betrayed, and jealous of Anu and her new consort, Bilé. When Anu discovered Maebhlaire was killing her children and stealing their powers, she demanded he stop. Meabhlaire refused and they went to war. Anu and Bilé ended up trapping Meabhlaire in a place between the realms."

"Was that when the elves split and went to *Endae*?" Charlie asked.

"No, that was eons later. The Fae-*Endaen* war only happened six thousand years ago. That had nothing to do with the gods."

"Six thousand. I can't fathom living that long." Charlie shook her head slowly with her eyes closed.

"Yes, well, to Hally, that's only five generations ago. It baffles my mind that your history has no records of this."

"If our Mother is Anu, why wouldn't we teach our people about everything else?" I flipped back to the beginning, looking for the first story. "Do you believe these to be true or just lessons?"

"Both, I think. There's some history to it, but it's been embellished to give them morals."

"And Anu and Meabhlaire's story?"

"I think it was bloodier and darker than what is written. Here." He found one of the first stories. "This is a drawn-out story of what I just told you." Quinn made sure I held the page down before he went back to the papers he'd collected. Right, we weren't here for a religious history lesson, but everything I believed about our Mother could be based on a lie or omission. I needed to look into that further. "Can I read this later?"

Quinn stopped pulling stuff out of the box and looked at the book. "How about I let you come read it here? As I said, royalty is given these books. Meabhlaire isn't known as a Gaelic god. If he's ever released—" Quinn squeezed his eyes shut for a moment. "I hope this has nothing to do with Meabhlaire. There are always fringe worshipers, like any other religion, but they're small. Ah, here's the information I have on the people Katie said were in the Westport house. There were at least ten people, but she only recognized four adults." He handed me the list, written in Katie's handwriting.

"Hey, Charlie. See if you can find anything on Caleb McPatrick and Sean O'Malley." Quinn handed me a photo of Ian with two other human-looking men around a table. Several stacks of what could have been packages of drugs were on it. "Katie took that picture. And this one." He handed me a photo of a familiar-looking kid. Although Ian and Katie had taken him twelve years ago, he looked about five years older.

"Is this the boy Katie told Zack about? Um, Darin?" I asked.

"Derrick, and yes. This was at the place in Westport. If Zack went to check it out, glamor could have been hiding it. I think it might be something Nolan and Drake could look into."

"No doubt." Once they showed back up, anyway. I riffled through more of Katie's notes.

"Here." Charlie handed over what looked like copies of bills. "Those addresses aren't in Westport. And look, there's a few from Mexico City and, oh! Tatie, London. Didn't you say Drake found one of Aswryn's labs in London?"

"Yeah."

"How did these get in here?" Quinn muttered and picked up a stack of photos from his box.

Pictures of Seamus's third birthday party at some public kids' party place. "Seamus probably put them in here. I bet there's a few with marker on them."

"No kidding. I'm so glad Ray is mostly out of that stage." Charlie reached for them. "Do you mind? Parent to parent?"

Quinn's face fell and his shoulders hunched at the reminder of Seamus's absence. His eyes changed from silver gray to black in seconds. I touched his hand, but it took him a minute to bring himself out of his thoughts.

"We'll find him, Quinn." I shouldn't have promised that, but what else could I have said, seeing that haunted look?

"Hey!" Charlie shook a photo. "This is one of our security guards. I know it's him because he was on duty the night Ernie got mugged and we had equipment stolen. Remember, Tatie?"

Charlie handed me the picture. "That's Drake. Charlie, this can't be—"

"Why would Drake work as a security guard somewhere?" Quinn asked. "Where do you work?"

"At the University of Washington. It's at the clinical research hub in South Lake Union. Nolan confirmed it was Aswryn who broke into my lab. The security guard, this guy, said there was nothing odd about that night's shift."

"You are absolutely positive?"

"He has the same neck tattoo." Charlie pointed at the tattoo visible in the picture.

"We need to talk to Drake. There has to be a reasonable explanation for his presence there." Quinn had his phone out a second after I'd given Charlie back the photo. His phone rang against his ear twice, three times, and then it went to voicemail. "Where are they?"

"Tracking magical signatures originating from the Capitol Hill house. He forgot his phone, but I can commu—"

Quinn's phone rang. He cleared his throat, then answered, "Drake?"

I waved at Quinn to get off the phone, then touched my communication *meril*. Quinn's eyes darted to my *meril* to the photo on the table, and then when he met my eyes, his mouth dropped open as realization hit, moments after mine had.

"*Nol,*" I willed my mental voice to extend through our *meril*. After we'd made them, we'd tried them out four or five times, but nothing long distance. Talk about trial under fire. "*You were right. Don't trust Drake. We think he's involved.*"

Quinn sat back in his seat, phone to his ear, but the smile on his face didn't reach his eyes as he spoke into the phone. "Nah, don't worry about it. It was a butt dial. I didn't even know it was ringing until it hit your voicemail. I gotta go."

"*How?*" Nol's thoughts in my head startled me as I'd lost focus watching and listening to Quinn. "*He's been nothing but helpful to me. I thought I was wrong.*"

Something past his thoughts made me think he was traveling in a car. Were they on their way back? "*You weren't wrong, Nol.*" I showed him my thoughts on what Charlie had discovered. "*Where are you?*"

Quinn shoved his phone back into his pocket and watched me with interest. Charlie whispered something to him, but I had to focus on Nol's conversation. Instead of trying to ignore the two in the room with me, I walked over to the window where nothing but airplanes and stars would distract me.

"*In Los Angeles. I've seen the lab, but there's nothing there anymore. Like the steam plant, this lab was in a vacant space, and now it has been renovated and sold.*"

They'd left for LA already? I wrapped my other arm around my middle as I kept my fingers on the *meril*. "*I don't like this. Why didn't you tell me before you left Washington?*"

I felt Nol shrug off my concern like he sometimes did when he thought I was overreacting. "*Drake took us through Faerie, and it has been fast-paced since we arrived.*"

"*Where are you going now?*" I closed my eyes and tried to see through his mind's eye, not to be nosy, but the feeling was like trying to remember an interesting dream. Impossible to let go.

"*We're taking a taxi to meet a friend and hopefully borrow their car. LA is huge.*" The even larger city piqued the curious side of my *muranildo*. He wasn't taking me seriously.

My eyes shot open, focusing on the night sky as I thought about his curiosity and all the possibilities a big city like LA could provide him. "*Nol—*"

"*I am taking you seriously, Hallë.*" Oh, Nol had read my mind. How helpful. "*See if Quinn knows where Drake lives, check his house for anything unusual.*" His mind started forming a list of tasks he would ordinarily carry out if he were going into a possible assailant's home, but he stopped when he realized I was "listening." "*Don't be reckless. Just feel for imolegin. Don't follow what I would do, Hallë. You're not Zayuri.*"

There was no way I was going to drive to Drake's house and walk around the yard feeling for *imolegin*. He knew me better than that. "*I'll be careful, but don't stay with him. You could be in danger.*"

"*I'll be fine,*" he said, dismissing my concern.

I squeezed the *meril* in my fist, but it wasn't an adequate substitution for strangling him. "*Please, keep alert at least?*" Perhaps my sincerity would win him over.

"*What did you say again? I'm a badass Zayuri.*"

"*Your head is expanding again. And Zack said that, not me.*"

"*Right.*"

"*You're a pain-in-my-ass.*"

"*Not as much as you are in mine.*" Their taxi stopped. The shift on his thoughts changed, ending his teasing. "*We're here. I will be careful, Hallë. If you go inside, look for evidence. Tell me what you find. I will arrest Drake if I need to, but right now, whichever side he's on, he is leading me closer to the children.*"

I ground my teeth as I stared out the window, unable to stress how certain I was. "*It's a trap, Nol, and you're falling right into it.*"

"*It could be, and I will be ready for it, thanks to you. Remember, we haven't tested our merili out when I'm working in the shadows—*"

"*What do you mean?*" Traveling through, I'd heard, but not working through.

Nol touched the door handle of the taxi cab, and I felt the fake leather brush his fingertips through his mind. "*If you don't hear from me at some point, it may be because I'm under shadows, or we could be coming home through Faerie.*"

"Wait—" I said out loud.

"*I have to go.*"

"*If I don't hear from you, I'm getting your uncle,*" I told him before he could cut off our conversation. Somehow, I felt his exasperation, perhaps a sigh or an eye roll, but at least I knew he'd heard me.

Sighing, I turned around to face Quinn and Charlie, who were both staring my way. Charlie rested her chin on the back of the couch, her brown doe eyes wide and curious. Quinn hadn't moved from his chair, but he held nothing as he waited for me to be finished. Thank the Mother I hadn't been watching them. What an awkward mental conversation that would have been with an audience. "They're in LA. He wants us to check Drake's house. He said if we sense any *imolegin* we're not sure about, he wants to know. Quinn, please tell me you know where he lives. Because I have no clue."

Quinn's mouth snapped shut, and a determined look filled his eyes. "Yeah, but there wouldn't be anything there. It's a condo on Mercer. If there's anything he wants to keep secret, I know that place, too."

20

Quinn turned the engine off. The rain pelted down so hard we couldn't see anything besides the yellow glow of a streetlight down the road. I still couldn't believe where we were. When he'd said he knew of another place besides Drake's house, I'd thought of some grungy, rundown place in the woods. Nope.

"Do you think if we wait fifteen minutes, the weather will change?" Charlie joked. Sort of. That was Washington's motto, but not always. Not in the winter or early spring—what was today? The equinox was any day now. I did the math. Holy shit, today was the first day of spring! Or was it tomorrow?

"Let's go." Quinn got out, invisible through the sheet of water.

"Fuck," I muttered before shoving the door open and shutting it just as fast.

Quinn ran ahead. I went to Charlie's side, grabbed her hand, and envisioned a bubble. I might not be able to make a ward to block out magic, but rain was a no-brainer. Nol said they were related, but I wasn't getting it.

We ran to the house—or more like a mansion, like a mini-Orlaith mansion.

"Quinn! Wait," I called out as it looked like he was about to kick the door in. Charlie and I made it to the large porch a second later. "Let me have a go at the lock before you break the door."

Quinn's lips pressed together, but he stepped back, exaggerating a welcoming gesture. Was he mad at me? Not the time to worry about that. He hadn't said much since I'd contacted Nol. I had no idea what was going on in his head. Hopefully, not nefarious thoughts, like how to get rid of our bodies. He couldn't be working with Drake. What if Katie, Quinn, and Drake had all been working with Aswryn? No, Katie's fear had been real when she saw Aswryn in my shop three weeks ago. Quinn could be working with Drake—no. I was doubting myself. First, my blind faith in a human stranger who'd turned out to be Aswryn in disguise. Then I'd put my trust in Drake. No wonder Nol didn't take me seriously.

I looked at Quinn until his face softened, and he nodded. What if he was thinking the same thing about me? He had no reason to trust me, no standing on my integrity. What he did know was that I'd been banished from *Endae*. I could only show him I was a good person, despite my history, through my actions.

The lock was easy. The alarm, on the other hand...

"There's an alarm. If I disarm it, could Drake get a phone call or text? I don't want to put Nol in more danger."

"The power could have gone out because of the storm," Charlie yelled over the rain.

I wiped my hair back as drips fell into my eyes. "To make that believable, we'd have to shut the power off."

Quinn set his jaw and gave me a curt nod. My magic followed the alarm's electrical current back to the breaker. That wouldn't do. Something told me he'd have a way of knowing. Outside, up the wires, to the transformer right down the road. I wrapped my magic around the electrical energy until mine replaced it and the line was severed. The entire grid went out. Sorry, everybody.

"Nice, Tatie."

I let the door creak open as we wiped our feet. If we were wrong, we didn't want to leave any clues. As soon as we stepped in, I felt several magical signatures. A lot of magic had been performed here. Quinn went around me, took three steps, and looked back.

"Do you feel that?" he asked.

I nodded. "They feel faint."

"I can't sense anything," Charlie said.

"You don't sense *imolegin*, love. Here, stay with Quinn, and I'll take this side." I pointed to the right side of the house.

"Do you know spells to protect yourself?" Quinn asked me.

I glanced at Charlie, recalling the frying pan she'd hit Aswryn in the face with. One side of Charlie's lips curled up. My globes were more of a nuisance, but hey, whatever got them off my back. "Um, sort of—"

Quinn looked between the two of us. "Right, different magic."

Sure, we'd go with that. "I've got this, Quinn."

Charlie pulled out her phone and turned her flashlight on. "Sorry guys, there's no way I can go through this house without it. Be careful, Tatie."

"That's the plan." I watched as the two of them went off to the left, through double doors. I waited until I couldn't see the light from Charlie's phone before I started moving. Subtle, high-end furniture and fixtures spread out, creating a well-designed, clean space—fake, all of it. A lie to fool potential visitors.

I wiped my finger on a shelf on the other side of the room and came away with a thin layer of dust. Yep, never used. The plush wall-to-wall carpet kept my steps silent. Not even a clock ticked. Past the bathroom, I detected a smell, faint at first, but after a few more steps, the smell of rot stung my nose. Shallow breaths. I needed to focus on the here and now. The smell wasn't bad enough that I could taste it as I breathed through my mouth, but it still brought unwanted memories to the surface. Another time, dried, mud-covered bodies—humans and horses littering the ground. Then the nightmare from the weekend surfaced.

No, get it together, Hally. I pressed my thumbnail into each finger pad until it hurt. I would not allow myself to be drawn back there. Not now. I knew what I'd find behind the first door—not specifically, but I prayed they wouldn't be children. Seamus's shy smile surfaced, and tears came to my eyes. Or maybe that was the sting of death in my nose.

The hinges didn't creak as I pushed the door open with one finger. Well oiled, the light thing swung open, but at my angle, I couldn't see inside.

Two shallow breaths. I stepped in front and took in the dark room: six cots, two lining each wall. The light from outside, behind the blinds, illuminated the room enough for me to make out the body-sized lumps. Two more shallow breaths. I did not step in. I needed to check out the other rooms. I prayed this was the only room like this.

Three more doors remained after the one with victims, all three without bodies. Medium and large boxes took up part of one room. The smell of cardboard and paper mingled with the decaying bodies across the way. I held my breath and swallowed a few times to keep myself from throwing up.

They kept hospital scrubs in a dresser in the last room, and soap and towels in the attached bathroom. Perhaps for the victims' use. That made sense. I wouldn't want to clean bedpans.

I didn't want to go into the other room yet. The bodies could wait until I had Quinn with me. Charlie would insist on seeing the room as well. I wished she wouldn't. I kept the same pace as I went back through my side of the house, even though I'd rather have run screaming—or crying—to the foyer and waited.

Five minutes ticked by, according to my phone. The house was large, but no way should it take them that long for a sweep. They'd found something. I peeked into the room they'd gone through, hoping to see Charlie's phone light, but discovered another wing of the mansion. A flash of light flickered under one door. I gave a tap and turned the knob. They'd found a long room, set up with not one, but four computer desks, with large monitors on each. File cabinets lined the back, the old-fashioned metal kinds. Charlie had one open, shining her light into the drawer.

"Looks like they didn't fully trust technology either," I whispered as I came to stand with Quinn and Charlie.

"Any chance you could turn the power back on?" Charlie asked without turning away from the cabinet.

I didn't laugh. "Maybe if we set up a ward and make sure Drake doesn't have something set up."

"Oh, he has a system," Charlie said. "There are external drives in one of these drawers, labeled with dates and organized by names of something. They mean nothing to me—yet. Hally, this will be very helpful."

I pressed my lips together and swallowed again, my mind still smelling the death of the room. "So there's bad news. There's—I found the victims."

Charlie stopped looking and met my eyes. We'd known what we'd find or expected to find, but it didn't make it easier.

"Six. I didn't want to go into the room alone."

"I'll go," Quinn volunteered. "You two don't have to. It's not your—"

"Aswryn did this. It's my responsibility as the only *enda* here."

As I expected, Charlie followed us, but she didn't go in, just stood in the threshold. Not that I went much farther. None of the bodies were covered. Some had IVs attached to them, but all of them had needle punctures and incisions. All of them were adults, thank the Mother.

"There're three elves in here," Quinn called, standing in front of the two cots on the far wall.

"Don't touch them." Charlie's voice cracked. "You need to have medical examiners document everything. I assume you have them?"

"Yeah," Quinn said after a few seconds.

"I want to be there."

Quinn looked at Charlie, his brow furrowed. Angry? Worried? "That's not your choice."

"There is more data here than at the steam plant lab. What if the key to developing the cure is here? What if the cure is here?"

"And how are you going to do that, human?"

"Watch it," I warned Quinn.

"Charlie, you were worried about what the queen would do if she learned about you. Now you're demanding to work with our medical staff. You'll be lucky if she allows you to be associated with our world."

Charlie *humphed* and walked away from the room.

"Finding the fae children and the people who took them is important, but finding a cure and saving my people is also important, Quinn. Sending me back to a realm riddled with disease would be a death sentence."

"Find the children and you get to stay. That's the deal. The queen likes you, Hally, but she doesn't know you, nor is she concerned about the people who betrayed us. I'm sorry, but you wanted honesty."

I held my tongue because he was right. I wanted honesty, even if it was harsh. The betrayal bit made me curious. Why were fae working with Aswryn? Who else was working with her? So many questions.

"What do we do?" I asked.

"We can't call Drake or his officers. Fuck. I don't know who to trust."

"Looks like it's a job for the Queen of the Fae."

Quinn grumbled but got out his phone, knowing I was right. Not that I was any happier about it.

Orlaith's elegantly manicured nails tapped on the marble counter of Drake's model kitchen. She stared at the refrigerator while Charlie, Quinn, and I looked anywhere but in the queen's eyes. One could say she was having a bad night.

Orlaith had brought Brodrick and Rowe, the blond fairy who had knocked Lewis out, in from the cold. Her most trusted agents. Quinn had even vouched for them. I wasn't too impressed with the people they chose to trust. How did they know these guys weren't helping Drake?

One of Orlaith's people had cast a ward so the neighbors couldn't see any goings-on. Light orbs flooded the entire property, inside and out, daylight bright. They'd been here for fifteen minutes and were ready to go as soon as Orlaith gave the word.

"The computers need to be scoured for possible evidence. I want undeniable proof that Drake is part of this. Don't say it, Quinn. Yes, this is his house, and yes, his magical signature mingles with the others. That isn't solid proof. Drake has people he could hide behind in other kingdoms. If he runs, I can't get him back until I have that proof to hand them. This conversation does not leave this room."

"What about Lord Gavin?" Brodrick asked.

"He can wait. Hally, have you heard anything more from Nolan?"

"The last I heard, they were in LA. They had visited one site and were going to the next one. I did warn Nol that if it went silent, I'd contact the *Zayuri*."

"Are you concerned Nolan can't handle himself?"

"Nol is a very skilled *Zayuri*. I've seen him fight Aswryn several times. If Aswryn hadn't had that vanishing *meril*, Nol would have—completed his mission much sooner. But I worry, not because I believe he can't handle himself, but because I told him Drake was trustworthy and when I contacted him last, Drake was proving himself to be an upstanding servant to the Crown. We don't know how many people Drake is working with. We don't know how big or powerful this cult is, but we know it's more than a few people."

"Do you have a way to contact the other *Zayuri*?"

"I do, Your Majesty."

Orlaith glanced at Charlie, then away as she tapped on the counter some more. "Before we go further, tell me about this." She waved at Charlie. "Hally, you introduced this human to me as your niece. If we are to continue honest, trusted communication, you'll need to tell me who you've told about our existence and the reasons behind it."

"I won't say anything until I have your word that they will be safe from repercussions. Most of it is due to Aswryn's intrusion."

She looked at all of her fairies. "As these fae as my witnesses, no harm will come to them, unless they do us harm first, including revealing us to more humans."

Fair enough. I stood up straighter across the counter from her and refused to fidget. "Charlie and her family are my foster family. They adopted me in 1893 after my family discovered me learning a trade as an orphan. All of my sister's blood relatives can sense what I am. I have looked after her dependents ever since."

"I can sense fairies as well, and I can tell the difference," Charlie interrupted with her two cents.

"Aswryn forced my hand in revealing myself and Gileal to Zack Thomas and my human friends. Drake has been keeping a lot of secrets from both of us, and I don't mean just this." I explained my relationship with Katie, Ian, and Drake, ending with how Katie had come into my shop days before she died.

"Is that all?"

"No." I tilted my head toward Charlie. "Drake confessed how you know so much about us."

Orlaith pursed her lips and tapped her nails again. "I see. Drake has been busy, hasn't he? I suppose, now knowing what I know about your family..." She sighed as I'd backed her into a corner. "After we learned there was an elf living in Seattle, we needed to find out more information.

"We have a spy, a goblin, watching you. Unfortunately, she was exposed when your little girl"—she looked at Charlie—"was playing outside. Feya was cloaked in glamor to hide herself. It makes sense now that I've learned your family is special."

Charlie smiled a slow smile. "Oh, I've known about your spy. I figured it out on Saturday. It's pretty obvious, isn't it? We learn there're fairies after my daughter's imaginary friend happened to appear."

"Well, no one was harmed in the process."

"So comforting. I want to be part of this investigation. There must be more information about the virus here. You will give me this for using my daughter and betraying her trust." When Orlaith shook her head to refuse her demand, Charlie quickly continued. "And I'll allow Feya to continue to visit if that's what the two want to do."

"The children are our first priority. The elves are of little consequence to me. How can you aid in this investigation?"

Charlie frowned and opened her mouth to argue, but stopped. "I know what it's like to have your child stolen. I can help look through the digital data and examine the bodies. I'm sure you have your own fae to do that. However, I have the unique perspective of being a human. I'm an epidemiologist and have medical training. The victims were hooked up to IVs, which tells me they used some human medical methods."

"We have fae throughout the human world, from medical fields to bus driving. Your expertise—"

"Yeah, fairies. You have little to no knowledge about the *endaen* health. You knew them what, almost ten thousand years ago? Did your people have the same technology as they do now? I've studied Hally my entire adult life. I'm more knowledgeable about the *enda* victims in there than any of your fairies. I have seen the virus that Aswryn made. You need me."

Queen Orlaith didn't strike me as the kind of person to lose an argument, but Charlie was right, and Orlaith knew it. "You better be as valuable as you say you are. I don't like being made a fool."

Charlie lifted her chin, one hand on her hip. "Neither do I."

"Brodrick, Rowe, bring the team in and pack all this up. Charlie will assist you. Hally, contact the *Zayuri*." Orlaith caught the look I gave Quinn over her shoulder. "What?"

"I won't do it here, and Quinn is my ride. And Charlie's."

"Where, then?"

"My house. Nol and a few others used my redwood to realm travel. It's a familiar place for the *Zayuri* to come through."

She huffed. "Quinn, take us to Hally's house."

"Your Majesty, being out here is bad enough. The place hasn't been vetted—"

"Fine. Send a pair of guards ahead of us, Brodrick. They have a five-minute window."

Brodrick looked as if he wanted to protest again, but thought better of it. "Yes, Your Majesty."

21

THE CLICK OF THE blinker filled the silence as Quinn waited for the light on North Beacon Hill near my home, a silence that seemed to expand into the quaint sleeping neighborhood at two fifteen in the morning. Orlaith rode in the front of Quinn's Porsche, ramrod straight for the thirty-minute ride. Quinn didn't turn the music on or talk while I kept thinking of ways I could break away to contact Yalu when we got to my place.

Queen Orlaith's phone rang as the light on 14th Avenue turned green. "Yes?" I heard the voice but couldn't understand the person's words on the other end. "We'll be there in a minute. Make a perimeter and wait." She hung up and slipped the phone back into her coat pocket.

"What's going on?" I asked.

"When we get there."

What the hell did that mean? I almost said something, but Quinn pulled up behind my house and killed the engine. I expected Orlaith to wait for Quinn to open the door, but she opened the door herself.

Quinn folded the seat forward for me but kept his eyes on Orlaith.

"What's going on?" I asked again.

Orlaith stood behind the car, looking at my gate as if she could see through it. Her eyes darted to me, her body tense. "I told you no other elves."

"There aren't—"

"There are five *Zayuri* in your backyard."

"I didn't—" It didn't matter if I didn't know. "I'll see what's going on. If you would have your people leave the yard, please?"

She pursed her lips, then murmured something under her breath. Her guards opened my gate moments later and took positions around their queen. Tolwe came out of my yard behind the last fairy, his light blue eyes trained on them, hands by his sides at the ready.

"Hally?"

"Tolwe? Excuse me, Your Majesty." I shuffled over to Nol's uncle and stood between the fairies and the *endao*. "What are you doing here?" I whispered as if the fairies understood *Aemirin*.

"The *Amura Ore* intend to blame you for the curse."

"I know. Yalu told me."

"You have until tomorrow night to prove your innocence. If you don't, you will either spend your entire life in prison or be executed."

My stomach dropped. "I'm not going back." My mouth said the words, but my brain didn't think them. Since when would I defy my country? Exiled or not, I'd always been loyal. "I'm *savilë*. They can't order me—"

"That's why we're here."

I narrowed my eyes and crossed my arms. "Are you warning me or waiting for their orders?"

"The *Zayuri* will not arrest you for a decision with no merit. However, this isn't a discussion to be had with a potential threat behind us. Why have you brought these people here?"

"I can bring whoever I want into my home." I put my hands on my hips, ignoring the cast. "And I don't like your tone."

Tolwe's eyebrow rose like his nephew's often did as he took in my words. "They tried to come into your home, ready to search it like they suspect you of something. Are they accusing you of something, too?"

"No. Queen Orlaith"—I waved my hand back at the fairies, palm up like Vanna—"is coming to my house."

Tolwe glanced back. "Their queen is amongst commoners?"

"Not all people treat their royalty like prisoners." The *Aeminan* royals were more like the ancient emperors of Japan. Our royals held little power, rarely left the royal compound, and never spoke with commoners. Blasphemy to even consider it. We just had to believe the *Amura Ore* were consulting the royal family. Tolwe went on to argue an old political argument that I had no right to fight any longer. "Forget it. We were actually coming to contact you."

Towle pressed his hand to his chest, eyes wide. "Me? Nolan could do that at any moment. If their queen it their ruler here, I wish to speak with her. Which one is she?"

"There's a situation with Nol."

Tolwe sobered, taking his eyes off the fairies and focusing on me. "He's shadowed himself, hasn't he?"

"If that means he hasn't made contact in a while, yes. He went looking for the fae children with their lead investigator on this. I talked to him by *meril* once. Now he's not responding."

Tolwe relaxed as if nothing I'd said mattered.

"He's with the fairy who tricked the queen. We discovered the fairy was working with Aswryn to help steal children for decades."

That piqued his interest. "Does Nolan know this?"

"Before he stopped responding, I told him what we suspected, but he didn't believe it. Nor does he know how involved that fairy is."

"That doesn't matter. He knows to stay alert and cautious. Now, would you introduce me?"

I groaned. "After we get out of the cold. I need coffee to function."

"Coffee?"

"You ask a lot of questions." I sucked in a quick breath of cold air as Tolwe gave me a flat glare. This was more than I'd ever conversed with him. In my childhood, the *endao* had scared the shit out of me. I'd thought he hated me, but it turned out the cold shoulder had never been about me.

Orlaith's guards checked the house. It passed. Shocking, I know.

No one else wanted coffee. After a tense situation of outmaneuvering the other team in the living room, I told everyone to sit at the dining room table, conference style. Fairies on one side, *endai* on the other. Two fairies sat on either side of the queen while Quinn winked at me from the corner of the dining room, furthest away. But when I looked back, he'd moved somewhere else. Two other *Zayuri* besides Towle stayed inside. One of them planted himself near the front door, where he could see down the hall to the back door. Fine by me.

Nol and Gileal had claimed that I'd willed a person to understand and speak the *Aemirin* language when we were young. I didn't remember, but even so, there wasn't a chance in hell I'd try doing anything like that now. So I played translator once again.

"Your Majesty," Towle began as he sat down across from the Queen of the Fae. "Nolan's and Hallanevaë's families are in your debt."

"Tolwe," I hissed to get his attention. "Wait!" I hadn't been ready. "She doesn't know *Aemirin*." She also didn't know my full name—not that it was a big deal at the moment.

"Nolan told me," he continued without listening to me, and I fumbled to keep up his commentary, "that you are allowing him and his *muranildë* to stay in this realm."

Orlaith's expression perked up as soon as Tolwe mentioned *muranildë*. She seemed to know that word as well as she knew *savilë*. I glared daggers at him as my face flamed. "And she also didn't know about our bond," I muttered. Nice going, General Tolwe.

"*Muranildë*? You and Nolan are a fated pair?" She turned to me before I could translate more than a few sentences. She waited for my answer, her arms folded in front of her. Orlaith's eyes widened. "How is it that a *Muranilde* pair is born to the Inara family and a *Zayuri* family?"

I shrugged. "I've stopped asking questions I'll never get answers to." Fate loved to fuck with people. That was my opinion. We would only know when the time was right if there was even a reason for it.

But Orlaith's look changed, like I was supposed to know why. We'd gotten that look at times when *endai* from other places had met us. Like we knew the secrets to the universe. Or we weren't normal *endai*, but something mystical.

"But I'd like to get back to Drake and Nol? If you know the term, then you know that if he dies, I die." Yeah, and if Drake killed him, I'd have enough time to make Drake wish he'd never been born.

"Does Drake know?" Orlaith asked.

"No."

"Good. Is there anything else you're keeping from me?"

"Yes, but it's not as pertinent right now." I'd sort of already told her about the others but had hedged around the details of who and how many friends knew about me because of Aswryn.

Orlaith let that go, focusing on this. "Tolwe? I understand why you hesitate to help your nephew, and I see you hold him in high regard." My jaw dropped as Queen Orlaith spoke to Tolwe in perfect *Aemirin*. Not rusty at all. "I don't doubt his ability or your instincts. I'm chagrined to say that Drake has fooled me for over thirty years now, or longer. Please, help us find them or we may never find the children."

"We were just at Drake's house, Tolwe," I added, still dazed that the queen had watched me struggle through the whole damn Estwyn thing for nothing. "Six bodies, three *endai*. And Nol doesn't know."

Tolwe cussed under his breath and looked away. "Contacting my nephew after he's shadowed himself isn't a straightforward matter. How far away and which way did these two travel?"

"Um, south?" I squinted. Showing him a map or telling him the mileage wouldn't help.

He frowned at my unhelpful answer.

"If we were to walk, it would take us over a full *Endaen* week," the queen added.

Okay, sure, being logical worked.

Tolwe winced. "That is too far to take the shadows directly, then. I'd like to try locating him, but there's interference here—Nolan has explained it, but..." Tolwe's eyes squinted. Yeah, Nol's explanations could be wordy and confusing to the non-geniuses of the world. Charlie would understand.

"This realm feels...thick and hazy. You and Nolan are used to navigating the energies here, and it's easier for you. If I spent more time here, I'm sure I would acclimate, but we don't have that time now. If you could guide me through the static and extend my spell to a wider area, I might be able to find him. The *metenya* spell does this. Are you familiar with it?"

"No, but I can't do traditional spells, anyway. Can't he do it?" I pointed at the other *Zayuri* with my chin, who shook his head.

"I have the same problem as *Basean* Tolwe. But sir? Is this safe, considering her history?"

Tolwe sat straighter and turned around to face his subordinate. "She's fine." So much more went into those two words, but the *Zayuri* didn't back down.

"*Basean*, my respect and loyalty to *Hasin* Twynolan is unbreakable. He is an honorable *Zayuri,* and I want to be part of this mission. I, too, believe he doesn't need assistance, and I also agree with Hallanevaë that there is a chance he could be in trouble. But we all know what she did to her friends. Asking her to cast a *metenya* spell is too much."

Okay, so he wasn't being as close-minded as I'd first thought. His concerns were valid, but damn it, we were right back at the beginning. They would never, ever trust me. Even if Nol got my banishment revoked, no one would believe in me. "He didn't ask me to cast a *metenya* spell. He asked if I could extend his spell with my magic. There's a difference. Tolwe, I can try, but I make no promises."

Tolwe studied me for a moment.

"Try to connect with him, and I'll feel around to see what I can do. Your Majesty? Are you comfortable with me attempting to assist Tolwe?"

"I'm interested to see you work, Hally."

"Oh—that's not." I held my breath. "We're doing what we can, Your Majesty."

I nodded to Tolwe, giving him the all-clear. Within seconds, he made a quick minute-hand gesture, the same one Nol made when he used his dagger to connect with him. Tolwe's *imolegin* spread out around us. Only knowing what Tolwe's *imolegin* felt like when he performed the spell and nothing about how it actually worked, I was lost. "I'm not sure what to do. How does the *metenya* spell work?"

"All magic travels on the waves of energy. Do you remember this from your school?"

Um, no. Contrary to what human stories portrayed about elves, we weren't some medieval society that had no knowledge of science. We merely chose a natural path with technology, rather than smelly cars and cellphones. But no, I didn't remember energy waves.

"Hally," Queen Orlaith interrupted. "What he's explaining is another wave on the light spectrum. You know, microwaves and sound waves?"

That's how magical energy traveled? Not wanting to look like the idiot I felt like, I nodded and turned to Tolwe, hoping he'd think I'd figured it all out. Shit. Light waves? He believed my lie and cast the spell again.

Imagining light waves traveling like water ones, I let Tolwe's *imolegin* wash over me. I was winging it here. Then I remembered Charlie talking about how big microwaves were, and how much bullshit it was when people freaked out about a microwave oven's radiation. In my mind's eye, I watched Tolwe's spell lift to the ceiling, like a cloud for the wind to carry—my magic being the wind, and his magic being the water.

"Allow me to direct it, Hally. It's not *Olauvë*."

Like I didn't know that already, but I gave Tolwe control of my magic so he could extend his spell. As Tolwe directed my magic, I felt him reach out. After a moment, I felt my energy build. If we didn't stop soon, the slave band—at the thought, I felt it siphon my magic into itself. Every time! I pushed and tried to close off the band's access. Big mistake. The thing started siphoning faster.

"Tolwe?" I whispered.

I didn't know how far he'd expanded the spell, but he hadn't found Nol yet. He still had his eyes closed, but they moved under his lids, searching through a fog of magic. Or was that the haze he'd described to me? I would never understand *Zayuri* magic.

"I'm getting tired," I warned him and prayed I wouldn't pass out again. The car incident with Quinn was embarrassing enough. Nol was right. I needed more practice to build up my endurance. I hated the feeling of my magic being drained from me, though. "Tolwe?"

Then, like a light in the storm, Nol's magic appeared from the fog of our spells. At first faint, then Tolwe homed in on it, speeding in his effort to get this over with.

"There," Tolwe whispered.

Through our connected spells, I sensed Tolwe mark Nol's location in his mind.

"See?" Towle said as he backed off, our energies speeding back through space, too fast like a diver swimming to the surface.

My head spun, and the band stopped sucking on my energy, but not fast enough. If I hadn't been sitting down, I would have fallen. Instead, my body tilted forward. Tolwe grabbed me before my head hit the edge of the table. After steadying me, he scooted his chair closer to let me lean on him. I rested my arms on the table and laid my head down.

"They're too far to use the shadows," Tolwe confirmed.

"It's a day and a night of travel in human cars." I kept my head on the table and looked up at him. "You know the big metal things that zoom?"

"Zoom?" But his faint smirk told me he knew what I was talking about. "Are they faster than dragon travel?"

"No. But dragons aren't here."

"And there is absolutely no way you're bringing any over," Orlaith added. "We can travel through Faerie, a land connected to this realm, yet separate from humans, where we can freely use magic." Orlaith paused, expecting Tolwe to respond, but he watched the queen, waiting for more. "Once in our land, it is possible to travel anywhere. You may take your *Zayuri* back to my manor, and I will send an entourage with you to LA."

"Their house is in that veiled fairy place," I whispered.

"It's just Faerie."

"That." I hitched my thumb toward the queen.

Tolwe nodded at Orlaith and locked eyes with his protesting *Zayuri* subordinate. "Will I have any problems with you going forward?"

"No, *Basean*." But the guy wouldn't take his eyes off me as he said it.

I looked away.

"Then we should leave now. While I felt no urgency or distress from my nephew, there is no point in waiting until morning. Unless your entourage needs time to prepare?"

"They'll be ready." Orlaith stood, and the two guards sitting next to her followed suit.

My house was too narrow to allow more than two people at a time to go down the hall, and Tolwe waited behind the others to walk with me. It was no surprise when he stopped me as we stepped onto my deck. "You shouldn't go, Hally."

Not that I'd given it much thought, but I assumed I'd be along for the ride. "But...I can take care of myself." I almost told him about our attack on Capitol Hill, but Tolwe's look kept me quiet.

He raised his cinnamon eyebrows, the same color as Nol's, with more than a bit of gray. "There are too many reasons for you to stay, and only one for you to come."

Tolwe was right, but what could I do while I waited? Translate Aswryn's damn notebooks? Even Charlie had more interesting things to do—not that I envied her. Dead bodies and science stuff weren't my thing. I sighed, then remembered Zack's evidence. Orlaith didn't know about that either.

"Aswryn left stacks of notebooks that I need to go through and translate. That's how we found the Capitol Hill site in the first place."

"See? That is being positive." Tolwe winked as he patted my shoulder. "I'll find him, Hally. I swear."

Sure, he'd find him, but would it be too late?

Tolwe squeezed my arm, right over the slave band. "He is fine. Have faith in him."

"Having faith in him isn't the problem, Tolwe." The sight of Nol lying on the ground, so close to death three weeks ago, resurfaced. Tolwe hadn't seen his nephew like that. If he had, maybe he wouldn't have been so nonplussed.

"I'll find him in time."

"The moment you find him"—I shook my finger at the high-ranking *Zayuri* who'd scared me as a kid—"you need to make him call me, or someone else needs to."

"You have my word." He held up his hand. I couldn't tell if he was being serious, or if he was placating me. At my glare, he gave me a sincere look and nodded.

Quinn came over after Tolwe had walked away. They were all moving to the gate and leaving. At least I'd have him.

"Where'd you go off to?"

"I was there." He gave me a sly smile. "You just didn't see me."

"Why—"

"Are you doing okay?" he whispered. "Remember, there are books to be translated."

"I know." So we'd go to his house. "We can—"

"I'm part of the entourage."

When had they discussed that? "But you're a foreign relations officer, not a soldier." If he got to go, why couldn't I?

He smiled, his straight smile with perfect teeth. "Remember?" He tucked my hair behind my left ear and leaned in. "I've been around the block a few hundred times."

Unimpressed and feeling abandoned, I pouted. "Everyone else gets to go."

"Everyone who can fight. I was a soldier for centuries. Can you get to my condo? I can have someone take you."

"What, you won't offer your Porsche?" I was getting a key to his condo, huh? I still didn't know how I felt about this prince, who might or might not be a spy for his brother's kingdom or his parents'.

Quinn chuckled. "Nice try. Here." He took my hand and pressed his house keys into my palm. "I'd like to talk after your *muranildo* is safely back home." His lips twisted in mild accusation.

My incisor caught my lip ring. "Quinn…it was just one date. No reason to have a break-up talk."

"I was hoping to have a different kind of talk. If…" He rolled his eyes to the sky. "If I didn't screw things up too badly to try again?"

"I…" What did I say to that? I couldn't stop the damn flirty smile I gave him. So much fucking trouble!

For a moment, I thought he was going to lean in and try to kiss me, but instead, he stood, touched my chin, and stepped away. "We'll find them both. Drake won't get away with this."

I shivered, remembering why this was close to Quinn. Drake's "Quinn's too close to this" excuse made more sense now.

I caught his hand and squeezed. "We'll find Seamus. I know it."

Quinn froze, deer in the headlights, unable to look away from me. He swallowed hard.

"Go. Find them. I'll look through Zack's evidence." That talk he wanted to have needed to include Katie and Seamus, too.

He shuddered. "Thanks, Hally."

"Why do you get to say thank you, but I can't?"

He winked before thumping down the stairs and catching up with everyone. The three guards who had arrived before us drove a Suburban or some other big-ass SUV that looked like it, but he, along with Queen Orlaith, slid into his Porsche.

I'd take a shower and go over to Quinn's.

22

WASHINGTON IS FUCKING COLD in the winter, and it rains ice. Which was what I got to ride my bike through to Quinn's house. The helmet kept the ice from stinging my cheeks and my jacket protected my upper body, but it was still ice pouring out of the sky. This was the first day of spring, damn it! What was wrong with the weather here?

Quinn's house had that hush to it that was almost its own noise. Quiet, not like a library, but like an inhale, waiting for noise again. That noise was supposed to be Seamus. Shivering from the cold, I shrugged out of my soaked riding jacket, took it into the bathroom and stepped into the tub to dry all my clothes off, knowing that even with magic, the water had to go somewhere. I pillaged around Quinn's coat closet and then wished I hadn't. While Quinn must have packed up Katie's belongings, I found a thin coat buried between Quinn's large ones. Even though it was smaller than Quinn's, I couldn't bring myself to use it. I picked one of his hoodies instead. Nice and comfy.

I found Seamus-sized boots and a few toys waiting for the little guy to claim them as soon as they brought him back. Granted, I liked Quinn, but he'd lied about being a prince and that had me uneasy. Or was it the fact that he was a prince that made me uneasy? I didn't know and I didn't have the time to deal with my issues. We'd figure that out during our talk, because as I found all the little accents of a dad waiting for his son to come home—cars, books, a lonely little sock—I decided I'd give Quinn a chance.

On the way over, I worked out in my head how I'd stay away from Quinn's little book of Gaelic gods he claimed was so close to my people's religious system. Though when I got down to it, sitting next to Zack's duffle and the box of lab books, I had no trouble ignoring it over there on the table next to the chair, waiting for me to compare similarities. Was *Aemina's* religion a lie? How close was it? So easy to ignore. Who needed to listen to that nagging at the back of one's mind anyway?

I decided to start off by calling the building owners in Germany again. Mexico City I had to try later—they were two hours ahead of us.

"*Gruß Gott*?" the gentleman on the line greeted me in German.

"*Ja, tag, mein Namen ist Hèléne Dubois,*" Yes, hello, my name is Hèléne Dubois. "I am hoping you can help me out with an issue I'm having. Do you have a moment?"

He inhaled through the phone. I bet he was an older guy and not a fan of technology. Would that be good or bad for me? "We're about to close for *Mittagen*."

"Oh, apologies," I continued in German. "I'm in the US right now. I'll be as quick as I can. I'm going over documents for a deceased cousin of mine, and I found some paperwork with your name. I'd like to find out if she was renting an apartment or something. I want to make sure her assets and bills are taken care of."

"*Namen*?" The screech of a metal file cabinet drowned out the word, but I could guess.

"Dana Isabell Miller. The lease says, *Streidhauß* thirty-eight, office suite one b."

"Wait, that place? It was demolished...*scheiße*." Papers shuffled, and the file cabinet screeched again. "*Frau* Miller has been paying on this address for ten years. How did I not catch this?"

"It was demolished?" I spoke in English as my throat squeezed shut, then repeated it in German.

"*Ja*. Ten years ago."

"Were there belongings left behind?"

"I couldn't tell you. Everything that wasn't claimed went to the trash or charity. Ah, here are some return posts for her notices. I'll cancel this. *Nein*, I will have my son get on the computer and cancel the deposits. If you give me your name and number, I will send out a refund slip."

"Um, no, that's not necessary."

"It's a reasonable sum."

"Take it as a donation. Get some windows replaced or something. If not that, find a charity of your choice to donate to. Please. *I* don't need her money." No, I needed the equipment. "I have no idea what kind of place this is. An apartment, storage? Like I said, I just found the paperwork."

"Ah, here! *Ja whol*! There was nothing in the unit. I found the documents. Would you like those sent over?"

"No. I appreciate your time. Have a good meal."

"*Danke, Hèléne*. Please call soon, and we'll get the death certificate in the paperwork, for audits and such."

"Absolutely." Not. "*Bis später*," *Until later*.

I almost threw my phone after I'd hung up. Useless dead end.

I weighed my choices: translate lab books or look at the evidence? I pulled the duffle bag closer to my side of the floor, farthest away from the chair Quinn had sat in with the not-interesting fairy history book next to it.

Lots and lots of Xerox-copied paperwork. Horrible handwritten notes and typed reports. Charlie's picture of Drake still sat on the coffee table, but Zack had tons more.

Then I found the pictures that Zack had shown me three weeks ago. The little boy in Arizona. "Derrick," I whispered, and I shook the picture. Katie had seen him in Westport. Well, if Zack had his picture, he could have some notes on the location. Feeling discouraged from the dead end and hoping to find something useful, I dug into the folder on Derrick. Three pages in, Zack had *Westport* written on a sticky note. His handwritten report stated why Katie had been there, gave a description of the property, and listed what he'd found and who was there.

According the Agent Thomas's notes Katie had gone to Westport at the request of one Riley Smith. She'd called and told Katie about Derrick and several other kidnapped victims. The only person Katie had seen was Derrick. The report gave the address of a one-story, three-bedroom house. Evidence of drug paraphernalia. No signs of victims on site. He'd arrested all five people. They'd told him nothing to further the investigation. And last but just as unhelpful, they'd made bail and were awaiting hearings. Zack's report didn't paint much of a picture.

Zack had pictures of twelve children of various ages. I checked the report—Katie had given all of these to Zack. She admitted she'd helped, under duress. Yes, she'd been addicted to drugs, but if what Drake had said was true, Katie, or rather Princess Catrina had been investigating Aswryn's trafficking ring. But had Katie *really* been investigating or helping Drake? And what about Ian? What about Quinn, then? I wanted to rip my hair out. No. I refused to believe that Katie and Quinn were on Aswryn's side, not with the haunted look Quinn had given me a few hours ago when I mentioned Seamus.

Katie had told me she'd tried enlisting other police, but none of them had helped. Now that I knew what Drake really was, I had a feeling he'd helped hinder that. How, I didn't know. Bribery and threats were my guesses. Again, all of us from California knew Drake wasn't one to cross. Lewis and his shop knew it, too.

I stopped shuffling. Lewis *didn't* know Drake was a fairy, but he knew Drake. I needed to know how they knew each other. I'd bet my best hat someone involved with Lewis's old shop knew about Drake, Katie, and Ian. Someone from Lewis's old shop was fae. Were they helping Drake? Yumi held the craziest hours as a nurse, and Lewis always stayed up to wait for her. But would they be awake at three forty in the morning? No harm in asking.

Are you up? I texted Lewis. If I woke him, he'd forgive me once I told him what was going on. I hoped.

I went back to shuffling papers and looking at the pictures of kids. Zack had gone back and taken other photos and statements of parents who'd agreed to talk to him—seven parents. Were they all fairies using glamor?

My eyes started drooping while I read one interview. How could I sleep without knowing about Nol? I didn't want to dream about the dead bodies in Quinn's condo.

My phone rang, loud crickets washing the fog away from a nightmare I couldn't remember. I rubbed my eyes and looked around while rubbing a kink in my neck. Quinn's place, crickets again. Lewis.

"Shit. Hey, Lewis," my voice crackled, thick with sleep. Dim light filtered in through Quinn's tinted windows with a distant view of Elliot Bay still misty and dim. Sunrise?

"Hally? Did I wake you? Nobody calls at three in the morning for a chat. What's going on?"

"Lots of shit." I wasn't a morning person, and my vocabulary didn't come back until at least my first cup of coffee. Did Quinn have a coffee maker?

"Hally?"

"Sorry." I took a deep breath and stretched. Papers slid off my lap, and my neck hurt on the left side. "Yeah, we need to talk." What time was it? Wow. Nine thirty-two.

Lewis grunted when I didn't elaborate. "Not a phone conversation, huh?"

"It's about Drake."

Lewis took a moment to respond. Only his deep breaths told me he was still on the line. "Hally, that's not—"

"It's got to do with Thursday night."

"Fuck."

"Yep. Got coffee?"

"Of course. Gimme a bit to get out of bed."

"'Kay. Half hour good?"

He grunted in the positive.

Fuck was right. This wouldn't be fun. I grabbed the photo of Drake as a security guard and got off the floor. Quinn had a coffee maker, but after staring at it for five minutes, I decided I was too tired to deal with such a complicated monstrosity. Why the fuck would a coffee maker need twelve buttons?

My riding jacket was still wet, but it was still raining, too. Harder. And I had to drive through downtown to get to Lewis's. I considered leaving the bike here and taking the bus.

"Fuck it." If I crashed, I crashed. Besides, what was the point of taking it out of storage if I didn't ride it? "Maybe I should put it back in," I grumbled as I looked up at the clouds with my helmet on.

23

"Absolutely not!" Yumi yelled, her bare, tattooed arms crossed as she stood in her living room. "Hally, I have nothing against you, and I love you, but you know you shouldn't involve Lewis further. These guys have already attacked him once."

Lewis sat on his couch, elbows on his knees as he looked from the floor to Yumi to me. "Babe, TJ might not even be one."

"The way things are going, he most definitely is a fairy. I have heard you mention Drake once and only once. This guy is bad news, and you left them all behind, Lewis."

"Yes. This changes shit. This queen lady, she could throw Hally out. Where would she go? These kids? You wanna tell me you don't care just 'cause you don't know 'em? I know you better than that. Hally needs my help. The shop, these guys, they don't know her; they won't trust her if she goes alone."

"They attacked you." Yumi shoved her short, blue hair back with both hands and moved closer to Lewis.

"I know." He reached out his hand. Yumi gave him her hands, and he pulled her in front of him. "But now that we know about these guys. We'll be more prepared."

"I'm scared." She leaned over and pressed her forehead against his. "I'm scared I'll lose you."

"You won't," he whispered back.

I looked away and around their small living room and down the hall, anywhere else to give them a moment. I tugged on the blanket

Yumi had handed me after laughing at the "limitations of magic" that I was cleaning up on her laundry room floor. I'd jumped in the small laundry room and dried my clothes again, making a puddle on their floor in the process. So I stood in their living room with a blanket wrapped around my shoulders, feeling like an intruder in their house for the first time ever.

The whisper of clothing brushing against clothing brought me out of my thoughts. Yumi came up to stand in front of me, close like before at the shop. "We had an agreement."

"I know."

"If anything happens to him, I will never forgive you. I love you, but I love Lewis more."

"I'll protect him with my life, Yumi."

"You haven't been doing a good job of it lately," she growled between gritted teeth.

"Yumi, that's not fair," Lewis said from the couch. "This is all beginning, and Hally never knew what to expect."

"She could have told us about herself sooner. We would have been prepared."

Taken aback by her harsh tone, I started and leaned away. Did I feel guilty for not telling them? Yes and no. It was normal to keep my identity a secret, but they weren't normal friends. I'd gotten so close to them all in such a short amount of time. So fast I hadn't realized it had happened until we were sitting down for Sunday dinner one night and my nephew Gérald called, asking about the family. He'd meant all of them. They'd only met Gérald once, when he came to visit from France, but they'd hit it off and my friends here had become part of the family I'd built.

Lewis stood and walked up behind his girlfriend. His larger fingers curved around her upper arms. "Yumi, it's gonna be okay."

"You—don't know that." She choked but refused to let the tears fall.

"I don't want Lewis to go with me, but I need him. There's no other way to get to TJ. I'm sorry."

Yumi's lip quivered, and she turned into Lewis's arms. He met my eyes, with his chin set and a hard look. I'd made her cry.

Mother, please don't let me lose them.

"Lewis, I—"

"Don't. Just don't, Hally." Lewis gripped the leather-wrapped steering wheel of his car. We'd left Yumi in their house for Tacoma and stepped into Lewis's past. I hated myself for making him do this.

We'd both known, in the beginning, that we had past issues we never talked about. I knew he came from Tacoma, and he knew I came from California. Done. Drake was our connection, and that's all there needed to be known about it.

"Hally?" Lewis shook my shoulder.

The rush of air and the smell of Old Spice let me know I'd fallen asleep in Lewis's car.

"What time is it?"

"Elven-oh-five. Here, I stopped and got us breakfast." He dropped a paper bag onto my lap.

"Coffee?"

"Ah-huh. It's cold, though. You didn't wanna wake up earlier. Tried twice and figured you needed the sleep if you didn't wake up to the smell of coffee."

I grunted and stretched my neck. Now I had a matching pair of kinks in my neck. Lewis liked food. I mean, he was over three hundred pounds and six foot four. I didn't doubt he'd bought himself at least three sandwiches from—I picked up the bag off my lap—Burger King. Oh good, they had those tater tots.

"French toast sticks?"

"Yes, ma'am."

"Don't call me 'ma'am' and don't talk with your mouth full."

"Yes, ma'am," he said with a chuckle.

I didn't rise to the bait, way too tired for all this shit. Nol still hadn't called or contacted me through the *meril*. Shouldn't they have found him by now? Tolwe had a lock on his location. Did I text him and tell him about TJ? Should I tell anyone? The lead might not even pan out. Listen to me—lead? Like I was any sort of investigator. Then what the fuck was I doing? Would everyone think I was going off on my own? Like when Aswryn had taken Ray?

"Lewis? Do you think this is a bad idea?" I asked as I picked up my medium roast Burger King coffee.

"Dunno." He raised his large shoulders, the satin and cotton Western-style vest moving with it over his dark skin.

Like any other tattooist, Lewis showed a lot of skin to display his tattoos. My favorite, though was his skeleton cowboy tattoo that started at the top of his head and went down his back, underneath the vest. Black and gray, with whites, blues, and reds. With his dark skin, he had to get it touched up frequently.

His other tattoos were one of the Duwamish tribe orcas as a tribute to Yumi, who was half Native American—with permission, of course—and a Japanese Hannya mask tattoo; Yumi had the same one. Plus, many others from before. Some he'd covered up, some he hadn't. His arms were covered fingers to neck. A themed sleeve on his right arm and a partial with various tattoos throughout his life on his left. He had one area along his left ribcage and over his heart that was reserved for me. We'd designed the piece and everything. Now all he had to do was get up the nerve to ask Yumi to marry him. Two years later...

"Whachu finkin' 'bout?" he asked with his mouth full.

"Actually? Tattoos. Since there're fairies here, and if I spend more time with them, I wouldn't need to hide as much."

He swallowed, then pulled his bottom lip up, his mouth curving down. "What would you get?"

"I don't know. It's just to get my mind off what I'm making you do. I hate this, Lewis. I hate it so much."

"You're doing right by these kids and yourself. This is all Drake and Aswryn's fault."

"Still."

"You wanna save Katie's boy?"

"Yes."

"So do I. Now let's go." Lewis pulled into the old shop in South Tacoma. Not the safest part of the city by any stretch.

"Is there anything I need to know?" I asked as we unbuckled.

"Yes, but it won't matter. They might remember you, but let me do the talkin' first."

We got out, and mist clung to my leather jacket and hair. I hurried to the door instead of flipping up my hood. There was no need to worry about makeup; it was faded after—how many hours ago now? Twenty-four hours? More? Didn't matter.

Lewis opened the door for me, and the buzz of their electronic doorbell went off, loud and jarring. Damn, that'd alert the neighbors if they had any. Under the heavy bass, rap music blared from the speakers in the back, but no one manned the front. Someone coughed. We waited. Pictures of people, cars, and tattoo conventions covered the dark green and maroon walls.

The shop looked nothing like ours, with our license plates on the lobby walls, a cowboy mural, and our giant gumball machine in one corner. They only had two chairs, those uncomfortable ones with blue fabric in the middle. Our "well loved" couches were luxurious compared to this place.

Lewis showed no sign of nervousness, like he had in the car. His own mask to hide behind. I bumped his arm with mine to show him I had his back.

A young man appeared from somewhere in the shop. His black hair was cut close to his head, and his beard was shaved so close to his brown skin that it looked like a tattoo. "What up, man. Be there in a minute." He tilted his head to the side for another person, and I could only see the straight, black cornrows on top of their head.

The one who'd greeted us sauntered out. His loose jeans, low on his hips and held up by his belt, swung back and forth in time with his steps. His army green tank top showed off his tattoos. One was a Polynesian tribal tattoo, and some belonged to another type of tribe that had nothing to do with any Native Americans. He walked past the counter and stopped in front of us.

"Come in to get your woman her first tattoo? Think she can handle it?"

"Why don't you try asking me that question?"

"Hally," Lewis muttered.

The guy's eyebrows shot up. He didn't expect me to have an opinion? He clicked his tongue and looked me up and down. "She's got a mouth on her." He looked back at Lewis, giving him a half grin.

"TJ in?" Lewis asked.

The guy's eyebrows shot up again, but in a distinctly guarded expression. "Got an appointment?"

"Nah." Lewis shrugged.

The guy lifted his chin. "Who'd be askin' then?"

"An old friend."

I snorted a laugh. Couldn't help it. That was the exact introduction Nol had used when he came into our shop that first day.

"Girl, what you laughin' at? This ain't funny."

Whatever. This guy couldn't intimidate me, especially after he found out I was part of the tattoo community.

"Brian!" the guy with cornrows lifted his head enough to shout over his privacy wall. He looked vaguely familiar. "Don't be talkin'—"

"Lou? Is that you?"

Lewis fidgeted in a way that gave the guy an answer.

"Is that Hally? *The* Hally? Shit, Brian, give 'em some fuckin' space. They ain't no customers. Get the fuck back here, Lou."

Brian looked us up and down again, still unsure of what the other guy was talking about. Apparently, Brain was new—ish.

The guy who'd invited us back put his machine down as we came around. He was working on another man's arm. I recognized a tattoo under his ear that matched one of Brian's and Lewis's friend here. He was at least twenty years older, with a black mustache and a long scar on his forehead and through his eyebrow. His patient, intelligent eyes watched over our discussion without introduction or acknowledgment. Was that a good thing?

"We can wait until you've finished," I offered. Yes, I was doing a crap-tastic job of listening to Lewis, but this was just rude of us.

The client waved his hand and shook his head while he found a comfortable position to listen to the conversation.

"Nah, all good." Lewis's friend stuck out an elbow with his gloves on, since he couldn't give him any other form of handshake or whatever guys called their secret man greeting.

"What are you both doing down here? Haven't seen you in years, Lou, not since lil Hally first came here." He looked at me and smiled. Soft and welcoming. A lie. "Half drowned from the rain, with that big tote almost as big as you are."

I smiled, remembering that day. Seattle had changed so much, and Charlie had still been getting situated with the baby. Drake had said Lewis was expecting me soon, so I'd hurried over, unsure of what to expect. They hadn't treated me like Brian, because I'd introduced myself right away before anyone could say a word. None of that "your woman" shit.

I crossed my arms and hummed with a smile of my own. "Yes, *bonjour*, eh...I'm sorry I don't know your name."

"Alex." He offered his elbow.

"Man, where's her ink?"

I turned, giving Brian a full frown.

"Brian don't know nothing. Sorry, Hally."

"Children." I crossed my arms and looked at the ceiling. I didn't look much older than Brian himself.

Alex chuckled. "She's allergic, broh."

"Once Tiger finds an ink I'm not allergic to, I'll get my second one." I pulled down the collar at the back of my neck to show him my shrapnel scars, which I told people was where I'd tried to get my first tattoo. No one asked questions after that.

"Shit, maybe you should try a different profession."

I almost let the comment go, but damn. "Do you think my talent is linked to my allergies in some way? You formed a biased opinion of me upon hearing about one quality—one I can't control. Disrespecting me as I step in the door."

"Hally—"

"No, Lewis. He owes me an apology."

"Girl, you be—"

"Brian, shut the fuck up," Alex snapped.

Brian clicked his tongue again, walked to his station, and pouted.

"Sorry 'bout him. He's—nah, I'm not gonna make up an excuse for him. So what you doin' 'round here, Lou?"

"Looking for TJ."

"TJ's out, man."

"Out? Where'd he go?"

"Think he's in Everett. Got a place, like you did."

"Contacts?"

As Lewis towered over Alex with a stern, unrelenting look, Alex tsked once, then looked at his client, who nodded to Alex. With that confirmation, he pulled his gloves off and went to the computer in the front.

"I don't even know if these are still good. He left a year ago." But Alex copied down the information on a sticky note. He handed it to me and lifted his chin to look Lewis in the eye. "It's good seein' you both. It's gotten better 'round here. And Hally, if you come in again, Brian won't be disrespecting you."

I gulped at his tone but squared my shoulders. Brian had gotten himself into trouble, and I doubted he would be reprimanded like any employee. No, with Alex's tone, it would be more.

"He's just a kid," I whispered.

Alex pursed his lips.

"Well! Thank you for your help." Lewis tipped his cowboy hat. "We gotta get goin'."

"For sure. But Lou, I'm gonna hafta tell Max 'bout you comin'."

"Do what you gotta do. Don't wanna 'cause trouble." Lewis held his hand out, and they did a complicated handshake, ending in a one-armed man hug.

I waved once, uncertain of what else to do. Lewis held the door open for me but didn't acknowledge me as I walked past him.

I hurried into the unlocked car to get out of the rain and plopped into my seat before Lewis had even reached the car.

"That wasn't horrible. It might not go so well for Brian, and I feel bad about that," I said as soon as Lewis shut his door.

Lewis kept quiet, staring out the window into the shop as he slid his seatbelt on. "Wanna call that number?"

"Do you want me to talk?" I asked.

"Put it on speaker."

His tone after we'd left his house had been so short and distant that I wanted to apologize again. He knew how bad I felt, though. After dialing the number and holding the phone between us as I put it on speaker, I watched Lewis. He checked the mirrors and backed up. My gaze shifted to a tattoo below his ear, one I'd done for him six months after we'd established Yula's Quill. The one underneath was the same as Brian's and Alex's. A heart with a chain around it, and a gun stabbing through the top instead of a sword. I knew what it was and what it represented, and I'd covered it. Drake had freed him, with no fighting, loss, or whatever else families like theirs did to get out—if they ever got out. TJ and Lewis had. But if TJ was a fairy, did that matter?

"I think TJ's a fairy."

"Why'd you say that?" Lewis asked.

"He got out."

"I got out."

"Yeah, because Drake knows I'm an *enda*. He said he thought I was some magic-less, runaway elf kid. Not something to start a war over. I wonder, though, if Aswryn was watching me even then? Did Drake send me up here on Aswryn's command? She was working for them. That organization, *Aiséirí an Meabhlaire.*"

"Alex gave us addresses. Home and work."

The line clicked and a male voice spoke, "Electric Ink, this is TJ."

My eyes locked with Lewis's surprised yet hopeful ones. Holy shit, how'd we get so lucky? Surprised and winging it, Lewis pointed at me. Pretend?

"Anybody there?"

"Yeah, hi!" I hid my accent as best I could and raised my voice, channeling my inner Cher Horowitz, Valley Girl. "I had it on mute. My bad. Yeah, I was wondering what time you close. I, huh, I'm just calling around, thinking of getting a tattoo."

TJ sighed into the phone. "We close up at midnight."

"Excellent. Can I schedule an appointment? I've got this picture I drew up with a monarch butterfly on a flower perched on the edge of an infinity sign. I was thinking blue and pink, with some green. Oh, and—"

"I'm gonna be straight with you. This might not be the shop for you. I can recommend some other shops that might be better suited for that kind of tattoo."

"Oh," I tried to sound taken aback. "But...you are an artist, right?"

"Everyone has their expertise. This ain't one of ours."

"Well, that's rude. Don't expect a good Yelp review from me!" I hung up and started laughing.

Lewis, now on South Tacoma Way, was laughing so hard he almost drove into a mini-van in the other lane.

"Lewis!" I yelled, still laughing.

He laughed louder. "What is with you and your goddamn Yelp reviews?"

Never expect a tattoo artist to copy someone else's art. Ever.

Lewis was still on the phone when I sat down with our bag of Subway sandwiches. "Babe, I promise, we're safe. It wasn't bad at all." He paused. "Yes, we're going there next. Yes, she thinks so."

My phone buzzed, the chirps of the ring tone muffled from inside zippered pocket. My thumb swiped the answer button as I lifted the phone to my ear.

"What's going on with Charlie?" Mateo started before I could greet him. "She's a wreck, and she wouldn't say a word. I haven't heard from you in days. Just a text that we'll talk later? And you canceled Sunday dinner. You never miss Sunday dinner."

"Hi, Mateo." I said his name for Lewis's benefit. "It's a lot to explain over the phone."

"Hop to it. I didn't let Charlie leave. I was scared she'd fall asleep with Ray in the back. If they ever got in a car wreck, Hally, I'd never forgive myself."

"They're there?"

"Where else do you think they'd be if I told you I didn't let them leave? Jail? Oh, speaking of, how's Nolan doing?"

I relaxed as Mateo talked, his drama scale up to the max, hiding his sincere and well-justified concern. We hadn't talked all weekend, too scared that the fairies were listening in. Would they be listening at a Subway in Federal Way? What if they had a spell to bug my phone? Unlikely as hell.

"There's lots going on, Mateo. I'll give you the rundown, but the details will have to wait. Have Charlie clarify. She knows."

"I don't see how that's fair," he grumbled. "And you brought Lewis into this. Do you know how upset Yumi is? I had to calm her down. I didn't realize how upset she was about the whole elf situation."

"Neither did I." I'd thought she'd forgiven me. I gave Mateo the Cliff Notes version of the last few days, which I'd already given Yumi and Lewis. "Thanks for making the girls stay, Mateo. I know Charlie'll want to keep going on this, but all the paperwork is at Quinn's right now and she can't get in."

"Yes, Prince Quinn." He flourished the name. "How'd Nolan take it?"

I played with my napkin and stared at my still-wrapped sandwich. "He's okay. Just missing Gil and…it's hard to see others moving on."

"*Ojitos*, you know that's not what I mean."

"Mateo, we don't see each other that way."

Lewis rolled his eyes and took a huge bite of his foot long.

I curled my lip at him.

"You're soul mates. It's supposed to happen."

"We aren't soul mates. The term means fated-friends. Friends, Mateo. That doesn't mean we'll be together every lifetime."

"I see the way he looks at you when you're not looking."

"Mateo," I growled.

Lewis took the phone. "Mateo. Give it up for now. She's got other shit to worry 'bout. You take care of them two girls for her, and we'll talk to you when we're done. When it's safe." Pause. "I know. It's not like she wanted me to get involved." Another pause, and he stopped chewing. His eyes bulged as they rose to meet mine. "I ain't tellin' her that, and you keep your nose out of it. No, I don't. I'm mindin' my own damn business, just like you should—"

Those two had meddled in my love life since I'd met them. Both romantics, both nosy, and both kind-hearted. Damn, I loved my friends.

"We'll talk about that later."

I dropped my sandwich as Lewis hung up. "Don't you dare meddle in this."

"He wants to know what Prince Quinn looks like."

"You don't know what he looks like."

"I'm bettin' I'm gonna find out real soon." He stared at me through another huge bite. Ugh, the insufferable pain!

"Fine, yes. He's—he's hot. Okay? He has this sly smile and—" I narrowed my eyes at his "gotcha smirk." "He's also a stepdad whose son's been kidnapped. It wouldn't have gone further than dinner. He was looking for...a distraction to the agony he's in."

Lewis's black-brown eyes kept watching me. I'd told him all of this before.

"I'm going to give him a chance after this is all over and Seamus is home safe."

He swallowed his food. "And you're sure Nolan's good with it?"

"I don't need his permission. But yes, we talked. About Quinn. Would you stop giving me that look? How did we even get on this subject?" I took a bite as Lewis picked the peppers from his paper. Say that five times fast.

24

"I should have taken you home first."

"And drive here on your bike—which, by the way is crappy that you hid that from me—in the freezing rain? Again? No. I'm helpin' you with this, Hally. These were my people. Or at least, I thought they were." He was right, but that didn't mean I had to like it.

I shifted in his car as we stared at TJ's shop, Electric Ink, in Issaquah. Not Everett. "Yeah, but I'm ninety-nine percent certain he's a fairy."

"So." Lewis waved his hand toward the shop from inside the car. "Doesn't mean he's working with Drake. Maybe he doesn't know, just like all your new fairy friends."

"They're not my friends." I settled down lower in my seat.

"Gonna be once you find these kids. They're gonna owe you a huge debt."

"That isn't the same thing as friendship."

His head turned away from the lights of the shop, and the whites of his eyes seemed to glow in the darkness of the car. "With you? It will be. I can see it. You're gonna like this Prince Quinn."

I covered my face. "Please stop calling him *Prince*."

"Ray and Seamus will go on playdates, just like you mentioned to Katie. Quinn and you will hit it off. Now, if Nolan is really okay with letting you go—"

"He won't be letting me go! Would you both drop it?" I think they teased me more about it than Nol, but their teasing needed to stop. "Look. If Quinn and I 'hit it off,' you need to drop the whole 'Hally and Nolan' bit. I know you like teasing me, but I don't want Quinn getting wind of it. He already asked if Nol and I were together. I made it clear to him that we are not involved and never will be."

"No. Never intend to be."

"He's leaving me in a year, Lewis!" I hiccupped, then held my breath. I'd said it out loud. "I—I need something to hold on to. The fairies might help—soothe the loss or whatever—when I lose him again. Please, please, stop. Nol isn't staying. We can't be together."

"Hally. I'm gonna ask you this, and I want you to give me a sincere and truthful answer. If Nolan stayed, would your relationship change?"

I rubbed my knuckles and tapped my lips in thought. Charlie had asked this once. "I think...I think the flirting is because we don't know how to act around each other. If he stayed, we'd level out, and we'd get used to each other again." I held my breath for a few seconds. "But he's not staying."

Lewis inhaled. "That's not—"

Then a tall, dark, and bulky guy with a huge afro walked out of the shop.

"Is that TJ? He fits your oh-so-thorough description."

"That's right. He ain't never getting rid of that afro. It's his pride and joy." Ugh. Men.

No, it wasn't midnight. Since TJ had been there in the morning, we'd taken a gamble and assumed he wouldn't stay all night long. Either TJ was taking a break or going home. Regardless, he was out of the shop.

"Is he a fairy? Can you sense him?"

"First of all, they have glamor, so I wouldn't know. Second, I don't sense people. It's the *imolegin* of magic that is detectable. Like a—"

"Stink of dog shit?"

"Excuse me?"

"You know? The shit is the magic, the eh-mol-eh-gin is the stink that wafts off it."

"I never would have considered that analogy, but that is accurate."

"So he has to do a spell for you to sense him? If he has his glamor up, can he do spells then?"

"I don't know."

"Could he hide the energy when he's under his glamor?"

"I don't know."

"You don't hafta answer every question, Hally. These are just things we need to find out. They'd be good to know, ya know? Like tonight would be good."

"What do you—"

He opened his door and stepped out while I tried to ask what he was talking about. I scrambled out as he slammed his door, catching TJ's attention.

"Lewis," I hissed. This wasn't part of the plan. He wasn't supposed to get more involved. He'd promised Yumi. I'd promised Yumi. "Fuck."

Lewis was next to him already, doing that manly handshake, shoulder-bump thing. I was still too far away, and my blood was boiling too hot for me to hear what they were saying. I jogged up in the rain, sweatshirt soaked through and hair plastered to my head. Damn it!

"Lewis Greene!" I came up and stood in front of them. Both men stared down at me, expressions blank at the small, drenched, pissed-off woman that I was. "You." I jabbed my finger at him and tried to find words that wouldn't give too much away. We needed to get him some place where we could talk. "I was still talking."

"Who are you?" TJ asked, fighting a smirk.

I shoved my hair out of my face and realized they were standing under the eave, staying dry. I stepped close to get out of the rain, but kept up my death glare. "Hally."

"Wait. *The* Hally?"

"Why does everyone keep saying that?"

They turned to each other, smirked, and looked back at me. Neither of them explained.

"Well?"

"You're Hally. The one who got idiot Ian off the street. Damn. It's nice to meet you." He held out his hand.

Not knowing how to respond, I placed my hand in his. My magic, as if it had a mind of its own, flowed down my arm and into him. Scared shitless because I'd hurt three people with my magic, including Lewis, I tried to take my hand back. TJ held on tighter. He gave me a knowing, almost-not-there smile. Fucking-A, he'd called my magic somehow. We'd do this here, then.

"Maybe you've heard of me from a different source?"

TJ's eyebrows rose, and his eyes flashed to Lewis.

"Hally? You good?" Quick to catch on, Lewis played dumb.

"I think I've seen him before. Maybe up at Avalon Winery?"

TJ rolled his eyes. "Maybe so. Haven't been out there in some time."

"Interesting. We should chat some more."

TJ tipped his head to the side in agreement. He looked at Lewis and clapped a hand on his shoulder. "Lou, my man. It's great seein' ya. I saw you got your own shop, and you inspired me to dream bigger. Beyond Tacoma. Got a fine thing goin' here. What'd you say you wanted to see me for?"

"That's just it. Ian, I mean. You heard he got himself killed?"

"So?"

"Me an' Hally been talkin'. We've been gettin' shit from that Agent Thomas, and we wanted to know if he's been harassing you, too?"

"Haven't seen him once. I'd heard Ian was in town, looking for Katie. It'd have been nice for her to let him see his kid, but Ian's an idiot. Went about it in a bad way."

We all agreed to that.

"You see, Zack-ass has been pestering us 'bout Seamus. He went missing after, you know, the incident."

"Mmm, shame, man." TJ crossed his arms and shook his head. "I dunno."

"Ian told me he had a run-in with Drake," I told TJ.

TJ inhaled and licked his lips. "He knew better than that."

"He was desperate. He attacked me twice."

TJ's eyes widened as he shook his head. "You did put him in jail."

"Meh, there're worse things I could've done."

Lewis scoffed. "Hally, you'd never hurt a fly."

I gave TJ a look to include him in my "secret."

"Is that all you wanted?" TJ asked. "I gotta get going. Food's waitin' at home. Hey, come by sometime—call first, though. It'd be good to get to know you, Hally."

"For sure. *Merci. Ravi de vous rencontrer*, TJ," *Thank you. It's nice to meet you*, TJ.

But TJ wasn't moving, even though he'd said he had to go. We moved toward Lewis's car. I slowed down and tipped my head at Lewis to make him go ahead of me. He frowned, but that's what we were here for. *Get in the car, Lewis!* My eyes said it all. As soon as Lewis grabbed the door, the rain stopped. The absence was so drastic my ears rang.

"You're not as magicless as Drake thought." A Gaelic lilt had replaced TJ's American accent.

"Is that what he really thought? Or...?" I turned.

The TJ I'd met a moment ago wasn't the TJ now in front of me. The surrounding night made it hard to distinguish his true skin tone, a possible midnight black. The afro was gone, replaced by short white hair plastered to his pointed ears and neck. His eyes were silver. He was still as big as Lewis, but without his glamor to hide behind, his bulk was pure muscle. Bodybuilder-style muscle. Not intimidating at all.

"Or what?" he hedged.

"Did you know Drake is missing?" What I really wanted to know was if he knew about his secret house of horrors, but we'd stick with the basics.

"I know a lot of things."

"Do you know about me?"

"What? That you're looking more and more like a threat?"

"Where are the kids?" I took a chance. Orlaith had said they couldn't create entrances, so he couldn't just open a portal and run away.

He tilted his head, sizing me up. Was I ready for this? I should have thought about that before opening my big mouth. TJ drew his hands together, cupping them, and pulled back. Energy built around him, and I had seconds to react. I pictured the wind and rain flowing through his little barrier and plowing into him—similar to what I'd done at the Capitol Hill house, except I had more than air and dust to play with. By the stunned look on his face, he hadn't expected my speed. No one ever did. My light orbs took longer, as I had to collect enough energy to throw at him. So I nicked that and went with something I'd done to Aswryn. Stalking up to him as he lay flat on the wet, dirty pavement, I willed my magic to flow out and coat his skin.

TJ slapped his arms, legs, chest, and neck as he felt me cover him with my magic. Then I squeezed, like cellophane tightening around a bowl. If he'd had enough air, he'd have screamed. He tried, but it came out as a mewling squeak.

"I'm not playing games, *TJ*." I spat his name. "I found the bodies at Drake's house. Either you tell me where the kids are, or I'll tighten my hold until I squeeze all the oxygen out of your lungs. Like ringing out a dishrag. Blink if you understand."

He blinked. I felt his glamor falter, and like a soap bubble, it popped. Rain pelted down, and after a moment, Lewis yelled my name.

"Two blinks for no, one for yes. Do you know where the kids are?"

One blink.

"Where?"

He hesitated, and I squeezed tighter.

"I can find others to tell me," I hissed. "My partner already has Drake in custody. My *Zayuri* partner. Trust me, you don't want him asking you."

He blinked once again.

I loosened my hold on his lungs so he could talk.

"Hidden," he wheezed out.

"No shit. Where?"

TJ didn't talk.

"TJ..." I warned.

"I can't—I can't tell you. Don't kill me, please."

"Oh, no, I'm not gonna kill you. That's no fun." I smiled, making it as ill-intending and threatening as possible. "You're going to take me to the kids if you want to keep all your body parts intact."

TJ's eyes hardened. "I'm not afraid of torture."

"Oh..." I pressed a finger to my chin. "Then let's get started." I squeezed his lungs again. "How attached are you to your magic?"

His eyes bulged and his lips opened and closed like a fish. TJ started blinking rapidly.

"What's that?" I loosened my hold once again.

"There's a house on Capitol Hill."

"I've been there. The kids were moved."

"No," he managed to squeak out. "Like I said, they're hidden. I can show you."

"Gee, that wasn't so hard, was it? Lewis!" I waved him over. "Help me get him in your car."

I picked up one of TJ's thighs while Lewis tucked his hands under TJ's shoulders. Together, we managed to drag TJ to Lewis's car and shove him into the back seat. I checked to see if we had an enraptured audience in the tattoo shop, but no one was looking. Not one soul had witnessed the abduction of their friend. What a pity. We scrambled into the car. Before I even had my seatbelt on, I was tightening my magic around TJ again.

"What'd you do?" Lewis asked as he started the car.

"Same thing I did to Aswryn."

He didn't say anything. Wait, I'd done several things to Aswryn.

"Oh, I mean, I have him held tight. Enough to breathe, but nothing more. Take us to Capitol Hill." Once I was done, I had the perfect place to put this fucker. And I didn't care if he was too big for that little room. I would make him fit.

25

"Can't you just wave your hand and float him in? There's nobody around."

We paused, staring down at TJ lying in Lewis's back seat. "I can try." *Endai* had a traditional spell that helped float things, or more like made things light so we could maneuver them around. It was related to the calling spell, but it required—

"Hey, you good?"

I shook my memories out of my head. "Yeah. Lost in thought." At first, I pictured my magic as hands lifting him and pulling him out of the car. It didn't work. What did I want it to do? I pictured TJ floating in mid-air. Now, how would that be accomplished with magic? With my magic? I wanted TJ out of the car—

"Holy fuck!" Lewis yelled.

"Shhh!" I smacked Lewis's arm as I maneuvered TJ. He only hit his shoulder on the door twice. "Grab his arms and pretend like you're holding him. I don't know how long I can keep this up before my band starts sucking energy out of me."

"You still haven't told Nolan it does that, huh?"

"Nope. It'll freak him out. He's already upset that it's on me. Now shut up and take his arms."

We parked on the same side of the street as the house, so it didn't take long to bring him into the crappy yard. But as we reached the steps, I felt the band pull. I stopped and focused. Holding on to both spells wouldn't be possible for much longer.

"Lewis, we need to carry him." I caught his legs at the last word. TJ's ass hit the cement, but Lewis held his upper body. I walked up the steps backward and almost tripped on the top step. I flung the door open, the wimpy lock was no match for my magic—I doubted it'd be much match for anything, really. We cleared the door as TJ slipped out of my fingers and his head slammed into the floor.

TJ's head hit the floor. "Oops." Lewis didn't look that guilty for dropping him when I did.

A moan escaped the fairy as he lay there, incapacitated by my spell. If only we had some of Nol's magical cuffs.

"Careful, Lewis. I know you can't see as well as me in the dark. There's a large hole on your side of the living room."

"What d'ya do? Knock the floor out from under them?" he teased.

"Yes. When asshole fairy number two got here, I ripped the floor out from under him so Nol could keep fighting fairy asshole number one."

"Ah, right." Lewis leaned over TJ. "So, don't fuck with Hally."

"Pretty much." I shrugged and conjured up a few light globes, but I stayed conscious of how much energy I was using. Always conscious. Three floating globes and a spell on TJ were about all I could handle. I loosened my magic around TJ's shoulders and upper chest and let him catch his breath. Three minutes later, according to my phone, I stepped up to his head and stood over him.

"Are you ready to talk, TJ?"

He blinked once.

"You can talk."

He looked off to the side, like he'd just realized he'd been breathing normally for the last three minutes. A real winner here. "What the fuck are you?"

"An elf? I thought you knew that."

"Not like one I've ever met."

The elves that he'd met? Like the victims on the cots I'd found last night. I didn't ask if there were more or what he meant. He couldn't know just how little information I knew.

"I'm not like other elves." I pressed my fingertips to my chest. "Why do you think Aswryn wanted me?"

TJ paused, debating if it was a trick question. "'Cause you're powerful?"

"Did she not explain the rest to you? I'm offended. I spent decades over here and that's all I get? Sad." I tsked.

"You're fucking psycho."

"No, dear. Aswryn's the psycho." I sighed. "Where are the kids, TJ?"

TJ lifted his chin, his eyes roaming what he could see from his position. "Go look for 'em."

I gave him a blank stare, but after a twenty-second pause, I pursed my lips and stood up straight. My neck was getting a kink anyway. "What would Queen Orlaith do to you if she found out about the little group you have going with Aswryn? That Drake and his lackeys"—I pointed to him—"have been lying to her for years?"

"She is part of the problem."

Here we went, another political drama.

"Do elaborate. I'm not up to date with fairy politics."

"It's not politics, girl. Orlaith and her family are descendants of Anu and Bilé"

"We all are. Meabhlaire's little swimmers can't swim without lifejackets." I included the *endai*, as Quinn had said we were part of the fae, plus I wanted to see how TJ would react.

TJ's lip curled as he squinted in disgust. How dare I mock his Meabhlaire. Or was it the *endai* issue? Please.

"When Meabhlaire is freed, he will rise above and reveal Anu and Bilé as the liars and deceivers they are—"

I covered a fake, loud yawn. "That's where you're wrong." I patted his shoulder. "Meabhlaire doesn't give a shit about Anu's children. You let him out, and he'll stomp on your puny black heart and take your magic from you."

"Not true."

"And you know this because? Did he tell you himself? Wouldn't you be a bit pissed about being trapped for eons? Your little fan club will get squashed if you even try. Besides, who are you to think you can undo anything Anu has done?" Phew. That pissed him off enough, which was good, because that was the extent of my knowledge. Thank you, Quinn.

"Wrong, elf! He will come for you first. The elves turned the natural world against him and erased him from your history." He paused, catching my expression. "You didn't know that, did you?"

"We didn't discuss about the losers in our history lessons, but that's not what we're here for, anyway." But internally I was reeling. Meabhlaire's power? We'd stolen it? How much of that was true? I felt the furthest away from the Mother than ever before. "Where're the kids? I have no doubt there are more than the ones Drake gave up in this powerless little cult of yours."

"It's not a cult. Meabhlaire will be rescued."

"Right."

"Aswryn was doing it, you know? The more power she drained from the elves, the more power Meabhlaire gained back."

What the fuck?

"Even now, that curse?" He smiled, seeing the fear in my eyes. "You thought killing Aswryn would end it, but you assumed wrong. All of you did."

"Where are the children, TJ?" I asked.

"Aswryn just designed the curse. There is no way you can break it."

I scoffed. "Your curse is useless."

"Then why is Meabhlaire still gaining power?"

I was going to be sick. "You sack of shit. Tell me where the children are."

He laughed, a small one but condescending as hell. "Open your eyes, girl. Where do you think we are?"

"I know they were moved, dipshit." I glanced deeper into the house.

TJ raised his eyebrows and shook his head, like I was some gullible idiot. It was exactly how I felt. "Were they?"

"I—" My voice faltered. "There's nothing down there."

"Just like you saw Drake was fae?"

"That isn't fair." I shook my finger. "I didn't have my magic then."

"What's your excuse now? You couldn't see through my glamor. You walked right past those kids and left them."

"Liar. There's nothing down there."

"Want me to prove it? Take me to the basement. I'll lower the veil."

"The veil is here, too?" I said before I could think better of letting my cluelessness slip.

"Faerie is everywhere. You just need to know how to lower the veil."

From what I'd read in stories and seen in movies, Faerie wasn't a place to be trifled with—if they were true. What were the rules? No eating food there, stay on a path (whatever that meant), and some other thing. Something told me all those rules were just to keep people out.

"Fine."

"Hally?" Lewis cautioned. "Don't trust him."

"I don't, but I also think he's talking out his ass when he says the kids are still in the house."

"Oh, no, I didn't say they're in the house."

A flash from my imagination: the kids dead and buried beside the tunnel Nol had found. *Please. Please, don't let that be it.*

"Show me." Like a rubber glove, I slid my magic down his body until the only place I still held onto was his torso, where an *enda's gin* organ would be. I didn't know if fairies had organs that converted nutrients into magical energy for them to use, but crushing any organ wasn't good. "One wrong move and kiss your magic goodbye. I did it to Aswryn, and I did it to myself. I can do it to you, too."

TJ pulled himself off the floor and paused, orienting himself now that he was free of my binding. Mostly.

"You really did that? I heard a rumor, but seriously?"

"Yes. I closed off each and every one of her *gin* cells until no magic could flow through her body. It's a painful process, so don't fuck with me."

"How'd you get yours back?"

"Painfully. Now move."

TJ led us around into the kitchen and down the basement stairs. I drifted my three orbs in front of us as we descended. Both guys had a hard time walking down the old wooden steps. Their feet were twice as long as the steps were deep. Lewis hit his head, first on the nonfunctioning lightbulb on a string, then again on a beam as we descended. TJ whacked his head pretty good on ceiling, when he straightened to his full height too early. It could have been that my light was blinding him or something else. We'd never know. Wood and dirt and asbestos-filled insulation covered the floor. Should we have worn masks? I'd inhaled a lot of that the first time.

"Lewis, you wanna wait upstairs? There isn't a lot of room, and this shit is toxic."

"Not a chance, Hally."

Irritated and imagining what Yumi would say if Lewis got a splinter, let alone asbestos in his lungs, I used my magic to push the debris to the edge of the room near fairy number two's dent in the wall. My globes blinked out as I went over that threshold and the band siphoned energy. Thinking he had a chance because my orbs had snuffed out, TJ turned and rammed me against the wall at the base of the stairs. My orbs popped into existence. TJ's forearm pressed into my throat, but Lewis's face was right there when the orbs blinked into existence again.

"What the fuck you doin'? You heard her. One toe out of line and your magic is gone."

TJ loosened his grip, insecure in his decision now.

Lewis punched the guy in the side of his head. "That means let go of my friend. Damn, ain't you smarter than Ian?"

"That's what I thought," I answered, voice husky from having my windpipe crushed. "Fucking-A, TJ."

TJ had backed up, his eyes widening as he rubbed his jaw where Lewis had hit him. He watched me, preparing for me to snap or wiggle my nose to take his magic away. Poof? Gone? No, I needed the loser still.

"There's nothing here. The tunnel is empty except for a few pieces of clothing. Where are the kids, TJ?"

The fairy pursed his lips and cocked his head. His hand went up, and as if grabbing a curtain, he pulled it to the side.

Silence.

A warehouse sized cavernous space lay before us, with the damp smell of earth and plants and the steady underground temperature. Spots of purple, pink, green, and yellow light floated around in the air like colorful fireflies. On second thought...one flew up to me, buzzing in my face. It was a fairy firefly. Interesting.

"Go on. They're in there."

I scoffed. Did he think I was *that* dumb? "You first." Like I'd trust a place like this not to have booby traps. With a magical place, assume magical threats.

TJ groaned, then walked through the basement, past the debris, into the entrance. I sent my orbs floating ahead of TJ and followed two of his body lengths apart. Lewis bumped into me as I slowed to give the fairy more space.

"Lewis, seriously. You need to stay here, on this side of the veil."

"No." He glanced over my head to where TJ stood.

"We know nothing about Faerie except what's in children's books. At least I have a chance to protect myself with magic. You're human. Please, stay here? Go to the car and wait. Guard my back? Keep your promise to Yumi and don't make me break mine?"

That last one did it. Lewis grumbled but stepped back. "Low."

I set my hands on my hips. "Yes, but it's a fact."

"You better come back out."

"Duh. Who'd schedule your appointments?"

He lifted his chin, and his lip stuck out a little. "I've been doin' fine these past weeks without you."

"Sure. Do I need to go back to last week's phone call?" He'd messed up the dates for two clients because he never wrote anything down. Needless to say, I lined it all up for him and smoothed it out over on the phone. Lewis still had the clients. Peachy keen.

Lewis pointed at me, but then he swallowed and his eyes softened.

"I'll come back, Lewis. Have that car ready." We would need to pile in a group of kids and quite possibly drive them to a fairy hospital.

Lewis tipped his chin toward TJ. Several meters into the space, TJ had stopped to watch us.

"Good idea, leaving the human behind."

"Shut the fuck up. Give me a reason why I shouldn't snuff out your magic like I did Aswryn's." I snapped my finger, and he jumped. My orbs floated ahead and kept going. I stopped them before the light was useless to us. We walked toward an arched opening that led to another dark space. "What's up there?"

"Faerie." He kept walking and I thought about smacking the back of his head. If only I were that tall.

"No shit? What's ahead?"

"We'll have to wait and see. Faerie likes to change."

"Really? That's what you're going with?"

TJ stopped moving and turned, shrugging like I was annoying him. "It's a living thing and has a mind of its own."

"What are you talking about?"

"Do you think Aswryn's curse was about nothing? Everything has a purpose in Faerie. Ebb and flow." Did that mean Meabhlaire was trapped in Faerie?

TJ turned to the left and disappeared.

"TJ? Fuck." I sped up, prepared to face a wall of skin and muscle if he came at me. No one was there. I spun around and faced a wall instead of the entrance to Faerie. Oh, fuck me.

I couldn't risk closing my eyes to focus on my proximity to TJ, to whom I still held that connection. He was there, somewhere. I felt him, or my magic in him, behind his glamor. "I can feel you, TJ. Torture isn't my thing, but if you leave me no alternative, I'll do it."

To prove my point, I willed that magic-like glove to compress his organs. He grunted to my right. Close. But it was only a wall. Like platform nine and three-quarters, I took a running start and rammed my shoulder into a doubled-over TJ and not a wall.

"I said," I panted, "don't fuck with me." I squeezed that organ once more and made him hiss. He wouldn't do well with menstrual cramps. I didn't do well with them. And humans had one every month. No thanks.

Wincing, he turned to guide me down a path. I could feel a breeze on my cheeks from both directions, but when I reached out, I felt the wall of earth I saw there.

"Faerie is believing more than seeing. You won't find anything if you don't trust your senses."

"I trust my senses just fine."

We pushed on ahead. The breeze blew against us harder. Was Faerie mad that I was here?

"Did Meabhlaire create Faerie?" I asked.

"Along with Anu, yes. Elves are foreign to this place. Looks like it doesn't agree with you."

"Like hell any natural thing will agree with you and your unnatural gang of misfits."

"We stand for Meabhlaire. He isn't unnatural."

"Yippie for Meabhlaire."

My orbs went out, and my connection with TJ closed. For one second, I thought my magic was gone again, but then I sensed it in my core. TJ laughed from twice the distance away than before, and all I could see and feel was blackness in front, behind, and at my sides. Was I in a box? A hole? But I could still feel the wind. I closed my eyes and focused. If TJ were to strike, now would be the time.

"Help me," I whispered to Faerie. If it was alive, I had to believe it wouldn't be thrilled with Drake's group using it to hide and torture kids. "I want to help the children. Nothing more. Let me take the children home."

The wind sped up, beating my hair against my head. My necklace chain hit my chin. The wind battered at my clothing, pushing, pulling, but never knocking me down. Then it settled back into a breeze. Something touched my nose, not like Nol's taps, but...I opened my eyes to find a fairy firefly on my nose. TJ was nowhere in sight, nor was the tunnel, the house, or any structure. A field of purple heather at twilight appeared ahead of me. Small animals and insects scurried through the leaves and air. A path in the heather led up to a curve, but before that stood a stone, taller than me but narrower, almost a pole. I walked up and placed my hand on the pitted, weathered surface warm as a sun-heated stone.

"*You seek the children, elf?*"

"I do, and only those victims taken by Aswryn and her conspirators."

"*Will you leave here again?*" Why did it feel so sad?

"Do you want me to leave?"

It—Faerie—didn't answer.

I closed my eyes and pressed my cheek against the warm rock face."Faerie? Will you aid me? I seek to do no harm."

"*But you will leave again.*"

Somehow, I didn't think it was referring to this place exactly. "If I don't bring Queen Orlaith the victims, she will send me to *Endae*."

Up the path materialized a dome of natural clay or dirt.

"*Take them.*"

26

A dozen people, some youngsters—I couldn't see Seamus—some older, in their late second century at least, huddled in the hut, about the size of the tent Mateo and Sam were considering renting for their wedding. The children all seemed relatively unharmed. We were just in a place separate from space and time. How would I get them home? Faerie trusted me to help the children, and I'd have to trust it to get us out. I walked right up to two people at the table. They appeared to be the oldest.

"My name is Hallanevaë, and I've come to take you all home."

"We're not safe outside these walls," the female said, her eyes a golden brown, her skin as white as printer paper. The other one, the male, had the lightest green eyes I'd ever seen and skin the color of the Arizona mountains.

"Where are your captors?"

The two older children frowned up at me.

One smaller girl came up and tugged on my shirt. "You can stay with me."

She brought me to her spot across the naturally carved-out room and leaned against my side as we looked around. Ten children of the twelve from Zack's photos were here.

The image of the table flickered, replaced by a different table and different fairies. These, no one would mistake as children. When they noticed I'd seen through their glamor, they stood together and walked toward me. The little girl was gone. Each light winked out of existence. I jumped up, ready for anything—at least that's what I told myself.

The female reached me first and took a swing. I dodged her fist, just to smack into the male, who shoved me to the floor. No way would I let them, or anyone, beat me like Aswryn had beaten me. I scrambled up and raised my hands.

"You should have left things as they were, elf."

"You left me no choice, bitch." I threw an orb at her, but it didn't have much energy built up. Instead, I'd meant it as a distraction in order to knock them both flat. My second move, using air to throw them backward, didn't work. Their bodies disintegrated, then re-formed.

"*Lie!*"

The mental voice of Faerie shattered my eardrums and dropped me to the floor.

The two fairies, not as tall or bulky as TJ, but over six feet tall, dropped to the floor as well. The sienna one, now as green as pine needles, and the other one, as brown as its bark, stood barring my way inside. Both had maroon eyes—not evil, just red. They had me in a corner and would take me down any second. Maybe Nol's focusing tool wasn't such a bad idea if we were going to keep getting into violent situations.

"I won't hurt them if they don't attack me," I whispered.

"*That is not what you said. Liar.*"

"It was...an oversight."

"Who are you talking to, elf?"

I ignored them, waiting for Faerie's response. When Faerie didn't respond, I knew it didn't believe me. These were all Faerie's children. If *endai* were a race of the fae, maybe it didn't want us fighting.

"Just let the children go. Drake has been captured. It's over."

The two fairies looked at each other, then laughed. They spoke to each other in the ancient Gaelic language.

"If you're trying to decide which spices I taste best with, it's pepper and thyme." I ran straight at them. Using no magic to hurt them, I grabbed two handfuls of earth and tossed them in their faces. Nothing magical about it, and nothing stopped it. Both fae rubbed at their eyes, and I ran, looking for the kids, while they were distracted. But the place was empty.

"I can't bring down their entire enterprise today, but," I whispered into the air, "my friend and I are willing to help."

"No magic shall be involved."

Oh, I was back to fending for myself, but I had one advantage: I was used to working without magic. They weren't. My back and forth with Faerie lasted less than a few seconds, because the next moment, the two fairies were racing toward me from opposite directions.

"Shit." I jumped to the side, but not in the best position to avoid the two.

One grabbed my ankle, the other grabbed my cast, and together they pulled me back to a corner. I relaxed and stopped fighting, giving them dead weight to deal with. Would Faerie be upset if I hit them the old-fashioned way? I'd have to try. They dropped me to the floor.

The female came close to me first, grabbed my uninjured wrist, and yanked it back behind me. Instead of waiting, I spun with it, just past her, then spun back until my cast-laden arm collided with her face. Dazed, she dropped onto her knees and shook her head violently as she tried to get her bearings. The male fairy moved around her, his arms stretched, ready to incapacitate me.

How could I stop these two? Lead them off in a different direction and run back to get the kids out? That was too short term. They'd just go get other fae to experiment on. If Faerie wanted me to stop them, I needed to start now. But how?

The male took a step closer to me, and I rolled away to stand up, a good eight feet away. The female followed close behind him. I did a running jump and went for his jugular. There was no way I could get his face. My left fist connected with the side of his neck. He stepped back, holding his neck. I had no doubt they knew how to fight, but by the looks of it, they weren't used to such a small person fighting back. My self-defense classes over the years had paid off.

The female lunged at me and grabbed my arm, but I moved in instead of out, and her hold on me didn't work. I used her weight against her as she became unbalanced by my move. My foot just happened to be in the way, and she fell flat on her back. Large people fall hard, and she was no different.

Her counterpart stepped forward just as she fell. He snatched my hair at the base of my skull, and a knee-jerk reaction had me sinking my nails into the back of his hand. His friend started to get up at the same time I stepped forward with my huge fairy hair accessory. I hopped over, and he tripped over his partner. He released my hair to save himself, but they both went down in a heap. I cartwheeled forward but managed to save myself from falling flat on my face. The two were already untangling themselves as I righted myself. I couldn't keep this up much longer.

"If you don't want me using magic, you need to help me out a little," I whispered to Faerie.

It didn't answer.

They weren't using magic either. It didn't want us using magic against each other, like a parent staying neutral while their kids figured things out—with boundaries. "Don't you see? Faerie doesn't want us to fight. It led me here to bring the children home."

"Faerie doesn't see things the way breathing beings do."

"It asked me if I was here to take them home and brought me here. That's pretty straightforward. Let them go."

"They're needed."

"For what?"

They didn't answer. Instead, the female threw out her arm, and a second later, I was soaring. I slid backward, my fingers sliding against...dirt? A strong wind came out of nowhere, shoving them to the ground as well. The scene had changed again. We were outside the dome, purple heather all around us. They'd fallen into large bushes and were tangled in the scratchy branches, purple petals falling on them. They struggled to get up. Then the branches started to move, encircling them and holding them in place.

It was helping me! I wouldn't gloat. The more the two struggled, the more branches held them, as if the bushes were growing, until their bodies were mostly hidden.

"Please keep them there, and I'll have someone retrieve them safely. I promise."

The wind died down, and the colorful fireflies appeared and swarmed them. Their screams stopped, their bodies settled, and they stopped fighting. Um...Faerie hadn't just killed them, right? I'd have to trust it.

I'd bring the *Zayuri* here after the children were safe—if we could get out. The wall that had closed off the arch gave me pause. What if we couldn't get out? No time for doubts now.

This time, when I entered, two older children stood up from their cots. There were ten children, all in different states of dress and capacity. I wanted to run over to the little guy facing away from me and see if he was Seamus, but two were walking toward me.

"Where did you come from?" the girl asked. Her hair could have been blond when it was clean. The locks that weren't matted into dreadlocks were curly. Her eyes were hazel, almost human but wider, and they seemed to glow under the color. Not a light, just...a glow. She wore what might have been a sleeping gown, but it was threadbare and ripped.

"What are you?" the boy asked. He, too, had dirty hair, blood red and caked with dirt. The parts that weren't bunched together went down to his shoulders.

"I'm Hallanevaë. Queen Orlaith sent me to find you. Are you well enough to help me gather the others? Do you know a way out of Faerie?"

"Faerie does as it wishes," the girl told me. "We are able-bodied. Can you prove Her Majesty sent you?"

"It's not like she gave me a shiny badge to wave around. Faerie guided me here. That will have to be enough. Do you have your magic?"

"They...suppressed ours." The boy looked away, swallowing hard.

"I have mine," a girl with blue and teal hair said as she walked into the light from the entrance.

"What's your name?" The girl couldn't be much younger than these two. "What are all your names?" Something told me they hadn't been able to share that in a while. It was about time someone started treating them like people.

"Marianna. I'm a water fairy, so it doesn't do much good in this dry area. That's why they weren't too worried about suppressing mine."

"I'm Patch," the red-haired boy told me. The three leaned in as if no one had talked to them in a long time—or believed what they had to say mattered.

"My name is Siobhan," the one with dirty blond hair told me.

"How long have you been here?"

"They took me from my home in nineteen ninety-three," Siobhan said.

I cussed under my breath. I didn't want to say it, but I had to. "It's two thousand twelve."

Siobhan's eyes brimmed with tears, but they didn't fall. A tough one, a survivor.

"They took me in two thousand five," Patch said. "I just want to go home. Do you have a way to get us out of here?"

"We have to walk out."

Marianna stepped up beside Patch. "A few of them can't walk. Molly's sick, and they beat Maneya three days ago in front of us when she tried to escape again. I think she has internal bleeding, but without water, I can't be certain."

"The little one back there." Patch pointed. "They gave him a potion not too long ago. It takes a few weeks to recover from that."

I acknowledge them with a nod. "Are you a healer, Marianna?"

"I have those qualities, but I'm not medically trained."

"It'll have to do. Is there anything we can use to transport the weakest ones on?"

The three fairies stared at each other, clueless.

"There are three in the corner—like you," Siobhan said. She pointed at a heap of kids lying ten feet away from us against the wall.

More *endai*? Why wasn't I surprised? How many had Aswryn taken? Nol had said he'd completed a few missing children missions. But there was no telling how many missions there had been besides his.

"They don't speak any language we know, and their ears are different. Like yours."

I nodded to show Siobhan I understood. "Would you take me around and introduce me?"

"Do you speak their language?"

I looked at the three she was referring to. "We'll have to find out."

"They treat them differently," Siobhan explained as we walked over.

"How so?"

She shrugged one shoulder. "At least they look us in the eyes."

"*Esamia*," I greeted the oldest, an *endao* around the same age as me. He held the littlest one against him while the third one, the one facing away from me, lay on her back.

Of course, they were all *Aeminan*. Aswryn was trying to decimate our country.

He licked his lips, looked at Siobhan, then back to me. His Caribbean blue eyes held thousands of questions.

"Are you well enough to walk?" I asked him quietly.

At first, his brow furrowed as he wondered how he could understand me. "Who are you?" he rasped.

"An *enda*. I'll explain later, when we have time to let our differences divide us. Right now, I need to know if you can help this little one. Are you well?"

He held his breath for a second, then looked at the *endaë* beside him. "We are all untainted by the curse, if that's what you mean. This is my brother, and my cousin…she won't make it." His brother couldn't have been over two decades old. Why would they take such little ones?

"What are your names?"

The *endao* set his jaw and didn't answer. If I wouldn't tell him mine, he wouldn't offer any of theirs.

"Hally." I made sure to emphasize the "a" and "y" the American way to make it less identifiable, which seemed to work.

"I'm Lalis, my brother is Aleanis, and my cousin is Maneya."

"We'll get you all out of here, Lalis." By his look, I didn't think he believed me. I walked around and crouched to be at eye level with Maneya, the girl they'd beaten three days ago. I doubted she was any older than I was when I was banished. "Maneya? Can you look at me?"

Her swollen face contorted until she could lift her eyes enough to reach mine.

"I've come to take you all out of here. I don't want to leave anyone behind. Can you hang on a little longer until we can get you to a healer?"

She took a deep, labored breath and looked back down at her cot.

I looked above Maneya and met Lalis's calculating stare. "I'll be back. I'm going to check on the other…kids." I'd almost said victims, but they were victims no longer.

"You know their language. What are you?" Siobhan asked.

"Isn't that a bit rude to ask?"

"You're the same as Aswryn."

"No." I stopped in the middle of the large hut where the light was brightest. "We are not the same."

"The same species."

"I know what you meant…" I heaved and got myself under control. "Yes, the same species. Don't ever compare her to us again. She was a foul person with no empathy."

"Was?"

I nodded but didn't elaborate. Siobhan's lip quivered, but this time I knew it was from relief. Seamus was asleep, level breathing, a little labored but not as much as Maneya's. With an unsteady hand, I reached out and gently shook his shoulder. I'd found him, so simply, and I couldn't break down or shout in joy. I had to be calm and collected. "Seamus?" He didn't move, so I tried again. If Patch was right, he was pretty out of it. "Seamus?" I shook again.

Seamus grumbled something and opened his eyes. When he saw an adult looking back down at him, he started crying. Rightly so. These people had taken away all their trust. Siobhan sat beside me, laying a hand on his hip so Seamus could see us both.

"Seamus? We're going home." She had to say it twice more before he registered her words.

His hand lowered away from his face, and their eyes met. When Siobhan didn't waver, when no other fairy appeared in front of him, he lowered his hands all the way with a hiccupped cry.

"Hey, Seamus. Do you remember me? You came to my shop. I knew you when you were a baby. I'm your mommy's friend. Remember?"

With another hiccup, he turned to assess me.

"Your daddy's waiting for you at home," I assured him, knowing he'd think of Quinn and not Ian.

"I want Mommy." His lip quivered. Ian had killed her in front of him. He had that hollow look that only someone who'd seen death could have.

"I know, baby. We all do. But right now, we have to be big and strong to get out of here and back home. Do you think you can be a big boy?"

He started to cry again, curling up into himself.

We walked away, and Siobhan crossed her arms. "You didn't tell us you knew him."

"I wasn't sure if it was him. I didn't want to get too excited."

"He'll have to walk," she said.

"He's three. He shouldn't be doing any of the things he does. Aleanis is just as little," I pointed out the obvious.

There were three other fairies. Most of them were able to walk. Like Patch had said, Molly couldn't. Her injuries weren't as obvious as Maneya's, but by the dullness of her eyes and the pallor of her skin, she wouldn't be moving on her own for some time. We walked back to Marianna and Patch, who were brainstorming ideas.

"I need to know, before we leave, are there any more of you? There's another boy I'm looking for. Derrick?"

"He's gone," Siobhan said, her emotions buried deep. "I mean—they took him away years ago, before Patch got here. I haven't heard his name in a long time."

"Faerie guided me here to take you home," I explained to the whole group. "Queen Orlaith has tasked my friend and me with rescuing you."

"Why you?" Patch asked after I'd translated for the *endai* children.

"My friend...he's part of an honorable league of...warriors. A *Zayuri*."

"Are you Hallanevaë? The one who killed her friends?" Lalis scowled at me, instant judgment. He was the sort who thought I was the worst person in the world—the majority of *Aemina*.

"I am all that you have right now, Lalis. You can stay in this hole if you don't want to be near me, but your brother and your cousin will come with me. Nol has Drake, and Aswryn is gone. Tolwe and other *Zayuri* are in this realm, and they can bring you home."

"Why should I believe you?" he spat.

I shrugged. "You don't have to believe me, but I am the only one offering a way out of here."

"I've never heard of *Zayuri*," Siobhan said after an awkward moment of Lalis's silent glaring.

"They're...they're elves." I kept going even when Patch tried to interrupt. "Three weeks ago, my friend, Nolan, found and killed Aswryn. That's why you haven't seen her."

"That's why the others have been scarce," Siobhan said, putting the pieces together.

"Elves aren't allowed here," Marianna said.

"No," I agreed. "But things changed when Aswryn came here."

"Drake is in charge of our detainment. Aswryn just complains that he doesn't bring more of us and that we don't give her the results she wants—wanted."

"Okay, well, we still need to get you out of here. The question is what to do with those two out there."

"Break their necks?" Patch said without hesitation.

"I don't think Faerie would like that. Plus, they don't deserve such an easy way out. Death isn't a punishment, Patch. It's a release. They need to suffer and see their failure."

Patch stepped back from where he stood by the table when he realized I didn't mean throwing them in a jail cell and letting them rot. Nope. These guys? I hoped they got a lot worse from Orlaith. And I didn't give one shit if that made me a bad person.

"If there's any chance of saving Molly and Maneya, we need to find the fastest exit. Faerie brought me right to you as soon as TJ guided me out of the...tunnel thing."

"TJ has less empathy than Aswryn," Marianna said.

"He's the one who beat Maneya three days ago for no reason. TJ knows Faerie, how to reason with it. He's not lost."

"He's waiting for us to come back," Patch added for her as Marianna lost control of her voice. Siobhan wrapped her arms around her when Marianna reached for her. "But he can open the veil."

"Wait, not just any fairy can open one?"

They shook their heads and looked around at each other.

"Okay. Would Faerie be able to?"

"You can't reason with Faerie, Hally."

"I refuse to believe we're stuck here. Faerie sent me to you. I'm trusting Faerie now." I looked around the room. Time to do this. "What are we going to use?"

"What about the table?" Patch pointed to the real table in the corner, not the one the adults had glamored.

"The table is too heavy," Siobhan said.

"We can use a cot." I knew what they were all thinking. Why hadn't I thought of this beforehand and brought something? "This wasn't planned, okay?"

They all looked up with varying emotions. "The moment I learned that TJ knew where you were, I made him take me immediately, so you'll all have to chip in. I'm asking you to help me help yourselves and get out together."

"You said your friend is a warrior?" Siobhan asked.

"Yes."

"You're not?"

"No, but I have skills no other of my kind has, and I'll use them against TJ if I have to. No matter what Faerie wants." Whether or not it understood, there was no way I could take TJ down without magic.

"Let's get Molly and Maneya on one cot. Maneya," I switched to *Aemirin*. "Do you think you can sit up?"

She didn't say anything to me, but Lalis whispered something and helped her while Aleanis got out of his brother's lap and watched them. The three *endai* were just as dirty as the rest of them. Did they ever let them bathe? How was Aswryn supposed to get clean results without clean specimens?

"She'll try, but the beating broke her collarbone and arm, and her neck is hurt as well." Lalis almost let go of Maneya when she cried out.

"We just need enough room to put Molly on."

Lalis nodded and tucked his cousin's feet under her to scoot her to the end. As he and Marianna got the girls situated, Patch, Siobhan, and I studied the cot. Depending on how much energy it took to lift the cot, the band could siphon my magic out and I'd fail them.

"Do you think you can manage a *majeta* spell, or will you butcher it like you did your friends?" Lalis walked up to me, his arms crossed and his eyes full of judgment.

I ground my teeth until I could speak in a level tone. "How is it that everyone seems to think they know what happened when *no one* is supposed to even speak my name? You know nothing about me, what happened, or what I can do. And right now, you need to back up, because I'm here saving your ass."

He scoffed. "Why can't you just be content with straightforward spells? You have to prove yourself, the all-powerful Hallanevaë."

I didn't need to explain myself to him. "The offer still stands, Lalis. You can stay and wait. Please say you will."

Lalis glared at me, but said nothing.

"You're just as closed-minded as the rest of them. Just do your part and I'll do mine."

He didn't respond with a snide remark, and when I looked over at him, his contorted, angry face was blank.

Shit. "How weakened are you?"

He stopped staring at the other kids, looking away into the darkened hut instead. "They haven't let us use magic since they took us."

"We'll get you back. Tolwe and Nol are in this realm, along with a few other *Zayuri*."

"Where are they, then?"

"Saving other children."

Lalis tilted his head in confusion, but I didn't give him anything else. No, he'd pissed me off.

27

Lalis didn't grumble, and I didn't ask him for help with his traditional *majeta* spell. Let him think I'd cursed the damn cot. Now that I wasn't holding TJ paralyzed, I managed without the band drawing energy away. Faerie wasn't making our exit as simple as my entrance. There was no telling how long we'd been walking. It felt like hours, but the sun hadn't moved from its spot far on the horizon.

Someone touched my fingers. I jumped and turned, finding Lalis, his face grave but apologetic, reaching over from his corner beside me.

"*Vesla uto gudinar*," *You need to rest*, Lalis said quietly, even though the only two others who spoke *Aemirin* were behind us. "I doubt you can hold a spell much longer."

Faerie hadn't spoken to me since we'd left the hut, even though I hadn't used magic like it had said, nor had I killed them, which was my personal line never to cross. Nope, they were back next to the hut. I was putting a lot of trust in an entity I'd never dealt with, communicated with, or even known was real before.

"We need to keep going." This whole place was one never-ending purple field—or seemed to be. Faerie had sent me to this field; I hadn't walked to it. Nothing seemed to change, even the distance from the curve in the path ahead of us. Was Faerie hinting at something? "Stop." I lowered the cot. "Is it just me, or are we no closer to that curve in the road than before? Why would Faerie keep us on this path if it didn't want us to go farther?"

"Faerie doesn't think like us."

"I've heard that before, but why doesn't it show us what it wants?" I grumbled. "It seems like it wants us to go back toward the hut."

"We should go back the way we came and see if Faerie leads us somewhere else," Siobhan suggested, looking back the way we had been traveling.

"What about the woods over there?" Sera, a three-foot-nothing, white-haired wisp of a girl, pointed behind me. Patch and Siobhan, who'd been looking ahead as if they could see TJ, whipped around.

Sure enough, in the distance toward the "setting" sun, a forest waited in the distance.

"That wasn't there before," I told everyone like they didn't already know. "Do we go off the trail?"

"No!" Patch barked. "Always follow the path. Let's go back the way we came. It will show us why the forest was revealed to us when it's ready."

"I'm tired," the quietest, least complaining fairy announced. "Can we wait a few minutes?"

"Nate, we're all tired, but we can't stop here," Marianna said.

"Why? Will Faerie swallow us?" I almost rolled my eyes. Why would it do that if it wanted the children safe?

"It might, or it could forget we're out here. There's no telling."

We'd keep going then. As I lifted the cot again, I felt the band pull. "Shit," I called out just before I let it go, a foot above the ground. I looked at Lalis and conceded, "I can't—I need a break. I'm sorry."

"You held that spell for hours," Siobhan said. "We get it. Patch, Marianna—grab a corner." Siobhan pointed to Lalis, then to the fourth corner closest to me.

I was tired, hungry, and thirsty, just like the rest of them. I caught movement beside me. Lalis was casting the *majeta* spell, but he wouldn't be able to hold it long. That was on him, though. We headed back toward the hut. I took another look at the forest, now to my right. The sun was above the treetops. Hadn't it been below them before?

"*C'yo!* Hally."

My head snapped around when Lalis cussed. The path was moving, veering off to the right—and into the trees. The freakiest thing in the world.

"This is crazy," I muttered, but followed the path.

Lalis nodded. "Can we truly trust this place?"

"*Sye voida sitam*," *I don't know.* "But there's nothing else we can do."

"The path is dividing!" Patch called out.

Dividing? Wasn't it moving? Sure enough, when I looked to my left, the other path was there, even though moments ago, it had been moving directions. It didn't matter. "Follow the divergence. There's something Faerie is trying to tell us," I said.

"You're sure? Is this the way you came?" Lalis asked.

"No, but the others say you can't fully trust Faerie. It has a will of its own. But it brought me to you, so I'm going to use it to get you to safety."

"I think Faerie is just messing with us," Patch growled, not at me but at the situation, or maybe he was hungry. The boy was sixteen. When was the last time these kids ate?

"How long have you been here?" I asked Lalis. I couldn't speak both languages at the same time, and talking to the other kids seemed to upset them. Lalis was old enough to see things objectively, I hoped.

"I don't know. The dome appeared soon after the little boy came. It would only let those two fairies come in. Did Faerie make the dome?"

"Yes. Like I said, it doesn't like what was done to you. Not that Tweedledee and Tweedledum were nice to you."

He smiled. "Those names sound funny. Is it a joke?"

"Stupid twin characters in a book."

He hedged, went to say something, then tried again. "I'm sorry. About earlier?"

I kept my eyes ahead, watching for anything resembling safety or an exit. The trees were getting closer, and when I looked behind us, I couldn't see the path. No going back now.

"My father is *Zayuri,* and we live in *Jinatrau.* My brother and I were born with the gene, but I don't want to be a *Zayuri* warrior. I saw Nolan after he accepted his heritage. I never wanted to cross paths with him. Some say he changed after you left."

"That's what I've heard, too."

Our surroundings changed in a heartbeat. One moment we were on the heather moors, the next we were on a path deep in the middle of an ancient forest. It almost looked like *Endae,* but the smell and trees were unfamiliar, assuring me we weren't.

"What happened?" a kid asked—Nate, the quiet one.

Another kid whispered in a panicked hush.

"Do you hear that?" Patch asked.

All the kids stopped talking. No one breathed. Something—not dangerous. Wind?

"It's water. That way." Marianna pointed to our right.

"Are you sure?" I asked.

"Yes. We'll find safety there." Marianna came to stand beside me. "I think Faerie is giving us safe passage."

"To where, though?" Siobhan asked.

"Some place away from TJ, I hope," Patch responded.

"It shouldn't be too much longer!" Marianna exclaimed. How long had it been since she'd seen a body of water? Since she was a water fairy, like she'd said, I imagined water was important to her, perhaps vital.

"Marianna, slow down. You'll tire yourself out too quickly."

She slowed. "It's just been so long..." Marianna whimpered as she scanned the forest ahead.

"We'll make them pay, Marianna. Queen Orlaith will want to talk to you, and she better give you all the medals or something."

"What good is a medal? I just want to see my parents and never go near a needle again." Her head swiveled, and she cleared her throat. "We're close."

"How is this place doing that? We were miles away a few moments ago."

"Faerie does what it wants. Even Anu can't control it."

"I'll check to see if there's a way across," I said since I was the only older one not doing anything.

"You're leaving us?" Sera cried. "I don't want you to go." Tears welled up, and I hightailed it over there before they were rolling down her face.

"Sweetie, I'm just going to be gone for a moment."

"You don't have to. The water knows a way." Marianna mumbled something to Patch, and away we went. "There's a waterfall. This will be wonderful!"

"Wait!" Siobhan called out. "Do you feel that?" She set her corner down, and the other three followed suit.

We looked from one to the other. Only Siobhan felt it.

"No one felt Faerie's pulse quicken?" She began to hyperventilate as she looked at the others' uncertain faces. The wind rustled the trees, thousands of leaves sounding like a downpour. Faerie had a pulse?

"Siobhan?" I kept my voice low as I tried to calm her down. "I don't think anyone else felt it."

"They're here!" she hissed, her hands to her mouth. "Drake is here!" The wind picked up, slapping our hair into our faces and picking up the edges of our clothes.

"Siobhan?" How did she know?

Sera yelped when the wind knocked her over, blowing her dirty, ragged clothing up her back. I tried to pick her up, but the wind almost knocked me over, too.

One of the youngsters asked what was happening. Aleanis. "Lalis! Mani!" he cried in the swirling wind.

Fuck this. I didn't know shields or wards, but I knew rain guards, and damn it, we needed a shelter. Without thinking, I expanded my energy out as Faerie pushed the wind inside. I willed my magic to create an extension of myself. I wanted to know how Siobhan knew Drake was close and who the fuck *they* were? Tweedledee and

Tweedledum? The wind stopped so abruptly that everyone but Lalis dropped to the ground. Not that he wasn't affected; he was just too heavy. I'd created my first ward. Well, damn. I'd have to tell Nol later.

"Let's get off the path. Lalis, can you pick up Maneya?"

Patch grabbed Sera. Siobhan and I grabbed Molly together.

"They'll see the cot," Molly croaked. "It's no use." I'd never heard the girl talk before.

"No, they won't. Siobhan, um—" I couldn't remember all ten of their names. "Take Molly for me. I have to take care of the cot."

"Hally, they're getting closer!" Siobhan's voice was a shrill whisper.

"Get as far as you can. I'll catch up. Do not come back."

They watched me, all ten of them. Three seconds...five...ten.

"Go!"

Lalis broke the trance first, and the kids moved. "Be careful. And Hally?" Our eyes met. "Thank you."

The wind would hit them as soon as they left my ward, but I couldn't lend it to them or anything. Before Lalis began running, I was reacting, picturing the cot's metal frame oxidizing at an accelerated rate. The metal rusted and collapsed within itself in seconds.

Next, I sank it partially into the dirt until it was barely there. It would have to do. I turned and ran. If I caught up, they could get inside my ward again. The wind uprooted several bushes to my right. I couldn't see or hear the others. Had the wind thrown them somewhere?

Was Faerie protecting them? Or was it just having a gay old time? "Come on, Faerie. Help me protect them."

The wind stopped again. Half-uprooted plants fell, and branches carried from other places rained down on me, bouncing off my ward.

"Hally?" a deep, familiar voice from my left called out. Drake moved in the forest, as if he was a part of it. His dark skin and dark clothes had aided in hiding him, but I saw him now. He came from the opposite direction the kids had run, thank the Mother, but now

I was in trouble. My knees buckled, because if Drake was in front of me, the *Zayuri* had failed.

No, I couldn't believe that. I touched my *meril*, but accepted that it might not work through Faerie. A pulse of energy responded to mine. Nol was okay—or at least able to respond. Then, what had happened? At first, I wasn't sure what I was feeling from my *meril*; it felt jumbled, like Nol was all right beside me, but then he was as far away as the moon.

"*Nol! Drake is going to get the kids. Where are you all?*"

For a moment, nothing happened. Then the *meril* sent a pulse—or rather, Nol sent it through. He was on this side of the veil and running this way. There was no telling if he'd heard my message, though.

"Hally? What on earth are you doing here?" Drake asked as if we were old friends.

"I—" What could I say or do to keep him interested in me and let the kids run? Hopefully, Faerie willing, they'd find a way out and away from Aswryn's cult. "I don't know. Someone...it's hard to remember. Where's Nol? Aren't you supposed to be in LA?"

He came over an arm's length away. "What did you do with the kids, Hally?"

"What do you mean?"

Drake narrowed his eyes and looked around the hushed forest. "I felt you enter the dome. What did you do with them?"

When I didn't answer, he growled and grabbed two handfuls of my borrowed sweatshirt. As he brought me closer, I saw the scratches on his face and dark blood dripping off his ear.

"What happened to your face?" This playing stupid idea wasn't working. "It looks like it hurt."

He lifted me off the ground and shook me. Quinn's sweatshirt was so loose I began slipping through. A moment later, he stilled. A smile spread across his face. "How'd you get here?"

"I stuck out my thumb and caught a ride."

He shoved me to the ground and would have kicked me if I hadn't kept rolling. I flung my magic out. A heartbeat later, I swept his legs out from under him, and he fell on his ass. Drake shook his head, his hair full of twigs and leaves.

"How did *you* get here, Drake?" But I didn't give him a chance to answer before I shoved him again.

Light flared in Drake's hand, and I flew back. "You aren't equipped to fight me, girl. Where are the kids?"

As I got my ass off the ground, I conjured an orb, but he snuffed it out before I could throw it. The next one I conjured was a decoy as I pulled the air out from under him with another thought.

I backed up again and dove behind a bush as he threw another spell. Heaving, I swallowed and tried to think of something to say. "Looks like we both want something. I'll tell you if you tell me. You go first. Where's Nol?"

Drake's next spell hit me in the side, and I doubled over. "Nolan's gone. Just take me to the kids, Hally. There's no way out of here."

Wincing from the pain of whatever fuck spell that had been, I rolled out of the bush and back to my feet. "Nah, I call that bullshit. You ran, didn't you? Did the *Zayuri* have you running scared? Had to use Faerie to hide?"

"Think you're hot stuff, do you? Such fast, powerful magic. It isn't all about power."

His next spell hit my shoulder. Oh, I needed to know how to cast a shield.

"Ow," I hissed but made my words as sarcastic as I could. "Why does everyone keep talking about power? I do not think I'm powerful! I'm—" I scrambled for a word because no one accepted "different" when it came to our family. "—divergent." I grabbed the first word that came to mind. Stupid, I know, but it made sense. "That's all it is."

Through the *meril*, I sensed Nol running and felt his mental desperation. Terrified he wouldn't make it, he reached out through our bond. We'd only ever opened it to soothe my nightmares. Drake wasn't a nightmare, but Nol had to fight him, and he was almost here. Just a little longer.

Taking a note from Faerie itself, I imagined the bush behind Drake wrapping around him, stronger than it should be, squeezing tightly and holding him there, just like the heather had wrapped around his friends. The roots of the next bush grabbed his kicking feet, and he called a spell, his fingers swishing to form a signal, slicing at the bush.

"Nope." More roots. I felt the surrounding power in the ground and trees. Faerie didn't like this much. I wasn't hurting him. I was just...detaining him, like it had done.

Drake called a Gaelic-sounding spell, and the plant material holding him exploded.

"Oh, Faerie doesn't like it when you destroy its babies."

"Fuck you, Hally."

I cocked my head. "No. Assholes aren't my type."

A mental picture of a spell popped into my head. Nol knew the traditional one, but he showed enough for me to finally understand the logistics of how he did it! And he was right. It was freaking easy as hell. Between Drake and me, close to my body, I gathered energy for a shield, and hopefully there was enough left over to fight Drake off. I hardened my magic to form a barrier above my skin. With a quick self-check, I figured I had enough to throw some back at Drake. Not as much as my fairy opponent on Capitol Hill, but I didn't feel close to being tapped out. I shoved the mass of energy I'd pulled in toward Drake, and his back slammed against the tree, even as Faerie tried to push back to keep him from getting hurt.

Drake grunted but wasn't fazed much.

"If he isn't stopped, he'll hurt the children," I muttered.

Faerie didn't like my conclusion. I felt it contemplate, considering what I'd suggested. Everything died, and everything was reborn. Balance and peace were better.

"No! That's not the answer."

Drake waited a beat against the tree, eyebrows all crooked as he looked from me to the surrounding nature. "Ah, Faerie isn't happy with your choices, is it? It's not as compassionate as you think."

"You're the one who exploded its plants."

At least I wasn't the only one Faerie had ever talked to.

Nol was ready. He saw the path in his mind. The distance between himself, me, then to Drake by the tree. He adjusted his grip on his sword. As he took the second step, I dropped. Nol jumped over me, sword on his left side. He swung, and the spell traveled through the sword.

I squeezed my eyes shut so the dirt from the backdraft wouldn't get in my eyes. He'd warned me that debris would fly once his sword started singing. Not in an audible sense, but by using the sword as an instrument to manipulate a spell and strike a certain cord to obtain the desired result. That's why *Zayuri* meant *Blade Singer*. Yes, he'd explained this to me before and would again after this fight, no doubt. Several thousand times until I could say the whole fucking sentence.

Nol's wrist moved a fraction another way, a word in his head for another sword spell. They came lightning quick. This was going to make me sick if I didn't close the link. Nol was too busy fighting. I could sense every move Nol's body made and when his brain told it to move. His wrist movements for spells, foot placement, and adjustments for balance.

Drake started a spell that Nol didn't know and couldn't prepare for. He slid back and waited, taking note. I had to get up to give Nol more room. The problem was detaching myself from what he was doing—how to keep him from feeling my movements as I scrambled away.

The fairies were unknown. He couldn't predict their spells by their movements like he could with *endai*. Every thought had to be on Drake and his unknown spells, leaving no room to think about closing our link. They'd fought before Drake ran through the veil. I saw it as Nol thought of Drake's injuries and which marks his sword movements had made. Drake made a move Nol recognized, and he countered effectively. Another hit and Drake had a matching injury on the side of his neck. Non-lethal strikes. Everyone wanted Drake alive.

Nol backed up again. He knew I was lying as still as I could, six paces behind him, ten paces away from Drake. One sword length. I sensed him thinking through non-lethal spells that would not hit me. I needed to move, but Nol wanted me to stay down. He needed to know where I was to focus on the unknown in front of him. Too late, I'd distracted him by picturing myself getting up. Drake moved, casting a spell Nol had seen Drake perform. Nol countered, but then Drake cast something new, forcing Nol back. Two paces in front of me. Drake ran and jumped over the river.

"Where is he going?" I asked no one while Nol ran after him.

The kids were in the opposite direction from where Drake and Nol had gone. The dome wasn't even over there. Then I felt it, a clap like thunder, and Drake appeared in front of Nol with a weapon.

Fuck.

28

While not as long as Nol's katana-like sword, Drake's weapon had a double edge and was just as deadly. From my viewpoint across the river, I watched them, poised to pounce, but I was also in Nol's mind with our link still open. He still couldn't risk the distraction. Nol stayed back, watching for Drake's next move. Through our link, I could feel the magic radiating off Drake's blade. Symbols covered every inch, indiscernible whether the magic came from the metal or the symbols.

Drake shifted, faked left, and swung his blade up and to the right. Nol kept his stance and blocked with a shift of his fingers. The fairy blade hit the shield Nol conjured just in time. When Drake slashed from the right, Nol deflected. A surge of power shoved Drake back three feet.

I couldn't hear through our link, but with Drake's clenched teeth and his determined look, I could imagine the words he spoke to Nol when his lips moved. My spot across the river, a few feet from the water, allowed me to see half their fight through my own eyes. We'd never had the link this open or for this long either. Dream sharing with him was much less confusing, and it didn't terrify me to move or look anywhere.

Drake knew what he was doing—I had no doubt he'd fought battles in his time—but his slashes were heavy and solid, while Nol's movements were swifter and lighter. At one point, Drake slashed to his left and followed it up with a jab. Immediately he spun when Nol built up a cone of power, ready to throw an invisible force Drake's way. Drake swiped his sword to the right and lifted it straight up.

Nol's sword left his hands. I saw the sword arc over his head and into the bushes obscuring their lower bodies from my view. But it didn't matter. I saw everything through Nol's mind as they fought. Nol reached down for the dagger in his boot. The same black-blue light as his sword flashed as he flicked his dagger one way and then the other. Drake slashed, but missed his target. Too quick to follow, Nol blocked Drake's blade with his much shorter one, inches from his face.

Nol jumped high, and similar to the grace of some fancy ninja moves, he planted a kick to Drake's chin. He landed and followed through with a shove, hands out with his palms facing Drake. But they didn't make physical contact. With the *Zayuri* magic that Nol possessed, along with the dagger's power, Nol conjured a spell that forced Drake back into a thick tree trunk. Pine needles of the ancient Faerie forest rained down between them as Drake pushed off the tree and lunged forward. But now there was a stiffness in Drake's movements. Still, Nol's range and tactics were limited by his dagger.

Nol needed his sword, but Drake was relentless. Hundreds of years of experience more than Nol, although his *Zayuri* training filled a large portion of that gap. With Nol's limited reach, Drake was getting closer. Three thrusts after I thought that, the tip of Drake's sword cut Nol's inner arm. He needed his sword back. Now.

Decision made, I bolted down the small hill, stumbled over the large rocks, and sank into the sand between them. The cold, rushing water covered the clashing of the blades. Nol knew what I was doing. I had the sense he didn't like it, but we had no alternative. As I hit the sand on the other side, Drake slid his sword down Nol's blade, cutting a diagonal slice from Nol's lower forearm to his wrist. He almost sliced Nol's left shoulder next.

That's when I learned the dagger didn't have the shielding capability like the larger, more powerful blade. And here I'd thought Nol was conjuring the shields. I dove into the bush closest to the river, where I'd watched the sword go, and snaked through the roots and branches. I started to panic when the blade was nowhere to be found. Then it fell on my head from where it'd been stuck between branches.

I wriggled out of the bushes and kept myself low until I saw them. Nol stepped back two deliberate steps to align with me. He didn't have time to sheath his dagger, though. With barely a thought, knowing I had the sword, Nol shoved Drake back with another forceful Zayuri spell and turned to me. I tossed his sword to him, and he tossed his dagger to me for safekeeping. In my peripheral vision, I noticed Drake pounce at me just as my hands wrapped around the hilt of the active blade. Why hadn't the blade disappeared like it was supposed to? No time for thought. Nol showed me a fraction of a second later what I needed to do as Drake made contact with me—a hair too far for Nol to reach in time.

Drake's large sword came down, in line with my collarbone. I brought the dagger up, close to my neck, and thrust out at an angle. The size difference between us played in my favor. Thanks to Nol's *Zayuri* reflexes, he saw the movement and showed me how to counter quicker than Drake could move.

I ducked under Drake's sword and swooped down and around, the dagger following in front of me, slicing open Drake's arm on its descending arc. As if Nol were moving through me, my blade swung forward as I spun until my back was to Drake. My body stepped back until I was inches away from his front, still under his arm, and before his blood could even drip enough to splash me, I swung the blade backward, under my arm and close to my side, just as my back hit Drake's front. The dagger stabbed him in the abdomen at the same moment.

I dropped the dagger as Nol collided with me. Several people descended on the area at once. My hands tingled with the sword's magic—magic I didn't have, magic I wasn't supposed to be able to use. My heartbeat drowned out all other sounds. Nol rose as two people—no, *Zayuri* came close. Where had they come from? The two *Zayuri* held Drake down, who appeared to be screaming, but again my heart thudded louder.

Nol turned to me, his face sickishly pale and eyes twice the size of normal. Everything slowed down. His braids whipped around, hitting his face as his mouth parted as if in shock. Granted, I was, too. How had that happened? The tingles of *Zayuri* magic crawled up my arms like ants marching and spreading throughout my body. My vision pulsed, and my stomach clenched. My knees buckled, and my body shifted to the side. I couldn't stop it.

"Nol?" Had I called for him out loud?

Nol darted forward, but I hit the ground before he reached me. He gathered me into his lap. Some of his hair, not in the braid, fell into my face.

"Hallë? Say something."

"Something," I croaked.

When he laughed, a few tears fell on my face. He tucked his hair behind his ears, the ear cuffs holding it there. Something was wrong. The tingling faded, replaced by...nothing. I was going numb, starting with my hands, where the magic from the active *Zayuri* blade had first touched me. Why wasn't that damn slave band sucking this magic up? That would've been too useful.

"Why didn't the dagger deactivate?" I asked.

Nol shook his head as he picked my hair off my face. "Don't leave me," he whispered.

Oh.

"What's happening?" A high, childlike voice rang out from behind Nol somewhere.

Murmuring commenced. How many people had come over? Where had they all come from? The kids...I'd told them to run. At least now they were safe with the *Zayuri* who had followed Nol into Faerie. If I lived, I wanted to know where the fuck they'd come from.

Two more tears fell from Nol's cheeks. I raised my hand to smooth the crease between his brows with my thumb.

"It'll be okay." I patted his cheek and held on. "*Olentame*, remember."

Nol nodded as he sniffled. "*Olentame*," *Beside each other, our bond is stronger.* We'd ride it out and see if our bond kept me alive.

"I don't understand!" Marianna—her higher voice getting louder. "If we take her to the water, I can heal her!" Her hand came into view as she touched Nol's shoulder.

Only then did Nol respond and lift his head. "Get her to the water."

Nol licked his lips and looked around Marianna. I felt pressure on my arms as someone else came to take me from Nol.

"*Sae*! If you take her away from me, she'll die!" Nol yelled at someone in *Aemirin*.

"Nol, I'm still conscious. I can't be that close."

"You are." He tried to force himself to smile. "But it's okay. We'll be together in the next one. It'll be okay." He said the last as if to convince himself. His voice wavered, and his eyes fluttered. Then I realized he knew, because we were both dying. Our link was still open.

"I'm sorry." I squeezed the words out of my constricting throat. "I didn't mean to." My fingers touched his ear cuff, then his hair. The loose strands spilled over my hand and arm. I spread my hand wide, my palm on his jaw, and my thumb touched his nose, then his lips.

"*Sitam*," *I know*.

"You shouldn't die. You have so much left to do," I whispered.

"*Nica astur*," *It's okay*.

"No, it's not." My voice warbled.

"*Ni motico astur*," *It'll be fine*. "It's just a little while apart."

"No." My chest heaved, and a sob escaped my mouth.

"*Ora udin lasi*." *You can rest now*, he whispered.

My hand slipped off his face, and Nol grabbed it, pressing it to his cheek. I was fading, and he wouldn't be far behind. "I tried so hard."

"You've done so well."

"Nolan." A *Zayuri* crouched next to us. She assessed me while she talked to Nol. "We could try pulling the *Zayuri* magic out of her. That little fairy over there, I think she means to heal her in the water."

"I can't stand," Nol whispered back. "And we must remain in contact."

The *Zayuri* turned and set her jaw tight. Then she argued with my very stubborn *muranildo*. "Forgive me for being crude, sir, but if you're both dying, what do we have to lose? Metryn and the largest fairy over there can carry you to the water. I'll carry Hallanevaë."

"We need to go." Marianna leaned over, looking down at me. She nodded at the *Zayuri* next to us.

"Let's do it." The *Zayuri* stood up, scooted over to my other side, and got her arms under me. "Hold on. We'll be there soon." With an exhale, she had me up in her arms, and with a hop to adjust me, she was moving, away from Nol.

"Jenne, wait," Nol called from where we'd left him. "Don't go too far ahead."

"The kid wants me to move faster," Jenne called back. "She's fading, Nolan. We have to get her to the water."

The farther apart we were, the weaker I felt, until I struggled to keep my eyes open. "Nol."

"They're bringing him. Promise." She hissed. "*C'yo*, this is cold."

I couldn't feel anything, but the water splashing on Jenne's neck and chin confirmed we'd reached the river.

"Put her in all the way!" Marianna's arm slid in front of my view to Jenne's face.

Drops of water blurred my vision, but I still couldn't feel it.

Marianna peered over me, her hair plastered to the sides of her head. Water dripped off her nose and blue lips. "Don't you dare die and leave us here. You're the only one who knows English in this bunch."

"You'll be fine," I whispered.

Marianna huffed and moved out of my view.

"Jenne?" I couldn't manage more than a whisper, and I didn't think she heard me. There wasn't enough left in me to call her name again.

"Hallanevaë? Nolan is coming, but I have to start..." Jenne jostled me. "...pull...*Zayuri*...as much as we.... Squeeze my hand if you understand."

I didn't squeeze. Whatever she had to do with the *Zayuri* would be too late. They'd kept us apart for too long. Nol was fading, too.

"Get over here!" Jenne shouted. "You have to hold on, Hallanevaë."

I felt Marianna's magic in my core, working with something else, something or someone.

Too late. But they didn't hear me.

A CROW CAWED IN the distance and was met with another's response. I inhaled as I felt the wind on my face and listened to the rustling leaves above me. My breath caught as I smelled the clean air—no exhaust, carbon dioxide, or any other pollution.

My eyes shot open. Where was I? The leaves, so far, far above my head, could have been touching the deep blue and yellow sky. Sunset? Sunrise? Where? Where on earth were there deciduous trees that tall? Nowhere.

I was still Hally, right? But that meant—gasping, I shot up. I was in *Endae*. No air on Earth smelled this clean.

"Nol?" I called for my *muranildo*.

"I'm here, Hallë." Nol sat in the grass next to me, plucking blades and rolling them up. How could he be so calm?

"Why are we in *Endae*. They'll kill me."

Nol lifted an eyebrow as he considered my words, like it was something to consider at all! "We're on Earth, Hallë. We're still on the fairies' land. Do you remember?"

I licked my lips and tasted the fresh river water from when someone...Jenne had brought me into the river. "Marianna did it?"

"Yes. And Jenne." He cocked his head to the side, like a crow studying a shiny object. "Do you remember yet?"

I swallowed. Oh, yeah. "Did I kill Drake?"

"No. He's alive. I made sure to show you a non-lethal sword combination. Jenne and Metryn are keeping him company. His wound is barely bleeding." I thought about our link and how he'd kept it open the entire time. It was the reason he'd almost died with me.

"The dagger. How? It's supposed to be impossible."

"*Zayuri* magic? Yes, it is...except with us, apparently. I think our open link is the reason my dagger stayed active. I didn't know, and I wouldn't have tossed..." Nol's words choked off, and he swallowed.

The hitch in his voice relaxed me. Not that I was morbid and glad that the thought hurt him, but his nonplussedness had been disconcerting. Like one of those robot movies where the freaky lady robot smiles, but there's nothing behind the eyes. Or Data, with the same head cock. Holy shit. Was I dreaming?

"Are you okay?"

The last I'd checked, he'd been dying right beside me. Now he sat next to me, the river we'd almost died in behind him, and he was talking like nothing had happened, or at least like it hadn't been that bad.

He gave me a slow, broad smile. "I'm fine. I've been awake for hours, waiting. Something about t's and i's before the Queen's Guard comes or something." The breeze blew strands of Nol's cinnamon-red hair in my face, tickling my nose. "While I don't blame her for making Drake suffer a while longer, I'm quite tired."

"Nol?" He wasn't fine. "What's going on? Have you eaten or drank any water?"

"Fairies came and brought nutrients around."

"How much have you eaten?"

"Enough."

Right. Meaning a nibble on an energy bar. The guy ate three hundred dollars in groceries a week at my house. "Nol. It's hypocritical to be worried about our near-death experience when you would be killing me if you starved yourself to death."

"It's been hours, Hallë. Not days. We're fine. The fairies are coming here to collect the traitors and bring the children home. Faerie is hosting us, apparently. I'm not exactly sure of the phrase."

"How are the kids?"

"Which ones? The ones you found or me?"

"You found them?" I grabbed Nol's arm and shook it, excited for a boy I didn't even know, but Siobhan had thought the others were dead. Did she know? "Was Derrick with them?"

"Derrick was with them, yes. You found ten on your own."

"Lewis and I figured it out together. The trip to Faerie wasn't planned." Yeah, with the traitor TJ, who'd bolted as soon as we got here. We'd find him. I had an amazing team of badass *Zayuri*.

Nol's brow furrowed. "Where's Lewis?"

"I made him stay behind at the Capitol Hill house. Guilted him with Yumi. She only said yes if I promised to keep Lewis safe."

"So this was a plot to go behind Tolwe's back?"

"Not at all." I grabbed the loose red strands in my face and tucked them behind his ear before I started sneezing. "Why didn't you call me back?"

He leaned back as I finished securing his hair. "I did."

I peered up at him, but got an eyeful of sunset instead. "I never got a call! Did you call again?"

"Several times. I think you were already here. We'll talk about all that in another con—"

"Conversation. You know, people don't say that."

"So? We're not talking about it until I know you're healthy."

"I'm not going to a fucking hospital."

"No. Fairies will check you out this time. Here...or possibly at Queen Orlaith's manor. I don't know. With me beside you the entire time. No hospital. I swear."

"Where is everyone?"

"Giving us a moment."

I scoffed.

"You died. I felt it."

"If I'd died—"

Nol grabbed my hand and squeezed. He dropped his chin to his chest and took a few shuddering breaths, but it didn't work. The tears welled up and rolled down his golden-tan cheeks. I scooted over and pulled him into a hug. He hadn't realized I'd come closer, and he started, but then he wrapped his long arms around me and dragged me onto my lap.

While used to close physical contact with my *muranildo*, what stunned me were the tears. I rested my head against his shoulder while he cried—for almost losing me, but also, I suspected, for the loss he'd endured from Aswryn's curse. Gil, An'di, and other close childhood friends of ours, I suspected. I knew he wasn't ready to talk about them. So I'd wait until he could talk and I'd give him the comfort he needed.

Nol sniffled, pulled me in tighter, and placed his chin on my head. He grabbed my hand again, resting in my lap, and played with the knuckles between his thumb and forefinger, lost in thought. I didn't stop him. He needed time to collect himself, and it felt like a hand massage.

"Marianna brought you back," he explained, his voice still thick with emotion. "She restarted your heart. You died beside me. Don't ever do that again. Ever."

"We die every life, Nol."

"Like you said, I have more to do. That involves you, you pain-in-the-ass."

I leaned back to give him the stink-eye. "Not as much as you are in mine."

Nol didn't smile like I'd thought he would. Instead, he studied me and dropped his eyes to my lips. My heart raced because it looked like he was about to kiss me. I tucked my head back under his chin and hoped I was wrong. We couldn't, just could not. He was leaving in a year, more or less. But the point was, he'd leave me. My heart couldn't take that. So I prayed that the awkward moment had just been mine.

"I was," he murmured, answering my unasked questions. "But I won't. We're not—" He swallowed.

We weren't. Not this life around. Things were too complicated.

"Just don't ever die on me again. Please, please, don't leave me."

I knew he meant dying, but leaving me here...wasn't that almost as bad?

Damn me. Damn my selfish choices. Damn my fucking exile.

29

"Lewis!" I yelled from the front steps as I shielded my eyes from the setting sun. How long had it been? "Lewis!"

He sat in his cream Crown Royal boat of a car, his head lowered—likely looking at his phone.

"Hallë, he has his music on."

I wrinkled my nose as I heard the bass. Nol pulled me down the steps as someone else walked away from the Capitol Hill house behind me. He hadn't left my side since I'd woken up.

"This is convenient," a *Zayuri* said after taking in a lungful of air. "Why didn't we go in through this one?"

"We didn't know it existed until now."

A thump and clatter behind us brought our attention to the house.

"Move," a fairy growled at Drake as he yanked him off the floor where he'd fallen.

Marianna had healed him, trembling the entire time for having to save one of her captors. She, like the other kids, had trailed behind everyone, not wanting to get close to him. I didn't blame them, but we assured them they were safe. When Aleanis recognized the *Zayuri*, he'd begun crying until Jenne picked him up. I was just thankful there were more adults than me to keep the children safe.

Drake stumbled again, right onto the porch. Blood drenched his shirt, tacky and drying now. While he was healed, I imagined the healing had zapped his energy. I still had a hard time with the fact that I'd done that with Nol's dagger. Nol had guided me, but if my stab had been higher, if Nol hadn't accounted for the height difference, Drake would have died. I would have killed him.

"Are you all right?" Nol asked above my ear.

I nodded and watched as they walked him out. Five fairies, three *Zayuri,* and the children waited in the yard. I kept referring to them as children, even though Lalis was only three years younger than me. Aswryn had wanted young, healthy people. I was hoping her notes would further explain what she'd been trying to accomplish with fairies and an *endaen* virus. TJ had said they were using *Aeminan endai* for their grand plan. Had she been injecting them with the virus? But none of them were infected, not even the *endai*. I could tell Nol had his own thoughts on it, but discussing Aswryn's research in front of her victims seemed...insensitive.

"They'll be here soon," a tall fairy with light blue hair and pale green eyes informed us.

"They?" I asked. "Who's coming?"

"A team." The fairy gave me a bewildered look like should have figured this out already. So I was slow. The whole damn thing confused me. Our fae escorts could only convince Faerie to take us this far. I wasn't sure who it was unhappy with, Drake, me...hell maybe it wasn't made all. Maybe Faerie liked to fuck with people as much as fate did. I wouldn't have been surprised if that were true.

"Where's Quinn?" I asked.

"He stayed with the group in California," the blue-haired fairy explained.

"Has anyone told him we have Seamus?"

Nol and the fairy looked at each other, then looked back at me.

"For Pete's fucking sake, someone tell him we found his son!"

"On it." The fairy pulled his phone out and walked away.

"How are they getting home?" I asked, referring to the other group in California.

"I'm not sure. That's Tolwe and the lead fairy's job. Quinn will be reunited with his son soon." Nol squeezed my shoulders. "Are you cold?"

Yes, I was cold, but there was no way I was putting my riding jacket on with Drake's blood saturating it. The thought of stabbing him disturbed me—the feel of the blade sliding in. I shook my head.

"You're shivering."

"I think I need coffee. And new clothes, these are filthy." I'd only been wearing them for…I didn't know how long we'd been in Faerie. Shit, all mighty. "Aren't you hungry?"

"Starving," Nol growled.

I smiled. Maybe reminding him of food would get his mind off what had happened. We were both shaking, but I wouldn't tell him. It might ruin his "badass" image of himself. No, I was not calling him a badass.

"Hally?" Lewis's door slammed shut. "Nolan? What the fuck?" Lewis opened the gate, and I ran to him.

"Thank you! For going to the car. For being here. I'm sorry—"

"Okay, calm down." Lewis grabbed my face and wiped at my tears. Relieved-to-see-him-safe tears. "What happened? Jesus. Don't you think for one fuckin' minute they're gettin' a ride."

I swallowed and stepped back. "We found 'em, Lewis."

"Yeah, I can see that. Anybody plannin' to come get 'em?"

I nodded and hugged him again. "You should go to Yumi."

"No, she made me stay here when you weren't back at lunchtime. Besides, she's at the hospital. I texted everyone that you're back. We're all good." Lewis reached around me and grabbed Nol's arm in a guy handshake. "Glad you're all right, man."

"Have you eaten?" I pressed. "I'm sure you're tired."

"Yumi fed me here. Chill, Hally."

Lewis pulled out a chirping phone—mine. "It's Charlie."

I took it, squeezed Lewis once more, and stepped away. Nol snaked his arm around my waist and kept me close to him.

"Charlie?"

"I'm so glad you're back. Did you find them? Are you all right? Tell me what happened. Lewis said you went into Faerie!"

"*Oui.*" I relayed everything to Charlie in French to keep it private. "Wait, love, someone's coming over. I'll call you later."

"As soon as you can, Tatie."

I shoved the phone into my pocket as the large fairy with leaf-green eyes and gray-brown skin stopped in front of us and cleared his throat. "The Queen wants everyone debriefed at the manor and the children will be seen by our doctors."

"I'd like Hallë to be looked at, as well."

"You both should be." The fairy socked Nol in the arm, then grabbed his shoulder. "It was an honor to fight beside you. I see why Her Majesty holds the *Zayuri* in such high regard."

"I am honored to hear that, and I will relay your praise to my fellow *Zayuri*."

"I hope Her Majesty lets you stay." He held out his hand.

Nol huffed a laugh as they grasped forearms. "At least long enough to try the mead you suggested."

Mead? Seriously? A white van turned onto the street, the new kind that's freakishly tall and should not be able to turn corners without tipping over.

"We're all going to fit into that?" I asked just as another came into view. "Oh."

"Nah, you and Nolan are comin' with me." Lewis jabbed his thumbs at himself.

"We have to go to the manor."

"And I'm comin' with."

"Lewis—"

"TJ and Drake were my acquaintances before they were yours, Hally. I might know shit they need to know that I don't know they need."

"What?" Nol asked. But I knew what Lewis meant.

"This is pulling you in way too far," I said.

"This isn't about you and me anymore." Lewis looked over at Drake, who was staring at Lewis. Creepy. "He looks...different."

"That's a nice word for it," I said.

"What happened to him?" Lewis asked.

"Hallë stabbed him in the stomach."

I stiffened at Nol's offhand remark. Almost murder. Nol pulled me closer and rested his chin on my head. His hands rubbed up and down my bare arms. I pressed his hand to my elbow when it became too much and the movement began tugging on my slave band. I let them talk as I watched the others. They filed the kids into the first van. Lalis was the last of the kidnapped to get in. Waiting for Jenne to step into the van with his brother, Lalis met my eyes. Someone from inside called his name and handed him a water bottle. They'd be okay. Drake met my eyes as well before he was led into the van. All the fairies and one *Zayuri* went with him.

"Nol? Do they need you?"

"No."

I leaned forward until I could see him above me. "Are you sure about that?"

"I'm staying with you."

"What's up with you two?" Lewis asked. "You won't let go of her."

"Hallë died. Her heart stopped beating for five minutes."

"What?" Lewis's voice echoed around the neighborhood. "You didn't think that was the most important detail of this entire circus? What the fuck, Hally?"

"We'll have their doctors look her over."

Lewis turned and headed for his car. "Let's get going. I can't believe you didn't say anything."

"It's not the sort of thing that comes up in polite conversations, Lewis."

"The hell it don't!" Lewis yanked on his seatbelt. It caught, and he fought with it while I strapped myself into the back. Nol had buckled in the second he'd sat down, before he even slammed Lewis's old car door closed. "You two need to stop tryin' to die on me."

"I'll take your request into consideration the next time someone threatens our lives."

"There ain't gonna be a next time, Hally!" Lewis won the fight with his seatbelt and started the car, grumbling under his breath as he drove out and turned toward the on-ramp. "Where's this place at?"

"Can we get food first?" I asked. "Maybe coffee, too?" I hadn't eaten since— "What day is it? It seems like we were in there for weeks."

"Same day, kiddo. Same day. But yes, I'll feed the two of you first."

"You're the best."

"Don't push it. You're still not forgiven for dying."

Nol laughed, Lewis continued his grumbling, and I got McDonald's coffee. Ba-da, da-da-da.

I BUMPED MY HEELS on the end of the patient bed as the black-eyed doctor pulled the stethoscope away. And I mean black, from the irises to the edges. Asking what kind of fairy she was, I thought, would be rude, so I didn't ask, but I found her fascinating, beautiful, and smart. Oh, and able to take Nol's freakout in stride.

Okay, he wasn't panicking, but he was so jumpy it made my hospital phobia ratchet up. Although the questions about my magic and not having to hide my identity eased my worry. We were in one of the four patient rooms they had in Orlaith's mansion. Not the same one Drake had brought me to. We'd passed that one. But it looked the same and smelled the same, with the same fluorescent lights and everything.

Molly and Sera and Seamus were being seen in the other rooms. I felt horrible, because no one was there to hold their hands—especially Seamus. Drake and Maneya had been taken to another area—their wounds being more severe.

The doctor hung her stethoscope around her neck. "Your heart sounds strong, and you've demonstrated your magic is at full capacity. All good here. Clean bill of health."

"What does that mean? Clean bill?" Nol asked.

"That I'm done," I told him.

"But her heart stopped. Marianna had to restart it. Can't you check it for damage? Bruises?"

The doctor glanced at me, clearly wondering if he was serious. I gave her a sheepish frown. She looked back to Nol. "I don't have that ability."

"Then let's go to someone who does."

"Nol!"

"That's unnecessary." She shoved her hands into her pockets and squared her shoulders. "She's fine."

"You don't know that for certain."

"Would you give us a minute, please?" I plastered on a smile that I hoped she understood as apologetic and annoyed with my *muranildo*.

Pursing her lips at Nol, she walked out. Oh, there was a limit to her patience.

"You are freaking out over nothing. I'm fine," I said after the door had closed.

"There could be problems, and they would know of them if they looked."

"I want to leave."

Nol stopped, realizing what that meant. I'd made him promise to make it all stop if I asked.

"I want to make sure—"

"If it makes you feel better, I'll do a check-in for a—"

"Month," he finished as I said, "Week."

"Three weeks."

"Three days."

Nol frowned, the crease between his brows deepening.

"Keep going and I'll say none."

"You were dead." He was too far away to press my thumb against the crease in his forehead.

"For a few seconds." I wouldn't say what came to mind. He'd been "dead" for two days. Granted, I'd been in and out of consciousness for some of it, and he'd been dying right along with me.

"Five minutes. They worked on you for almost five minutes."

That sent a shiver through me. Nol nodded as I accepted that chilling truth. "Fine, a week."

He came over and pressed his head to mine, spreading his legs so he didn't have to bend over much. "This would sound like a weird request by anyone except us. I'm just not sure if I can sleep out—"

"You can sleep beside me tonight."

His body slumped. "Thank you." His mouth went to the top of my head. He shuddered and stayed there. "Promise. Every day?"

"Every day," I agreed. "Now call the doctor back in and stop pacing; it's freaking me out and irritating her."

Nol held his breath, almost said what he was thinking—probably to argue—thought better of it, and called the doctor in.

"Okay, we good now?" she asked.

"Would it be okay if I came in to get checked on for any issues for the rest of the week?"

"You agreed to a week." Nol crossed his arms and pouted. Pouted like a child. "That is nine days."

"In *Endae*! Seven. Could I come in for six more days?"

"Um." She looked at her tablet. "I'm not here Saturday or Sunday. My nurse, Maisie, could look you over?"

I lifted my chin and glared at Nol, daring him to say something as I answered the doctor, "That's fine."

"I will leave a few notes for her so she knows what's going on." She wrote something down on the tablet then smiled up at me, ignoring Nol.

"Thanks. I'll see you tomorrow?"

"Fantastic." She let out a sigh of relief. Yep, Nol had broken through her limit.

I got off the fairy examination bed.

"I'm starving." Nol stretched his long arms up high. "Could we have pizza for dinner?"

I checked my phone as we left the office. "Not yet. We can make it to the debriefing."

"It's really only for the Los Angeles group."

I stopped and glared up at him. The Los Angeles group hadn't even arrived yet. "No. Orlaith needs to know what I have to say. From me. Plus, I'm not leaving Lewis and Charlie alone." Orlaith had wanted them both in there, giving their accounts. I wanted to know how pissed Orlaith was about Lewis. I needed to come clean and tell her about Mateo, Sam, and Yumi. My humans were assets. I just hoped she saw that.

"The doctor said you need to rest," Nol informed me.

"It's not like I'm running in a marathon. It'll be fine."

"There's no need. Really."

"Shut up and come with me. Or don't, and you won't find out any details. I'm not repeating them."

"Like you won't tell Mateo."

"Nope. He's getting the Cliff Notes version."

"Bullshit."

30

A FAIRY GAVE US instructions to the meeting room before leaving us in the hospital wing. We passed at least two conference-sized rooms. At some point, a teenager came around the corner in her pajamas, talking to the cat I'd seen bolting across the hall the other day. What seemed like hours later, Nol reached around me and twisted the ornate knob, allowing me to take in the entire room, unobstructed.

"*C'yo*," Nol whispered.

I had no words. Past all the discussions and decisions to be made, the window wall displayed the mid-Cascade Mountains in all their magnificence. A vast field of resting grape lands spread in every direction until it fell out of existence into the wilderness. Snow-capped mountains looked close enough to touch. I could stare at this for hours—days.

"Hello, you two," Queen Orlaith called out. All conversations ceased. "Find a place. We'll need to hear your accounts soon."

Then I noticed the people in the room. They sat in a semi-circle facing away from the window toward a small podium that no one was standing at currently.

Four of the *Zayuri* who'd been in Faerie occupied their own space next to the queen. At the end of the *Zayuri*, Charlie sat with her ankles crossed, engaged in the debriefing. And there, lounging like this was another day at the office, Lewis watched the proceedings, his head swiveling between the queen and me. Big, tattooed arms hung over the sides, while one ankle rested on the other knee. He watched and waited, much more nonchalant than I'd expected.

Ignoring the beautiful scene before us (or trying to), I shuffled over to Lewis and glared at Nol until he sat. He sat by me instead of the other *Zayuri*. I would have teased him and asked if he'd lose badass points for sitting next to me, but even with our link closed, I knew the scene at the river was on repeat in his head. Nol sat looking straight ahead, eyes focused on the fairy's shoes across from him.

I reached for Lewis's hand across the tiny table between our comfy chairs. Lewis turned his head, his frown deepening the wrinkles on his face. The whites of his eyes, bright against his dark skin, rolled as he studied me, like he wasn't sure who I was. Until he took my hand and winked, I'd wondered if he was under some fairy spell. What did he think of all this shit?

"You okay?" I mouthed, but in response, he turned back to the fairy who was giving his report to the queen. Orlaith didn't look irritated, and the fairy didn't seem nervous. Perhaps she'd take my admission well.

"Nineteen people, mostly children, were rescued in total. While Nolan had the situation under control, our entourage and the *Zayuri* coordinated the victims' safe travel. Drake had been keeping them in the basement."

"How did Drake get away and escape to Faerie?" Orlaith asked.

Good question.

"We should have assigned more people to hold Drake. Nolan handed Drake into our custody, as expected, but Drake outmaneuvered us. We thought nothing of it at first since he was going deeper into the basement. He had an entrance to Faerie in the basement. I didn't know he could do that."

Orlaith looked at me. "It seems very convenient—or not—that Hally was rescuing the children within Faerie at that moment."

"He sensed our escape through the wards when Hally took us out of the hut, Your Majesty," Siobhan said. I hadn't noticed her sitting between two much larger fairies. She was the only one of Aswryn's victims here. "Our captors designed the enclosures that way to alert them of who went in and out." Drake had mentioned he'd felt me enter the dome. So the kids had known and hadn't mentioned it. Then again, we'd had other issues to consider at the time.

"I know Drake is apt in sensing where the veil is thinnest. He's not as skilled at creating entrances. There are several fae who are talented in that respect. Terric's skills lie in that direction..." Orlaith tapped her finger on the arm of her chair. "His powers have diminished since we came to the New World. Or so I thought." She sat up straighter. "I want to know how they did this and why. They shouldn't have been able to hide this from me. Sean, May, that is another thing you need to get out of them."

"Yes, Your Majesty," a female, I presumed May, answered.

"Perhaps he has a mentor?" a male fairy eight chairs away from me suggested.

"Siobhan?"

"TJ is attuned with Faerie. Drake managed the enclosures and kept us contained. I'm uncertain who created the entrances, but I will provide descriptions of all the fae who came close to me. I remember everything." Her words trailed off at the end, and a haunted look entered her eyes. I wished, someday, she could forget. But if they were anything like *endai*, they had very long memories.

"Hally." I jumped in my seat when Orlaith called my name. "Explain how you came to discover Terric."

"Terric, Your Majesty?"

"He calls himself TJ here, Your Majesty," a fairy inserted respectfully.

"Charlie recognized Drake as a security guard where she works." I went on to explain the events that led up to the kids' discovery.

"You forced him to?" Orlaith interrupted as I got to the part about threatening TJ in front of his shop.

"Well, yeah. I guess."

"You guess? Was it or was it not threatening?"

I sighed and shifted in my chair. "He attacked us first, but yes, I fought back. I'm not usually a violent person, but when it comes to the safety of my family—"

"The fae children are not your family," another fairy informed me.

"No, but Katie was my friend." I made eye contact with the fairy who'd butted in. "We endured Ian together, her more than me. He killed her, and Aswryn took Seamus. So yeah, while she wasn't family, per se, I cared about her and Seamus."

"Ian didn't kill Katie," Queen Orlaith said.

"Drake said Aswryn had, but I don't see how. She arrived at my shop before Ian, and he had blood all over him."

"And that proves his guilt?" the queen asked. They were defending Ian? I'd seen his eyes! Bloodshot and...

"That doesn't prove it, no, but those who have killed before. I..." I waited, sorting through my memories of what I'd seen the War do to people. "I'm not saying I'm an expert in this, but I've seen the eyes of someone after they've killed another person. It can be sorrow and guilt, but there are also the ones—" I looked down at the floor, remembering those soldiers who'd gone numb, gotten used to killing others. "Aswryn didn't have that in her eyes. She was determined to take me."

"Aswryn was—"

"It wasn't Aswryn," I interrupted Orlaith.

No one said anything. Ian had had Katie's blood all over him. At least someone's blood. There was no way to tell if it was really hers, though. But Ian's panic...had that been from murdering the mother of his child or discovering her murdered? Or something else?

"It might not have been Ian. I thought it was, but now...I'm not so sure. Ian was panicked. But he was high, like really high. I haven't experienced a murderer high—other than morphine."

"Just how long have you been here, elf?" The same fairy who'd interrupted me earlier sneered.

I didn't owe this fairy one iota of an explanation. Did any of these fairies know about me? Orlaith sat watching me like everyone else, giving no clues. What was the best answer?

At that moment, I realized I was angry with them. Not that it was their fault. They hadn't known about me, but if I'd met the fae, and if they'd permitted me to live, my life would have been different. I would never have met Emma and the Dubois family. I felt abandoned by both the *endai* and the fae. I knew the wound would heal in time, and I still hoped Orlaith would let me stay, but for now, it hurt.

"My name is Hally, not elf."

Nol coughed beside me, failing to hide his laugh.

"My whereabouts and involvement are classified. I am not at liberty to discuss my actions or previous engagements until Her Majesty and *Aemina* permit it."

"Your Majesty, she is a spy."

"That is enough, Siegel. Hally is right. Her involvement is classified. Right now, we owe the *Zayuri* and Hally a debt for saving our young ones. I have heard quite enough for tonight. Once the records are noted and looked upon, I may have follow-up questions. Hally. Nolan. Stay here. Lewis, Charlie, you as well."

With that, the collection of fairies rose and hustled out. No one argued or pleaded for more details. Orlaith didn't even move after everyone had left, didn't look at any of us, just stared out the window.

Oh, she wasn't happy.

"Lewis, when did Hally involve you in this?"

"This? Hally needed me to introduce her to my old tattoo shop. Drake's contacts align with some of mine. I wouldn't be surprised if I knew more fairies than I realized. Um...Your Majesty," Lewis fumbled at the end.

The queen lifted an eyebrow and watched him. "Elaborate on your relationship with Hally. Please." Oh, look, she added a magic word.

Lewis didn't even look away. "That could be a long while—"

I nudged him with my foot so he'd stop messing around. There was a reason Lewis and I got along.

Lewis's shoulders slumped—oh darn, no playtime for Lewis. "I met Hally through Drake, when she came up from California. But I learned the rest when Aswryn attacked us at Hally's house."

"Upon learning what Hally is, how did you feel about her?"

"There's 'no upon' about it. She's Hally, my friend and business partner. Nothing's changed with her and me."

Orlaith looked between us, trying to pry us open with her mind. "Lewis, you will need protection until Drake's associates have been apprehended."

"There's no reason—"

"I suspect there are many more of these Meabhlaire followers than I ever imagined. Drake has been busy. There is no telling how many of your tattoo friends are a danger to you."

"Um, that's very kind of you." It looked like someone had taught Lewis not to thank the fairies.

"Charlie? Has your time at Drake's house given you your data?"

Charlie sat up straighter and looked around the room. "What I've found looks promising."

"Hally and Nolan, we do owe you a vast debt. You and the *Zayuri*. The problem is, every corner I've come around with you, I find more that you've hidden from me. These omissions make me wary of granting you asylum. I can't trust you."

"Your Majesty—"

"I will need to think about how to proceed. Some of what you've held back was for *Aemina's* desecration, which you have made clear; however, I grow weary of pulling the truth out of you."

"Your Majesty? If I may?"

Orlaith sighed and waved her hand, granting me permission to speak.

"You're right. I haven't been honest. I have been afraid—for my friends and myself. Trust doesn't come easy, and I thank the Mother I didn't tell Drake everything. There are a few human friends who know the truth, thanks to Aswryn."

"It was my fault, Your Majesty," Nol interrupted. "I persuaded her to tell her friends."

"Nevertheless, they know. I was hoping you'd tell me on your own. There are..." She shook her hand, pointing at each of us.

"...three others, if I remember Feya's report correctly. She said you were a 'tight-knit' group, as humans say."

A knock on the door echoed around the room. With only the five of us, the room felt cavernous.

"Enter." Orlaith didn't even raise her voice.

A black-haired fairy, who came up to my chest, poked her head in. "Your Majesty, the others are back."

"What took them so long?"

"They had an issue navigating Faerie. Apparently, it wanted to play."

Orlaith groaned. "Bring them in."

"Ah." The fairy held a finger up. "Prince Quinn said he isn't coming—"

The Queen of the Fae adjusted her shoulders but showed no other sign of emotion. "Bring the others in."

"Also—"

"What is it, Seri?"

"Lord Gavin is demanding a moment of your time, as this has interrupted your meeting."

"Bring him in as well."

"At...the same time, Your Majesty?"

She switched her crossed ankles, and Seri nodded, ducking out of the door. "I won't need you for this. You will be informed of my decision later this week."

With a few awkward bows and an awkward curtsy from Charlie, we shuffled out. Gavin shoved the door open as Nol grabbed the handle, hitting him in the shoulder.

"Your Majesty? Why wasn't I informed of this meeting? As a representative of King Lorcan, I must insist on being—"

"You are an uninvited guest, but I assure you, you'll hear everything, Gavin."

Gavin noticed the four of us when Nol slipped by, as Gavin was blocking most of the doorway. Lewis would have to make him move.

"I see. I presume my presence was unwelcome due to the company in attendance."

"Presume away. They were just leaving."

"Where did you get that?" Gavin asked someone, his tone much less whiny and much more concerned.

Charlie followed Nol, turning sideways to scoot around Gavin. She rolled her eyes at me, and I had to hold my breath to keep from laughing. Whatever had made his tone change, I didn't care to know. I didn't have the energy to listen.

"Hally?" Queen Orlaith called.

We stopped. "Your Majesty?"

Orlaith still sat on her chair in the front, ankles crossed, but she'd leaned forward, taking an interest in me.

Gavin walked around Charlie, who stood between the two of us. He reached out and almost touched my arm. The doorknob pressed into my back, unable to open any wider. Nol stepped up to my side as Gavin intruded on my space.

"Where did you get that?" Gavin pointed at my arm. At the slave band.

Startled by the hint of urgency in his voice, I didn't speak. If he was going to accuse me of helping Aswryn because of this—she was making my life a living hell, even from the grave.

Gavin stood there, eyes glued to the band.

"What is it, Gavin?" Out of the corner of my eye, I saw Orlaith stand.

He didn't answer her. His eyes flicked away from the band to my eyes. He pursed his lips and continued to wait for my answer.

My tongue stuck to the back of my throat. "It's…"

Orlaith was walking toward us, her expression growing more serious.

I had to swallow several more times to force my tongue to unstick. "Aswryn said it was a slave band."

Gavin didn't breathe, and Orlaith's sharp inhale filled the silent room.

"I can't take it off. My grandmother is still looking for information on it."

"Do you know anything about it?" Nol asked, a tad accusatory.

"That is an ancient relic—parts of it." Gavin's brow furrowed as he seemed to work something out in his head. "How did she get a fae slave band?"

My knees weakened, and my hair stood on end.

"Tell me everything," Gavin demanded. He stepped away, into the room, ushering us back in. He looked out into the hall, then shut the door.

"Gavin, explain what you know." Queen Orlaith followed Gavin back over to the chairs while the four of us stood like idiots by the closed door.

"The relic is pure evil, Your Majesty. They aren't supposed to be out of the catacombs."

"Catacombs? She got this off a dead person?" My voice came out as more of a squeak, but who'd blame me? Charlie reached for my hand, or maybe I reached for hers, but we squeezed our interlaced fingers.

Gavin nodded, quick shakes that could have rattled his brain. "I was a boy when my mother was finally freed from one of those monstrosities. They were outlawed over eight thousand years ago and I haven't heard of them in use since before the elven war."

How could it possibly be that old? How could *he* be that old?

"Are you certain, Gavin? That's a long time to keep the memory." The queen's question mirrored my thoughts. There was no way.

"I'm certain, Your Majesty. Our clan was the last to be freed, nearly... ten thousand years ago." Gavin walked over to the closest chair, but instead of sitting, he tried ushering us over again. "It cut into her arm whenever it was pulled too far from her skin. I will never forget the feel of those things. Now come sit down and tell me everything.."

I took a deep breath, torn between learning more and hopefully getting the damn thing off, or leaving just to irritate Gavin. With a rush of breath, I gave in and walked back over to the chairs. "She tricked me and hid it inside my regular bracelet, which she'd stolen. When she kidnapped Ray, she left my bracelet with a note. It guided me to Ray...and Aswryn."

"You willingly put a slave band on?"

"No! I just told you, she tricked me." I pinched my bracelet, holding the luggage tag with my sister's name on it. "I've had this since my sister died. Aswryn stole it, and when she gave it back, she somehow hid the band in it. When I put my bracelet on, the band slithered up my arm and attached itself. I don't know how to get it off."

Charlie came around behind me and found her seat while I glared at the stuck-up fairy who wasn't listening to me. Lewis's hand on my shoulder jolted me. He nodded once. Was I good? I nodded back. He walked over to stand behind Charlie's seat, arms draped over the back.

"Does it draw energy from you when you use your magic?" Gavin hissed in a sharp whisper that drew my attention away from my friends.

"If I use..." I paused and found Nol staring at me from an arm's length away. "...a lot of magic. I don't know why. I mean, she's dead, so it's collecting magic for no reason."

Gavin looked away from me. His eyes grew wide as he nodded. "There's a reason."

Nol touched my shoulder and leaned in close. "You said it wasn't doing anything," he whispered.

"I knew you'd freak out if I told you," I sort of whispered back. "And you can't do shit about it. Besides, it's not all the time."

"What is the reason?" Nol asked Gavin.

"Aswryn was killed that night, yes?" Gavin said.

I nodded, rattling my own brain. He was scaring me, and I didn't want to know any more. Tears built up, and my head swam. My worst fear was coming true. Someone still had control over the band. Please, not Drake. Please, please no.

"Accidentally, or did someone kill her?"

Nol and I looked at each other for a moment. "I killed her. She was attacking Hallë when I came into the room."

Gavin paled and walked around to the front of his chair and sat down. "You...you should sit down."

"Why?" Nol barked, his voice uncharacteristically loud.

Gavin lifted his head out of the palm he'd been resting it on. "You need to sit down." His hand was shaking. Why was his hand shaking?

"Gavin?" Orlaith went over and knelt down in front of him, her hand on his forehead. "Cousin?" she whispered. "Tell me what has you so shaken."

He patted the queen's shoulder. "They need to sit before I explain. Have the boy sit."

Nol gasped. "No."

Slower to react with my head swimming, I saw Gavin's and Orlaith's heads turn, as if in slow motion. I followed their gazes.

"No." The back of Nol's legs bumped into a chair, but he didn't sit.

"What?" Orlaith asked, and I echoed her. Somehow, Nol had worked out whatever Gavin wasn't saying. His genius brain was always a handful of steps ahead of everyone else's.

He walked across the room to the window as he pressed his palms to the sides of his head. "Are you certain?"

"What did you figure out?" I asked. Nol's panic had cleared my head.

He paced from one side of the windows to the other, his shadow passing over the closest chairs.

Orlaith sat on the chair arm next to Gavin as she looked from the panicking Nol to the shocked fairy representative.

"When the slave owner dies, the slave is freed. But if the owner is killed by someone, the ownership of the slave is transferred to the one who killed them."

Charlie gasped. It took me a moment to work it through. I couldn't breathe, and my ears began ringing as I finally let myself accept Gavin's words.

"There's a way to get it off," Nol said, almost too quiet for me to hear above the ringing. "There has to be a way to...free..." His voice died. "I can't own—This can't be possible. I can't own another person. I can't own Hallë." It took me a moment to realize Nol was whispering in *Aemirin* as he paced.

"What do we have to do to get it off?" Charlie's calm voice pierced through Nol's whispers.

Gavin's whole body was shaking. Orlaith was rubbing his back, not in any way regal, but now I saw through the politics into the family dynamic. Orlaith whispered something to Gavin, and his terrified eyes didn't waver from hers. Gavin nodded.

"An owner has a phrase or a word of power that will release the hold on the band. It is unique to the owner."

"But Aswryn's dead. How will we find the word?" My voice sounded too hollow and distant to be mine.

"I'm sorry, child, but if you can't find the phrase, it will stay attached."

"Nolan can't just make up his own phrase?" Charlie asked. "There isn't a spell that'll override Aswryn's orders? There has to be a backdoor."

"It isn't a computer program." Gavin wiped his hands down his face, then rubbed them on his knees. "My mother was freed when her owner died from an infection. I don't remember the details."

"Would my father know more?" Orlaith asked.

"He was born after their use was outlawed. They were dark times. The human Middle Ages have nothing on this time in our history. How did she get hold of this?" Gavin hissed to himself. "I'll need to go back and investigate this. Someone must have granted her access. Whatever Drake and this elf, Aswryn, were up to, it has spilled onto our coasts."

"Or it started there." Lewis's deep voice startled everyone.

Nol stopped pacing and whispering.

Lewis's eyebrows went up as everyone stared at him, listening to his opinion. "It's not some cult you're lookin' for. This is deep and a hell of a lot more organized."

"I want my father to hear this from me, Gavin. You will leave immediately and start looking for any connection to the *Aiséirí an Meabhlaire*, but I'll call him and explain everything."

"But Your Majesty, we need to discuss the elves who are here."

"They saved the children and dealt with Aswryn. We'll save the specifics for later. Hally has my protection."

Gavin pressed his hands to his thighs and stood. "I'll leave right away. If you would be so kind as to call him before I reach the tarmac?"

"I have a feeling this will be a long conversation," Orlaith said.

"*Zayuri*?" Gavin turned to Nol, who stood frozen, watching us all with his emotions hidden. He bowed low to Nol, one arm in back, one in front. "You have my deepest thanks. Prince Quinn is my best friend, and you saved his son's life."

"Hallë saved him. We found some children in California. Hallë found ten inside your Faerie world."

"Hallë?" Gavin asked.

"Hally. They are *muranildi*," Orlaith told him.

"As I live and breathe. We'll never know if it was you, but I knew a *Muranilde* pair."

"It wasn't us," Nol interrupted.

"You wouldn't remember—"

"It wasn't. I feel no familiarity with you."

Gavin fidgeted but dropped his argument. "Your Majesty." Gavin bowed. "Until our next meeting." He stopped as he reached for the door. "Take care—the two of you. Don't cross realms separately with that band on. Hally will be sucked through, and I'm not sure if she'd survive that." He looked at the floor, his brow furrowed. "I am sorry this has happened. I would never wish this on anyone, human, fae, or elf."

"Gavin, keep me informed of what you learn," Orlaith said.

"Yes, Your Majesty. I will promptly inform you."

With that, Gavin left.

No one spoke. Charlie's fingers slipped into mine. Nol paced some more. He'd need to leave to think soon. The door clicked. Lewis jumped in my peripheral vision. Charlie's hand spasmed. Tolwe, with his cinnamon and gray hair, took in the room, but homed in on his nephew, his expressions blooming as he went from *Zayuri* general to uncle.

"*Maca?*" *What happened?*

Nol bent forward, his hands on his knees. He said nothing, but Towle stopped the other *Zayuri* from entering, pushing them out of the door before he ran to Nol. In harsh whispers, Tolwe learned what had happened. He reached for Nol, his hand pressing Nol's head down to his shoulder. Being the same height, Tolwe was the perfect size for Nol to fall apart on.

Tolwe's head turned and found me across the room. His face morphed back into the emotionless *Zayuri*. Did that mean Tolwe blamed me for Nol being stuck here for who knew how long? Maybe years...or even a lifetime. Charlie pulled me against her, but I didn't cry, too shell-shocked to even think beyond staring back at Towle's pale blue eyes.

31

WE MADE IT TO the mansion's great room in less time than it had taken to get to the meeting. Something told me Faerie was still in a playful mood. Eighteen out of the nineteen rescued kidnapped victims huddled together in the middle of the room. Patch was red-faced, tears streaking his cheeks as he held the boy I recognized from Katie's photos. Derrick squeezed Patch right back. They all talked and hugged, a hint of a smile in some, but most looked like Patch and Derrick, crying for the kids they'd been reunited with.

The other *Zayuri* sat in a group off to the side, watching the kids until they noticed us. Jenne's inquisitive look shut down as soon as she saw Nol and Tolwe, with their own masks in place. None of them asked why they'd been kicked out of the conference room, but Tolwe and Nol walked over to the other four, and they made their own huddle.

Several fae stood on the outskirts of the room, watching for what? At this point, they probably had nothing else to do. Gavin was gone, and the queen was on the phone. If they didn't trust the *Zayuri* now, it was a personal problem. They'd proven themselves trustworthy to at least most of the fae here.

"Tatie." Charlie nudged me. "Tatie," she hissed again. "Isn't that Quinn?"

My head swiveled away from the *Zayuri* group. Charlie tipped her chin toward the kitchen and the entrance to the garage. Sure enough, Quinn stood leaning against the door, with Seamus by his side. Quinn smiled and started toward our little group, but Seamus wrapped his arms around his dad's legs. Quinn's face fell, and he knelt in front of his son. Seamus shook his head as they talked, and he refused to lift his head and look around the room as Quinn pointed out everyone who was there.

"Excuse me," I whispered to Charlie.

Jenne and Tolwe noticed me as I walked toward them, but they didn't acknowledge me further. I kept walking. They could be as angry as they wanted. I wouldn't try to calm them. I wasn't happy with myself either. I reached Quinn soon after, who was still kneeling in front of Seamus.

"Look, bud, someone's here to see us."

Seamus didn't look up. All he wanted to do was hold his dad.

"Hey," I whispered as Quinn gave in and picked him up. "Seamus was such a brave boy. He walked all day, even when he didn't feel good at all. I'm sure it's very scary to talk about it, and there are lots of people he doesn't know." I tried to look under Quinn's chin to make eye contact with the three-year-old. He buried his eyes as soon as he saw mine. "I'm so proud of him for helping and being a really big boy. Maybe in the future, after Seamus is feeling better, he could come meet Ray? She's my niece, and I'm sure she'd love to meet him."

"Hear that, bud?" Quinn jiggled his arm, which Seamus was sitting on. "Think you'd be up for that later?"

Seamus shook his head against his dad's shoulder.

"Ray had something really scary like this happen to her. Just a few weeks ago."

Quinn's eyes got big as he realized that Ray had been taken only a few days after Seamus. I leaned over and kissed Quinn's cheek and rubbed Seamus's back.

"When you guys are up for it, gimme a call, and we can have that talk."

"We can do that." He gave me a grateful smile, kissed the top of his son's head, and sighed. "We're actually waiting for Brodrick. Like everyone is, actually. He's fetching a car seat for Seamus. Then we're going to my house to see Mr. Piggles."

"Mr. Piggles?" At Quinn's house. That's when I realized Seamus and Katie hadn't been living with Quinn. There were so many changes ahead of him.

From behind Quinn, the garage door opened, and Brodrick came in. He jerked backward, not expecting us to be so close.

Brodrick cleared his throat and looked at each of us. "A booster seat has been acquired, Your Highness."

Quinn kissed my cheek. "I'm glad we caught you," he whispered before he headed out to take Seamus home.

Brodrick lifted his head and looked out at the entire room. "The van is ready for the elves."

While the kids were a close-knit group, Lalis and Aleanis broke away with a few quick goodbyes. The group parted, and Maneya stood up from a chair in the center. Her arm was in a sling, her face was still swollen, and she didn't move fast, but behind those puffy eyes and cheeks, her face lightened at the prospect of going home. She stumbled, and several of them reached out, prepared to catch her. The experience had been horrific for them all, but the camaraderie between the two species gave me hope for the next generation. Then I stopped. Lalis was my age. Nol and I would've fit right in. That next generation was us. It was about time to read that damn treaty.

Tolwe and Nol were the first to enter the garage. I didn't know what to say to Nol as he passed me going out of the kitchen. He hadn't said a word since his uncle had come into the meeting room. Nol hadn't touched me, and he'd barely looked at me, staying by Towle's side the entire time. Now it looked like it would continue that way to the house. He made a beeline to the open van and climbed into the front passenger seat, and there he stayed. I walked Lewis and Charlie to their cars before I climbed in after everyone else.

"I'll see you at home—unless you changed your mind? You can come with me." Charlie offered.

"No. I'll stay with them. I don't want to put any more stress on Nol, not with what he just..."

"It wasn't just him, Tatie."

"It affects him the worst. He's angry and when he's angry he prefers to be left alone. Making him be the translator for the driver isn't fair."

Charlie went to say something and I placed a hand on her shoulder. "It's okay, love. Thank you for the support." I kissed her cheeks and opened her door. "Go home."

Lewis patted my shoulder as Charlie started the Volvo. "We'll figure it out."

How? Aswryn didn't strike me as the kind of person to write down her passwords on a sticky note, let alone a slave-freeing secret code. I went to tell him just that, but he needed to get home to Yumi. I waited for him to shut his door before I climbed into the back of the van and found my seat next to Tolwe. Nol didn't even grab the oh-shit handle on the way home.

"How are there so many people?" Maneya asked as she looked out of the van's window at the glowing lights of the interstate traffic and the tall buildings of Bellevue.

I smiled a small, brief smile. It was good she was feeling better after the fae had looked her over and set her collarbone, but that didn't hold back the depression and guilt about the slave band for long.

Lalis said something quieter to his cousin as they pointed out the window, but they didn't try to ask me. Perhaps they realized I wasn't in the mood to talk. Aleanis's head poked around between two taller *endai*, Jenne, the *Zayuri* who'd carried me to the water, and Lalis, his brother. I was told that Jenne hadn't left their side since their reunion. Three *Zayuri* sat behind me. I'd never seen this many *Zayuri* in my life. In fact, Tolwe was the only one I'd ever met—Nol didn't count.

Brodrick drove the van into the alley, and the moment he killed the engine, Nol was out. The sliding door of the van behind us slammed shut. I led our entourage up to my back fence and to the tree. I almost asked if anyone needed to use the bathroom, but I didn't have the positive energy to offer.

Aleanis ran up to my redwood and placed his small hand on the bark. I saw the look. How the hell were they supposed to travel through such a small tree? Well, I had news for the kid. I walked over and knelt next to him.

"They don't have as big of trees here. I planted this one ninety years ago."

"Can we go home through it?"

"Yep, it works fine. You take care of your brother and cousin back there." The rescue would be a surprise in *Aemina*. I patted Aleanis on the head and walked up to Lalis. "Would you—" Maneya came to stand next to her cousin, and I fidgeted. I had to do this, though. "I have a favor to ask. I'm not asking you to speak on my behalf or give a character witness for a *savilë*, but I hope that when asked, you'll tell them I wasn't involved."

"Why would we do that?" Maneya asked. "You don't want them to know you rescued us?"

"They're trying to claim I helped Aswryn. That I'm involved with the curse."

The two *endai*—closer to my age than Nol, even—gave me blank stares.

"Aswryn took us from our home almost ten years ago," Maneya said. "I met you for the first time today, and that is what I will tell anyone who asks me. You have my word."

Lalis watched the two of us talk, and when Maneya was done, she kicked her cousin in the shin. "Ow! *C'yo*. What she said. *Majut, endaë!*"

Something caught Lalis's attention, and I turned to look.

Four feet away, Tolwe clasped arms with Nol, then rested his forehead against his nephew's. "I will report to *Atrau* as soon as I can."

Nol nodded and backed up. Tolwe grabbed my arm as I was looking at Nol. He pulled me close and rested his forehead against mine, his expression grave. "I will make sure to add your part to the report. This will help your case." While he gave me a close farewell, his tone suggested something else.

"Tolwe," I whispered, "I didn't know. I swear."

With a deep-set frown, Tolwe dipped his chin against my head, but he didn't meet my eyes. Did they all think I was somehow in on the slave band? That I'd trapped Nol here on purpose? I was responsible, unintentionally, but I'd put the band on and its existence was keeping Nol from leaving. From Nol's cold shoulder, I knew he blamed me, or wanted to.

The back gate's creak drew everyone's attention. Ray popped through the opening before Charlie even pushed the thing open. Charlie hadn't mentioned getting Ray. Her little whisky-colored eyes widened as she took in the *endai* in front of her. She didn't move, even when Charlie tried to encourage her to walk in farther.

Charlie crouched and whispered in her ear, reminding me of Quinn and Seamus. Ray leaned into her mother and wrapped her arms around her neck. Even though she'd been welcoming to Nol and Gileal when she'd met them, so many fairies and *endai* surprising her had brought out her normal shyness.

I walked over to Nol. "Would you go to her?" The crease between Nol's brows deepened. He didn't want me to talk to him. "You can be mad at me all you want, but do not extend that anger to Ray."

Nol inhaled but chose not to comment when I glared. Ray didn't look up from her mom's shoulder until Nol was a few steps away. He stopped and crouched where he stood, just out of reach. She looked around him, taking in each *endai*. Then she wrapped her little arms around the second most important person in her young life.

Their shared kidnapping had drawn them closer—the same way the kids' capture had. I looked over at Lalis, Aleanis, and Maneya. Would they miss the fairies? They were a *Zayuri* family; maybe they could sneak them over to spend time with Siobhan and the others. If Orlaith let me stay, I'd ask if the three could visit. Unlikely, but it never hurt to ask.

With Ray in his arms, Nol stood and walked back, Charlie by his side. Once they got close, Tolwe went over and reached for Charlie's arm. She nodded after Nol had translated something to her, and then he pressed his forehead to hers, then to Ray's. Tolwe came back to the redwood and stood by Lalis.

"We're ready," Tolwe announced.

Lalis grabbed Aleanis's hand, but the little boy twisted away, ran to me, and wrapped his arms around my hips.

"Thank you, Hally." He ran back and grabbed his brother's hand again. Lalis smiled at him, looked up, and nodded to me. One *Zayuri* grabbed Lalis's hand and touched his *meril*, and another grabbed Aleanis's hand. They walked in a chain through the redwood. Tolwe didn't even look back before he left.

The two fairy drivers stared at the emptied yard, fidgeting. Guessing from the way their portals worked, I doubted they'd ever seen anyone walk through a tree. After an awkward moment, Brodrick turned to see the four of us.

"I'll be on my way," Brodrick announced like it was a big deal. I would have laughed at his awkwardness if my mind hadn't been focused on Charlie, Ray, and Nol. They stood out of reach, maybe ten steps away from me, and they didn't move as everyone left and the sounds of our neighbors' nighttime routines divided us.

I wanted to yell that I hadn't known. Apologies wouldn't work. That I'd made Nol a slave owner tore me apart. The seconds passed, the wind blowing between us, picking up Ray's red hair, and my chest tightened until I couldn't stand their judging glares. I turned. Walking wasn't fast enough.

"Hally!" Charlie called after me, but I didn't want to hear her. Would she patronize me? Suggest I leave? At that moment I knew she'd taken Nol's side. Everyone did. Gavin and Orlaith didn't believe that I hadn't known anything, had suspected nothing, or that neither of us had drawn that conclusion.

32

I couldn't even draw. I stared down at the blank page and charcoals, but I didn't have the will to pick them up. My phone buzzed.

Mateo.

Again.

I didn't have the mental energy to talk to him.

CALL ME, he'd messaged in all-caps. It was his fifth text. I reached for the little black rectangle and stared down at the gray comment bubble. I held down the button on the side and turned it off. Why hadn't I before? Well, I hadn't thought about it.

My eyes drooped, and I rubbed them. Yes, it'd been a while since I'd slept, but how could I justify sleeping after discovering I was responsible for this? Nol couldn't leave, and I couldn't get his words out of my head from three weeks ago, when he'd thought there was no way to get home.

My head dropped into my folded arms. I let myself cry in my art room, where no one could see me. Where I could have a pity party by myself—not that hiding in my room, pouting and refusing to take responsibility for my careless actions, didn't show everyone how big of a pity party I was throwing.

Someone pounded on my door—hard. I jumped, standing and staring, trying to orient myself. Out of my window, the sun was kissing the tips of the Olympics as it rose over the Cascades, shining straight at the smaller mountain range. Another pounding on my door startled me. My face was probably swollen as I'd fallen asleep crying.

They wiggled the locked doorknob.

"Hallë, you must come out here. The *Amura Ore* are in the backyard. They are demanding to speak with you."

What? I shoved my hair back and rubbed my face. Time for me to suck it up. I unlocked the door and threw it open. "Are they threatening the girls? Have they accused you of anything?"

"*Ma? Sae,*" *What?* No. "Listen, when we get out there, don't take the blame for anything or apologize to them," he spoke quickly in *Aemirin* as he walked beside me through the second floor. Nol's emotions weren't tamped down, but he had a calm business demeanor, as if he'd done this a thousand times. He grabbed my shoulders and stopped me at the top of the stairs. He studied my face. "What they're doing is illegal. I read the declaration—"

"What are they declaring?" I almost broke down in tears again. "Do they think—I didn't mean to trap you here! I didn't know. I'm sorry."

He paused and searched my face. "It doesn't matter what the declaration says. They're not taking you anywhere."

"You want me to defy the *Amura Ore*?" I would have stepped away from him if his fingers hadn't been pressing into my shoulders.

"*Sae.* Their orders aren't legal."

"I can't—I can't calm down." My body was shaking.

"Look at me. Breathe in." I followed suit as he inhaled. "Breathe out. Again. See? It's working."

"No, it's not."

"Eyes here, Hallë." He pinched my chin and moved my head to look at him. "They want you to go with them, which you won't do." He moved my head back and forth as he shook his head no.

"If I refuse, they'll use it against me."

"*Tameseb rama savilë,*" *They made you savilë.* "You don't have to listen to a fucking thing they say."

"But—" I hiccupped as I tried to calm down. "It'll be my word against theirs. They'll win." I shuddered and looked at the floor, squeezing my eyes shut. "They always win."

Nol shook my shoulders, getting my attention. "Calm yourself. Face them level-headedly, without panic. Trust me, nothing will come of this."

"What does the declaration say, though?" I wished he'd let me go downstairs. How long would they wait before they took things a step further? Would they break down my door?

"They've demanded you come outside."

"Then let's go!"

"Not until you promise me you won't go with them."

That's what this was about? "Are there capital guards?"

"Yes, four."

"Four?" I squeaked.

"Don't worry. I won't let them take you."

"We can't stop four guards!"

Nol scoffed. "You have so little faith in me? I can take on twelve before I even unsheathe my sword."

"Don't use your sword! Nol, if they—"

"Everything will be fine. Look at me. Deep breath." He said it a few more times, trying to make me follow him in a deep breathing exercise. It wasn't working.

"Are you really going to kick me out next month?"

I held my breath and focused on his pale blue eyes with a glimmer of mischief—but it wasn't real.

"Not working?"

My hair hit my face as I whipped my head back and forth.

He came closer. I thought he was going to rest his forehead against mine, but he paused when our noses almost touched. He set his palm along my jaw, and his thumb brushed my lips. I needed to stop him. He tilted my head one way. My heart pounded in my ears. I was too afraid to move. Was he going to do it this time? His cold cheek slid against mine, narrowly missing what I thought was his target.

Nol's smooth chin pressed against my neck, his lips just touching my earlobe. His warm breath in my ear stopped my own.

"You need to calm down," he whispered.

This wasn't calming me down. It was distracting, but for a completely different reason. He was not doing this right now. I closed my eyes as I tried to ignore his hair touching my face, some cinnamon strands in my eyes. Why was I getting light-headed?

"Breathe, Hallë."

How the fuck was I supposed to breathe while he whispered in my ear? If he told me to breathe one more time—

"Breathe," he whispered again. When had his hand moved to the back of my neck? Shit, shit, shit. My lungs burned, and I realized I hadn't taken a breath since he'd leaned into me. I took a deep, shuddering breath. He nestled in closer, and his lips pressed against the front of my ear.

"You need to back the fuck up, Twynolan," I said. "That isn't funny."

"No, it is not. But it's distracting you."

"Not in any way we both agreed."

He swallowed, his Adam's apple bobbing against my throat. "We do need to discuss this, though."

"Yeah, we need to talk to Mateo. He needs to stop meddling."

Nol pulled back to meet my eyes. He cupped my face in both palms and looked at me level, his emotions masked while he thought about Mother only knew what. We needed to get moving, but finally, he came to some sort of inner conclusion. "And we can't do that if you let them take you, now can we?"

"No."

"Mateo isn't the only—"

He was right. Distracting me had worked. I grabbed his wrists and pulled his hands down. "It's not time for a heart-to-heart, Nol. You have issues to get through, and I'm here when you're ready to talk. But we have to get outside. Where are the girls?"

"Waiting in the mudroom. I told them not to go outside." Nol thumped down the stairs ahead of me.

"And you think Charlie will listen to you?"

He stopped on the landing. "Ray is scared, so yes."

"Is Estwyn out there?"

"What do you think?"

"Fuck."

"Nolan?" Charlie poked her head through the door and looked right at us on the landing. "Tatie? I called Queen Orlaith. They're on their way."

"Good thinking," Nolan said.

"What? Why?" I asked.

"Estwyn knows he's not supposed to be here, remember? None of them are welcome in this realm."

"If he even told the *Amura Ore*, which I doubt." The arrogant prick. Okay. Time to be pissed, not scared, guilty, or upset. I expelled the last little shakes through my body, not from my panic attack, but from Nol being a pain-in-the-ass. "Let's go." I shoved my hair back again.

Ray came into the house and attached herself to Nol. He knelt down and whispered, "You need to stay here with mommy, okay?"

"Are they going to take you and Tatie?"

"No. Never." He tucked her hair behind her ear. "No one will take us. Charlie," Nol said as he stood. "I don't want either of you to see this."

"I—" She went to argue, but noticed Nol's hands on Ray's shoulders. "Okay." Then she jumped over and hugged him. "Don't let them take her."

"I won't."

"Swear it."

"I gave you my *Idorem* oath weeks ago. There were no stipulations when I promised that."

"That's what that means?" Her eyebrows shot up.

He licked his lips and hugged her tightly. "Yes." Nol tapped her shoulder and reached his hand out to me. "How long do we need to stall before the fairies get back here?"

Charlie shoved her hands into her back pockets and rolled up onto her toes. "Forty minutes or so."

"Forty? Can't they use Faerie to get to Capitol Hill?" I asked.

"With what car would they travel from there, Hallë?"

Okay, he had a point.

I took his hand before he pulled open the door to the mudroom and, beyond that, my backyard. As we stepped out from under the eve, Nol cast a ward to protect us from the rain—but I didn't know if it did more than that. I wouldn't ask.

"By the way, yes, I am kicking you out next month. That just proved my point up there."

Nol growled and squeezed my hand as we looked off my deck at the four guards and three *Amura Ore* members waiting for us in the drizzle under the trees.

He looked at me and dropped the calm mask. "We need to talk." No flirting or mischief, but a "holy shit, he wanted to have a talk" look. Um, anything but that. But he didn't look away, and his expression didn't change. Not until I acknowledged my understanding did he turn toward the *endaen* issue below. We were so not having that conversation.

The seven *endai* stood fidgeting underneath their ward, protected from any rain that got through the branches. One guard flexed his hand, and another glanced down at our joined hands as we stopped in front of them.

"Finally. *Savilë*—"

I balled my hands into fists at my side. "I want to see the declaration, Estwyn."

"That is *Loret* Estwyn to you, *savilë*."

I shrugged off his demand. Orlaith was probably right; they'd sent him because he was the most expendable. I bet he annoyed the council as much as he annoyed us. "The declaration?"

The two guards standing on either side of Estwyn looked at each other. One of them reached into the jacket of his uniform and stepped forward. Nol tugged me behind him.

"Don't give it to her," Estwyn hissed.

The guard stopped.

"I have a right to read it, just like Nol did."

"Give it to me," Nol said tonelessly. "I'll give it to her."

"That is not necessary. *Hasin* Twynolan, you've been informed. We will take the *savilë,* and you may follow if you choose."

"Her name is Hally, and you don't have the authority to take her anywhere."

"Yes, I do," Estwyn snapped at Nol.

"This isn't a good choice, Twynolan. Protecting a *savilë*..." the assembly member next to Estwyn warned Nol.

"You know my *muranildë* is under the *Zayuri's* protection, not just mine."

I was? Were the *Zayuri* and the *Amura Ore* at odds with each other? Had I misread the entire situation when my grandmother and I talked?

"How many names does there need to be to make an arrest, Hallë?"

I stepped up beside Nol again and raised my voice to be heard over the ten feet between us and the rain getting heavier by the second. "Seventy-seven, and forty of those must be senior members, um...including..." I drew out my words as I tried to remember. "...all twenty-five of the judiciary committee, and ten of those must be senior members as well."

"How dare you try to attempt to instruct me on our laws. I am an *Amura Ore* representative, and I am ordering this *savilë* to surrender herself for her role in casting the deadly curse. If she refuses to lift the curse, she will be executed nine days from today. By order of these here members—"

Nol lifted his chin and raised his voice over Estwyn's. "*Loret* Estwyn, you do not have enough signatures to carry out the arrest. Come back with a senior member in charge and then we'll talk."

"You can't possibly know how many sig—"

Nol interrupted Estwyn again. "There are nineteen names on that paper. All of them are junior members. Shall I name them? I have quite a good memory."

"That isn't necessary. The order was fast tracked."

After a moment, I pulled some answers from my almost thirty years of political classes and fifty-some years of private instruction with my grandmother. Once I'd told Yalu I wanted to change the *Amura Ore* for the better, she'd dropped ten books in front of me and told me to have them read in a week. I'd been seventy-five.

"Loret Estwyn, and other esteemed council members, I understand the graveness of the situation."

"Hallë," Nol whispered. "Don't agree with them."

I ignored him. "However, there are still rules to follow, even when a declaration is fast tracked. Nol says you have nineteen signatures, and they're all junior members."

"He can't possibly know that."

"Yes, he can. Twynolan's ability to remember such details is well known. Do you deny that you are all junior members?"

"You are coming with us, *savilë*," he told me instead of answering.

"Her name is Hally." Nol spoke up to be heard above the rain, but I heard the anger building.

"I know that look, Hallë." Nol kept his voice low as if they could hear us through the rain. "Don't give in. You're not going."

I stepped in closer. "Do you?" I asked Estwyn. "Be warned, if I go with you and what you say is false, you will be held accountable and my case will be thrown out."

"I know *Aeminan* laws, girl." Oh, that was a step better than *savilë*. "Yes, we are all junior members."

"Fast tracking requires twenty-five signatures and twenty of them must be senior members. You don't have enough."

"It is treason to refuse *Amura Ore's* orders."

No, it wasn't. I could go to prison, but now he was just pulling things out of his ass. How long had this guy been in office? "You are the one committing treason, *Loret* Estwyn. You and the members behind you. And the officers you've taken along are accessories." My eyes narrowed, and I stepped past Nol, or tried to. His left arm snaked around my waist, and he pulled me back to his side. "How could you? For your own pride? What a shameful action."

The four guards looked at the three *Amura Ore* members in turn, and I knew I was right. They hadn't been informed of how illegal their presence was.

"Not only that, but you are also defying the orders of the Queen of the Fae of this realm. She ordered you to stay in *Endae*. No other *enda* is welcome without permission from Queen Orlaith." Now it was the other members glancing at Estwyn. Yep, I was right. He'd let his pride get in the way and hadn't told them about that tiny detail.

"Speaking of the queen." Nol pulled his phone out of his back pocket and unlocked the screen. "An entourage of the fae is on its way here now."

"No, actually. We're here." Ten fae walked single file through the back gate—three of the guards we'd seen at the manor, plus Brodrick, Queen Orlaith. Two faeries walked in right behind them that looked almost identical to the fae girl, Sera from the hut, with their with smaller, whimsical features, long white hair and pale skin. A stocky, two foot tall fae with earth-brown skin and tightly curled blonde hair followed close behind them. The last two towered over my eight-foot fence and had to turn sideways to fit through the gate. They were built like boulders and had the skin of them, too, lined with oranges and whites, even a bit of purple, like layers of deposits in rocks.

At the sight of the boulder fae, the four *endai* guards positioned themselves in front of the *Amura Ore* members, pretending to be prepared for battle, but the hand of the one closest to us was shaking right above the hilt of his sword.

"Estwyn, violating my orders?" the queen said in perfect, yet accented *Aemirin*.

"You can speak *Aemirin*?" His face paled now that he knew she'd heard everything he'd told me. Every last snide remark.

"I can't show all of my cards at once."

He didn't get the reference. As the *endai* weren't facing us, I couldn't see Estwyn's expression. He cleared his throat and fidgeted. "We are here to take the *savilë* back to stand trial for her role in the deadly curse killing our people."

"So I've heard. Yet she's not connected to Aswryn."

"We know Aswryn wasn't working alone—"

"True."

"Only one other *enda* is powerful enough to have helped disperse the curse."

I wanted to argue that comment, but at some point, you just get tired of correcting people's assumptions.

"Before she was two hundred, she killed two people with her magic. It is clear Hallanevaë was working with Aswryn."

"Is it? As I've learned, Hally, as she prefers to be called, was without magic for over one hundred years, up until three weeks ago. Aswryn cast the curse over thirty years ago."

"She could have helped in other ways."

"So prove it. Hally is my chosen *endaen* liaison."

"She's an exile—"

"I have granted her asylum," the queen announced. "Here are three copies of the Earth-*Endae* treaty. I will await a formal, written apology from each nation for entering this realm. You have one *Aeminan* week."

Estwyn sputtered, claiming that wasn't enough time. One of the other members took the papers from a tiny fairy who'd pulled them out of a briefcase.

"Any time after that, I will consider it a breach of the treaty and an act of war. In the documents, you will also find my permissions and demands until further notice. No other *endaen* may stay in this realm besides Hally—Hallanevaë Inara—and Twynolan Madoraen *Rudairn, Hasin Zayuri*. Furthermore, any *Zayuri* are also welcome. They have a long-standing respect with my people. Plus, Nolan and Hally found the missing fae and *endaen* children and apprehended two fae who were working with Aswryn. And I assure you, they will confirm Hally had nothing to do with the curse. Once I receive the letters of apology, we can discuss the Aswryn situation further."

"*Endaen* children?" the same junior member who'd taken the papers asked. "Why haven't we heard of this?"

"Because my fellow *Zayuri* left this realm just a few hours ago, as you know, since you waited until they were gone to try to take Hallë illegally."

"You'll hear all about it in their reports," I added. "You should probably get back there before that happens."

"It is time for you and your party to leave my kingdom, *Loret* Estwyn."

"How are we to get formal permission to come here if we can't enter to ask you?"

"You can arrange that through the *Zayuri*."

"Your Majesty?" the third member, who hadn't spoken yet, called out. "I understand you want Hallanevaë as your *Aeminan* representative; however, with the *Savile* title, she can't contact anyone."

"For now, she's my *Endae* representative, and you can't banish her from *Endae* as you can't speak for the other nations. Either figure it out internally or you will need to contact one of the other nations to receive information."

Estwyn's eyes bulged, and the other two whispered something, then nodded.

"Thank you for your time, Your Majesty," the assembly member who'd warned Nol not to protect me said. "We will be in touch in a week."

"Now wait one moment—" But they weren't listening to Estwyn any longer. He'd embarrassed them, and they'd been called out for their treachery. Those guards looked pissed as they grabbed his arms and hauled him through the portal.

"Whew, what a rush." The queen swung her arm out then clasped her hands together. "I almost had to ask you for help."

"Me? With what?" I let go of Nol's hand and walked closer to the group of fae. I wanted to meet every one of them. Gaelic was next on my language list.

"Translating into *Mellorian* and *Pequwynian*. I called in a few favors." The queen turned and leaned forward toward the small wispy fairies. "These fae had their work cut out for them."

The smallest of the wispy fairies smiled proudly.

The queen stepped closer to me, meeting me under the cover of my redwood tree. "Do you drink coffee?"

I blinked, trying to comprehend not just the fact that a royal fairy was in front of me asking about coffee, but also that said queen fairy had saved me from my own people. I was safe? There had to be more to it.

All the fairies stared at me with their colorful, inhuman eyes. Leaf-green Brodrick wasn't doing a good job of hiding his smirk, enjoying my political stumbling. Shit. The wispy ones seemed to be lawyers of some sort with their paperwork, and acting like a dumbass in front of them all wasn't the impression I wanted to give as the representative of *Endae*. At least until someone could convince the queen otherwise. No one was going to accept a *savilë* as their rep. I realized the queen was still waiting for an answer. "Coffee, Your Majesty?"

"We need to discuss your schedule and I'm not about to discuss things standing in the rain!" Orlaith waved her hand, frowning at my confusion. "You'll be meeting with several other nations in the next few months. Not all of them are sold on your asylum. Technically, you can't leave my kingdom until your asylum is approved everywhere else."

"Are there any areas where there aren't fae?" I asked, hopefully.

Orlaith tsked as she raised an eyebrow. "Not one."

"I assume your father is first on the list?" I scrunched my nose, thinking about the tension I'd picked up on between Gavin, Quinn, and Orlaith.

"Actually, no. Quinn's mother is interested in meeting you."

"Huh." She didn't hint at anything and I didn't know if she knew about the date Quinn and I had attempted. "They're from—"

"France. They are interested about your time there. How about it? Do you have time for coffee this morning?"

"Your Majesty." Brodrick walked up between the large rock fae and came to stand beside his liege. "This wasn't part of the plan."

The look Orlaith directed Brodrick's way gave him a jolt, and he held his hand to his chest.

"Of course, Your Majesty is always able to see to her own schedule however she so chooses." Brodrick's face turned red as he bowed until he was staring at his toes.

"Do you have somewhere to be, Brodrick?"

"Um..." He straightened, his brows knitting on his bright red face. "No...no, Queen Orlaith."

"Astrid, take Brodrick and the Corrigans home. Red Caps, your presence here accomplished exactly what was needed. If your lord has need of me, please don't hesitate to call."

The two Red Caps, whatever they were, bowed to Orlaith. Something bright and shiny caught the light, and a drop of red fell on my lawn. I stepped back and bumped into Nol, and that was fine with me.

"Is that blood pouring from their heads?" Nol whispered in my ear.

"I think so," I murmured back. "I want to know what Corrigans are."

"Not now. I'm too tired to look after you."

I turned to glare at him. "What? You don't 'look after me.'"

"You are so oblivious. I've saved your life at least twenty times since I've been here. That first night in the alley? There were people waiting for us to come out."

"There are lots of homeless downtown. Just 'cause you saw people doesn't mean—"

"One of them had a knife in his hand."

He had to be making this shit up.

"Last week, leaving Pike Place Market, you almost walked into traffic."

"When?"

"I just told you, after we left." He pulled me closer so we were standing side by side in front of the Queen of the Fae, who wanted coffee. "We'll talk about it later. Let's just say, some of the times I distract you are for your own good."

"I beg your pardon!"

He shook his head and looked over at the three fairies in front of us. The others had left while Nol and I had been bickering. My face flamed, and I ducked my head. "I—I apologize that you had to see that display, Your Majesty."

"On the contrary, I need something normal and mundane, and honestly, you two are adorable together. Nolan, Hally, this is Paige, and she likes coffee as much as we do. And Feya, who doesn't like coffee, would love to play with Ray. Would you mind if we invited ourselves in?"

We were going to have royalty for morning coffee, and my house wasn't nearly clean enough. Then I looked past what she was and paid attention to what she was wearing: blue jeans and a Nike hoodie? Not something I'd ever consider a fairy queen to even own.

"Um, right this way, Your Majesty, and, um, Paige?"

"Orie, please," Orlaith asked. "Just between us."

"You're allowed to do this?"

"Sure. After all, I am the queen."

Nol stepped away, taking his rain shield with him. The heavy rain pelted down on me before I could get my own up, my hair and shirt getting soaked. The only thing dry was my jeans. If the fairies hadn't been here, I'd have given him a piece of my mind. Instead, I shook my fist at his back as he made it to the stairs. Nol took the steps two at a time and reached the door in seconds flat.

As soon as we were close enough, Nol opened the door for the queen. "Your—Orie, I just reset the ward. This is my normal one. If you and your subjects intend to visit without calling, I'll need to make you some amulets to see through it."

"How interesting." Orie looked up and around as if she could see the ward. "I doubt I'll be able to come over much, but today's circumstances played out perfectly for a brief visit."

I stepped through last, and he smiled as I walked by. "You are such a pain-in-the-ass."

He tapped my nose and pulled me close. "Not as much as you are in mine," he whispered in my ear.

The move and the feel of his breath on me seized my lungs, and only when he straightened and turned my shoulders could I take a full breath. There was no way we were having a "talk." Nope. He was headed to the loft, where we could get some distance. It would all be smoother and calmer once that happened. Oh, and the talk with Mateo would happen as soon as we got Orie out of here.

33

"I can't believe you had coffee with the queen and didn't invite me." Mateo bounced his leg in his seat at the Pizzeria on North Beacon Hill. "Do you think I can meet her when they visit for protection detail?"

"What? The queen isn't going to guard your house personally." Charlie rolled her eyes for dramatic affect.

"You got to meet her!" Mateo threw a napkin at Charlie. "I should, too." Mateo stuck his tongue out as Charlie laughed at his hissy fit.

Orie had visited until eleven yesterday morning. Yes, we'd drunk coffee, but we'd also come up with a raw idea of a plan. As it so happened, Paige was her secretary and had the queen's calendar with her. Can we say *setup*? She was now in the process of approving, coordinating, and refining our Zoom meetings with the other kingdoms.

My first official duty would be a Zoom meeting on Monday with several heads of state and defense ministers. Not that I was prepared for that. I'd made sure she agreed that I did not need to act officially in my day-to-day life—otherwise, I'd be wearing a freaking pantsuit to my tattoo sessions. No, thank you. Mainly, I'd need to look professional when I went to meetings and during my time in Faerie. Oh, and the best part (read the sarcasm between the lines here), I was to be called Ambassador Inara or Madam Inara. Inara. Honestly, I think it was Her Majesty's way of thumbing her nose at *Aemina*.

Sam walked over to our table, carrying seven drinks. I jumped off my stool and grabbed three before they fell. "Is he still going on about meeting the queen?" Sam asked. "I thought you were past this, dear?"

Charlie scooted around everyone's stools, squeezed my shoulder, and wandered off.

"Past it?" I asked. "It's been a day."

"Oh, no, he's moved on—"

"Doesn't seem like much movin' on to me." Lewis chuckled as he pulled his and Yumi's drinks over to them.

"I am equally eager to meet Prince Quinn." Mateo wiggled his eyebrows.

I pointed my finger at him. "Do not call him that."

"What am I supposed to call him?" Mateo asked, knowing full well that's not what Quinn wanted to be called.

"Quinn," Nol and I said together.

"And you'll meet him once he gets Seamus settled in. However long that takes."

Mateo grumbled but couldn't argue. The little boy had lost everything. It'd take a while.

"Hi, Tatie." Ray wrapped her arms around my hips.

"When did you show up?" I looked around the mostly empty pizzeria for an answer. "Weren't you at Natalie's house?" Ray, in Ray fashion, ignored me to go to Auntie Yumi, who had squealed and demanded hugs.

Most of the tables, like ours, were huge round ones, unless they were bench seats, which were closer to the front. I loved it for the memories it stirred up, but also for the smell of the old wood tables and walls mixed with pizza herbs, dough, and sauce. Perfect combination. Mixed with all my friends, a rarity for the middle of the day, but it happened.

Charlie sauntered up behind Ray, a smirk on her face. She twisted around and looked behind her, then met my eyes once more. At first, my brain didn't register who the black-haired guy was that Nol was shaking hands with at the front door. Not until they were walking over did I realize it was Quinn with Seamus in his arms.

"Oh, look, I guess I get to meet him sooner than you thought." Mateo beamed with excitement.

Quinn followed close behind Nol but kept that sly smirk on his face as he watched my reaction. I got up before they made it to the table.

"What are you doing here?" I leaned in and gave Quinn an air-cheek kiss. "I didn't think I'd see you for weeks."

"I couldn't say no to Nolan's invitation, late notice, as it was."

"Invitation?" I frowned first at Quinn, then at Nol as he snaked his arm across my shoulders and pulled me back to the table. Everyone was standing, holding their drinks, when I turned around. Sam scooted around and handed Quinn a glass of beer from somewhere.

They all lifted their drinks, and as one, they called out, "Happy Birthday, Hally!"

I froze.

"That's right, Tatie! Nolan gave up your birthday." Charlie took a sip of her drink while she gauged my reaction.

"Hallë?" Nolan whispered, only loud enough for me.

"I need a moment, Nol."

I shook my head and left the table, heading straight for the bathrooms. I would not freak out in front of everyone. I shoved on the restroom door and locked it behind me—then belatedly checked to see if there was anyone else in there. Check. Placing my hands on the sink, I leaned forward and stared at myself in the mirror. My freckles were hidden under my makeup, heavy with black eyeliner, glitter, and dark red lipstick, and today I had gray and teal eyeshadow. I could handle a birthday, right? Celebrating Hallanevaë's birthday. It wasn't that bad. Then why was I freaking out?

"You can do this, Hally," I told my reflection. "Go over, thank them, and smile. Fuck, it's been too long." I took one more big breath and went to face my friends. I unlocked and yanked the door open to find Nol waiting for me at the entrance to the bathroom hallway.

"Hallë—hear me out."

"Did Charlie tell you why I don't celebrate my birthday?"

"Yes, and it's shit. It's time for you to start living your life for you. Emma's children are grown. Her descendants can take care of their own babies—with an auntie's guidance—and you're not just living for me."

"Nol—"

"Everyone has forgiven you. They understand it was an accident. Hallë, please, hear me. Go celebrate your fucking birthday."

"I was going to until my annoying, pain-in-the-ass *muranildo* stopped me in the hall to give me a pep talk."

Nol stopped, mouth open, prepared to argue more. "You will?"

"Being Hally Dubois has helped me find something different and learn about myself. And Charlie keeps pestering me."

Nol's smile grew as he realized I was serious. "Good." He moved over and gestured for me to go in front of him back to the table.

"Oh good, you didn't clobber him!" Mateo called out from a few tables away.

"He's not even on my shit list for it."

"Does that mean I don't have to move out?" Nol asked.

"What's this now?" Sam laughed. "You're kickin' him out?"

"I'm offering him my loft to stay in. And yes, you're still moving out!"

"Have I not been behaving?"

Everyone laughed, knowing Nol would never "behave."

"Tatie, I knew you would feel uncomfortable with all the attention, so we brought the kids some presents for your birthday."

"You know me well, Charlie. But now I look like the schmuck who didn't bring her niece a present."

"What's a schmuck?" Seamus asked as he sat beside Ray to color as they waited for their food.

"My Tatie, who didn't bring presents, duh." Her wide amber eyes were serious in her almost four-year-old face. "She just said that." With the attitude behind that comment, most of the adults had to turn away before Seamus and Ray saw our laughter. "So we get presents now. Right, Mommy?"

"If you say thank you."

Ray stopped coloring long enough to roll her eyes. "Thank you."

"Oriane Caroline Roux!" Charlie chided, but she tickled Ray at the same time.

I inched over and nudged Quinn's shoulder with mine. "Thanks for coming."

"Are you okay about the birthday thing?" he mumbled.

"No," I mumbled back. "But I'm working on it."

Ray squealed. I hadn't realized the unwrapping had commenced. "Thank you, Nolan!" It was a My Little Pony stuffed animal and a My Little Pony movie.

"Oh boy." I patted Quinn's arm, scooted around Mateo, and stood next to Nol. He beamed at Ray and Seamus and the presents they'd already opened on the large table. "You know you're in trouble, right?"

Nol looked away from Ray, his eyes still dancing with the glow that this little girl brought to all of us. "Why?"

"You're one of the most important people in her life."

The crease between his brows dinted in. "All right." He shoved his hands into his hoody pockets. "She's important to me, too."

I sighed and shuffled closer. We watched Ray for a moment. An afternoon sunbeam shone down through the tinted glass of the mostly empty pizzeria, lighting her orange eyelashes. I paused to figure out the way I wanted to explain this. "Ray goes to you when she's scared and trusts you to fix things. She asks you to look under her bed at night. Leaving will be hard on her. She loves you."

Nol fidgeted and looked around the table we were standing next to, but apart from at the moment. "I love her, too."

"Don't you see?"

"I'll stay here longer." Nol shrugged. "What's another ten years?"

His words snatched my breath, and my lungs refused to inflate. Even though his words had sounded flippant, I knew he meant them. When had he decided this and why hadn't he told me?

"What?" Nol frowned and leaned down. "Breathe, Hallë." His whispered words reminded me of yesterday on the stairs before Estwyn's visit. We still hadn't talked. Or, at least, I'd avoided it as best I could. "What have I done now to make you breathless?"

I glared at him. "You don't make me breathless. How corny is that? But seriously, you'd really stay for her?"

"I said I will." He glanced up at Ray for a second. "And yes, I do. I don't have enough fingers to count the times—"

"Shut up, Twynolan. It isn't about you," I grumbled.

"Tell me one thing—"

"Twyn—"

"Why are you more delighted with me staying for her than you were when I said I was staying for you? Even though I just said another ten years. What do you think that means?"

He hadn't just said that, had he? "You said you'd stay for Ray."

Nol pulled on me to get me to follow him. We went to the empty back patio just as the rain started up again. He headed over to the first covered area, away from the door. "I want to stay here because of you. I never said how long that would be for. Do you hear what I'm telling you?"

Oh shit. Not this. "Nol, now is not the time."

"Things are—" He looked away, but he couldn't go far without stepping into the rain. "I haven't been this happy in a long time. And that's all because of you. This gives me peace. You give me peace. Does my presence give you peace?"

"Of course, you give me peace. You're my *muranildo*."

He turned away, staring off into the constant stream of cars on Beacon Avenue.

"Why won't you talk to me?" I asked.

Nolan closed his eyes as if counting to ten.

"I know something's—" I reached for his arm, but he stayed where he was. "Something is troubling you, hurting you."

"I can't," he choked. "I want to be here, right now, where it's peaceful."

"Where you don't have to be reminded of it? To face what's tearing you up?"

He shook his head. "It will hurt you. I'm afraid you'll see me differently."

"Have you talked to anyone about it?"

He continued to stare into the distance and didn't need to shake his head for me to know he hadn't.

"You can talk to me. I'm your *muranildë*, remember?" I tugged on his arm. "We can talk about anything."

"I know. But...there are things that neither of us wants to talk about. About the way we keep flirting? How breathless you get when I do it? How your reaction makes me happy? Let's talk about that."

I ground my teeth as he deflected. "Raj is dead, isn't she?"

Nol froze.

"Is that why you don't want to tell me anything about home? Is anyone left?"

"I don't want to tell you. Not yet. I want to have someone in my life who doesn't know. I want to play ponies with Ray or lay my head in your lap on the floor, watching movies all night until Charlie's snoring becomes too loud to hear the movie. I'm terrified you'll never forgive me for what I did. I'll need to tell you eventually. I know. Can't that be later? I'll move out, whatever you need me to do to feel safe, but please don't shut me out—"

I slipped under his arm, like I always used to, and wrapped an arm around him. "I won't shut you out. You just need to find..." I threw my hand out at the cars. Did I really want to say this? Yes, because it would help him. "...something new. I think you need to get laid."

He lifted his arm and turned to face me. "What?"

"You know, to relieve stress." When he still stared down at me with that blank, clueless expression, I scrambled for a better explanation. "Not like, develop a relationship with someone." I waved my hand around as I floundered. "Have you ever heard of a one-night stand?" Of course, he hadn't. "It's a date with someone, and afterward, you go your separate ways."

"To not know anything about them? Where would we have sex?"

"Oh, jeez." I looked up at the canopy protecting us from the rain. "Their place, your place, it doesn't matter. There's more to it—not just that. You'd take them out, get to know them a little."

"But I'd be having sex with a total stranger? Do you think this will resolve some of what I feel? Will it help your reactions to me as well? Your reactions start it."

I stepped back, shocked at the accusation. "I don't do anything."

"Bullshit."

"I do not."

"You do so! Your eyes deepen to an even darker green and you know I love your eyes."

"You've always wanted to have my eyes."

He chuckled. "No. I love your eyes and always will. I could stare into them all day." He turned, leaning in so he was staring at me from eye level.

Now he was being a shit. I laughed and pushed on him. "You're doing it again!"

"I don't know what you're talking about." He thumped my nose. Then he turned somber again. "All right. We'll try it that way first."

"Good! Charlie, I'm sure, can hook you up with someone at the U-dub. Lots of smart people you'd connect with."

"Oh, really?"

"Yeah. Here's the game plan—"

"Game?"

"Just shut up and go with it. You're moving out. Don't give me that look. I'll help you find a job. We'll talk to Mateo. You can go out on a few dates and have fun. I know you haven't had that in a long time. If you like someone enough, maybe you can bring her over for Sunday dinner. Oh, and those are non-negotiable. You're still going to those, no matter what. You want me to forgive myself?"

He nodded his agreement.

"And I want you to find peace within yourself. That way, maybe you'll be able to tell me what's been troubling you so much. Otherwise, Nol, we won't discuss anything else. But I truly believe that a lot of this is just nerves and outside influence. Do we have an understanding?"

"I think this will help clear some things up."

"Yeah?" I stepped over and hooked his arm in mine. "Or did it just confirm how conflicted you are about life?"

"Life is conflicting—especially with you."

"That's fair. But at least I'm not boring." I pulled him back into the pizzeria, where Ray and Seamus were running amuck between the empty tables and the adults were talking over the pizza that had arrived while we were gone.

"You two doin' okay?" Mateo asked as we reached the table. "You left His Highness out here to go talk privately."

"Yes, we did." I lifted my chin and looked around the table. "And everything is fine. We've just decided a few things."

Everyone stopped talking and stared. Quinn stayed still as he sat on the stool closest to me. "Nol is moving out because he wants to stay here for a while—"

"How long is a while?" Charlie asked.

"Two decades, at least," he told everyone. "So, I need to think of a job I can do."

"And nothing to do with the *Zayuri*. He'll have enough of that working with me and the fae."

"Stripper," Mateo joked. "No, no, seriously, I could find you a job at my company. They're always hiring people."

"Okay, new job. You said a few things?" Yumi asked.

"Nol is going to find a date. It's high time he had some fun. I told him he could bring her to Sunday dinner if he likes her enough."

Mateo leaned away from the table and closer to Nol, but spoke loud enough for everyone at the table to hear. "Who said it has to be a her?"

"It doesn't," Nol teased right back to Mateo's surprise. "Humans put labels on things, Mateo. Love is love. We don't have that divide."

"Cheers to that." Mateo held his glass out for everyone to click.

34

Nolan

Bellies full, the two youngsters were sleepy and fighting it. Charlie let Lewis and Yumi take Ray back to the house to put her down while Quinn wrestled Seamus into this booster seat. Hallë stood by the door, watching and waiting with a contented smile on her face.

"You sure you're okay with this?" Mateo asked Nolan as they watched the three of them.

"More than fine. Mateo, I need you to stop." Sam frowned up at Nolan, protective of his partner, but his tension eased as Nolan explained. "You see it, I know you do, and you're right. Hallë and I see each other the way you think, in a way. We have centuries ahead of us, though. We need to live and find joy with ourselves and others before we settle down."

"Wait—you're telling me you guys are planning to be together later?"

"No. If Hallë finds someone else, that's fine. I was fine with Gileal and her—though she always knew they weren't meant for each other. Our relationship is strange to everyone but us."

"What about you?"

"I have issues I need to resolve on my own, and I don't know how long that will take or if I'll ever resolve them. Let her be happy. Let her be with Prince Charming. Hold back on the matchmaking comments. I can't say what the future holds, but if Hallë and I come together, it won't be anytime soon."

"It'd be nice to see you two together before I die, though!"

"It could happen, but that would mean she'd have to put up with me for—" How long did humans live for? "—seven hundred years! That's a long fucking time."

"You have a point." Mateo crossed his arms, assessing the pair in front of them. "All right, I'll tone it down."

"Aw, don't pout." Sam nudged his partner, making Mateo stumble. They righted themselves together—just like in life. "Hey, Nolan? We keep meaning to ask," Sam hedged.

"What?" Nolan gave the guys his full attention.

"If you're gonna be here, we were hoping you'd be part of the wedding."

"Wedding? Where people get married?"

They both nodded, letting him work through it, which he appreciated.

"How are others part of someone else's wedding? Aren't there vows to each other?"

"You'd be in it. We have an odd number in the party, and you'd even it out."

Nolan tried to imagine a reason for other people to be in a wedding meant for them. "What would be my role?"

"Walk up the aisle with someone else and stand at the front when we say our vows."

"Interesting. Yes, I'd like to be part of that."

"Hey guys! You didn't need to wait for me." Hallë, bright-eyed and a little red-faced, jumped onto the curb beside Nolan. Quinn honked and waved through his window as he drove away. "Well?"

"Well?" Mateo asked.

She waved her arms at Mateo, then in the air. "What do you think?"

"He's okay."

"Okay?" She gasped. "Just okay?"

"He's not Nolan, but—"

"Mateo," Sam warned, backing Nolan up.

"I've been asked to tone it down." Mateo rolled his eyes dramatically. Hallë said he did it to deflect sometimes.

"Have you now?" she asked Mateo, but looked at Nolan. He saw the relief in her, and he could do nothing but smile back. This was going to work.

"And he said yes!" Mateo added, as if starting up an old conversation.

"Yes, to...oh, the wedding! See, I told you he would." Hallë knocked her fist on Mateo's shoulder, then started walking back to her house.

"It was your idea?" Nolan asked her. He hadn't seen that coming.

"Uh, yeah. They've been searching for an eighth friend, and I kept telling them you were the obvious choice."

"Obvious?" Nolan felt his eyebrow rise. He wanted to hear this reasoning.

"Sure. They've pretty much adopted you. They do that."

"Watch out, or we'll keep you longer, too, Nolan," Sam warned.

Hallë laughed. "Wouldn't it be the other way around, since you wanted to move with me?"

"Potato, potato."

"Do you have a plan in place?" Nolan asked, getting interested.

"We're working on it." Mateo huffed. "Don't give me the stink-eye, Nolan. We're trying to decide where we want to go."

"I was thinking Scotland or Ireland," Hallë said.

Mateo stopped for a moment to glare at her. "Really? Last time we talked, you didn't want to—said the weather was too much like here."

"Yeah, well, I've decided my next language is going to be Gaelic. If I'm going to play diplomat, I might as well learn the language."

Nolan shook his head in disbelief. Hadn't she just been complaining that she didn't want the job? The light turned, and they began walking again. "I'm honored to be part of your family, Mateo and Sam. And we'll have to wait and see what the future holds. As long as we're there for one another, nothing can break us apart."

"Nol, be careful. You might jinx us."

"Yeah, a bit too optimistic," Mateo agreed with Hallë. "Although, I like the *being there for one another* part. That I can get behind."

"Very well. Now let's go home. I'm getting hungry again."

"No! We just ate."

"I didn't get to eat much. Ray and Seamus distracted me."

They laughed and kept walking. Things would be fine. He'd work on finding that peace Hallë wanted him to find. Charlie was positive they'd find the cure in Aswryn's notes, and then they'd work on the slave band. Things would be just fine. Even with the terrorist group of Aswryn's that Hallë and the queen had talked to him about. He'd start working on that problem tomorrow.

"Hey?" Hallë came up and slid her arm around his waist. "You all right?"

"I'm fine." Lots to do. But it would be fine. It had to be.

Epilogue

The mailbox key and the spare key clinked together as I unlocked the loft apartment above Yula's Quill. Other people lived in the building, but mine was on the top floor and the only one with roof access. I'd owned most of the building for decades now—sort of. My niece, Amelia, ran her real estate business in France, and I owned it with her. Call me the American face of the company.

Nol shoved himself off the wall next to the door as the lock slid.

"You will need to be conscious of heating, especially in the spring and summer. It'll get too hot in here, but mornings are chilly." I looked back the moment I stepped inside, hoping to catch a glimpse of Nol's first reaction to the place. He walked in past me as he looked up at the fourteen-foot-high ceilings, exposed beams, and the tall windows that provided all the light. Nothing. Not one reaction. He'd said all of two words to me on the way over. The point was to give him a place to stay, not find a place he liked. That didn't make me feel better, though. He hated the idea, but damn it, we needed our spaces. He needed a bed.

He touched his fingertips to the back of the futon. His boot tapped the bottom of the beanbag chair that I liked but had never found the best place for. His boots made little noise on the hardwood as he walked to the far windows, where he looked down onto Yesler Avenue. Still, he said nothing. The entire corner, most of the front wall and a quarter of the adjacent wall, were all floor-to-ceiling window panes.

"You'll have to get groceries—"

"You've said that already," he mumbled, deadpan.

The kitchen, a counter along the wall under the bedroom platform, was simple enough. No propane or fancy buttons. Next to that was the bathroom and laundry room, then the wrought-iron staircase that led above. I kept that floor carpeted. It opened to below, with a wrought-iron railing protecting me from falling. Yes, it had saved my ass once.

"And the fans?"

I blinked away from the memory as I registered Nol's voice. He pointed to the ceiling fans.

"Oh, the switch is against the wall, but there's also a remote—that would be good to show you." The remote for the place was supposed to be with the TV remote on the entertainment console. I checked the drawer and even behind the console. Odd. "It can't have gone far. This place isn't that big. I'm looking for a silver remote. That is, I think it's silver." I kept rambling as I looked, first in all the drawers, then in the coffee table compartments. "Shit."

"I'll find it later," Nol said.

"Sure. Anyway, it controls the fans, the lights, and the curtains."

"Curtains?" Nol examined the windows.

"Yeah, they're the roll-down ones. See, at the very top? There's one on each, including the ones upstairs. There's not much up there—a bed, stand, and closet—but it is a loft, and lofts aren't supposed to have rooms."

"I don't think I'll pull down the blinds. I like the light."

"You say that now. Try at five o'clock in the morning after you've gone out with friends and the sun is directly in your eyes. It's no fun then."

I tried to stay out of the way and let him look around the little place. He stayed clear of me as I stood in the corner by the refrigerator. I looked down below and watched the people and vehicles coming to and fro like silent ants. This place had excellent soundproofing, and I prayed it would help him sleep.

"There isn't much room to practice." Nol came to stand next to me.

"That's because it's outside. Come on." We had to go up to the platform and out onto the attached balcony off the bedroom to get to the rooftop. It was a bit of a pain, but at least he had a place away from others. Once on the tiny balcony, a small wrought-iron staircase against the brick-and-ivy building led us up to the rooftop. Most of the space was empty, with a shed on one side that held the electrical box, and close to that was the other set of stairs that led to the street access, which I kept closed.

I clambered up the platform stairs and took the pole out of the sliding glass door. The city barged in, the rush of cars, their horns and brakes. Planes and people, boats and even birds, not that those were as invasive. I stepped onto the private balcony, which I didn't use much. Nol came out right behind me, so I couldn't turn to climb up the other stairs. I pointed to them instead.

"Up there." I let him go first since he was closer, and he was the one touring the place. It took him a second to see the black metal steps against the dark brick and leaves, but once he did, he took those steps two at a time. Four steps and he stood atop the world. "I figure you and Tolwe could set up a ward and have it all to yourselves. You won't have to worry about interruptions. You can practice spells—within reason—up here."

He walked to the front, right above the spot by the fridge, and looked straight down onto the street below. I walked to the public access and glanced at the calmer Post Avenue. I wanted to know what he thought, but that made it sound like he had a choice. He was not staying at the Beacon Hill house.

"And you think this will help?" Nol spoke right against me, having snuck up behind me.

"You are such a shit!" I shoved him. If I'd been a jumpier person, I could have fallen. "Yes. This'll give you privacy away from us girls. Did you notice how quiet it is in there?"

"I am surprised at that, yes. This is a nice place. A bit...girly, though."

"Girly?" I tried to see my space differently and compared it to Quinn's place. "Yeah, I guess. It's also pretty dated. The last time I lived here was in the nineties. We can all help you update it." I walked back down the steps onto the balcony.

"Where are your paintings?" Nol asked as he followed me back inside.

"I wasn't painting back then, and I never thought to bring any here." I climbed back down the bedroom steps. "Hally Dubois will go away eventually and, with her, her art."

"It's part of you. I want a few pieces here and pictures of our friends."

"Totally doable. The only thing you won't be changing is the flooring. The rest is up to you. Are you feeling better about it?"

Nol didn't say anything as he walked over to the windows. He turned to look at me and leaned against the panes in the corner. He watched me for a moment, then beyond me to the surrounding loft. He sighed, lost in thought.

"Nol?" He didn't look at me. "I'm sorry. I didn't know there was even such a thing as a slave band. I mean, I knew there was something malicious going on when my bracelet showed up with a letter, but you were dead, and Ray was missing."

"Hallë—"

"I never intended for you to be stuck here. Stuck—" I looked up at the ceiling fans.

"Don't say it. I don't blame you. There was no way for you to know what would transpire that night."

"Maybe not, but I know you don't want to be stuck here, and this is as stuck as it gets."

"The queen made a valid point. The *Amura Ore* can't exile you from all of *Endae*." He held his hand up to stop my argument. "I'm not asking, not even considering making you leave here. But what I am saying is, I know I'm not stuck here. We could go to *Pequwyn*. That's close enough to home for me."

But he was stuck with me. "I'll find out how to get it off."

"We will, because I don't like how it takes energy from you. But getting it off is our lowest priority at the moment."

"Yeah, curse first."

"Nope." He shoved off the windows, using his core, held his arms behind his back, and stalked up to me. Oh, shit, now what? "Wards and shields."

"Pardon?"

"You said you made one in Faerie. Show me. You're not going home until you can block me."

"Now?"

"Uh-huh." He held up a finger. "You want me to live here, you have to be able to do this without me."

"But you have the one around the house. It's why we have these." I tapped the string of *merili* around my neck. One of them granted me access to the ward around my house. It sounded a bit odd when said like that, but without it, the closest I could get to my house was the tree in my backyard. Nol had increased the ward's strength after Estwyn had visited the first time. I hadn't known that was the reason the *endai* couldn't go farther than the tree that morning. Nol had said that if I'd been calmer, he would have explained that to me.

"Either you show me a working ward or—"

"Or what?" I was going to kick his ass if he tried any funny business.

"You'll miss Sunday dinner two weeks in a row, and we both know Mateo won't be happy about that."

I rolled my eyes. We had hours before Sam and Mateo showed up. It was going to be Quinn's first Sunday dinner, too. Our second date had gone much smoother.

So we would practice spells. Fine. Since meeting the fairies I was practicing magic daily; building my magical endurance and holding more energy before the band began to siphon it. But since the fight with Drake I hadn't had much time to work on wards. Or rather, worked with Nol to test my wards. I gathered my thoughts of why I'd needed to make that shield in Faerie. I'd wanted to keep us safe from the storm. I nodded to Nol. Too easy.

A zap, like a nine-vault battery shock, slapped my knuckles, and I jumped back. "Ow!" I zapped him back, the same shit Gil and he used to do to each other all the time.

Nol laughed and threw another one.

"I wasn't ready!" We'd be here for a minute more than I'd thought. We were not missing dinner again. Another zap. "I blocked trees from getting into my bubble, you know. Twynolan!" I yelled after a third zap.

He laughed again.

Whatever. It was nice to see him laughing. Like I said, we had a while, and I was more than happy to zap him back. Talk about shock therapy. The little shit.

Maybe sometimes we all needed a little shock therapy to get us through the hard times.

Author's Note

Thanks so much for reading Jaded Loyalties. Haven't read the rest of the series?

Check them out now: A Twisted Fate, Book 1, Shattered Fate Book 1.5 (novella)

And of course, if you're not already, subscribe to my mailing list so you don't miss out on news and book release updates: https://subscribepage.io/kristineendsley

If you enjoyed this book, why not help me out and leave a review? Reviews are essential to a book's success and they're a great way to show your support for your favorite authors.

The third novel in The Exile's Paradox will be out in 2025

Acknowledgements

If it weren't for the people here, I would never have published my first book, let alone the rest. Thank you.

My critique group at Café Noir in Silverdale. My partner at CritiqueMatch, Rachel. Katie Cross, you are super woman! I wouldn't have done this without your encouragement and advice from you and G.S. Jennson. Thank you both.

My betas! I begged and bugged you to read this and give me your honest feedback. It was crazy this last summer and everyone got busy, I get it. April, Cassie and Nikki thank you so much.

Adam, I love you. Thank you for coming with me to Miscons; listening to me rant or ignore me when I talk to myself; not complaining when you get up for work and I've just gone to bed and for being my partner for the past twenty-two years.

My boys, you are my world. You amaze me; you inspire me. How did I get so lucky to be your mom? Thank you for being there, for the hugs and Eskimo kisses.

My editor, Elizabeth Darkley. Thank you for making it look professional, you know it'd be a mess without you.

My cover illustrator/designer, Cristiana Leone, thank you for making this book look so magical!

About the Author

Kristine Endsley lives in Western Washington with her husband and two boys, two old lazy dogs and two wild black kitties. She works as a substitute para-educator to fund her writing habits.

Yula's Quill
TATTOO STUDIO
OPEN
Tuesday –
Saturday
PIZZERIA
ITALIA
TIGER'S

Milton Keynes UK
Ingram Content Group UK Ltd.
UKHW031354011224
451755UK00004B/320